W9-BTS-691

Blodgett Memorial Library
District of Fishkill
37 Broad St.
Fishkill, NY 12524
845-896-9215

THE LIST

ALSO BY MARTIN FLETCHER

Walking Israel

Breaking News

THE LIST

a Novel

Martin Fletcher

Blodgett Memorial Library
District of Fishkill
37 Broad St.
Fishkill, NY 12524
845-896-9215

THOMAS DUNNE BOOKS

ST. MARTIN'S PRESS ✻ NEW YORK

This is a work of fiction. All of the characters, organizations, and events portrayed in this novel are either products of the author's imagination or are used fictitiously.

"Refugee Blues," copyright © 1940 and renewed 1968 by W. H. Auden, from COLLECTED POEMS OF W. H. AUDEN by W. H. Auden. Used by permission of Random House, Inc.

THOMAS DUNNE BOOKS.
An imprint of St. Martin's Press.

THE LIST. Copyright © 2011 by Martin Fletcher. All rights reserved. Printed in the United States of America. For information, address St. Martin's Press, 175 Fifth Avenue, New York, N.Y. 10010.

www.thomasdunnebooks.com
www.stmartins.com

Library of Congress Cataloging-in-Publication Data

Fletcher, Martin, 1947–
    The list / Martin Fletcher.
        p. cm.
    ISBN 978-0-312-60692-3 (hardback)
    1. Jewish families—Fiction.   2. London (England)—Fiction.   3. Palestine—Fiction.   4. Jews—England—London—Fiction.   5. Jews—Palestine—Fiction.   6. Jewish fiction.   I. Title.
    PS3606.L486L57 2011
    813'.6—dc22   2011024814

First Edition: October 2011

10 9 8 7 6 5 4 3 2 1

For Nicola and Julian,
for Guy, Daniel, and Jonathan,
for Lynne and Susan,
and Tony and Betsy

Acknowledgments

Above all, thank you, George and Edith, my parents. I didn't intend to use your names, but somehow I just had to. I wish you had lived to read this story about a moment in your lives. The same goes to my brother, Peter, too.

Hagar, thank you for supporting my need to spend six months alone in a room.

I owe a tremendous amount to Marcia Markland, Kat Brzozowski, Carol Mann, Robbie O'Hare, Merle Nygate, Eliza Dreier, Gen Carden, and my son, Guy Fletcher. Your comments on the first draft helped me understand how to move forward and your support throughout the entire research and writing process made it a pleasure. And special thanks to Carolyn Hessel for your support, enthusiasm, and insight.

The Association of Jewish Refugees in London opened their archives to me, and introduced me to the wonderful old folk at their day-care center in Cleve Road; their memories were a great source. The British Library newspaper archives in Colindale has the most patient and helpful staff one could wish for. Catherine Shepherd shared her master's thesis on postwar fascism in Hampstead. Anthony Grenville helped me understand how the refugees adapted to their new home. Ivor Gabor introduced me to Martin White, a treasure trove of anecdotes who opened the doors to a dozen colorful former Eastenders and Jewish ex-soldiers who fought the fascists in London's streets after the Second World War. Thanks also to the former terrorist for your frank and comprehensive account of how you planned to murder Ernest Bevin. I'm glad it was called off the night before.

Thanks to Daisy Roessler in Israel for explaining how she repaired nylon stockings in 1945. And to Thelma Klein for her hilarious account of giving birth to my mate Jeff in London right after the war, and to Rachel Goldman in New York for her more sobering description of Braxton Hicks contractions.

Another great resource was the Mass Observation archives at Sussex University. The thousands of wartime diaries kept by Britons provided priceless contemporary color, from wartime recipes to children's games, where German Jews always played the Nazis. And that great advice on how to survive German bombs: Put a bucket on your head.

I have nothing left of my past, then, but what I carry in my head.
—*The World of Yesterday* by Stefan Zweig

THE LIST

ONE

London

May 8, 1945

VE Day

"Give 'er one! Give 'er one!"

Up on the bronze plinth of Eros a soldier with a red beret embraced a blonde, his leg locked around hers. She strained into him, their lips fused: an erotic sculpture against the leaden sky. His hands entered her blouse. The crowd below roared and clapped. Will they fall off or copulate? Right there, in the place of Eros, carted off years ago to be hidden from German bombs. The elderly drunk shouted: "Give 'er one! Give 'er one!" as she lurched toward a beer truck inching by, honking, while men and women swarmed over it, pulling bottles from the stacked crates. The driver took a swig, waved his bottle and yelled, "Where's Jerry now!" The call to give 'er one faded as the drunk staggered away, waving a beer. The truck backfired and a man in a red, white, and blue paper hat called out, "It's okay, it's one of ours!"

There was somebody up every lamppost in Piccadilly Circus, hanging from every balcony, dancing on every car, denting their roofs, people yelling and screaming and kissing strangers. At the top of Pall Mall two boys banged dustbin lids when they could, for there wasn't space to spread their arms, there were so many Londoners pushing toward Buckingham Palace. Under the plane trees, soldiers in khaki kicked their legs and nurses in white lifted their skirts, dancing, holding hands, and shouting, "Knees up, Mother Brown, knees up, Mother Brown," while others pulled their hands apart to join in "Knees up, knees up, knees up, knees up, knees up, Mother Brown!"

The red glow over London wasn't burning buildings but bonfires of joy, and the flashes streaking through the sky weren't V-2 rockets but fireworks. London was ablaze with celebration; the searchlights no longer hunting Nazi bombers but burning a V for Victory in the clouds over St. Paul's Cathedral. Buckingham Palace shone in floodlights for the first time since 1939. Dots appeared on the distant balcony and a roar erupted from the crowd: "God Save the King!" King George VI, with a chest of medals on his Royal Navy tunic, waved and smiled, the Queen at his side in powder blue, while the two princesses, coats buttoned against the chill, beamed down at the people. Their prime minister joined them. A man yelled "There 'e is, the bald old coot!" and called out, "Winnie, Winnie," and everyone joined him, and broke into a chorus of "For He's a Jolly Good Fellow."

A hushing sound like a gentle wind silenced the people, and they crowded around their wirelesses to hear their monarch's victory address:

> *For five long years and more, heart and brain, nerve and muscle have been directed upon the overthrow of Nazi tyranny. There is great comfort in the thought that the years of darkness and danger in which the children of our country have grown up are over, please God, forever.*

"Hear, hear!" could be heard along the Mall and around the fountain, followed quickly by "Shut up, mate, let's listen!" But nothing, certainly not George's hesitant lisp, stirred the British like Winston Churchill's splendid growl when his speech to Parliament was relayed by loudspeaker:

> *Almost the whole world was combined against the evildoers, who are now prostrate before us . . . but let us not forget for a moment the toil and efforts that lie ahead. Japan, with all her treachery and greed, remains unsubdued. The injury she has inflicted on Great Britain, the United States, and other countries, and her detestable cruelties, call for justice and retribution. . . . Advance, Britannia! Long live the cause of freedom! God save the king!"*

"God save the king!" The roar rolled across the capital and the country and before the palace the crowd burst into yet another chorus: "For he's a jolly good fellow . . . For he's a jolly good fellow . . ."

Halfway up the Mall, a speck in the crowd, Georg stood behind Edith, his arms around her waist, nibbling her ear, as she jiggled her shoulders and tapped her foot and sang along, "And so say all of us, and so say . . ." The nape of her neck felt damp and her loose hair itched his nose. He smoothed it back and whispered again, "Dit, please, I keep asking you." Edith jumped and waved her arms in the air and shouted "Winnie!" Georg put his mouth into Edith's ear to be heard above the crowd: "Dit, you know you must be careful, this time."

"Ouch!" Edith jerked her head away, and her shiny auburn hair settled with a wave. "You almost made me deaf, I told you, Schorschi,

I'm fine!" She swung him round so that he stood before her, took his hand, pulled him tight to her body, kissed him full on the lips and pushed him away again, swinging her hips and shouting, "Come on, let's dance!" Georg apologized to the soldier whose foot he stood on, but the man only laughed and yelled, "If you don't want to dance with the lovely lady, I will!" and took Edith's hand and twirled her round.

She threw her head back and they jigged, as best they could in the crush, Georg trying to join the fun but fearing for Edith. Now all three had their arms around each other, kicking their legs, and Edith pulled in Ismael, their Egyptian friend from the boardinghouse, who hadn't sung a word. He was as reluctant as Georg but when two other women grabbed his hands and joined the jig he smiled at them and also raised a leg. They laughed and teased him: "Where you from then, handsome? Arabia?" Ismael grinned and shouted to be heard, "Guess!"

"Oooh, mystery man," one said, laughing. "I do like a good mystery!" Her friend elbowed Ismael in the side. "Me too!" and they shrieked with laughter. "My name's Doris," the redhead said, "and this is Rose—she's blooming mad!" They hooted and pulled Ismael between them, dancing and singing.

The dancing tapered off as a song rippled across the Mall, rising high, fifty thousand voices calling to the skies, which would no longer rain bombs and death. Everyone knew Vera Lynn's ode to the marching boys; it had been a hit throughout the war.

We'll meet again,
Don't know where,
Don't know when.

But I know we'll meet again
Some sunny day.

Doris and Rose sang with Edith and Georg, and the nation joined, calling for the safe return of their fighting men and women.

Keep smiling through,
Just like you always do,
Till the blue skies
Drive the dark clouds far away
So will you please say hello
To the folks that I know,
Tell them I won't be long . . .

As they sang the first verse again, Doris looked with sympathy toward Edith and Georg. Their accents had given them away:

Ve'll meet again
Don't know vere,
Don't know ven
Ve'll meet again,
Some sunny day.

"Jewish, are you, then?" Doris asked, putting her hand on Edith's elbow. "You're from Germany, are you?"

Edith shook her head. "Austria." Her body stiffened, her shoulders seemed to drop.

"Same old, same old. But why you suddenly looking so sad, then? We won the war!"

Edith tried to smile, but it didn't work anymore. Her face tensed and she felt nauseous as she thought of her family, everyone. Who's alive, who's dead? Georg put his arm around her shoulder. "The war's over," he said. "You celebrate, you mourn." A great roar rose from the crowd as the song ended: *"Some sunny day."* "Doing both isn't easy."

"You what? You feeling queasy?" Doris shouted. "I can 'ardly 'ear you. Wouldn't wonder at all. But cheer up! We won, we won!" She shook Edith's elbow hard and peered into her face. "Ve von, ve von," she shouted, "you can go back to Austria now, ducks, it's all over! Ve von! You can go 'ome!"

Edith looked up at Georg, who pulled her closer, feeling her shudder. Home. That graveyard. *Sicher!* To live among those Nazi swine? Where? And who with? Who's left?"

We'll meet again, don't know where, don't know when.

Oh, I hope so!

They'll be happy to know that as you saw me go I was singing this song.

No, I wasn't. Edith didn't even dare wave good-bye as her parents saw her go; she had been too scared of the plainclothes Nazi police at the Wien Südbahnhof, and she hadn't heard from *Mutti* and *Papi* for nearly three years, since September 1942.

We'll meet again,
Some sunny day.

Another roar erupted: a black Humber was inching through the crowd, heading for the palace. From the backseat a large man rolled down the window and waved to the crowd. People swarmed forward, calling out "Ernie, Ernie, bless you, Ernie!"

"Who's that, who's coming?" Edith asked, standing on her tiptoes. "I can't see."

"It's a cabinet minister," Georg said. "It's Ernest Bevin."

"Who is it?" Ismael, a head shorter than Georg, but twice as stocky, asked. "It's Bevin, really?"

"Yes."

"You know why he hates the Jews? Because . . ." It was the setup for another one of Ismael's tiresome anti-Semitic jokes. Georg was about to interrupt when Edith gripped his arm and yelped.

"What? What is it, Edith?"

Her face contorted as she bent over, putting her other hand between her legs. "Oh, no," she said, "oh no!"

"Edith, what?"

Her eyes brimmed with tears. Her mouth trembled.

"Edith, please, what is it?"

"I think I'm bleeding."

"Oh, please, no! Not again!"

Her knickers felt warm and wet beneath her stockings, thickness oozing on her skin. "I think so. Oh no! I need to see. Quickly! Get me out of here." She gripped Georg tighter. He looked around, his eyes wide in alarm. The crowd was massed all the way to the Palace one way and up to Trafalgar Square the other. Revelers were packed in all directions, singing, swaying, dancing, laughing, shouting. It would take hours just to reach the trees.

"You all right, ducks?" Rose said.

Oh, why did they come, he told Edith she needed to rest. Why didn't she ever listen?

Georg bent down and yelled into Ismael's ear. "Ismael. Let's go, Edith is bleeding."

Ismael looked Edith up and down, surprised now by her tears. "Bleeding? Where?"

Georg shouted, "We already lost one baby in the fifth month, get it? Please, help."

Georg's arms supported Edith while burly Ismael forced his way through the crowd shouting "Emergency, medical emergency!" Two strangers helped, one shoulder-to-shoulder with Ismael, ramming through the people, clearing a path, the other linking hands with Georg to form a seat for Edith. Georg and Edith looked in shock, white and drawn. Panting and terrified, they fought their way to a medical team close to Kensington Gate. The young medic in white pushed Georg back and rushed Edith into his tent. Georg thanked the Englishmen, who left with knowing pats and nods, and waited outside with Ismael, who held his hand. Georg could barely stand. "She's only in her eighth week," he said to Ismael, with tears in his eyes. "We've had bad luck in the past." Ismael nodded, tight-lipped.

It didn't take long. Edith reappeared, walking unaided, shy and tentative. Georg and Ismael rushed forward. "Are you all right?" Georg asked, his voice catching. "Please, tell me you're all right."

Edith glanced at Ismael, shrugged one shoulder with a sweet smile, and took Georg aside. Behind her the medic grinned. She raised her chin and pulled Georg down so that she could whisper into his ear. "Schorschi, I'm fine. I was just getting too excited. I'm afraid I wet myself."

TWO

The 7:21 from Dover to Liverpool Street rattled through the rising mist, hooted past sleepy English towns. Through gaps in the orange-tinged clouds, sunlight flashed and glinted off the speeding train. Toward the front, Anna breathed onto the window of her compartment and traced the outline of a head. Frowning, she added pigtails with bows, and two outward-curving lines, to form a neck. She leaned forward so that her own face fitted in the outline and looked back at her. Now she had pigtails, too. Like Elsie, Edith's rag doll without the eyes.

Her face stared back, with Elsie's pigtails, from the glass. She watched her warm breath fade as it left her face, staring, without the pigtails. Her head was long with tight curly hair. It had been nine months now. She didn't know why her hair wouldn't grow back. It had been so lush and black and shiny.

Anna turned and sunk into her seat. As she did so the woman opposite looked away. The man reading the newspaper lowered his head.

Anna looked out of the window. It was drizzling now; droplets slid across the window. They were passing low houses and untidy little gardens and her reflection stared back, unmoving, as the background of grimy buildings and washing lines flashed by. She thought, *Am I stuck in time?* But time moves at different speeds. She already knew that.

I already know that.

She trembled as she saw herself. Naked in the snow, hunched up, shivering, teeth chattering, jumping up and down, her breasts heavy. Guards laughing. Then time is like a stagnant river. Blood barely flows and it aches as it struggles through your veins; it throbs. Fingers and toes feel like they'll burst. Gums ache from grinding teeth. While when you're warm, oh, how quickly it passes, please don't end. I'll do anything to stay warm. Hold me. Please.

They'll ask questions. Everyone will. What can I say? Where shall I start? How can I explain? How many lifetimes went by in the last five years? How many people died? And the way they died. And I didn't die. Or did I? Here I am. That's proof I didn't die. What other proof do you need? But can your body and your mind and your heart die at different speeds?

Anna's eyes met the lady's opposite and held them for a moment. They both looked away.

She took the telegram from her coat pocket. SEE YOU AT THE STATION STOP EDITH. She hadn't understood why Edith had written *station stop*. Was it a misspelling? Should it be "shop"? Should they meet at the station shop? It must be a big station. Was there only one shop or were there many? Or did "station stop" just mean the stop at the station? So why didn't Edith just write "station"? It didn't make sense. But then, what did?

Anna closed her eyes and hoped the gentle rhythm of the train would help her sleep, but it didn't. Her mind was grinding, bouncing. When did I last sleep well? I can't remember. It's not that I see things. I don't see anything. Only darkness. But I hear. Footsteps, the clack of heels on wood, doors squeaking and slamming, girls whimpering, screaming, begging for mercy, guards jeering, dogs barking, thumps, engines, and more darkness. What's next for me? I feel so empty. Drained. Nothing. Nothing. If they ask what happened, if they ask, how did you live, what can I say? Will they ask? Of course they will.

Anna looked at the window. She stared at her staring eyes as the peaceful countryside slid by.

"Mostly I remember Anna's eyes, such sparkling green eyes, she's always such fun, you'll love her," Edith smiled in excitement, as Georg handed her his steaming cup of Bovril. "And her hair, we were all so jealous, so thick and long with natural shiny waves. Thank you."

She cupped the drink with her hands and blew into it. Georg looked along the empty rails of track 14, which curved out of sight. He checked the big white clock hanging below the cavernous glass roof of Liverpool Street station. He smiled. "I saw the minute hand move. Click. I always love that. It's like time stands still for a moment." A whistle shrieked and clouds of steam hissed from a locomotive pulling into the next platform. A guard waved and guided the train to a halt, its massive black rubber nose bumped into the thick wooden barrier at the end of the track. Doors swung open, passengers jumped down before it stopped. Two trains pulled out from other platforms at the same moment, a lurch and a rattle as they picked up speed. A man ran after one, dragging his case.

"She'll be here in a moment," Edith said, between sips. Georg looked at the clock. "Twelve minutes, if it's on time. Are you nervous?"

"Oh, yes."

· · ·

It was all so sudden.

The day before, kind Mrs. Wilson from Bloomsbury House, which housed most of London's Jewish refugee organizations, had telephoned Edith. "I think I've got some good news for you, dearie," she had said, almost singing. "Can you drop by?"

Silence. Edith's hand dropped to her belly, cupped it. She could hardly breathe. Good news? Is there such a thing? From Bloomsbury House? All news from the past had been bad.

Georg kept two lists: his relatives and hers. One by one he crossed them out when the phone call came, or when they found the names on a Red Cross list, or when news, definite news, came from friends on the Continent. Edith's uncle Max had a heart attack in Budapest and was taken to the hospital the day before the SS emptied the wards of Jews; they were ordered to the woods and shot. The Red Cross found his name on a list of the murdered and it matched a checking form at Bloomsbury House. Georg drew a thick lead line through Uncle Max. Edith's brother Ernst somehow existed two years in the Sobibor death camp before a guard clubbed him to death because he couldn't stand. A blockmate who survived told a mutual acquaintance who wrote Edith. Georg crossed him off. Georg's mother and father were gassed in Majdanek, with his sister, grandmother, and two aunts. He even knew the dates, from the German records. His tears had stained the paper as he drew wavering pencil marks through their names, as if cutting their bodies in two, though he felt he was cutting off parts of himself, this leg, that arm. For years rumors and reports, of massacres, death camps, gas chambers, had prepared them all for the worst; still, you were never really ready. Sometimes he vomited. Edith cried with him, and they carried on, because what else was there to do? There were some relatives on the list without a line through them.

And now this. Five months after the war had ended, with the unfathomable number of six million Jews said to be dead, their first sign of life. Anna, Edith's cousin. The beautiful one.

She had moved in with Edith's parents and sister in Vienna when Anna's own parents and brothers and sisters were removed to Poland's second-largest city, Lodz, where they disappeared, presumably to be gassed in Auschwitz, like so many others from the Lodz ghetto. A large copper frying pan, a prized one, had saved Anna's life. She had left the house to collect it from a friend in Hietzing who no longer needed it, as all her friend's family had been taken. She had stayed to chat. When she returned home the neighbors told her: the SS took your family. She brought the frying pan to Edith's parents, her aunt and uncle, for now she, too, had no use for it.

From that day Anna slept in Edith's bedroom, with Edith's eyeless rag doll for company; until the maid's family requisitioned the grand apartment, heirlooms and all, for the Third Reich, forcing the four of them to live together in the little maid's room upstairs. Censored letters became scarcer and less informative. They talked of failed attempts to procure exit visas, affidavits from guarantors in America that didn't arrive. How hard it was to go for a walk because Mutti's legs hurt and Jews weren't allowed to rest on public benches; Mutti's teeth trouble because no dentist dared help her, and Papi's anger at not being allowed to work in his medical practice, and their blossoming garden that they could now enjoy only through the top-floor window, and which friends had disappeared and who still came to visit; until finally there were no more letters. The very last communication from Edith's father was to a Christian friend in Vienna who had forwarded it to Edith in London via Marseilles. Eight words on a postcard dated June 1, 1942, in the doctor's hurried scrawl. It read: *"Wir müssen fort, alle vier, innerhalb einer Stunde."* We must go, all four of us, within the hour.

Everyone knew what that meant.

Only the day before Mrs. Wilson called, Georg had struck two more names off his list. Edith, looking tired, was lounging in the window alcove at Bloomsbury House, listening to her sultry friend Gina, she of the languid, fluttered hand, when Georg, who was making his way down the list of names on the wall, said, "Dit, Esther Lemburger—is she one of yours?" Edith edged past the other refugees scanning lists in the narrow corridor. She put her finger on the name. "If she's from Kaiserslautern? Could be." Mrs. Wilson looked at that morning's file from the Red Cross. And there it was: Lemburger from Kaiserslautern. Edith's mother's aunt, whom she had never met, had that name and lived in that town. Next to her name was another name—Stutthof. The concentration camp near Danzig. Farther down the list was Hilde Truedhof—the married name of Esther Lemburger's daughter.

A week earlier Gina had found her youngest sister's name, Rosa, alongside Treblinka death camp. She burst into tears and almost pulled Edith to the floor with her. It was the last of her sisters; her only brother had been shot in Budapest. Edith and Georg helped her up and took her into one of the rooms and stayed with her until she was empty and then they all went to Lyons Corner House for tea and carrot cake.

Now it was Gina's turn to hold Edith, but she didn't need to. Edith didn't cry. She made herself think, *I didn't know them anyway.*

Back home, Georg crossed Esther Lemburger and Hilda Truedhof off Edith's list.

And then Mrs. Wilson's call.

"I begged her, finally, some good news, tell me now, over the phone, I can't wait," Edith told Georg, who had leapt down the stairs three at a time when he heard her shout. They were on the first floor, by the front door, next to the phone attached to the wall. Edith was shaking her head in wonder, a huge smile. "And she said it's my cousin Anna, she's in Paris, she's coming to London. Tomorrow! They matched our names. I don't know anything else." Georg held Edith while she trembled and cried. "She was with Mutti and Papi and Lisa, they were all taken at the same time." His shirt became damp with her tears. His eyes burnt. He understood. If Anna was alive, maybe Edith's parents and sister were, too.

The loudspeaker echoed through the immense concourse: "Seven twenty-one from Dover arriving platform nine, platform nine." Georg threw his head back, drained the Bovril, walked to the trashcan and threw in the paper cup. Edith stood up, too, smoothed down her dress over her swollen stomach and buttoned her coat. She turned up the collar, thought better of it, and turned it down again. Opened her bag and pulled out a little mirror. Gave her hat to Georg while she found her brush and tidied her hair. Dug around in her bag again and came up with her lipstick and dabbed some on. Looking into her pocket mirror, she pressed her lips together, pursed them, pressed them. As she put the lipstick and mirror back into the little leather bag and snapped it shut, she tried to smile at Georg. He took her hand but she shook him away and with both hands put her hat back on. Georg followed her to platform 9.

Edith couldn't remember the last time she had seen Anna. It must have been in her garden, which had become the meeting place of all her friends. Anna, at seventeen, was a year younger than Edith, and the whole crowd, a dozen school and family friends, was within a year or two of each other in age. They had made the best of things.

When Jews were no longer allowed into the swimming pool, or into the park, or the cafés, or even into most of the shops, their world had shrunk until they could only meet at home. They were like dying people confined to the space around them. Edith's garden was the largest and had an alpine shed with a bed and cooking fire, and three benches under a large oak tree whose thick canopy gave them shade that last hot summer of 1938. It became their universe, where they talked and read and courted until one by one her friends disappeared. Some were lucky. Willi's family got a visa for America, Berndt's family to France, while Betty's family just vanished and finally turned up safe in Switzerland. Some were not lucky. Albert and Benno were arrested and couldn't be traced. Addie was beaten in the street and died in the hospital. And then, on February 6, 1939, a rare sunny day, it was Edith's turn to vanish.

At six o'clock in the morning the Nazis came for her father. They pounded on the door until the maid pulled it open, the same maid who would later steal their home. Five SA stormtroopers in brown shirts with swastika armbands and high leather boots pushed past her into the lobby. She fell against the sidetable and a prized Annamese dish, exquisitely veined, one of a pair, crashed to the floor. Edith, woken from a deep sleep, at first didn't understand the commotion downstairs.

"Max Epstein! *Raus!* Out!"

"Doktor Epstein," the maid corrected automatically.

"*Jude* Epstein! Jew Epstein!" One of them shouted, "*Sofort,* immediately, *rrrrraus!*" The Nazi *rrrr,* that boiled up from the gut.

The whole family scrambled to the lobby in their nightclothes as the Nazis tried to pull Doktor Epstein from his home. Edith's mother,

Josephine, cried and begged. "Please, why? My husband is a doctor, the people need him."

"*Rrrraus!* Out, now."

"He was in the army, an army surgeon!" Josephine, desperate, ran from one Nazi to the other, pulling at their shirts. "A hero! He has a medal from the Kaiser! I will show it to you! Wait!" She ran into the salon, to take the imperial award from its case in the glass display cabinet.

As Edith rushed down the stairs she saw Lisa, her sister, gripping the arm of one of the Nazis who pushed her away so that she fell against a chair, screaming. The brown-shirted men shouted for Epstein to come with them and two of them dragged him by the arms, stretching his pajama sleeves. They all stumbled into the sidetable, shattering the second Annamese dish.

Doktor Epstein pulled back, insisting he be allowed to collect his clothes and identity papers. "Surely your officer will want to see my documents," he said, with as much dignity as the occasion, and his breathlessness, allowed. "Permit me to fetch them."

"Here, here!" Josephine called, her nightgown open, her crinkly hair disheveled. "See, look, the Golden Service Cross, for bravery before the enemy. Doktor Epstein was a hero in the Imperial Austrian Army in the Great War, this is his medal. He saved lives. Austrian lives. Leave my husband alone!" She sobbed, holding out the gold and white cross in its purple quilt case. "Look. Here is the imperial seal. Leave him alone." A stormtrooper struck her arm. The medal clattered to the floor.

Edith, who had paused on the bottom step, now pushed past her mother. "Where are your papers?" she shouted. "Where is your arrest warrant?" Everyone knew the new Nazi orders: All arrests in Austria, even of Jews, had to be made with the proper papers.

"Papers! Papers! I'll show you papers!" one of the Nazis shouted and pushed Edith in the chest. She fell against the maid but quickly recovered.

"I'll have you arrested, I'll call the police," Edith shouted back, and slapped his face.

Everyone froze. Shocked. Edith's fortune was that the Nazi pulled back and her fingertips merely grazed him. He put his hand to his cheek, eyes wide.

The two men pulling Doktor Epstein's arms relaxed their grip. He pulled his arms free. Josephine stopped crying. The maid stepped back toward the kitchen.

Edith slapped a Nazi? Everyone looked at the brownshirts' clubs; they didn't carry guns. Edith broke the silence in a low, determined voice. "If you take my father without an arrest warrant I will call the police and you will be arrested yourself. All of you." She held their stares, a slim Jewish girl against six Nazis with clubs. But she could hardly breathe.

Everyone knew the police wouldn't do a thing. But Edith was right. They needed papers, and they didn't have any. There was a pause. Max drew himself up, a dignified man with calm eyes, even now. He automatically twirled one side of his grey moustache, his nervous tic. "We will be back," one of the men growled, "and we will have the papers."

That evening they returned with the papers. Not for Doktor Epstein. The arrest papers were for Miss Edith Epstein, eighteen years old, trainee-seamstress. By then, however, Edith was in Czechoslovakia. She was the only member of the family with an exit permit. Until then she had refused to leave her parents. Now she had no choice. As soon as the door slammed, her parents rushed her to her room, where she sobbed from frustration and fear. They helped her pack—

not clothes or shoes, but memories: letters, photos, the drawing of a black cat that hung over her bed, the school yearbook signed by her friends. Every second counted.

Edith last saw her parents at the station. Max and Josephine squeezed out every last instant of seeing their little daughter, as she trudged with her small suitcase to the ticket window to buy a one-way ticket to Prague. They followed fifty yards behind as she walked slowly to the train that would take her to the border, and safety. They treated her like a stranger, they couldn't acknowledge her, let alone hold her, or kiss her good-bye, or even wave, and she couldn't wave to them. Plainclothes security where everywhere, especially at the train stations, looking for Jews leaving illegally. Although Edith had the correct permits, who knew if her name wasn't already circulating on some arrest list? They mustn't draw attention. They could only look at each other, from a distance, through the crowd. And as the train whistled and picked up speed, Edith leaned out the window and saw her parents becoming smaller and smaller in the fading steam until they appeared as one distant hazy outline. Only as the train entered the bend, when she couldn't see them anymore, did Edith dare wave good-bye.

Six years on, brakes screeched and sparks flew along the steel brackets of track 9. The train's giant black rubber nose edged the final inches and rested amid a sigh of steam against the wooden wall. Edith looked up just as the clock's second hand twitched to 12:10. She tried to smile, said "I saw it move, too," and put her arm into Georg's. She felt her stomach churn.

From a dozen carriages passengers passed bags through the windows, helped one another down the steep iron steps, scanned the crowd for family and friends. Within moments the empty platform was a mass of people, disappearing in the steam and reappearing like ghosts, hurrying toward the exit, where Edith and Georg stood behind the metal gate, trying to spot Anna.

"It's been such a long time," Edith said. "She was a year younger than me, seventeen." Georg only knew Anna by Edith's description. The most beautiful girl in the family—all the friends flirted with her, and she adored the attention. Ludwig, an artist, painted three portraits of her and everyone knew he was really making advances, but he got nowhere. Where was he now? And the paintings? She had long, shiny black hair, and perfect curves. She was funny and lively, a good student until she was banned from school; she always climbed highest on Edith's oak tree. Georg's gangly height gave him a good view over the crowd—he was looking for an attractive twenty-two-year-old woman walking alone, probably carrying a small suitcase. But who knew what she looked like now? What she had been through? How she had survived? Lucky ones had found shelter passing as non-Jews in Christian homes or even in convents. Maybe she had been lucky?

The crowd of passengers funneled through the narrow exit gate and swelled again on the other side, Anna carried along with them, right past Edith and Georg. She walked to the shops, wondering if Edith had meant the newspaper shop or the café. Or maybe station stop meant the station exit? But she didn't recognize anyone there, either. People were lining up at the bus stops and leaving or were entering the station. She felt she was in a daze, swept to and fro with the crowd. Only when she reentered the concourse and looked back toward the platform exit, which was empty again, and saw the pregnant young woman in the hat holding hands with the tall, thin man in the long overcoat and flat cap, both looking around, as if searching, she about twenty-three, he a couple of years older, and stared, and their eyes met, and they took small steps toward each other, did she recognize Edith, and at the same moment, Edith thought she saw something familiar in the frail woman looking at her.

Georg didn't know what he had expected. A celebration? Joy? Stamping of the feet and squeals of delight and hugs and kisses like it used to be in Vienna? To go for a cup of tea and *Schwartzwäldische Kirchentorte mit Schlagsahne,* everyone's favorite cherry cake, and get all the news? Answer all the questions. Mysteries solved?

It wasn't like that.

The two women stood opposite each other, unsure, and didn't say anything or take each other's hands. They just looked. Trying to remember, staring through time. Is this Anna? Can it be? The most they did was take another step forward. They looked into each other's eyes for a long time, silently, seeking something. It was the heaviest silence. Anna knew Edith; but it was all so long ago, in a different world, beyond the gulf that suddenly loomed. She must have had a good war. In fact she looked better, somehow warmer, with shiny auburn hair, and what a lovely tummy in her tight coat, pregnancy suited her.

But Edith wasn't sure. The sparkling emerald eyes were brown and lifeless, as if no one was home, the sparkling dark hair was short and frizzy and neglected. This woman was painfully thin, with pale, dry skin, almost sickly, and her face was blank, with no sign of recognition. She could be thirty-five, and poorly preserved at that, not twenty-two. They looked at each other, two strangers, as travelers pushed by, seeking their platform, meeting friends, going home. The stationmaster called, "Twelve-forty for Manchester, leaving platform twelve, platform twelve."

As Edith, shaken and unsure, glanced at Georg for support, the other woman, her face muscles immobile, murmured, "Edith?"

Edith burst into tears.

Anna leaned forward and touched Edith's belly and whispered, "Edith, you mustn't upset the baby."

On the bus, Georg explained. "Edith cries a lot now. She didn't used to. I think it's being pregnant in her seventh month." He smiled to himself, couldn't help it. Twelve weeks to go, eighty-four days, and he'd be a father, God willing. He glanced at Edith's stomach and kissed his baby's soul. *Stay safe*, he thought.

"Fayers, pleeese. Thenk yuh," the conductor called. After paying for three tickets to Swiss Cottage, Georg added, "We're so excited, having a baby." He shrugged, laying his hand on Edith's thigh. "But it's hard. We're getting so much bad news, too. Happy, sad—we're all mixed up."

Edith and Anna shared a bench, side by side. Edith held Anna's hand and was surprised at how rough it felt, like a laborer's hand. She hoped Anna would volunteer something about her parents and sister, but Anna had hardly spoken. She seemed strange and distant, blank. She didn't smile, her face never changed. Was something wrong with her after all she must have been through? Was she hiding something? Edith didn't dare ask. Can they still be alive? All night Edith had hardly slept; the last she'd ever heard was the postcard: *We must go, all four of us, within the hour.* And now one had returned. And the others? Could Mummy and Daddy and Lisa be alive? Edith's heart pounded as she worked up her courage. Finally she pressed Anna's hand and brought it to her chest. As the bus slowed at a crossing, Edith asked, "Anna, can you tell me, please, what do you know about Mutti and Papi and Lisa? What happened? Where are they? What do you know?"

Georg, on the bench in front, stiffened.

Anna looked away, shook her head and withdrew her hand. Edith felt that each second of silence pressed her closer to the ground, made it harder to breathe. A minute went by before Anna answered.

"Nothing. I don't know anything."

"Nothing? Nothing?" Edith felt faint. After a pause, she said, "You must know something."

"No."

"But you all left Vienna together, isn't that right? Papi sent a card, where did you go?"

"Lodz," Anna said.

"Where?"

Anna didn't answer.

"Litsmannstadt, in Poland," Georg said, over his shoulder. "Lodz is the Polish word. Most Viennese Jews were sent there." Georg paused, before adding, "And then from there to Auschwitz."

Anna's eyes flickered.

He knows.

But he knows nothing.

The bus passed through the dingy streets of Clerkenwell and crossed Grey's Inn Road toward Euston. Anna stared out the window at the bombed buildings, piles of rubble and collapsed walls, and scorched door frames poking out at angles like arms calling for help. It was drizzling and grey and the streets were slick with rain. People hunched forward under umbrellas like damp mushrooms while bicycles sent a spray of water behind them. Anna looked at her reflection in the window, unmoving, as the streets flashed by through the image of her face.

At first Georg snuck sidelong glances at her, not wanting to stare, but slowly he turned and studied her face more directly, wondering what she was thinking about. He had so many questions, but best to take it slowly. After a moment he gave a little cough. "We live in Hampstead, one of the prettiest parts of London, but not our part. Swiss Cottage, it's a nice place, though," he began, but trailed off as Anna still stared out of the window. After a minute or two he tried again. "Nice people there—arty, intellectual, it's famous for writers. Hey, Sigmund Freud, he lived up the road from us, well, maybe not so close but . . ." Anna remained impassive. He exchanged looks with Edith, who raised an eyebrow. Georg turned to Anna. She must have been in Auschwitz and Auschwitz was the worst of all the death camps. No wonder she seems so . . . damaged. After five minutes of silence, it just came out, unplanned. "Anna, would you mind if I looked at your arm?" He was shocked at hearing himself ask.

As if her neck hurt, Anna slowly turned her head from the window to Georg. The conductor called out, "Fayers, pleeese. Thenk yuh," and counted out change for the old lady opposite.

Anna held out her right arm, and sighed. It seemed with relief. She pulled back the sleeve of her coat, and nodded to Georg to roll back the cuffs of her cardigan and blouse. Edith stared as Anna's wrist and then her pale forearm were exposed. She recoiled, shocked. They'd seen it at the pictures and now, there it was. Like an extra set of blue veins: M-23501. Edith looked away and felt the bile rising. It stopped on the way out and she swallowed the burning stuff. She closed her eyes in pain: Mutti? Papi? Lisa?

Georg whispered, "We'll talk later?" There was the barest, almost imperceptible nod from Anna. She turned back to look at her face in the window.

Minutes passed. As they all leaned to the left on a bend, it was Anna who broke the silence. "What about my family? Did you hear anything about Mummy? Daddy?"

Edith had been so worried about her own family she had forgotten that Anna was just as worried, maybe even more so, because she knew what had happened in the camps. "No," Edith managed to say. "Nothing. We check almost every day, but no news. No good news, anyway. Until you." She squeezed Anna's hand, which lay limp in hers.

It had stopped raining by the time they arrived at Swiss Cottage. Georg carried Anna's small bag down the hill, a tall, thin man with spectacles, habitually stooped from fatigue, following a step behind Anna and Edith, who walked silently hand in hand. Anna spoke first. "How beautiful," she said, as Belsize Road reached the roundabout at Fairhazel Gardens. In its raised center stood a solitary tree, its lush canopy stretching and falling in a circle of deepest green, raindrops on the leaves glinting in the dim streetlight.

"*Trauerweide.* It has a lovely name in English," Georg said. "Weeping willow."

At the pair of red telephone boxes they turned left into Goldhurst Terrace, a curving line of tall Victorian homes scarred by three gardens crowded with piles of bricks and doors and broken glass, with exposed basements full of dark rainwater. "Bomb sites," said Georg as they passed. "Nobody was hurt, they were all in the shelters." They stopped outside the blue door of 181. The house was built of rust-colored brick and the porch had stained-glass windows and colored tiles. "This is it," Edith announced, and led Anna up the steep steps. She paused, to catch her breath. "This is where we live, and—"

"And this is the new girl!" a woman's shrill voice interrupted as the door opened from within.

"Hello, Mrs. Barnes, I'd like you to meet—"

"Goodness, look what the cat's dragged in," Sally Barnes said, beckoning them in. "So you're the new girl, you look as if you could do with a cup of tea, dearie. Where've you come from then, Siberia?"

Georg tried to take over. "Mrs. Barnes, this is Anna, Edith's cousin. Anna, this is Mrs. Barnes, our landlady. I think we'll just show Anna to the room and—"

"A good cup of tea, that's what you need. Come in, ducks, come in. You look awful."

Georg carried Anna's bag into the narrow entrance hall and headed for the stairs, but Sally called out, "Albert, they're heee-yer."

"Cuuu-miiing," a voice sounded from below, followed by heavy footsteps and wheezing, and Albert appeared. Big and balding, he offered Anna his hand. "I want to tell you you're very welcome here. Ismael told us all about you, come from them concentrations camps. Well, you're safe now!"

"There really isn't much room in the corridor," Georg said, "I think we'll just—"

"Of course, dear, come right on into the lounge," Sally said. "We want to hear all about it."

Squeezing past Albert, who sucked in his stomach while she turned hers, Edith said, "We must go upstairs first, Mrs. Barnes, and get organized, and then we'll come down and chat. We'll join you for tea later."

"You know, dearie . . . what's your name again?"

"Anna."

"You know, Anna, just yesterday we were at the waxworks up at Oxford Street, they had all these figures of Hitler and Mussolini and them, just like in real life. You had to pay to get in. They had a concentration camp, too, but you had to pay another sixpence to see it. We'd already paid sixpence to get in. And they wanted another sixpence. Bloody cheek. So I says to Albert, didn't I, Albert, I says, let's not bother, Edith's friend'll tell us all about it anyway. Straight from the horse's mouth, so to speak."

"We'll talk soon," Edith said, "I promise," and she guided Anna toward the stairs.

"No, just a moment . . . ," Sally said.

"That's all right," Albert said. "You must be tired from the journey. No need to rush things. I know how you feel. Our Eric, no picnic for him, either. He's been in the Airborne this past year. Sergeant. In Palestine. Bit of bother with your lot. He's been in an army camp, too. Terrible conditions, you know, don't know how people can survive like that. So hot. Well, carry on. Catch up later, then."

Georg carried the bag up the stairs, followed by Anna, with Edith trailing. Pity they lived on the third floor. It wasn't so easy anymore to walk up the stairs. She was into her seventh month and it was a lot of extra weight to carry. Put on twenty pounds already and only weighed 110 to start with. Doctor Goldscheider said it looked like being a big baby. Edith paused, holding on to the railing, breathing loudly. No more belly dancing for her in the lounge, she was thinking, that's for sure, or wrestling with Otto in room 5, let alone carrying the laundry down to the washing machine. Take it easy, Doctor Goldscheider had said. Only last week she had phoned him about her stomachaches and he'd insisted she come straight to his surgery up the road—*sofort*! He had come from around his desk and sat next to her, put his hand on her knee. She liked him. A family doctor from Berlin, he had the same moustache as her father, and also closed all three buttons of his jacket. He looked like a stuffed doll with a kind face. "I'm warning you, Edith," he had said. "If you don't slow down you could endanger the baby. After you lose one it's easier to lose the next. You must try not to work so hard, and not to worry so much. I know it's hard for you, it's hard for all of us, at this moment, with so many worries, but if you want to keep the baby, I would advise you to spend as much time as possible lying down. Even stay in bed. It's the best thing."

With Georg earning so little in the button factory there was no chance of that. Edith's money mending stockings paid the rent. "That work on the sewing machine isn't good," Doctor Goldscheider went on. "All that movement of your legs, up and down, and moving your arms all the time, it puts strain on your middle region. The next few weeks are critical and it could affect your . . . well, it puts strain on the baby and, well, we don't want to lose another one, do we?" Edith shook her head and thanked the doctor and didn't tell Georg. The only advice she followed was to swallow a soup spoon of cod liver oil a day, and drink her extra ration of orange juice.

When Edith reached the room, panting, Anna was sitting on the sofa. "That's your bed, then," Georg was saying. "Only for a bit, I'm afraid it's the best we could do at such short notice. I hope you don't mind. Another room should come vacant soon."

There were eight rooms in the guesthouse, as well as a shared kitchen, bathroom, and lounge. The landlords lived in two rooms on the ground floor, where there was a coal shed and a communal washing machine. "Half the residents are refugees, we're all friends," Georg said, "then there's an Indian, from Delhi, I think, we don't see much of him; two English people who just moved in, they share a room; and Ismael, the Egyptian. Strange fellow, comes and goes at all hours, but friendly. Says he's a student but doesn't seem to study. He's been here about six months. Doesn't say much. The refugees—"

"And what he does say isn't very nice," Edith interrupted, falling onto the sofa next to Anna. "He doesn't like Jews."

"The refugees all stay. But the others turn over quite a lot. I'm sure a room will soon be vacant. I hope you don't mind . . . ?"

Anna shook her head, looking around the little room. "It's warm."

"We left the electric heater on so you wouldn't be cold," Georg said, and smiled.

Anna removed her cardigan and rolled up her sleeve, revealing her tattoo. Georg couldn't stop looking at it.

She took three steps to the window. There were tall trees but the leaves were brown and spare. Through their bare branches she saw the rear of another row of terrace houses, whose back gardens were separated from the gardens of Goldhurst Terrace by a low brick wall covered by moss. On it she saw a grey-white squirrel. It bounded onto a tree and clambered along a branch. Its curled bushy tail, which had dragged along, now quivered and stood straight out. It had seen something. She followed its stare and from behind another tree a second squirrel appeared, gripping with its little claws, before darting up and leaping onto the same branch as the first squirrel. They moved toward each other in nervous starts and climbed on each other and rubbed noses, then rolled to the ground, and one chased the other back up the tree trunk. Anna gave a little laugh. Edith joined her at the window. She smiled. "It's a nice room, lots of light and sun in the mornings. Faces east. In the summer the landlord lets us sit in the garden. If it isn't raining."

Anna took Edith's hand and said, "It is very beautiful here."

Edith laughed. "I wouldn't say that, exactly."

Georg said, "It depends what you're used to."

"We had squirrels in our garden in Vienna, too," Edith said. "Remember?"

Anna said, "The last time I saw a squirrel was in Poland. It was dead in the snow. We ate it." There was silence for a moment.

"Well," Edith ended the pause, "not too sure what to say after that. Except for, Georg, what's for dinner?"

"Boiled rabbits."

"Ummm, yummy. We ate that during the war at Christmas."

"Really?" asked Anna.

"Really," said Georg.

"What were they like?"

"Fried rabbits are better. But whatever we had must have been a feast compared to you . . ." He let it hang, hoping Anna would open up.

She didn't.

Edith emptied a drawer. Anna's clothes filled half of it. "Is that all?" Edith asked, as Anna hung up her coat. "We must buy you something to wear. If we have any money. I'll try to get some extra work this week."

The door opened as they heard the knock. "Hello, hello," said Ismael.

"Did I say come in?" Edith asked.

Ismael ignored her and fell on the bed, leaning on one elbow for support. He looked at Anna, leaned forward, and stretched out his hand. "So you're the survivor," he said.

"Ismael!" Edith said, punching the word.

Georg took Ismael by the arm. "Not now, Ismael," he said, and tried to direct him toward the door.

But Ismael wouldn't budge. His hand was still extended. "I'm glad to meet you," he said. "We have the same hairstyle." Ismael's thick curls were dark and tightly cropped, emphasising his glowing swarthy skin, which gleamed in the electric light. Anna's short dark hair only set off her pallor. Their eyes met, and held. "It's all right, Dit," Anna said, using Edith's nickname for the first time. "Is that the word you prefer?" she asked Ismael as she took two steps toward him. "Survivor?" And stretched out her hand to take his. He stood as they shook hands. Their eyes were still fixed on each other and Ismael raised an eyebrow and smiled until he looked down and saw the blue tracks of her Auschwitz tattoo. "Oh!" he said, deflated. His eyes darted away and back again, riveted.

"Satisfied?" Georg said. "Now, would you mind?"

Ismael tried to recover as he turned toward the door. "I didn't mean to disturb. I'll see you later. I'll be in my room. I just, uh, just, wanted to say hello. . . ."

"Hello," Anna said, as she watched him leave and the door close.

THREE

It was dark outside and drizzling again. Damp air cut in through the rotting wooden window frames and when Edith opened the door to go to the kitchen she sucked in a cold blast from the freezing corridor. Georg fed another shilling into the gas meter, struck a match, and lit the fire. He and Anna huddled around the yellow flame, blowing on their hands and rubbing them. To break the silence, Georg said, "It's getting cold."

"This is cold?"

A few minutes later Edith returned carrying a salad bowl and buttered Wonderloaf. Georg fetched three plates and forks and set them on the low table by the fire. Their faces flushed in the heat while cold air brushed their necks. "Lettuce, radishes, beetroot, mustard, and cress," Edith announced. She passed Anna a slice of bread. "There's honey, if you like. And some milk. It isn't much to eat, but . . ."

They ate in silence, shadows from the fire playing on the flowery wallpaper. They heard footsteps above and the stairs creaked as residents walked by, and the toilet flushed, and from the bathroom next door came the stream of running water, followed by the gurgle through the pipes. "If you want a bath," Georg said, "you can only run five inches. Once a week. Rationing. We wash in the sink."

Anna didn't answer. *We wash in the sink . . .* She shuddered, and then again. Georg took her hand. Edith looked on in alarm. Anna's body trembled, as if icy. A tear left her eye, a glistening snail track.

We wash in the sink . . .

Standing in icy water, no towel, naked women running through snow to the barracks and to their filthy clothes covered in lice. Dogs chasing. Biting. Guards with sticks, yelling, cursing, beating.

It isn't much to eat, but . . .

Soup—tepid, dirty water with bits of hair and mice bones, and fighting over chunks of mouldy bread crawling with tiny worms.

Urine. On hot days soaking in a cloth to keep cool, on cold days to keep warm. Squeezing the cloth and drinking the drops.

Georg and Edith looked at each other, startled. What's happening?

Anna started and looked around. She blinked and shook her head. It was always so sudden, and so real. She could feel it, see it. Or sometimes, the opposite. So unreal. Am I imagining this? Could this really have happened to me? Was it just a nightmare?

Old people worry about losing their memory; the true tragedy is when you can't forget.

She took her cup of milk and emptied it. "I'm very tired," she whispered. "I think I'd like to go to sleep."

Georg went to the lounge as Anna undressed down to her under-wear and hung her clothes over the chair. As she brushed her teeth and patted water under her arms and on her face, she didn't stop looking at herself in the mirror over the sink. She touched her hair and tried to smooth it with water. She took a long drink. She went to the sofa and lay down, her legs bent. The sofa was too short. She rolled onto her back and pulled her legs up. Edith tucked her in under two blankets and kissed her brow. She stroked her hair. It felt damp and spiky and coarse. "Your beautiful hair will grow back," Edith whispered. "I'm so happy you are here. I love you."

With her heavy belly Edith couldn't bend for long, so she turned off the light and sat down on the sofa's edge. Anna pushed back into the cushion and pulled Edith closer. Now they lay together, Edith's body barely fitting, but held safe by Anna's arms tight around her. Their heads touched and they listened to each other breathing. Anna whispered, "Do you want a boy or a girl?"

"A girl. But I don't mind," Edith answered, wriggling even closer. "Just healthy. We're so excited. All our friends are. First baby of the next generation."

"Of course, it's wonderful."

They breathed almost in unison, for minutes, their bodies tight together, looking at the orange gas flame in the dark, its flickering shadows, beams of silver moonlight filtering in through tears in the curtain, dotting and playing on the walls as the curtain gently rustled, swelling and falling with the draught, until, finally, Anna murmured: "Dit, there's something I have to tell you. I couldn't tell you before. I know I should have told you straight away."

Edith felt the blood drain from her face. Her muscles tensed. She swallowed hard.

"Dit, I'm so sorry. You asked me about your family. I'm so very sorry. I have to tell you. Mutti and Lisa—they're gone."

Edith felt clammy, felt sweat rising through her pores; waited for her heart to stop pounding. For three years she had waited for this moment, ever since the postcard.

"Gone?"

"I'm so sorry."

"Where?"

Anna stroked Edith's hair, pulled her fingers through its softness. "I'm so sorry."

"What about Papi?"

"I only know that near the end of the war he was alive. We were together in Auschwitz."

Georg opened the door to a dark room. There was a sound, like mice scurrying and whimpering. Sometimes they got stuck in the walls or beneath the floorboards and there was a scratchy, squeaky yelp as if they were calling for help. These decrepit terrace houses were 120 years old, and they had more mice and rats than people. He kicked off his slippers and judged the distance to the bed so that he wouldn't need to switch the light back on and wake the girls. He wouldn't brush his teeth. He shouldn't have spent so long chatting in the lounge with Ismael, who felt bad about what he'd said to Anna. As he closed the door, careful not to make a noise, the corridor light narrowed until the last shaft fell on the sofa. It wasn't the squeaking of mice. It was Edith and Anna, hugging and crying in the dark.

They shared the bed, Edith in the middle. She and Georg lay on their backs, holding hands, listening to Anna who sat against the wall. For years Edith had agonized, sometimes in despair, sometimes in hope, desperate at German advances, encouraged by Allied successes, exhausted by not knowing, a world war reduced to its essence: What happened to my family? And now it wasn't a film at the pictures or a story in the paper or a rumor at the Austrian Center. Anna had been there, and come back. She knew. The last thing Edith knew was the postcard. It was Georg, the unemployed lawyer, who had got Anna to break her silence. "Nobody knows what happened there," he had said.

He was leaning across Edith, looking intently at Anna, almost beseeching her. "Only rumors, secret reports, newspaper headlines. We never knew what to believe. We always hoped for the best. And then suddenly, three months ago, they started talking about this number—six million. Six million Jews. What? What kind of number is that? It must be everyone. Were there no survivors? And then you came, like a present from God. And you can tell us the truth. About what happened. We've been tortured for years, nothing like you, of course. But Anna, please, I know how hard this must be, or rather, I can't possibly imagine. But can you tell us, just tell us what happened to you, since you left Vienna? We're desperate to know."

The room was dark, with wavering thin shafts of silver moonlight. The house was silent, but for creaks and moans of shifting timber. As Georg and Edith waited, gripping hands, Anna's voice came, stony and monotone, from a dark place.

"In Vienna we went to the station with our best clothes and jewelry, they told us that we should bring our valuables, that we would work, we thought everything would be all right. We traveled in second-class carriages, it wasn't so bad. But as soon as we crossed the border into Poland it got worse. Of course, they stole the jewelry. And for three years, every time we thought it couldn't get any worse, it got worse." Anna's voice trailed off, as she remembered.

"The train stopped at Lodz in Poland and we all walked to the ghetto, thousands of us. The windows were full of Poles, watching. We lived there for almost three years. Everybody was starving. People fell dead in the streets. Bodies lay there for days. The smell! The Nazis kept taking people to kill them, hundreds of people at once, sometimes thousands, putting them on more trains and sending them off. Once they took twenty thousand children. At first we thought they were going somewhere better but one man escaped from the train. He went all the way to Auschwitz, and then hid in the piles of clothes and came back. He told us, so we knew. We knew we would all die, in Lodz or in Auschwitz. Papi kept us alive because he was a doctor. They needed him. And he worked so hard. But he came home. Huh. Home! We were three families in two rooms. He came home with food—potatoes, potato peels, sometimes a can of fish, a strip of old meat. We ate any little thing, and so we didn't starve.

But in the end they emptied the ghetto and put us on trains without windows, they were cattle cars. There wasn't room to stand or sit, everybody brought so many suitcases and bags. Again they told us we were going to a better place. We just leaned on one another, for four days. The four of us were together. And Grodzinski the baker was with us, and his son and some of Papi's patients. They kept asking him to do something, to speak to the Nazis, wasn't he a war hero, after all? It was stinking, and freezing, so cold that there were icicles inside. Some old people died right next to me. It stank. Mutti was too tired to stand so she sat on a dead body, and she wasn't the only one. They took everyone to Auschwitz and other camps.

Mutti was very sick. Lisa and I helped her, but by now Lisa was sick, too, she kept vomiting. Papi was all right. I think of all the families that went to Lodz, maybe we were the only ones still intact. But when we got off the train, there were dogs and guards shouting and they made us stand in lines. We walked past Nazi officers at a desk. One of them was the worst, the chief, his name was Mengele, a doctor, too. I was with Lisa and Mutti. They wouldn't let us help Mutti, they hit me with a stick. Mutti couldn't walk, she was so ill, and just as Lisa passed the officers, such bad luck, her chest heaved, she wanted to be sick. I was behind her. Mengele was disgusted, he said 'Stinking Jew.' It was such bad timing. They were sent one way, I went the other."

They heard footsteps upstairs and the scraping of a chair's legs.

The tap ran. Otto was washing and brushing his teeth. Edith and Georg didn't dare move, lying side by side, holding hands. Waiting for Anna to continue. The stony voice went on.

"They were taken where they all were taken. They said in Auschwitz there was only one way out—through the chimney. Papi saved me many times. He had the greatest fortune. We were together till the end, and all because of one man. After Lodz Papi looked old, his hair had fallen out, and he was sent to the line to die."

Edith's hand was gripping Georg's so hard he squirmed and had to pull it away.

"But a man behind Mengele, a man with a deep hollow scar on his throat, saw Papi and saved him. Later he told me why he saved Papi, and Papi told me the rest of the story. This is what happened, this is why I am here now.

"You know in the Great War Papi was a doctor. He was the officer commanding one of the hospital trains that brought our boys—huh, our boys!—back from the Russian front. It was terrible, so many wounded, dying soldiers and so few people to treat them and so few medicines and bandages, and all on the train. It was a freight train. Papi said the worst thing was the smell, they didn't even have windows, just small vents. Well, one day, the train was going through the Carpathian Mountains, slowing down at a bend, when the Russians attacked. It was a furious attack and the guards fought back. One of them was shot in the throat. He almost died. They rushed him to the surgery and Papi took the bullet out. The man was dying. Even though the train was rocking and flying along, and the Russians were shooting and everyone was screaming and yelling, and Papi was operating on three soldiers at the same time, he was walking in blood, still he kept coming back to that young soldier and treated his wound and held his hand. He was groaning and sweating and struggling to breathe. Papi thought he must die but he didn't. Papi held his hand and the man didn't close his eyes, he just kept staring at Papi, into his eyes, pleading for his life, and Papi helped him and stayed with him. And that man never forgot the man who saved his life. And he was the man behind Mengele when Papi said to Mengele that he was a doctor and he could help. Papi told Mengele that he was a captain in the Imperial Army, commander of hospital train 9 from the Russian and Galician fronts, that he had won the Golden Service Cross in 1915. Mengele laughed and said he was just a dirty old Jew and they had too many doctors already. He sent him to die. But the officer with the scar asked Papi his name. He told Papi to stand on his own and he whispered something to Mengele. Then he told Papi to get in line with the people who would not be killed. That man was an SS Haupt-sturmführer but one little bit of decency, or honor, must have been left. He was good to Papi and he saved me, too.

"He got Papi a job in the clinic. And he gave me work, too, light work. That man looked after us. But he left the camp. He gave me to another man who gave me the same work. Papi stayed at the clinic, and so he had food, and heat. He was always lucky. I wasn't so lucky, but I found a way to live.

"Then the rumors began. The Russians were getting close. The officer I was with left. We began to hear explosions. The camp I was in, the women's camp, we didn't know what to be afraid of first. Every-body was falling sick and dying. We were afraid the SS would kill us. Or that when the Russians came they would rape us, they raped everyone—every female, they didn't care about anything, old, young, skin and bones, sick, they raped everyone. We knew what to expect. But the SS forced us out of the camp. We started to march. There was deep snow, and frozen mud, it was so cold. I can't tell you what it was like. Most people had no shoes or just one, and they didn't fit, they wrapped their feet in rags. My fortune was I had boots that fit, a matching pair, Papi got them for me a few weeks before we left, they saved my life.

"He stayed behind. They forced everyone out, to run away with them from the Russians. Except for the very sick in the infirmary and the isolation ward, they stayed and Papi stayed with them. That's the last I saw of him. He was always trying to help but by then he was very sick, too. I don't know with what—it may have been typhus or scarlet fever; there was diphtheria, everyone had dysentery. There was no food or water, the guards took it all. Everyone said the last guards had orders to shoot the sick, too. No survivors. No witnesses. No one left to say what happened. But I don't know what happened. I couldn't say good-bye to Papi, we were in different camps.

"We walked for days through the snow, on the road, through the trees. It was so cold. People dropped dead all the time. If they fell over and couldn't carry on, the guards shot them. Somehow, I kept going. Each time somebody died everyone else jumped on them and took their clothes. Every dirty rag meant the difference between life and death. I wasn't hungry. I was too sick to eat. I drank the snow. Thousands of people began that march. Only a few hundred finished it. I don't know why I didn't die. Papi got me good boots."

Anna stopped. They could hear her heavy breathing. The black-out curtains didn't quite meet and the moon cast a thin line of bluish light into the room and onto Anna's upright body, as if cutting her in half. Edith pulled herself up and arranged her pillow for support and sat next to Anna. Georg didn't move. He was lying on his back, thinking of his own parents and brother and sister, dead in Maydanek. What about all the aunts and uncles and cousins and grandparents—would anyone else come back? And Anna. She had been seventeen when the war began, about eighteen when she went to Lodz, a beautiful young girl, Edith had said, with shiny black hair and sparkling eyes. What had those Nazis done to her? She just gave the outline; not a word about what happened to her in all those years. Light work? What does that mean?

Edith broke the silence. "Then what happened?"

After a pause Anna gave a huge sigh. "Oh, they put us on a train, to Germany. Another filthy freezing cattle train. It was bombed. Four of us jumped off. We hid in a barn, nobody lived there. It didn't have a roof. One day Americans found us. They put us in a camp. Some young people from Palestine came, from the Jewish Agency, and I wanted to go there with them. I thought it wasn't possible that anyone else from my family could be alive. I just wanted to go away. Somewhere safe. For the Jews. Anywhere. Palestine seemed easy. But I couldn't even go there. The British wouldn't let us go. I could have tried to get in illegally, we prepared for that. I was on a secret list. We were waiting near Paris. But there were so many Jewish survivors who wanted to go to Palestine, hundreds of thousands, I had to wait my turn. And then I heard about you. I knew you had gone to London but I couldn't believe that you were still alive, or that I could find you. I didn't believe it. So the Red Cross sent a letter. And here I am."

She sighed again. Edith had never heard such a loud, drawn-out, shuddering sigh, as if Anna's very soul was squeezing through an open wound. Edith felt that Anna was struggling to contain herself, and when Edith kissed her cheek Anna dissolved, the dam broke. Her body shook as if it would fall apart, and she cried out in pain and reached for Edith who held her as tightly as she could. Anna screamed and Edith covered her mouth with her hand. Georg felt his own tears stream down his cheek and raised himself and hugged Edith from behind, felt her crying, too, his hands resting on Anna's head, her coarse hair. But just as suddenly as she started, Anna stopped, panting. "It's all right," Edith said, stroking Anna's wet face, "you can cry."

But she didn't anymore.

All three held one another as Anna stared into the dark.

She knew that whenever she looked in a mirror or saw her reflection in a window, she would not see herself, but that other Anna, the one she wanted to forget. Staring back from that place. She was still young and her hair would grow back and her body would fill out again; she was only twenty-two. Time would pass and they say that time heals, but Anna knew that what she saw with her own eyes would never change because what she had done to survive could never be forgotten, or forgiven, or even talked of, not now or ever, and the wounds she had suffered were not the kind that could ever heal.

Edith held Anna and Georg held Edith. They were like one body, sharing their strength. They breathed together. Moonlight reflected from the mirror over the sink onto them and threw their single shadow, like a giant rodent, onto the wall behind the bed. They stayed locked together for a long time and the gas and electricity ran out and the room became cold. The house was silent, but for the light rustling of wind and creaking beams. They could hear mice pattering in the walls.

At last they separated and arranged themselves for the night, turning, pulling sheets and blankets, covering themselves. Georg thought, as he got comfortable, *I'll have to cross Mutti and Lisa off the list. I'll do it when Edith isn't here.*

"Good night," he said.

"Good night," Anna answered. In the middle, Edith lay on her side and stuffed a pillow under her belly to support the weight of her baby in its warm liquid sac and snuggled her back against Georg, whose hand cupped her breast. As she drifted off to sleep, a hazy distant image formed in her eyelids and seemed to come closer and closer and to grow and bring with it the sweet aroma of apple-mixed tobacco and she saw cheeks that hollowed and sucked and the growing haze became clouds of bluish smoke rising from a long curved pipe and she murmured, in a wondering voice: "Papi? Papi? Oh, where are you, Papi?"

FOUR

Palestine

October 2, 1945

Above Elijah's cave on Mount Carmel, a young man with a backpack waved from a gap in the trees; he pushed through a bush and wriggled into the densest thicket, where he sat down to wait. Below, where the Haifa road meets the steep path that winds up the hill toward the British army base behind Stella Maris Church, the boy at the bus stop turned and took off his hat. Observing this, the woman sitting by the rocks at the first bend in the road stood, lit a cigarette, and walked back to her home. As she passed the two men in the dusty red Renault on the corner, she took a last puff, coughed twice, and flicked the cigarette away. The driver, a short, thin man with a tense, sharp face, turned the ignition key. "All set," he said, and started back to Tel Aviv.

In Haifa's port, even the brisk Mediterranean salt breeze couldn't sweep away the fetid, dank stink aboard the Greek-registered *Martina*. The mouldy smell rose from the hold and stuck to the sails. Three hundred and fifty passengers, nineteen days at sea on a thirty-five-foot schooner, with no water to wash in, at anchor off Haifa for three days with no permission to land—*No wonder they smell,* thought Sami Sapriel as he trod carefully among the wretched human cargo. After years in concentration camps, months in displaced people camps, and now weeks at sea, the Jewish survivors were filthy, hungry, with sunken, staring eyes and pleading, ravaged faces. At least thirty were pregnant women and another hundred were children.

Soon the British troops would board. Sami had assessed his chances of organizing resistance: Nil. The hired Greek crew didn't care whether the stinking Jews got into Palestine or not, they just wanted to offload them, sail home, and get paid. The two Haganah agents on board were so sick with dysentery they could hardly move, and the male refugees were exhausted and demoralized. Sami had slid off the dock at night, swum through the British cordon and climbed aboard, but there was nothing he could do. From the boat's prow he watched the British tug pull them to shore.

He saw a platoon of the feared British "poppies" lining up on the dock. Poppies—red on the outside with a black heart. A good nickname, he thought. They were fierce and efficient troops. Their maroon berets were replaced by helmets; instead of rifles they carried wooden clubs. He looked out to sea. Two patrol boats aimed their automatic weapons at the *Martina.* A line of trucks waited on the dock to transport the Jews to the internment camp at Atlit where they would rot for God knows how long, and there was nothing Sami or anyone could do about it. Yet.

He saw the officer briefing the soldiers. They stood at attention and snapped a salute. You have to hand it to them, Sami thought, they're a tough bunch. British paratroopers from the Sixth Airborne. They'd landed at Normandy, fought all over Europe and North Africa and for their pains got police duty in Palestine. Soon they would throw up a gangplank and board. It wouldn't get bloody this time, though. He looked down at the ragged concentration camp survivors, lying like corpses around the deck. No, nobody would fight back. Not here and now. Soon, though. His job was to blend in, go to Atlit with them, and organize from the inside. He'd done it before.

He knew the order had been given when the platoon formed into three squads. The soldiers marched toward the boat, holding their clubs out. At the same time a megaphone blared, with a clipped officer's voice: "Let's do this in an organized manner, ladies and gentlemen. You will line up and descend in pairs and walk straight to the trucks on your left. No running. You will be taken to a reception center were you will be taken care of, receive food and water, and there will be medical attention for those in need. Easy does it, thank you."

Nobody moved. But when the soldiers spread out along the decks and their heavy boots thumped by the heads and hands of the tired Jews, they didn't need their clubs. The refugees had had enough. At least they would be on the soil of Palestine, even if it was behind barbed wire again. Who knows? Something will happen. They'll get out one day. Like a centipede moving all its legs, the mass of people shrugged and pulled itself up, men carrying bags, women carrying babies, the sick supporting one another, dragging their bodies past the poppies to the promised land.

"Well done, lads," the young lieutenant said after the last truckload had departed. "Good job, well done. No trouble, for a change. Tomorrow, same time, same place." The men groaned. Another refugee boat was anchored at port and British gunships enforcing the immigration blockade had spotted two more small boats packed with concentration camp survivors sailing across the Mediterranean from France and Italy. The soldiers stuffed their clubs into a large canvas bag, checked their rifles, and climbed onto three open vehicles, ten men in each plus the driver, and set off along the coast road back to base.

For most of the journey they sat in silence. This police job wasn't what they'd signed up for, pushing around those miserable bastards. They had another six months to go before three years was up, which meant they'd get a home leave, back to Blighty. Four years and they could go home for good. War in Japan had been over since August and they were still stuck in this boiling godforsaken place keeping the Yids and the Ay-rabs apart. It was a mess. The Jews don't want to stay in Europe, fair enough, who'd want to after what they'd been through? Too many in England already, though, and the Yanks and the Aussies don't want them, either. Nobody does. But neither do the Ay-rabs. Supposed to be a hundred thousand Jews waiting to come here. Crikey—there'll be smelly boats till kingdom come.

The convoy turned left at the junction leading to Stella Maris and began to climb toward their base. A soldier said, to no one in particular, "Could do with a cold shower. Christ, it's 'ot." They lost speed, the engines roared as the drivers double-declutched into second gear. When the lead vehicle entered the first bend none of the troops sitting in the back paid attention to the boy who was a hundred yards behind them, the boy at the bus stop who put on his hat.

But the man in the trees did. He'd been waiting seven hours for the sign. He flicked a switch and a current shot from his battery along the wires to the bag with the two land mines by the rocks, three yards from the first truck. They were big mines, antivehicle, stolen two weeks earlier from the British police station in Petah Tikva. The man looked down from the mountain, tensed, waiting for the explosion. It should be massive—take out a truck and maybe two. The boy flinched and began to run, but pulled up short, surprised. The man on the hill stared. All he heard was the throbbing army engines laboring up the hill. The second truck trundled past the hidden land mines and the failed trigger, followed by the third, and the convoy continued all the way to the coils of barbed wire in front of their base. A corporal saluted, pulled the barrier to the side, and the three trucks drove in without stopping. Thirty British soldiers who didn't know how lucky they were leapt down and headed for their bunks and showers.

The man in the woods cursed—lousy English mines! He stuffed the battery and rolled-up wire back into his backpack. Shit! The plan was to kill the poppies and avoid roadblocks and patrols by hiking through the thick forests toward Zikhron Ya'akov, hiding in a cave if necessary. Now he had to walk anyway—those were the orders—hitchhike back to Tel Aviv. He'd have to tell the boss—another failure.

Two days later, on schedule, the man saw a teenage girl in a yellow skirt on the corner of Allenby and Bialik streets. He followed her, at a discreet distance, until she turned into a hotel. He was surprised. The Savoy hotel, near the beach. Nice. He went to the lift, where the girl whispered a room number and left the hotel. He went up alone. A young man with a beard watched him from the balcony at the end of the corridor. He knocked on the door.

He had never seen the face of the man behind the curtain in the dimly lit room. The house changed and the area changed and the voice changed—there must be several bosses—but always the closed shutters and the curtain in the dark. Jimmy began to explain, "It was the explosive, or maybe the trigger device, the setup worked like clockwork—"

The voice interrupted. "I know. It wasn't your fault. We'll make sure it doesn't happen again. Our people recovered the land mines, they are examining them now. Now you and your friends should prepare for another operation, and very quickly."

Already? He'd only been back at work for two days. He couldn't keep taking time off from the hospital, they'd get suspicious. Already the chief porter kept asking how come he had money to keep going away on holiday. He had told him his mother was sick in Haifa, but there was a limit. He might have to find another job. Maybe the boss could help. He waited.

"It is a big job," the voice said.

"I'm ready," he answered.

"You know Sami." It was a statement, not a question.

"I know several Samis."

"Our Sami."

"The best," he said. Sami had recruited him. They grew up in the same neighborhood of Tel Aviv, Shuk Ha'Carmel. Their fathers, both Egyptian Jews, worked together selling vegetables and the boys had played together among the stands. The families were close. The boy's hero was Sami's elder brother, a tough bastard who had showed them the tricks of the market and showed them girls could be fun, too, but he had disappeared when the war in Europe began. As Arabic speakers with dark skins, most of their friends were local Arabs. The two boys had drifted apart but when Sami looked for a smart friend to help him stick up posters against the British at night, he had sounded him out. That was years ago. Now they were both tough, experienced, and even at their young age, eighteen, senior fighters for the underground. "What about him?"

"The British caught him. He was badly beaten."

He felt like he had been punched in the stomach, the air sucked from his lungs. "Badly? How badly?"

"Very badly."

"So what's the operation?"

"Maria will contact you."

He usually sniggered when he heard "Maria." Somebody had a sense of humor. Maria was a huge man from Belarus. They all had code names to protect themselves—Sami's was the only real name he knew—but Maria? Who came up with that? But this time he only felt sick. "Where is Sami?"

"Atlit police station."

"Do we have anyone on the inside there?"

"No. No Jews."

"They didn't take him to the hospital?"

"No."

That could be good or bad: good if he didn't need to go, bad if they weren't ready to take him. That meant only one thing—torture. He was sure of one thing.

"He won't talk," he said.

"We can't take any chances. He knows your name and where you live. You need to disappear for a while."

"So that's why you called me here?"

"Yes. But also, the operation."

"Can you give me an idea? Anyway, if it's urgent I'll know soon."

The man behind the curtain had a raspy voice, as if recovering from a cold, but it always sounded the same, and set him apart from the other leaders. He spoke decent Hebrew with a rolling, lilting rhythm and sharp vowels—Polish for sure. He didn't say much. This was their longest conversation ever. Usually they just brought him to a room somewhere and it was over in moments—the boss never waited anywhere for more than a few hours, and no doubt other people came from the shadows to see him. The strange thing was, there were no bodyguards. Just a couple of men with long beards like rabbis, him in a dark room, and then gone. Same with all the leaders.

"Eye for an eye."

Okay. They beat Sami. We beat them. Won't be the first time.

"Maria will be in touch. It will be very soon, sooner than you think, and we will need you for a few days. You will abduct an English soldier and beat him. Do not kill him. Beat him and keep him. Maria will know where, we have a place ready. It's good for you because you have to lie low anyway in case Sami talks. And the soldier should be an officer. Like last time."

"You mean whip him?"

"No. We whipped those officers because they whipped our men in prison. This is a beating, a bad one. But no killing. And it must be quick. If we want to help Sami, they must know that whatever happens to him will happen to their officer. That's all."

Someone touched his shoulder. He gasped; another bearded man; he hadn't even noticed anyone else in the room. The meeting was over. He stood and, as always, the man behind the curtain said, "Good luck. God be with you."

He left the building and was quickly swallowed by the crowds and bicycles on Dizengoff Street. Two olive army jeeps were parked at Frishman Street, poppies standing next to them with their weapons cocked. They were looking for someone. He didn't hesitate, but walked straight past them heading toward Arlozoroff Street, where he lived in a small room. It was another hot day and his room would be sweltering.

He felt torn—should he rush home and pack a bag in case Sami talked and the poppies came for him? He could stay with Bella for a few nights, she always wanted him to sleep over. Or did he have time for a cold lemon tea at Café Cassit first? A boy on a bike raced past, brushing him. "Careful!" he shouted, throwing out an elbow that missed. He was wound up. Sami. His friend. His best friend, really, if he thought about it. What were those cold bastards doing to him? Rescue was out of the question; Atlit was one of the few really secure British police stations. They were all surrounded by road-blocks, barbed wire, patrols, sentries, and what have you—Bevingrad—and they'd still broken into quite a few, dressed up as police or Arab workers. But Atlit—there was a hill right next to the camp and it con-trolled the whole area. You'd have to take out the sentries first, and they were inside a concrete bunker. Could be done, maybe. But no time. *Sami, stay strong.* They'd beat him bloody for sure and break his bones. Always do.

Cassit was full. He stood amongst the crowded round tables, and saw an empty seat on the sidewalk, a good spot in the shade of the trees. He edged around the knots of people to the chair outside. "Is this free?" he asked. The elderly man and woman both nodded and reached over to remove their bags. He lowered himself into the seat and looked up to thank them. Maria was leaning against the tree, watching.

"Lemon tea, you must be joking! No time to get a bag, either," Maria said, "they could be watching your place already." They walked quickly to the bus station. "We're all set, we're going to a place we've got and we'll take delivery of the package. Today."

"Package?"

"Code talk, Jimmy."

Jimmy laughed. Maria smiled as they walked. He liked Jimmy. Nobody looked less like a Jimmy. He was short, dark, strong. A Jimmy was tall and thin, pale, spotty and from Scotland. This Jimmy was from Shuk Ha'Carmel.

The bus to Lydda was just leaving. They ran after it and jumped on. It was full of noisy Jews and Arabs and the radio was blaring, Mozart or something. The driver was the only Ashkenazi on the bus and refused to switch the music. British soldiers used to ride the buses, too, in groups, but not anymore. Not since they'd been ordered to hit the Jews where it hurts most—in their pockets. They didn't go shopping, go to the pictures, spend money in the cafés, or on the buses—revenge where it hurts most, they said, for the terrorist gang attacks against innocent British soldiers.

At Lydda, Maria led Jimmy twenty minutes through the streets to a small separate section of low stone houses, some abandoned, at the edge of the eastern orange groves. There they followed a track through the trees that was wide enough for a single car. Maria had to duck beneath the branches, until they reached a clearing with a single decaying wooden hut once used for storing tools. As they approached, two men, one from each side, emerged from the trees. "Jimmy, Maria," one said.

The other one took them to the tree nearest the hut. At its base there was a plastic bag with two pistols. "Just in case," he said, and pointed with his chin to the hut. "He's all yours."

Jimmy looked at Maria. Already? They took a gun each, brown-handled Czech CZs, checked the rounds and ducked into the hut, Maria first.

He was tied to the rafter with a noose around his neck, his hands bound behind his back, a canvas hood over his head. He stood on a wooden log. If he kicked it away to try to escape, he'd hang. He was naked. His clothes were folded in the corner, with his maroon poppy beret neatly on top. His shirt sleeve showed one bar: lieutenant.

"What's your name?" Maria asked. Silence.

"I said, what's your name?" Maria tapped his gun barrel by the man's shriveled balls. He jerked.

"I don't speak Jewish," he said.

"Name—your name?" Maria said in English.

"Fuck off."

"Oh!" Maria smiled. "A brave one. Look, we don't want any information from you, just your name."

"Why am I here, then? What do you fuckers want? Let me down."

Maria sat on the floor against the wall. It was a small dark space; the only light came through the open door. Dust motes flashed. A few rusty, broken farm tools were stacked against the wall next to him. Maria took a pair of shears and tried to force open the wooden handles. The blades were rusted together to form a single blunt point. He leaned forward and poked the man's stomach. "What's your name? You're allowed to give me your name."

"Lieutenant Jimmy Sanders. That's all you're getting."

Jimmy laughed. "Really? Another Jimmy? Where are you from?"

"Fuck off."

"Just tell me where you're from. Scotland, right?" His body was pinky-white with a sunburned neck and forearms. "Please say you're from Scotland."

Silence.

"Let me down. What good does this do? I can't run away anyway. This is no way to treat an officer."

Maria said, "I'm sorry, I have to do this. Especially to an officer."

Jimmy looked at Maria; he didn't look very sorry. Maria put his gun on the floor and took off his shirt so it wouldn't get bloody. The big Belarus held the rusty shears before him, testing the weight. Jimmy said, "I'll be outside."

He joined the other two men. It was a cinch, they said. Last night. Four of us. Knew his routine for weeks. He had a girl, a Jewish girl, in a room in the building next to one of our boys. She liked him a lot. He'd come out of her house and stopped to take a leak in a dark garden. Perfect. Coshed him on the head, dragged him to the car, and that was it. Changed cars a couple of times. Couldn't be easier.

The two men left Jimmy and went back to their room in the last of Lydda's houses near the fields, where they'd stay until this escapade was over. They had rented the room a month earlier after finding the isolated hut among the trees—a perfect safe house ready for a moment like this. When it was over they'd move out and set up another safe house, for the next time. Their job now was to warn of any suspicious activity in the area, to give Maria and Jimmy time to run. Jimmy's job was to stay with the English officer, babysit him till it was time to dump him somewhere, close enough to a hospital to get him immediate care.

As for Maria, after ten minutes, his job was done.

Jimmy's job was the worst. The soldier cried for days. He was in terrible pain. Jimmy had cut him down and he lay on the floor where he had fallen, his hands still tied behind his back with the bag over his head. He was naked beneath a blanket one of the men had brought. His right ankle was huge and bruised, and the right foot pointed outward. His left knee was also swollen and discolored. Thick weals and blood clots covered his body. Some of his fingers seemed to be broken. The hood wasn't discolored, though; no blood there. Maria had avoided his head. Jimmy the soldier breathed a little more easily through a hole Jimmy had cut for his mouth and nose. But when Jimmy sometimes heard a choking rattle instead of breathing he wondered whether Maria had whacked him on the Adam's apple. He hoped not. He didn't take the hood off to look. He didn't want to look at the poor soldier's face, and the soldier certainly mustn't see his.

Jimmy sat on the floor next to the soldier. Sometimes he told him not to worry, everything would be fine, soon, it was just a matter of time.

The only time the soldier answered, his words were barely audible, but Jimmy made out "Fuck off, Jew bastard." Jimmy thought, no hard feelings, I'd say the same if I was him.

Jimmy dabbed water through the hood's hole onto the soldier's lips, and tried to feed him, but he didn't eat. He seemed feverish; his lips burned, and he hardly moved. If he felt sorry for the soldier, Jimmy thought of Sami. What had they done to him? The longer he was in the police station, the worse it would be. He'd be in a dark corner somewhere, all beaten up, hoping for a rescue. No chance. As for this officer, Jimmy knew the drill. The resistance would have called a British police switchboard and warned them to call off the search for the kidnapped soldier, broadcast the same warning over their clandestine radio and plastered posters all over the country with the promise that whatever happened to Sami would happen to the officer. If they freed Sami, they'd get their man back. It had worked before. The more public the humiliation, the less the British could take it. You could do anything to their men as long as nobody knew about it. Ridicule was the real threat. It encouraged more resistance. If the British looked stupid, they couldn't be unbeatable.

They'd let Sami go.

It was just a matter of time.

Early the next morning, Jimmy heard one of the men whistling La Marseillaise. It was the sign that they were approaching and not to worry. If they whistled a waltz, time to run. Jimmy came out of the hut, stretching, hoping they had brought some coffee. They emerged from the trees. His heart sank—no breakfast. Instead they had brought Maria, ducking beneath the branches, his wide body catching on twigs. Not a good sign. Maria didn't call out his usual cheery greeting. He looked grim.

"I'm sorry, Jimmy, I know you two were close," was how Maria delivered the news.

The terrorist had jumped out of a window and died, the police announced with regret.

Everyone knew Atlit police station was a bungalow.

Eye for an eye.

Maria entered the hut.

The next morning long before dawn, the two men left the hut with the still naked, hooded body rolled in a blanket, and crammed it into the backseat of the Renault, along with its uniform and maroon beret. Maria and Jimmy walked through the orange groves toward the Lydda bus station, while the other two set off with the body in the back. The hawk-faced one drove and the other man sat silent and stony next to him.

Dizengoff Circle was deserted when they arrived an hour later. Soon it would be the busiest junction in Tel Aviv. They drove round twice, making sure there were no police or troops, then the driver slammed on the brakes. In a flash it was over: They pulled the body out, dropped it to the ground, removed the blanket, lay the folded uniform over the bare, bloodied groin and set the beret on the corpse's hooded head like a stuffed Guy Fawkes, snapped two photos for the local press, and raced off.

Just in case they'd been seen dumping the body, the two men drove to the Yarkon River and set fire to the Renault. They'd get another one, bigger. Not yet, though. Better lie low. The poppies wouldn't like this. Oh no. Not at all. The shit was about to hit the fan. Big-time.

FIVE

London

October 9, 1945

Edith held up the nylon stocking with her left arm, squinted against the light, found the long ladder, and in one quick movement hooked its stem with the crochet and pumped her foot on the pedal. The rented Vitos sewing machine hummed. Edith guided the thread along the ladder, back and forward, back and forward, closed it and sealed the end. A shilling. She examined the carroty orange stocking again, folded its foot around her forearm, fed it back into the Vitos, picked up a smaller run with the crochet, and the machine hummed again. Sixpence. There were three more runs. Threepence each. Another stocking had a hole that couldn't be sewn, so she decided to cover it. She reached into her basket, pulled out some nylon scraps, and cut a matching pink-beige piece into shape, stretched the stocking over a wooden mushroom, glued on the patch, and sat on it. Sixpence.

She clocked up her earnings automatically: It bought her peace of mind. She no longer wondered at how her life had changed, at all she'd lost, even her diaries, which she had forgotten in the rush. They were hidden under the bed. Who found her secrets? Who read them? Who cares now? All she wanted now was enough money to pay the rent, eat, and drink. If her thoughts took her back—to Mutti knitting in the drawing room, sewing little green and yellow men onto the corners of lace serviettes, while Papi smoked his pipe and read *Die Freie Presse* in his deep leather chair next to the cabinet with his collection of oriental porcelain and Bohemian glass—if all she had taken for granted and lost popped into her mind, took it over, colonized it so that for a moment she was back home, real home, and she imagined she heard the little bell ringing for lunch and she and Lisa ran in from the garden to wash their hands; if always being the stranger in London, the person with the funny accent, the outsider, the alien, made her feel lonely and frightened; well, she always came back with a start to her dirty, slithery nylons. Adding up the pennies. Hardly building a new life, but at least surviving. Making the best of it. Saving to buy her own Vitos, but something always came up that was more urgent. Now it would be baby clothes. She smiled and patted her belly. Doctor Goldscheider had told her not to work so hard. Papi would have said the same. All doctors tell expecting mothers to take it easy. Easily said, with a nanny, a cook, a cleaner, a mother, a sister, aunts, and cousins by the dozen. Here there's just poor worried Georg, who still can't find a real job.

Edith shrugged. *Don't worry, Papi, I can cope.* But as she thought it, she raised her right shoulder to rub the muscles, searching for the stiffness. She dug the side of her finger between the vertebrae of her lower back and arched against the ache; there was a persistent throb that stretched round to her abdomen. She knew it came from her leg constantly pumping the motor of the Vitos. It put pressure on her stomach. Don't tell Papi!

As Edith leaned down to pull another torn stocking from the pile,

Anna entered the lounge. "It's so warm!" She pushed out her lower lip and breathed onto the tip of her nose. "It's freezing in the corridor. And the carpet's loose, it's the third time I've nearly fallen. Is there any tea?"

"You've adapted quickly! Mustn't grumble, you're in England now," Ismael said from behind his newspaper. "I'll get it, how many sugars? Four, for a girl so sweet?"

"I'll get it myself, thank you," Anna said. "You're in a better mood. You've been very quiet the last few days. Hardly seen you."

"Yes," Ismael said.

"Working early?" Anna said to Edith as she poured the tea. "You want some?"

"No thanks. The newsagent called. He had a pile of stockings and I went to collect them. This is a big day."

"Why?"

"We're going shopping. I'm going to finish all this, get the money, and buy you a coat."

Ismael sniggered. "Why, are they selling them cheap?"

"Leck mich am Arsch," Edith said.

They all laughed. Ismael wiped a slice of Hovis over the last of his watered-down strawberry jam, smacked his lips, and cleared away his breakfast plate. They hadn't sat a moment when the door flew open and Albert stormed in, waving the *Daily Graphic*. "Have you seen this? Have you? Have you?"

"What?" Ismael asked.

"Bloody terrorists," Albert shouted. "That's what they are. Nothing less, nothing more. Should hang 'em all."

Edith's foot pumped, the Vitos kept humming, and Anna sipped her tea. "Look at this," Albert went on, slapping the front page. "This takes the bloody cake!" Ismael took the paper.

A two-inch headline screamed: HUNT THEM DOWN! A photo-graph covered half the page. It showed a bloody and bruised naked man with a neatly folded uniform covering his private parts and a beret on his hooded head. "How dare they? How *dare* they?" Albert snatched it back. "Look at this," he shouted, shoving the newspaper at Anna. "See?" She flinched at the photo. "And they've got the bloody effrontery to ask for help against the Arabs. We're trying to help them and look what we get! Typical! Let them all bloody die, that's what I say. About bloody time!"

"Hear, hear!" Ismael said.

"Not you lot, mind," Albert said, "I don't mean you lot, of course, you're different. They're just a bunch of thugs."

After a moment Edith asked, "How is your son, Mr. Barnes? You must be very concerned."

"He's all right, thanks, he can look after himself. Got a nice letter just yesterday. Just a few more months to go. Kind of you to ask."

Sally came in. "What's up, Albert? Can hear you round the corner."

"Palestine," Albert said, dropping down next to Ismael.

"Oh, what a to-do," she said. "You know what, if you ask me? We should stop trying to keep the Jews out, and move there ourselves. That's what. The English should go live in Palestine and let the Jews have England. They own half of it anyway!"

Ismael roared with laughter, smacked his thigh.

Albert showed her the newspaper. Sally took it, smoothed the paper out on the table, and put on her glasses. She gasped. "Oh, my goodness."

Albert looked at her and shook his head. Sally said, "Oh, dear, I do hope Eric is all right. I do hope he comes home soon."

She looked at his photo in the silver frame on the mantelpiece, grinning in his uniform, holding his weapon, his red beret nestling on his shock of light brown hair. Eric was their only child. Because he was in his midteens when war broke out he hadn't been evacuated so far during the bombing, only to a farm near Welwyn Garden City just outside London, so whenever Albert got free time from his job as an air-raid warden they would try to visit him. Only once had Albert and Sally stayed over at the farm, and that was the very night the big bomb fell on the houses down the street. Luckily nobody was killed, but the residents were trapped in their shelters while firemen fought the flames above them. Neighbors were in a panic as they heard the screams. Albert was crushed. "The only night they need me, and I'm not here." Nobody held a grudge. They were Albert's friends. Albert had been born in his house and had a heart of gold. He'd help anybody, his neighbors said—look, even got a house full of Jews. But there was a limit. Fair enough, Mr. Rogers down the road had said, during the war, but now he asked why Albert didn't turf them out—make way for the lads coming home from the front. "Because Jews need somewhere to live, too," Albert had said. The neighbors were beginning to talk. Tapping their noses. Rubbing their thumbs and forefingers. Know what I mean?

At eleven o'clock the door opened and Georg came in. Anna was slumped on the sofa, half dozing and bleary-eyed, following Edith's foot pumping away at the sewing machine. She'd been at it for three hours nonstop. Edith looked up. She had heard the phone ring, heard Sally's summons, followed Georg's footsteps down the stairs to the hall, and now he brought the news. "Gina would like to meet us at the Cosmo."

"No work today?" Edith asked.

"No, I may have a shift in two days. Too many soldiers being demobbed. They always get the work first. Anyway, Gina would like to meet."

"You go, I want to finish this lot. Then I want to take Anna out. We're going shopping!"

Anna had been in London a week and hadn't left the house. She said she was cold but they knew that wasn't it. There were no secrets when three people slept in one bed. Anna's groans, her gasps, the moans and sighs, like a whimpering kitten, the sudden turning: They could feel her lying awake, sense her anguish, and when Edith asked if she was asleep, Anna would turn around and not answer. Georg would try the sofa but it was too short. Edith would try next but the sofa was too narrow for her belly which she supported with a pillow. Whenever Anna offered to sleep on the sofa, they wouldn't let her. So they slept together in the crowded bed and the springs creaked and the mattress rose and fell as Anna tossed and turned. When she did sleep, she mumbled and called out. They tried, but could never understand a word. In the morning she was soaked in sweat.

If Anna was haunted by what she knew, Edith was tormented by what she didn't know; her sleep was almost as restless. She fidgeted and squirmed and holding Georg's hand would squeeze so hard it hurt. She dreamed of her father most nights, and if she didn't have dreams about him, she dreamed of the baby. Mostly she sensed the pain of birth: pushing and squeezing of her organs, the effort. She couldn't remember the details, just the finality of it, the end of waiting, the end of a journey, the new beginning, but somehow the baby dreams merged with her father dreams, one roiling mixed image of pain, helplessness, waiting, and, above all, hoping, that Papi would come, that the baby would come, and that all would be good again altogether.

Georg slept well. For him, it was easier. He knew. He had been the first of everyone to find out. Gassed in Majdanek. The whole family. He didn't want to know what *gassed* really meant, what terrible things happened on the way to being *gassed*. What a word. But at least it was over. He didn't have the anguish of not knowing, the torment of waiting, for a phone, a letter, a rumor, searching the lists. Some refugees had joined aid groups so they could look for survivors themselves. A soldier had found his own mother in Bergen-Belsen. One refugee with enough money for a rail ticket had returned to his family home in Vienna and been chased away by Austrians who were living in it. He asked if any other relatives had shown up. They shouted and threatened to kill him if he came back.

Hundreds of thousands of refugees were looking for millions of relatives all over Europe. They were learning too slowly who was alive and who was dead. But Georg knew his family's fate, and while what he knew could not have been worse, now at least he could think of his future, not only his past. Others were frozen, in limbo, paralysed by not knowing. For them the present was just a way station between past and future. But Georg's whole focus now was the future, starting again, with the baby.

He was scared for Edith, though. Ever since Anna had told her that Papi may still be alive, she had been crazed, had called everywhere: the Red Cross, the Austrian Center, the Association of Jewish Refugees, Bloomsbury House, Woburn House, the Quakers, the British army information center and the American army public information office, and all gave the same answer: Fill out the tracing forms and wait. There is nothing else to do. When the Americans and the British liberated concentration camps they had listed the names of all the survivors and were slowly matching their names with other family members across Europe and in America. But the Russians kept no records, just opened the gates, and the survivors trickled out and drifted off as best they could. Anna was the first to return, a living phantom.

But where was Papi? Anna said he had been sick; that was nine months ago; by now he must be better. He was a soldier, a doctor; if anybody could survive, he could. But then why hadn't he been in touch, why hadn't he found them? One call to the Red Cross and they would have traced her. Why hadn't he done that? Where was Papi? Many Jews had been hauled off to Russian jails—maybe he was a prisoner? Was he sick somewhere, lost his memory, did he need help? She had written to a Christian friend in Vienna asking him to visit the house, to see if anybody was there or if neighbors knew anything.

Edith lay on her back next to Anna, staring at the ceiling. They were both silent and sleepless, their minds racing. Edith squeezed Georg's hand so hard he winced.

"Gina didn't say why she wants to meet," Georg said. "But I think she must have some news."

Edith sighed. There was only one subject that counted as news. And if it was good, she would have said so on the phone. She counted the stockings. She had been working for three hours and almost finished the assignment. "All right. I'll just finish these and drop them off on the way to the Cosmo."

Anna wouldn't come. "I'm cold and tired. I think I'll try to sleep." She heaved herself up.

"I think it would do you good to come out for a change—" Edith began, but Anna snapped, "No!" Edith flinched. "But I think Gina would love to meet you, and . . ." She didn't want to say that everyone was dying to hear from Anna what the camps were really like.

"I said no! I'm too tired," Anna said. "And I'm not interested!"

She slammed the door. They heard her heavy tread up the stairs. Edith spread her hands: What was that all about? She said, "You know, she doesn't eat much at all. I'm worried about her."

Georg shrugged. "Let's go, Gina will be waiting. Finchleystrasse awaits."

There were so many German-speaking refugees in the area that bus conductors didn't call out "Tickets!" anymore; they said "Passports." St. John's Wood was Johanneswald and Baker Street was Beckerstrasse. The refugees joked about it but for a lot of locals it wasn't so funny. Just the day before Georg had overheard Sally at the door, yet again turning away a young man looking for a room to rent. Otto from upstairs had walked past them into the street and greeted them: "Good day," he had said, but pronounced it "Gut day."

"Who's that, then?" the man had said.

"Oh, he's been renting a room for years," Sally had said, "one of those refugees."

The man had snorted, and said, "Yes, he's all right. While I've been fighting a war for five years so that he can stay here safely. And now I'm living in a Nissen hut while he's got a nice warm room. It isn't right." Sally apologized and closed the door. She'd been hearing a lot of that lately, and it didn't sit well with her. She felt sorry for the man. But it didn't do to throw the Jews out, either. Not with what they're going through, looking for their families and all, not knowing who's dead or alive. And that Edith, about to have her first baby, she looks so young, and sad. Still, it'll be all right in the end. Always is. That's what got us through the Blitz, through the war. As she went downstairs to her little flat, Sally thought of Eric. I hope he's all right, over there. What a mess. What a horrible photo.

Georg held Edith's coat as she slipped her arms in the sleeves, and waited as she buttoned up and pulled on a woolly hat. At the newsagents she dropped off the stockings and came out with a smile. "Twelve and sixpence! And there'll be more work in a few days."

"Good," Georg said, and smiled back. But he didn't feel good. His rare translations earned a few pounds and the occasional shift in the button factory didn't bring in much more. They were lucky to have such decent digs, but otherwise they needed to earn more money. But Edith was obsessive; she never knew when enough was enough, it worried him. On top of the stockings Edith had even asked about waitressing at the Austrian Center and the Czech club on West End Lane but he'd been against it; in her condition that was out of the question. She should be resting in the last few months, not working harder. As for him, he couldn't work in a law firm without sitting for the British bar exam, and anyway, the British made it hard for refugee lawyers and doctors to work. And what if their number came up in the American quota? They'd move to New York and he'd have to take his bar exam there, too. All he could do was wait and see. And make buttons, if he got a shift. One thing at a time, he told himself. See who's alive. Have the baby. One thing at a time. And then we can get on with the rest of our lives. But Edith was becoming more and more nervous, frustrated. "Surely there's *something* we can do to find Papi," she kept saying, in an accusing voice. "Can't you think of *anything* to do, we can't just sit here and *wait*."

Oh, shut up, Georg heard himself think. *What do you think I can do?* But he knew if Edith wasn't as big as a medicine ball, she'd do something, she wouldn't rest. After all, she hadn't given up on him, and that had saved his life.

They had met before the war in Prague, in a line of anxious Jewish refugees that stretched around the British embassy, all applying for visas, all stamping their feet and blowing into their hands: It was a frosty January morning. "Do I know you?" Georg had asked, raising an eyebrow, in response to her steady gaze. He stretched and stressed the vowels in a lilting, fastidious manner, like her father. Viennese. Edith hesitated, and then smiled. There seemed little point in standing on formality. "Well, I know you, at least I think I do," she replied. "You have a niece called Dorli, is that right?"

"Yes," he said, delighted. His moustache rose sweetly as he smiled. "She's lucky, she got out, on her way to America. My name is Georg."

"Lucky her. I'm Edith," she said as they shook hands. "Gosh, your hand is cold. Pleased to meet you."

"The pleasure is entirely mine," Georg answered, rubbing his hands, and they both smiled as they took another step with the advancing line. They laughed at the coincidence that Edith and Dorli had been classmates in the secondary school in Wenzgasse in Hietzing. Georg was twenty-five, seven years older than Edith. She took in the three-piece woolen suit under his fawn coat. "You're very well-dressed," she said. "You should have some gloves." She shivered in her heavy sweater and overcoat. It was a bitter morning, all the colder for the sharp blue sky and biting wind. Georg paused, as if considering how to respond.

"Well, truth be told, I don't have any other clothes." He stopped suddenly and this time the pause was awkward. Edith saw his eyes briefly redden, moist at the corner, but blinked away. "How long have you been here?" she asked gently.

"I arrived this morning. I came straight here."

Another pause.

"Do you have anywhere to stay?"

"Not really."

"How did you get here?"

Georg hesitated, and looked around at the people standing with them. He shrugged and breathed out hard. "Maybe later?" he said, watching the steam of his breath. Before they reached the front of the line the embassy closed. They were given numbers and told to return the next morning.

"It happens all the time," Edith said. "The French open at two o'clock. Very convenient. Everyone goes there in the afternoon."

Wind that blasted through the avenues turned their cheeks red, their lips blue. They hurried inside the first café they found in Wenceslas Square, a scruffy place with a black-and-white tiled floor that needed sweeping. Cigarette butts, crumbs, and dust. They sat at a square wooden table with uncomfortable metal chairs and looked around. Couples playing chess, men reading newspapers, a long table of noisy, laughing youngsters. They were still looking at the menu, looking for the cheapest items, when two policemen in long leather coats entered and stamped their feet, surveying the room. They walked to the noisy table nearest the door and one of them put out his gloved hand, saying something in a challenging manner. Georg watched a young man half rise as he took his wallet from his pants, and with a bored look hand over his identification papers. "Quietly, slowly, let's go," Georg whispered. Edith didn't need to ask why. Half the Jews in Prague didn't have papers. She placed the menu back on the table, pushed back her chair without scraping it, stood up, smiled apologetically at the waitress and followed Georg deeper into the room. He walked to one corner, slid the glass side door open and without looking round, slipped out. Their pace quickened as they distanced themselves from the café. They didn't talk. Georg turned his collar up against the wind.

They continued to walk silently along the square until they were swallowed up by the crowd. Edith gave Georg time, knowing he would speak when ready. She could feel his nerves. She glanced at him. Now she saw he was exhausted. She hadn't noticed the dark bags under his set eyes before, or the worried frown. He was tense. She moved closer and gently slipped her hand into his. He started a moment, felt a different tension, and smiled. "I have no idea where we're going," he said, and laughed. How different things already look, he thought, holding her hand, stealing a glance.

"Me neither."

They had left the big crowded square and walked through quiet side streets until they came upon a pretty garden among tall, narrow homes with gabled roofs. It had thick trees and ferns and a paved path that led to a bench inside a hut under a cherry tree. They sat down, out of the wind, still holding hands. There was a high-pitched warble as one bird called to another.

"Actually," Georg finally said, "the thing is, I don't have any papers. And if they catch me they can send me back to Austria. And you know what that means." He looked sideways at her, and hunched forward, running his free hand through his thinning hair.

"How did you get in, then?" Edith asked, knowing how scared she had been passing through the Austrian passport authority on the border. The guard had flicked through her passport page by page, glancing up at her face repeatedy, before handing it back. The Czech guards hadn't been much friendlier. They had surprised her by asking where she would stay, whether she had any family in Prague, and how she would support herself, but her spontaneous answers must have satisfied them. They didn't see that she was Jewish.

"Otto Ballek. He's connected," Georg answered.

"Otto! I know Otto," Edith said, "our parents are friends."

"How come we never met, then?" Georg said. "Vienna is so small, let alone Hietzing. Otto is my best friend. He saved me. Twice, in fact."

"Really? How?"

"Twice the Gestapo arrested me. Once I tried to help a friend when they arrested him, and they took me, too. Paul Somlo? You know him?"

"No."

"Well, Otto bought me out after two days. This time I was inside for a week. They threatened to send me to Dachau. I was terrified. Then they suddenly released me. Otto paid someone off. He was waiting with this fancy suit I'm wearing. That was yesterday. He told me to put it on, gave me false papers, and put me together with a group of businessmen who came here to explore a beer export venture. That's what he told me to say, anyway. When we all got in, at the road border crossing near Brno, we stopped for a drink. It was past midnight. One of the men collected everyone's papers, said he'd need them to get the next batch out, and we were on our own. That's the story. I got a bus to Prague and arrived early this morning. I didn't even get a chance to say good-bye to my friends."

"What about your family?"

"I said good-bye at the house, very quickly. I grabbed a few things and left. They're still there. I have to find a way to get them out. I must."

"That's another thing we have in common, then," Edith said.

"Us and every Jew in Prague," Georg said.

She hesitated, and added, "Lucky they didn't send you to Dachau. My uncle died there. They burned his body, then charged my aunt ten marks for his ashes."

"Thanks," George said, with a snort.

"Don't you have a suitcase?" Edith asked.

"No."

Edith watched two sparrows hopping together on the path and waggling their wings, until one darted up and settled on a branch and the other one strutted away, turned, and flew to join it. She said quietly, "I'm staying at a lodging house, it must be near here somewhere."

Their eyes met, and Edith looked away shyly. When Georg didn't respond, Edith looked at the bird that was twittering in the tree, and then back at Georg. "We could see if they have an empty room for you. If you like?"

They were still holding hands. "Beggars can't be choosers," Georg answered, squeezing her hand softly.

"Good, that's that, then," Edith said. "Now all we have to do is find the place."

Waiting for a visa wasn't unpleasant; Edith and Georg walked in the woods and along the icy Vltava River. They sat in cafés with other refugees who were dribbling out of Austria and Germany. The earlier refugees brought suitcases of clothes and even money, and often bought coffees for the latest who came with just the clothes on their back. Time was like a roulette wheel: The ball flashed by on the outer rim, while the center barely budged. The Nazis built up power at terrifying speed, while the refugees' plans to escape got bogged down. They were trapped in Prague, their families were trapped in Vienna, and Hitler's evil grip closed around them all. They could only wait in line at a dozen embassies, fill out forms and plead with clerks, and each day they felt more helpless, losing a shade more control of their lives. They knew Hitler would invade Czechoslovakia. Could they get out first?

"We could be brother and sister," Edith said, so similar were their family histories. Each generation had moved westward. Each had great-grandparents from Ukraine, grandparents from Poland, and parents who had been born in Vienna. "And we'll go—" Edith began.

"To anywhere that will take us," Georg finished.

Edith's father was a doctor, Georg's a lawyer. Georg didn't know what to do with his life, so like all aimless Viennese Jews, he studied law. But nobody dared hire him, so he hung around the house with his friends, all seeking a way to escape the Nazis. Otto had helped him leave. But how to get the rest of the family out? They had left it too late. All their parents' letters from Vienna talked of was the worsening situation for Jews and their failed attempts to escape. That was all anyone talked about—how to run away from Vienna and where to go. And then in Prague, for hours Edith and Georg huddled and plotted with friends, walking the streets, waiting in lines. England, France, America, South America, China? Australia? Every day the choices narrowed. Every embassy either said no, or had a quota that was filled.

And then, quite suddenly, four weeks after she arrived in Prague, and a week after Georg moved into her boardinghouse, three days after he moved into her room, Edith got a brief postcard. "Please report at the embassy and ask for Mrs . . ." First prize. A visa for Britain. It would save her life. They made love for the first time, hugged all night, cried, and the next day she was gone.

Five weeks later Edith was reduced to knocking on doors, beseeching neighbors in Leeds, where her sponsor employed her as a domestic servant and baby's help. Please, she pleaded, give my friend a job, any job, even for no money, just help him get a visa to Britain. Please! She looked pitiable, with her thin wool coat and brown hat in the damp cold, pleading in a thick foreign accent. The northerners were kind and clucked in sympathy, some even invited her in for a cup of tea. One or two wanted to help, but couldn't. *Sorry, dear, we've got our own problems.*

But Edith wouldn't stop begging and telephoning, calling the aid groups and church groups. She spent the pittance she earned on phone calls from the post office, working her way, person by person, through the entire members' register of the Leeds and Harrogate synagogues, until one day in late February Miss Wolff, a kindly, middle-aged lady with a constantly preoccupied air, telephoned her from the local branch of the Jewish Council of Refugees. "Don't get your hopes up too high, ducks, but come on over and we'll see what we can do. We've been working on your case, darling, and we hope to get some news. So come tomorrow morning at ten." Edith's heart was thumping as she put the phone down and hurried to her employer, Mrs. Franklin. She had given Edith a small room next to the kitchen with a lumpy bed and a lumpy pillow. It was hard. At home in Vienna she had grown up with two domestic servants, a cook and a maid. Now Edith was both, and she also helped with the children. She was busy from the moment she got up until she dried the dishes and stacked them late at night. Everything was new—the strange food, the way they cleaned, even the way they washed the babies, with olive oil. And all in a language with which Edith was barely familiar. But she tried hard and Mrs. Franklin appeared satisfied enough, even though Edith could not bring herself to address her as ma'am.

"Mrs. Franklin, tomorrow morning I don't work, rendezvous."

"Oh, no, that's no good," Mrs. Franklin replied. "I need you tomorrow morning, you can't go out."

"But is important, you know about Georg and the Nazis, maybe I help him tomorrow. Only two hours. Please?"

"I'm sorry, no, not tomorrow morning dear, it's out of the question. I have a hairdresser's appointment."

"But is so important."

Mrs. Franklin's voice was shrill. "Well, it will just have to wait."

"I must to go." Edith was close to tears. She clasped her hands in supplication. "I cannot not to go. It is about Georg. Is his only chance." She looked so frail in her little black dress and white socks. She had refused to wear the white cap.

"No. I already have an appointment. I am so sorry, no, I need you here, I'm sure it can wait. I must get my hair done."

The next morning when Miss Wolff arrived for work at the Jewish Council of Refugees, she found Edith waiting at the door, looking upset and disheveled. "My dear, what on earth has happened to you?" Miss Wolff asked in alarm as she climbed the steps. She put her arm around Edith's thin shoulders. "What's wrong? You look like something the cat's dragged in. And why have you brought your suitcase? Did you sleep in the street or something?" Edith burst into tears.

Three weeks later, on March 15, 1939, the Wehrmacht occupied the rest of Czechoslovakia. Jackbooted Hitler reviewed ranks of helmeted stormtroopers in the courtyard of Prague Castle. He marched inside and vetted crowds cheered him as he waved from a belfry window. Outside, a quarter of a million Jews were trapped. But thanks to Miss Wolff's sponsor, Georg was not one of them. He had escaped with two days to spare. Edith met him at Liverpool Street station with her new friends Margit and Gina, and they bought him his first cup of English tea at Lyons Corner House at Marble Arch. "That's a nice three-piece suit you have on," Margit said, with a teasing little wink, stroking Georg's arm. "Don't see many of those around these days."

"Hands off!" Edith said, laughing.

SIX

London

October 9, 1945

As soon as Gina saw them enter the little café, she started to cry. Not weeping or sobbing, just silent tears running down her face. Edith saw her turn her head away and pull out a hanky. They hung up their coats, greeted a few people in German, and sat on the black leather corner bench with Gina. Edith ordered *Apfelkuchen mit Schlagsahne,* saying to Gina, "It's for you." Gina managed a crooked smile: apple cake and cream. Everyone knew the buttery cake with apple and raisins was her favorite. Cosmo did a delicious one, even though it wasn't real butter, the apples were from a can, and the cream was thin. Ah, Budapest, she would say, where an *almas pite* really is an *almas pite.*

In Hungary Gina had been a prominent writer and beauty, dark and sultry, exotic in her trademark black and red head scarves and big silver earrings—a Jewish gypsy, though she had no Romany blood. But here she was just another lost, sad exile, drained of inspiration and energy, which hardly mattered as no one could understand what she wrote anyway. The only language even related to Hungarian is Finnish. She was only a decade older than Edith yet her hair was already turning grey and her eyes were sunken. Their shared loss threw them together like sisters. Still, when she was on form, Gina could liven up a party like a gypsy queen, laughing and singing. Now, however, Gina took Edith's hand with a sigh that welled from her stomach. "You are so lucky."

"Why?"

"To be having a baby."

Edith sighed, too, with satisfaction. She folded her hands over her stomach and gave it a little pat. "I can't tell you how lucky I feel. And how happy." But she shook her head and added, "Sometimes." The waitress brought their coffees and apple cake with cream and laid three forks on three napkins. *"Danke schön,"* Edith said, pushing the plate toward Gina. They sipped in silence and shared the cake until Georg said, "Gina, you called, so what's new?"

She put down her cup too hard, it clinked on the saucer. "I got a letter. From a neighbor at home. She survived the camps." Edith unfolded the thin blue airmail paper and began to read the single-line type. In places the keys had been hit so heavily they tore the paper. She began to read aloud but quickly fell silent.

"Dearest Gina, There is no pain like the pain I know you will feel now. Your mother and I suffered terribly together in Treblinka, until . . ." Edith read till the end, her lips sometimes moving, and handed the letter to Georg, her hand shaking.

Word was spreading from the death camps, like ashes with the wind, choking the hearts of the living. How many ways are there to say there is no pain like this pain? . . . *It is with the greatest sorrow that I must . . . If only I did not have this terrible duty to inform you . . . Please know that in this most difficult moment you are not alone . . . I hope it is of some comfort to know that your mother did not suffer as I did . . .* yes, but . . . Dead. Murdered.

Edith handed the letter to Georg and covered Gina's hand with her own. "Gina, I am so sorry." Georg finished the letter and felt his eyes burning and stopped a sob as it reached his throat. Now Edith was crying. They were all losing everyone, like trees shorn of their branches, leaving logs that would roll away. The people at the next table tried not to look. It was the same for all of them. Phone calls, letters, rumors, a name on a list on a wall. Years of awful suspense, and a last shred of hope shattered, followed by weeks or months or years of despair. How long the grief and darkness? Nobody knew. Such a calamity was unknown.

"I already knew about my brother and sisters," Gina said, and sighed. "But I didn't know Opi and Omi were in Treblinka, too." Her eyes were red and tears fell. Looking in her little pocket mirror, she dabbed at the runny black mascara with her stained damp hanky. "It is too much to bear. They were all right until last August. They lasted so long. They nearly made it. It isn't fair. That is why I say you're so lucky to be having a baby. You have so much to look forward to."

Edith wiped her own tears. "Yes, I am so happy. And so sad. I never know what to feel." Now she was sobbing and her body shook and the loud chatter in the room trailed off as people looked at the crying pregnant young woman. Edith took Gina's hands and put them on her belly, on her baby. She struggled, to say, between sobs, "If . . . I feel sad . . . I feel I'm betraying my baby . . . and if I feel happy . . . I feel I'm betraying . . . my mummy." Gina held her and cried with her. Georg drew his hand across his eyes and pushed back his hair. "I'm glad Anna didn't come," he tried to joke. The waitress brought three glasses of water.

"You *are* lucky," Gina insisted, trying to calm Edith. "I wish I was

having a baby." She hadn't seen Bennie, her husband, since she had
fled Budapest in 1943, leaving him to follow a week later. But they
had cut it too close. The Germans invaded and swept to the capital
and arrested him at the train station with the whole underground
courier network. Gina had been one of the last to escape. She knew
the Jews of Budapest, who had stayed behind, were among the last
in Europe to avoid the transports, but they, too, had finally been
shipped off to Treblinka, Auschwitz, and God knows where else.
Maybe Anna knew Bennie in Auschwitz. Maybe. If she could survive, maybe he . . . She wanted to ask Anna, but Anna wouldn't talk.

Georg sensed a change in the light, the slightest fading, and looked
up to see the large café window filled by several English women.
They peered through cupped hands, squinting against the glare, as
if judging the food. The tables were all taken, but there were a few
empty places along the L-shaped bench. When the café was full
Hilda, the owner, guided customers through the low door to the ad-
jacent restaurant. The Cosmo was renowned for its authentic Wiener
schnitzel in the finest bread crumbs, and potato salad with the light-
est mayonnaise; when there was no veal they used chicken breast.
While it wasn't the same, nobody complained. Times were hard in
war and you even had to compromise with Wiener schnitzel. The
Cosmo's only real competition was the Dorice, over the road and
down a bit toward the swimming pool. The Dorice had better cakes
and was a heavier, darker, more intimate place—more Hungarian.
The Cosmo was lighter, airier, more cheerful—German and Austrian. The Dorice served a delectable gundel palacsinta, its paper-
thin layers of pancake filled with ground walnuts, raisins, candied
orange peel, cinnamon, and rum. And chocolate sauce. The Cosmo
had Palatschinken, equally luscious pancakes rolled up with apricot

or strawberry jam and sprinkled with confectioner's sugar. Their competition was intense and the mutual insults of Hilda and Dorice were vicious, but in truth their pancakes were equally delicious and anyway, nobody frequented either for their pastries. In exile, refugees clung to their memories, grasping what little remained of their old life, trying to re-create it, too exhausted and drained and uncertain to try building new ones. Everybody sought out countrymen or even townspeople, yearned for anyone who remembered what they remembered, who shared memories of the brook gleaming beneath the arched stone bridge, the evening walks around the cobbled square, being roped in to form a minyan in the gloomy synagogue. Nobody called Palatschinken or palacsinta a simple pancake.

Elsa the waitress smiled at the women in the window and beckoned at them to sit down, but it didn't look as if they wanted to enter. On the contrary. The tall thin one with grey hair pulled tight into a bun had a disapproving look, and as she leaned forward she positively glared. A shorter, rounder woman peered so closely to the window, her breath fogged the glass. An elderly man sitting inches away on the other side was startled by her looming grim face and said something to his table companion, who looked at the women and laughed. The short woman seemed insulted and jerked back. She took a piece of typewritten paper and waved it at them, straightened her back, said something to the taller woman that provoked a grimace and off they marched.

Georg recognized the taller woman with the bun and knew what was on the paper. He had seen her the day before outside the Finchley Road station, by the taxi rank, on his way back from another fruitless job interview as a lawyer's clerk. Sorry, thank you for your interest, but you know, overqualified and well, our boys coming back from the war need work, you understand. . . . Georg was becoming bitter. He couldn't get a job anywhere, yet everyone complained that the Jews have all the good jobs. It's becoming more like Vienna every day, he thought: lies feeding hatred.

Half a dozen men and women were standing around a folding table in the street, and the taller woman, the one with the bun, was calling on passersby to sign a petition. He saw a rather distinguished-looking gentleman wearing a brown trilby lean over the table and sign while a middle-aged couple stood and remonstrated. They all seemed quite animated. He had walked by without stopping, but accepted a flyer from a tough-looking young man in a torn army jacket. As he walked down the hill he had glanced at the paper, about to throw it away, when he stopped in his tracks. It read:

URGENT PUBLIC MEETING
When: Thursday, October 11. 7 pm
Where: Community Hall, 78, Hampstead High Street
Subject: Send the Aliens Home

How he hated the word *aliens*. It made him think of the moon and little green men with tentacles. Georg looked around, almost guiltily, and read on:

WE CALL ON ALL HAMPSTEAD RESIDENTS TO SIGN
THIS PETITION AND TAKE BACK THEIR HOMES

The HONOURABLE PETITION of the undersigned inhabitants of the RESIDENTIAL Borough of Hampstead asketh for HAMPSTEAD HOMES for HAMPSTEAD PEOPLE and prayeth for the prompt repatriation of the thousands of Austrian and German refugees who have taken up residence here and have turned so many of these houses and flats into factories and workshops, which same houses and flats are now sorely needed for our returning daughters and sons and for our evacuated daughters and their children.

Georg had crumpled the leaflet and thrown it away. He hadn't mentioned the petition to Edith; she had enough to worry about. But sitting in the café with Edith and Gina, now both thankfully recovered and chattering at the same time, their heads almost touching, his own sadness enveloped him. Seeing the skinny woman peering through the pane had done it: as if he was still being watched, like in Vienna and Prague, as if nowhere was safe. It was the pain of not being wanted, of having no secure place, a barely tolerated visitor, a vulnerable bird of passage, waiting for the hawk to swoop. In Austria, once his home, his natural habitat, countrymen stamped his passport with a big red *J* for Jew, setting him apart. The officials even took his identity, changed his name on the passport from Georg to Israel, as they did to all Jewish men. They renamed all Jewish women Sara, as if all Jews were faceless, interchangeable. It wasn't even the Nazis who had the idea of stamping *J* on their passports. It was the Swiss who insisted upon it, even before the war, so they wouldn't allow Jews to enter their country by mistake. And then, as a last resort, after no other country would take him, thanks to Edith, England finally gave him grudging refuge: for six months only.

Georg felt in his inside jacket pocket and took out his Certificate of Registration, Alien's Order 1920, which he kept neatly inside a protective paper cover. He opened the little booklet and sighed at the photo: a scared, starving rabbit. He'd arrived in the country the day before. The photographer had told him to smile but he couldn't. It was the vacant stare of a lost, beaten man. A man with no rights, begging for a favor: Let me in. An official had asked about his professional qualifications. He had answered: doctor of law, fluent in seven languages. But he wasn't allowed to work in England. So under "Profession or Occupation" the official had written, *No Occupation.* A nobody. It was the beginning of his transformation from a subject to an object.

He turned the page:

> Permitted by the Immigration Officer to land at Croydon on 28/3/1939 on condition that the holder registers at once with Police and does not remain longer than six months and does not enter employment paid or unpaid in the United Kingdom.

As the six months ran out, his fear grew. He could be arrested and deported, but where to? He couldn't go home; the Nazis would kill him. Nowhere else would take him. Every day he worried more. He lost confidence, became distrustful. He felt he was losing possession of himself, like a cork in the sea, tossed at another's whim. War saved him. Weeks before he had to leave, when it looked as if he would have to go to the Dominican Republic, wherever that was, Germany invaded Poland and Britain declared war on Germany. Britain was stuck with him. Until then he had been classified merely as an alien. Now that changed. He read, *Georg Fleischer: Enemy alien.* He drew his finger across the description stamped below his new status: *Refugee from Nazi Oppression.*

They married in a Spartan affair, with two witnesses, Gina and Margit, at Hampstead town hall, Georg in his three-piece suit, Edith in her soft wool dress with white lace lapels. They felt no joy. How could they, with Europe at war, no contact with their families who could be dead or in prison, and no future. They lived off Edith's wages as a domestic servant, and her work on the side cleaning two houses. She never complained. As he weakened she seemed to grow in strength. She learned how to mend stockings to make more money. Their only furniture was a single bed, an orange crate to sit on, and half an old door for a table, and that was more than most of their friends had. He looked at her, smiling and chatting with Gina. A rush of warmth rose in his heart. Where would he have been without Edith? Dead.

Five weeks after they married, there was a knock on the door, two policemen, and before he could say *Hupfingatsch,* get lost, he was behind barbed wire on the Isle of Man. He hadn't even known there was an island in the Irish Sea. All Jewish male refugees were interned. "Collar the lot!" said the new prime minister, Winston Churchill. Possible Nazi spies. How stupid was that? Edith hadn't rested a moment: She wrote to Churchill himself, to members of Parliament, to the newspapers, appealed to the refugee organisations. And it worked. He was among the first to get out.

He turned the page. Another stamp with a handwritten note:

Recruiting Officer 28/12/1940

DOUGLAS

Isle of Man

Enlisted into Pioneer Corps

Digging trenches, filling sandbags, trying and failing to march in step. His poor hearing and what the orderly called "a dicky heart" kept him out of more active duty. All he'd thought of was Edith. She'd kept his spirits up with care packages of home-baked cakes and dried flowers and daily letters filled with accounts of life in the guest-house she'd moved into in Goldhurst Terrace: an Indian man, Mr. Patel, always courting her, trying to kiss her. *"I box him in the stom-ach, but if you don't come home who knows what a lonely girl may do. . . ."* Otto upstairs had created a scandal in the house by giving three girls a bath. *"The landlady, Mrs. Barnes, shouted, 'Water! You're only allowed five inches! Rationing!'*

After his discharge came at last the coveted permit:

Permission granted for employment 18/2/1942
As . . . trainee optical framemaker
With . . . United Kingdom Opticals 19 Britton St. E6.
Subject to review as necessary

He'd been all thumbs, but it was work. And finally he made it, the passport stamp that meant he was safe and sound behind the white cliffs of Dover. Printed on the last page:

AUXILIARY WAR SERVICES 20/8/1944
NO PERMISSION TO LEAVE THE UNITED KINGDOM
CAN BE GRANTED UNTIL AFTER THE DATE ON WHICH
THIS PERMIT HAS BEEN CANCELLED BY THE AUXILIARY
WAR SERVICE DEPARTMENT HOME OFFICE

First they wouldn't let him in; then they wouldn't let him out. And that was just fine, Georg thought, just fine. He felt safe at last.

Until that thug gave him the flyer, and now that woman looking through the window, waving her piece of paper.

It's just a petition, he thought, just a petition; a list of names. Who are they? There's a good government here. This isn't Germany. Ger-

many lost. But Otto had told him the petition already had hundreds
of signatures. The refugees were getting scared, Otto said. A lot of
English people agreed with the petition: the Jews came as refugees
from Hitler; Hitler was dead, the war was won, so why don't they go
home? He remembered VE day, the celebrations outside Buckingham Palace and the women who made fun of their accents: *ve von, ve
von.* They said we could go home now. They meant well. But these
people don't. Not at all. He sensed a fight was beginning. To stay in
England. Not to get kicked out. They think we're taking their jobs.
He snorted.

Georg hadn't wanted to bother Edith. First he didn't want to upset
her. But most of all, one thing he knew about his bride was that she
wouldn't sit back and take it. She'd fight back. And she had to stay
quiet, calm, relaxed; for the baby's sake. *The baby,* Georg thought,
nothing must harm the baby.

He didn't blame her, it was nobody's fault. But Edith loved to dance,
to fool around. It was one of the things he loved about her; so different from him, he was too stiff, too worried what other people thought.
But Edith always did the first thing that came into her head, and
when Otto had passed her on the stairs and turned as she climbed up
and pinched her bottom she had whipped round and without thinking jumped onto his back. But he was quick, and also without
thinking leapt out of the way. Ten steps. He heard her shout and
rushed to the door. She was sprawled on the floor and already bleeding
between the legs. They called a cab and rushed to the hospital—too late.

The doctor said it would have happened anyway; there were
severe signs of umbilical cord stricture.

But whatever the reason, Georg was scared. He wanted Edith to
take it easy this time and even hoped secretly that he could persuade

her to stay in bed until the baby was born. He hoped to get her to work less, even though she earned a lot more money than he did. She must stop worrying about Papi. Even as he thought it he despaired, and felt a surge of affection for his beautiful wife, who wouldn't be tamed. He leaned over and kissed Edith on the cheek while she was talking. So smooth and warm. She smiled and stroked his face without missing a word. Gina pursed her red lips, raised her long fingernails to her mouth, and blew him a kiss. Behind the bar, drying a glass, the waitress smiled.

"The meeting's tomorrow," Otto was saying to Frieda, who lived in number three, when they came home and entered the lounge. "Let's go."

"What meeting?" Edith asked, struggling out of her coat and throwing it over a chair.

"You haven't heard? The meeting to throw us out?"

"What do you mean?" Edith said, dropping onto the sofa. "Ooof, my feet hurt—I've put on twenty-three pounds already."

Ismael said, "They've had enough of you here. Too many of you."

"Give me a visa to America and we'll leave tomorrow, how about that?" Georg said.

"What are you talking about?" Edith said, pulling off a shoe and rubbing her foot. "What meeting? It's chilly here, anybody got a shilling?"

"No," everyone said together.

"Come on, it's freezing."

Ismael stood and walked to the meter. "You'd all rather freeze to death," he said, slipping in a coin and twisting the lever. "You know what, don't all fall over, here's another shilling," and he put another coin in the slot and twisted. The coin clanged into the box.

"Where do you get your money from, anyway?" asked Edith. "You never work, I never see you study, if you're so rich, what's so large about putting a shilling in the meter? Two shillings, cripes!" She loved to use these English words. "Golly, you're so generous, the generous Arab. Oh sorry, Ay-rab." When Ismael made his little anti-Semitic slurs, Edith always gave it right back. It was a kind of game, though Edith never knew how seriously to take it. Although he had a very hard edge to him, Ismael was more jokey than nasty. Also, he was outnumbered. "I have an idea," Edith said. "I'll bring you some stockings to mend. The smelly ones."

"Have you seen this?" Otto said, handing the flyer to Georg.

He glanced at it. "Yes, at the station. People were signing it."

"I just came from the Austrian Center," Otto continued. "Everyone's talking about it. It's been growing for a long time. But now this petition, it's building up steam."

"What are you talking about?" Edith asked.

"You didn't hear?" Otto said. "There's a petition to throw the Jews out of Hampstead. Of course, they don't say Jews. Refugees."

"Oh, that," Edith said. She'd also heard about it. "They can't be serious."

Otto had a copy of the petition and read it out in an exaggerated English accent, pulling out the vowels in a high-pitched female voice: "Hoooonooorable petiiition . . . prooompt reeeepaaaatriaaation . . ."

Frieda asked, "Do you really think they can make us leave?"

"Of course they can," Georg said, "we're not citizens, not naturalised, we're just temporary."

"They want us to go home," Frieda said.

Edith snorted. "Home! What home?"

Otto stood by the fireplace. "In Poland, Jews went home and the Poles who had stolen their homes killed them. Can you imagine?

Surviving those concentration camps, make your way home for months, and then what do the neighbors do? Kill you. My God."

Ismael stared at Otto and seemed about to add something when he saw Edith looking at him, daring him. He shook his head.

The door opened and Anna came in. She went straight to the gas fire and stood over it, warming her hands in the rising heat.

"So what's the meeting?" Edith asked again.

"Tomorrow, at seven o'clock. Here." Otto waved the flyer. "Send the aliens home," he read. "That's you, by the way. Alien."

"Hey, don't put me down," Georg said. "Enemy alien."

"Sorry, correct, enemy alien." Otto laughed. "I say we go and listen."

"No," Georg said. "No!" He looked at Edith, rubbing her feet. He knew what was coming. Why hadn't they gone straight upstairs?

"Of course we're going. If someone wants to throw us out, we must go there. We must all go there. We must speak up for ourselves. No one else will."

"Edith," Georg said, "first of all, in your condition, you're not going anywhere. Second, plenty of other people can go. Let's just—"

"No. We're going. That's that. I know what everyone's saying but I didn't know about a petition—"

"It isn't everyone," Georg interrupted. "Not everyone agrees with—"

"So why don't they say so, then?" Edith said sharply. "If we don't stand up and talk for ourselves, who will? We must go!"

"Edith, no!"

Otto said, "Georg, haven't you learned yet? You're going."

Georg stood. "Dit, come on, let's go upstairs."

"Uh-oh," Ismael said. "Trouble in paradise."

"What's happening? What are you talking about?" Anna asked.

Nobody answered. As Edith and Georg gathered their coats and left the room, they heard Ismael begin to explain. "There's this petition to throw out the Jews. . . ."

Georg closed the door and they climbed upstairs to their room. Edith went first, resting on the landing and again halfway up the next flight, holding the rail with both hands, hanging her head, catching her breath. Georg waited, his hand resting on her bottom, leaning forward, pushing her up the stairs. "Come on. Three months to go," he said. "Less. We'll make it. We'll have a baby soon. That's all we care about."

Edith took three more steps, rested, exhaled loudly. She closed her eyes in a grimace. She felt more tired than usual. And then Papi came. Papi, his face, calling from a great distance. He should trim his moustache. Just as quickly, he faded away. She raised her head, sucked in air, ready to set off again, breathing deeply, while Georg waited, his hand still on her bottom.

SEVEN

Hampstead Community Hall, London

October 10, 1945

We the undersigned petition the House of Commons in a request that aliens of Hampstead should be repatriated to assure that men and women of the Forces should have accommodation on their return.

"I don't think so, thank you," Edith said, taking the petition from Otto and handing it to Georg, who passed it to Ismael who passed it on to the ruddy-faced country-type man sitting next to him. He licked his lips as he signed, ending with a flourish underlining his name, and passed it on. Edith leaned across Georg: "You didn't sign, Ismael; I'm surprised."

"I'm full of surprises," he answered, "and anyway, *Kul kalb biji uomo*. You know what that means?"

Edith shook her head.

"Arab proverb. Every dog has his day."

"Meaning what?"

"Everyone gets what they deserve."

Edith still didn't get it, but she shrugged and sat back. She hoped the Nazi dogs got what they deserved. A line of people were taking the stage. Tough-looking young men filed into the front of the hall, their arms tensed at their sides, scanning the audience, while from the arc lights above them hung a long banner with the organisation's name: Face the Facts. Onstage half a dozen men and women sat behind the trestle table, as a young man distributed two jugs of water and six glasses. In the front row an intense man from the local newspaper, the *Ham and High,* the Hampstead and Highgate express, snapped photos as a tall, thin woman pulled the microphone toward her. She banged it once with a finger and looked up as she heard the hollow pop. The pop heard round the room, Edith thought, and sniggered. Satisfied with the sound and the turnout—about three hundred people, all leaning forward with upturned faces—the woman bent toward the microphone and discreetly cleared her throat.

"Welcome," she began, and Edith immediately laughed. The woman sounded just like Otto. Edith put her elbow in his side and he acknowledged with a nod. "Wil-cum!" he whispered, and they both giggled.

"Thank you for coming this evening. My name is Margaret Crabtree and I am speaking to you this evening on behalf of Face the Facts. And I call on you, before it is too late—to face the facts." An approving murmur rippled through the hall.

"This country, after six years of war, can provide neither homes nor food for all its nationals, nor jobs, and is therefore in no position to offer homes or food or jobs to large numbers of refugees." She paused for dramatic effect, looked across the audience, noticed the assenting nods, and continued.

"Our finest young men and women are now returning home in large numbers and finding those homes occupied by others. Jobs have been taken by others. It is not inhuman or uncharitable to prefer our own homeless people to these others who have already had a home here for six years." Jewish refugees in the audience began shifting uncomfortably, looking around for support. Edith thought: *That's me. I'm an "other."*

"Yet when we draw attention to the iniquities of this sad situation, when we venture the slightest criticism of the Germans amongst us, we are immediately assailed as 'fascists,' 'anti-Semites,' 'un-Christian,' 'un-British.' I believe on the contrary, the most unsavory feature of the situation is the callous exploitation of the sufferings of those who remained in Hitler's power to promote the power and privilege of those who escaped over here. This is distressing and distasteful."

A shout from the audience: "Vat you talking about? Translation!"

"Go home," a man called out.

"You go home!"

"I am home."

Edith waved and called out, "Get to the point!"

A large man with a florid face in the front row turned round and glared at her. "Be quiet! Disgraceful!"

Georg pushed Edith's hand down. *"Dorftrottel,"* Edith said. She leaned across to Ismael and translated. "Village idiot." She was beginning to enjoy herself.

Mrs. Crabtree continued, unperturbed. It's easy for the English to ignore hecklers, Georg thought—they don't listen anyway.

"We decided to get up the petition because we are so fed up with the housing situation in Hampstead . . ."

Otto whispered to Edith: "Hemp-stid."

"We are not anti-Semitic and we are strictly nonpolitical. Our only interest is to see that fair play is given to our dear boys when they come back for jobs and houses in Hemp-stid."

A man called out, "Why not build more houses, then? Fix up the bombed ones? There's hundreds of empty houses—why not let people live in them?"

"May I ask what is your name, sir?" Mrs Crabtree asked.

"Benzi Krodszinski," he answered.

"I thought so," she jeered, and most of the audience roared in appreciation. Edith clasped and unclasped her hands, not enjoying it so much after all. She was getting nervous. For six years she had lived with the supercilious sneers, the veiled rudeness, the sense that you'd just been insulted but didn't quite know how. Even the pleasant newsagent didn't say *Here are more stockings.* Instead he said *Here's more money, here's more of the folding stuff.* She knew he would never have said that to an English repair girl. She still didn't have one English friend, none of them did.

"If I may continue," Mrs. Crabtree said, gesturing for silence with both outstretched hands. "We have given every shelter and help to our foreign friends, and rightly so. We have done our duty and much more, more than any other country. But now the war is over. We won! And now our fine fighters need help. We do not think it would do any good removing the aliens just from Hampstead, because they would infiltrate again. The longer they stay here the more children there will be and the greater the problem of their removal."

"Hear, hear!"

"We hope our campaign will influence other boroughs to carry on the good work."

Edith suddenly rose and yelled, "What good work? Send us home? There's nothing there, don't you understand!"

"Sit down!"

"Shut up!"

A man stood up and shouted across the heads of the audience, "Put a sock in it, Jew bitch!"

Edith flopped down, panting, her lip trembling. Georg was horrified. "Dit, stop it!"

But she shot back up, without thinking, her belly heaving as she struggled for breath. "Don't you know what they've done to us? What did you fight for? To send us back? Are you mad?" She sat down again, gasping, tears welling in her eyes. Heads turned as people strained to see who was shouting with the high voice and foreign accent. A woman behind her laid her hand on Edith's shoulder and leaned forward. "There, there, dear, don't listen, they're just fascist animals. Don't listen. There's plenty of us as won't listen to them. And you're expecting, too. It's all right, my dear, nobody's going to throw you out."

Georg thanked the lady with a tense smile and put a restraining arm around Edith, ready to force her down. "I knew we shouldn't have come."

Edith thought of something else to say and tried to stand but Georg wouldn't let her up, helped by Otto on the other side, who was also alarmed. Ismael's jaw muscles twitched. His hand balled into a fist and his neck muscles swelled. He liked Edith. She was a fighter. When Georg had asked why he wanted to come, Ismael had smiled and said, "Protection." He seemed ready. Georg knew how strong Ismael was, even if he was short. He was built like, in one of Georg's favorite new English phrases, a brick shithouse.

"That's right, sit down, sit down and shut up," another man called out, "this is England, go back to Germany! They know what to do with you!"

Two of the bouncers came from the front and leaned over toward Edith and one pointed at her. He was big with a scar on his temple. He wiggled his finger as at a naughty child, put his finger to his lips. Then he drew his thumb across his throat. She looked away, *Nazi dog,* fixed her eyes ahead, and so did Georg; but Ismael glared at the man. Their eyes locked until the bouncer, looking at Ismael, again drew his thumb across his throat and swaggered back to the stage, protecting Mrs. Crabtree.

"Don't let him scare you, ducks, they're just thugs," the women whispered from behind. "They didn't even fight in the war. Fascists were in jail where they belong."

Mrs. Crabtree's high, piercing voice went on, magnified through the speaker system. "All refugees who entered our wonderful country signed a form agreeing to leave later on. Now the war is over. Will they honor their signature? The mass of German Jews came here in transit. We shared with them our food, gave them shelter and protection. But today, we know no difference between German Jews and Germans."

"Shame," a woman called, "shame on you!" She stamped her feet and a few others joined her. "No difference indeed! Jews aren't Nazis! You are!"

"Shut yer face," said a man who stood up near her and leaned across, "or I'll clock yer one!" The feet-stamping died out and Mrs. Crabtree continued.

"We object to these refugees being given licences to open shops and restaurants. We object to them being allowed to use British names. We object to the way they are buying our freehold and long leasehold property. We strongly object to the way they turn our private houses and flats into factories and workshops. We object to the number of them in the medical profession.

"We protest against the naturalization of these refugees . . ." Mrs. Crabtree went on and on, her voice growing in volume and shrillness, until she ended, "Friends, face the facts. Sign the petition. Take back your homes and jobs!"

The hall erupted in applause and feet-stamping and calls of "Hear, hear!'" Mrs. Crabtree returned to her seat on the podium, beaming broadly, nodding, acknowledging the audience. A man called, "Turf 'em out!"

When silence was restored, a beefy man with a mop of unruly silver hair stood up behind the table and said, "And now we'd like to ask you for any questions or comments. And please, let's keep this orderly. One by one."

A man in the front row shot up his hand. It was the same red-faced man who had earlier called for quiet. He labored to his feet and said, in a raspy, nicotine voice: "I just want to say that I heartily endorse everything Mrs. Crabtree has said this evening. I signed the petition. . . ."

"What a surprise!"

"Yes, I signed it! And let me tell you, I have not observed any sign of persecution of our Jewish friends in Hampstead. They are better housed and better dressed and their restaurants have better foods than any of our English people. They are always in the front of the queue and get all the best rations. Ask anyone. I'm just saying what I have seen. An inspection of the foreign-owned restaurants in Finchley Road will prove this. . . ."

"Finchleystrasse!" Laughter and clapping.

"Those who came from European countries should return and help rebuild them. They have been here long enough, they are healthy, fit, and strong. That will give them advantage over everyone else across the Channel, and we know our alien friends always look for every advantage. . . ." He sat down to cheers and laughter.

Mrs. Crabtree added, "There are more Jews here than the government figure of forty thousand would have us believe. I challenge the government's figure and say there are more like two hundred and seventy thousand Jewish refugees here, not forty thousand. The only gentleman in office today who speaks honestly and fairly about these people is the honorable Minister Ernest Bevin."

"Hear, hear!"

"How many refugees are there in Hampstead, then?" someone called out.

The beefy man with silver hair answered. "About twenty-five thousand aliens, out of seventy thousand residents, and that's the town hall's official figure."

"Ridiculous! Who let them all in?"

"Where do they get all the food from? Have you seen the cakes in the Dorice? What about the rations!"

"I can't afford them!"

"Nor can I!"

"Not even kosher!" Laughter.

"Hitler should have finished the job, that's what I say!"

Clapping, feet-stamping, laughter, cheering.

Her heart thumping, Edith rose slowly to her feet, so slowly that Georg didn't think of stopping her before it was too late. Now what was she doing? He couldn't very well yank her off her feet, much as he wanted to. She was supposed to be taking it easy! Oh, why did he let her come? She stood, her lips pursed, surveying the packed room. Her eyes were red. Georg heard her heavy, even breathing, and knew she was trying not to explode. Her tummy rose and fell with her breaths. Bit by bit, section by section, the murmuring and chattering faded and people turned and pointed and Edith, just by standing, attracted the room's full attention: the pretty pregnant girl in the black woolen sweater tight against her jutting stomach. With her slim frame and wavy auburn hair and artless looks, she was always taken for five years younger. She looked the picture of an innocent and demure mother-to-be. A lovely girl. Could she really be Jewish? Now the hall was silent, all eyes on Edith, even Mrs. Crabtree's, from the stage. Edith let her gaze wander across the faces, her eyes lingering on the hostile, suspicious eyes of the Jew haters, feeling herself grow stronger. But there were so many, until she looked directly at the leaders on the stage. Now Georg's heart was thumping so hard he began to pant. He was sweating. He looked at her belly, so close, the hairs of the sweater grazed his head, and he imagined his growing baby inside, a curled sleeping fetus, and he felt his own stomach tighten. Doctor Goldscheider said to relax! Otto was leaning upward toward Edith, his face intent. Ismael didn't take his eyes from the scar-faced bouncer, who was looking murderous.

Everyone was now looking at Edith. It was one thing jeering at an absent enemy, but face-to-face, eye-to-eye, one-on-one—here was a Jewish refugee, not just a caricature. The moment extended, and the silence grew, until it was unbearable. Later Otto said it felt like if Edith didn't speak, the silence would explode like a crashing glass.

As if she had second thoughts, as if overwhelmed, Edith began to lower herself back into her chair. She had no idea why she had stood, what she wanted to say. But, as she touched it, she sprang up again.

She looked sadly at the stage. "Mrs. Crabtree," Edith said finally, and paused, gathering her courage, her thoughts. "Look at me. I am going to have a baby. My first. She will be so lonely." Edith swallowed hard, but felt a strength that came from somewhere deep. This was her chance to speak up. To do something. She looked down at Georg. He wouldn't do it. She met his eyes. They were pleading. But his fear gave her strength. Someone must say it. She continued in a rush. "My mother and sister and as far as I know all my cousins except one, all my aunts and uncles and grandparents, will never see my child, because Hitler, the Nazis, murdered them. In ways I can't begin to imagine and don't want to know. My past is a graveyard. My neighbors in Vienna wouldn't even sell me food or say hello, and for all I know now they have stolen my home." She paused, breathing deeply, sucking in air. In that moment an image flashed through her mind, Auden's poem of a thousand doors, which Georg had read to her a dozen times. Closed, slammed, locked. "To them, I am less than an animal. They feed a dog. Me, they'd let me starve to death, or kill me first. And you want to send me back? That's my home?"

From the stage the speaker used a microphone and a loudhailer system, yet Edith's trembling voice penetrated every corner of the transfixed room.

"Is it so awful for you to think that my baby will be born in your beautiful country that was so good to me and my friends? Do you know that if my baby will be born here, my baby will be English? That's all it takes to be English. And then she will be English like you. Is that what you're afraid of, that my baby will be like you? Jewish and English? It is so easy to be English, and yet you hate me because I'm not."

Edith spoke with her hands resting on her belly. She stroked it as if receiving strength, and looked around at the audience. A few were looking intently at her and as their eyes met, they nodded encouragement and several smiled and gave her a thumbs-up. Not only the refugees, some of the English, too. But most were slumped back in their seats, legs out, arms folded, grim-faced, staring at their legs or the back of the heads of the people in front. In the pause, some started to mutter, but fell silent when Edith continued.

"How is your father, Mrs. Crabtree? I hope he is healthy and well—" Edith's voice caught and she faltered and Georg looked up in alarm. He took her hand and squeezed to give her courage. Still, she couldn't talk and she struggled to control her breaths and it seemed as if she would break down. Her heart fluttered as she suppressed a sob and the corners of her eyes heated with welling tears. The room was silent, the hearts of some going out to the pregnant suffering girl, the hearts of others like stone. Georg raised Edith's hand to his lips and kissed it and she looked down. She heaved a huge sigh, and licked her lips and swallowed. She wiped her brow with her other sweating hand.

"My father, Mrs. Crabtree—I don't know where he is. I know he was in Auschwitz where hundreds of thousands of Jews, maybe more, were killed. But he may still be alive. My cousin saw him near the end and he was alive. If he is alive, he may be sick, lost, or wounded. He may need help, calling out, and I need help to find him. He may be in a prison in Russia—apparently many are, in Siberia. Maybe he's in a hospital in Poland. I just don't know. There are many, many people like me and him. So many. Mrs. Crabtree, you say you are not anti-Semitic, you're nonpolitical, you just care about homes and jobs. But do you care about me, the hundreds of thousands of Jews like me? Why don't you just say the truth. You don't care about us. You would close your door in my face. For you, we are dogs in the street. Don't hide behind jobs and houses.

"Why am I saying all this? Mrs. Crabtree, it is very hard to know that in spite of everything we have gone through, you still hate me and you hate my baby. Haven't enough Jews died? But you know what? Most English people are not like you."

She sat down heavily as if in mid-thought but out of strength. A sigh swept across the room. A single voice said, unchallenged, "Hear, hear." People pulled themselves up in their seats and unfolded their arms, as if an ordeal was over. Some looked around and when their eyes met someone else's, they looked away.

Mrs. Crabtree, sitting at the long table, leaned into the microphone. "My dear, we're all very sorry for you and your father. I hope he's well. And by the way, mine is just fine, thank you. But all you lot have to understand. We looked after you when you needed help, we did our duty, we shared everything, and now it's over. You just don't belong here. It's time to go home, just like our brave boys and girls are coming home."

"Hear, hear."

But it seemed halfhearted now.

There were a few more comments and an announcement about more Face the Facts meetings, all aimed at collecting support for the petition and ejecting the refugees from the country. An old grey-haired woman limped to the piano while everyone else stood at attention to sing "God Save the King," and the audience began filing out, a row at a time. They gathered in the lobby, signing the petition, exchanging comments which the dozen or so refugees filing out tried not to hear: "I'm sorry, I don't agree, she was just embarrassing"; "They do keep to themselves, you know, don't try to mix, it's unpleasant"; "Mind you, you'll never catch one with his coat off, work is a four-letter word."

The refugees were shocked. "Can they really throw us out?" Otto murmured as they shuffled onto the street. "And there's so many of them," Georg said, handing Edith her coat.

"Edith, you were amazing," Otto said. "I've never seen you like that before."

"I have," Georg said with a halfhearted chuckle.

She was stunned herself. From where had she gotten the strength? The words? Her cheeks felt flushed, hot. But inside she was smiling. Such a relief! At last she had stood up, done something. Georg didn't know if he was angry or proud. Maybe both. He knew he needed to stop Edith from getting upset, and this evening he had failed. He could still see her tummy going in and out and thought of his baby inside. But good for her, so typical. He'd never have dared.

All were lost in their thoughts as they turned right and headed down the hill toward the bus stop. They had planned to stop at a café for a drink but nobody was in the mood. Their energy was gone. So much hatred in that room! How widespread was it? They'd soon find out. Now they just wanted to go home and get into bed.

A voice came from behind. "Well, look who it ain't," it said. "Lost your dad, 'ave ya?"

"Oh dear, what a pity," another voice said. "Gonna lose your Jew-baby, too, if you aren't careful."

Edith felt her skin prickle. She hurried forward.

"Come on, don't look round," Georg hissed in German. Otto hesitated, unsure what to do. His heart raced. He felt adrenaline pumping, and so did Georg. His hair stood, his pores opened, he quickened his step, keeping up with Edith, Ismael at her side. "That's right, Jew boys, piss off before you get 'urt." Georg gripped Edith's arm, his tall, thin frame becoming stooped. In front, Otto walked faster.

But the two big men lengthened their steps and overtook them and turned around, blocking them. It was the scar-faced bouncer and a friend who was just as big and mean-looking. Both had dark blue combat jackets buttoned to their throats and cropped hair and cruel, hard faces.

They faced the refugees, who couldn't walk by.

Georg glanced back, hoping for help. They were alone, down the hill from the community center where a crowd was still gathered. It was too far to call for help, even if anyone there was so inclined, which was doubtful. Worse, the two men had timed it well. They'd stopped them in the shade of a tree and in the dark they were all but invisible. Clearly these men knew what they were doing. His heart pounded, felt like it would burst out of his ribs. They were helpless before these brutes. Why did they come? Oh, why did Edith come? Why did she draw attention? The baby . . .

"Quite a little speech, darlin'," the bouncer said. "Almost 'ad me in tears."

The other one laughed. "Where you pieces of shit from, then?"

"We're from Austria," Georg answered. "Please, we don't want any trouble. My wife is pregnant, six months pregnant, please, we're just going home."

"Up the spout, eh? Ain't that nice. Who's the lucky feller?"

"I told you, she's my wife, please, leave us alone." The police station was half a mile down the road on the other side. He could see the blue lamp glowing in the distance. Oh, why don't they ever come when you need them?

"That don't mean nothin', pretty girl like you. Eh?" the bouncer said, his hand reaching out and stroking Edith's hair. She jerked her head away. "Eh? Look at me, I don't bite."

"Much. Unless you like it," his friend said, and they sniggered.

Now the bouncer looked at Georg and Otto, who wouldn't meet his eyes. They knew brownshirts in Vienna. The bastards. But in London?

The bouncer snorted. Wankers! He turned to Ismael, whose hands were in his jacket pockets. Ismael looked back, into the hard man's cruel, stupid eyes. The bouncer stared back and pushed his neck forward and tensed, but Ismael, shorter by a head, didn't flinch. They stared at each other. Edith tried to step forward past the bouncer and the other one but they didn't move, and she stopped rather than bump into them.

"Please . . . ," Georg began, but the bouncer grunted at Ismael, "Who you fuckin' lookin' at, then?"

Ismael, on Edith's right, removed his left hand from his pocket and gently pulled her backward by the arm, a step out of harm's way, and glanced at Georg, who moved with Edith, and Otto stepped back, too. Now Ismael was closest to the two men. He turned slightly, his side facing the bouncer, and brought his right hand from his pocket and stared back, unblinking, into the big man's eyes, and eased his weight to the forward leg.

"Didn't you 'ear me? I said who you fuckin' lookin' at, you Jewish git?"

Ismael said, "Who are you calling Jewish?" and spun forward, throwing all his weight and solid muscle behind the knuckle duster on his right fist, a metal blow that smashed the bouncer's cheekbone so hard and with such ferocity and surprise that the bouncer's head jerked back and crashed into his mate's nose with all the power of a jackhammer. Blood poured from the broken nose. With one punch both big men were down. Ismael leaned back and kicked them both in the eyes, leaned over them and gave them each a short knuckle duster chop to the Adam's apple. It was all over in three seconds.

"See you at home, walk away quickly," Ismael said and ran. Within seconds he had vanished around the corner.

Astonished, Edith stared at the two men writhing and groaning on the ground. They couldn't call for help. They were gripping their throats, croaking and gasping.

"Quickly," Otto said, "the bus is coming." They stepped into the light and ran to the bus stop fifty yards away and jumped on the number 24 to Chalk Farm, from where they'd get the 31 to Fairhazel Gardens. They sat in a row, shocked, as the conductor called, "Fayers, please, thenk you!"

"Did you see that?" Edith murmured, shaking her head, as Georg bought three tickets. He was speechless. Edith said, "I don't understand. I thought Ismael would have signed the petition."

EIGHT

Tel Aviv, Palestine

October 18, 1945

Jimmy had felt safe, in Bella's arms. He'd been in them, one way or another, for five hours, and he hadn't planned to move. She exhausted him, as usual, in the nicest possible way, but she fell asleep first, her gentle breathing, her fleshy warmth, her breast against his cheek where he lay curled on the damp sheet, his left hand wedged between her moist thighs, his right hand groping for the gun on the floor.

His grip closed around the handle. His neck muscles tensed as he inched his head up from the bed and gently slid his hand from Bella's crotch. She sighed and moved to grip him but now he had swung his feet to the floor and the bed gently creaked as he sat on the edge.

It was dead quiet outside: three a.m., curfew, a quiet room facing trees in the back garden. The window opened onto the thick branches of a giant eucalyptus whose leaves rustled and sent moon shadows moving on the walls of the curtainless room. He was alert. There shouldn't be one moving light, but there was. If an army convoy patrolled the streets, there would be several beams flashing along the walls, and an engine drone, but not just one alone. There was only one reason for a single, silent beam: a car stealing up on a raid.

So Sami had known about Bella after all. How?

Jimmy leapt to his feet, pulled up his shorts, jerked into his T-shirt, and slipped into his shoes. He bent to grab his backpack but there was nothing in it he needed. Gripping the gun, he crossed to the window in two steps and climbed onto the sill. He'd long planned this and now it was for real. He had seconds. They'd be up the stairs with a man or two out back in the time it took him to—

"Open up! Police!"

In the same instant the door crashed open, Bella woke up screaming, and Jimmy jumped. Onto the branch, swung down and through the foliage, swung down from another branch like a monkey and hit the ground running. Leapt over a bush, swung round the building's pillar, left arm pumping, right arm gripping the pistol shoulder high, suddenly a flashing shadow and a big man crunched into him, both of them crashing to the ground, rolling over, the man's arm around Jimmy's throat, calling for help, *"I've got 'im, over 'ere!"* Jimmy pulling free, pushing his gun into the policeman's face. A flash, a roar, his head reverberating, warm stuff spurting, and Jimmy rolled, leapt to his feet and sprinted round the garbage cans, grabbing for leverage, sending them flying, and racing down the street, heart bursting, away, away.

In Palestine there were no high mountain chains with miles of secret caves or endless desert expanses with hidden valleys and dry river-beds where a man on the run could hide from the British. Nor were there distant farming communities in forests with isolated huts where he could live undisturbed for months or years. There was nowhere to hide, except in plain view.

Jimmy found an open building, ran to the top floor, and passed the rest of the night beneath a dripping water tank on the roof. In the morning, when the streets were full, he stopped at a small grocery store and begged to use the phone for free. The owner sniffed, "You've got one minute," and handed him the speaker.

Thirty minutes later, at a discreet distance, Jimmy followed the girl. This time, as he passed a café, a boy stood up, bumped into him, said "Follow me," crossed the road, and led Jimmy for a mile until they reached the corner of Ben Yehuda and Gordon streets, where a woman said "Jimmy" and led him up the stairs to her apartment on the third floor, beneath the roof. She gave him a towel, and he showered in the welcome cold water, his skin pocked with goose bumps. When he came out she gave him a plate of cheese and spinach bourekas and strong black tea and showed him to a small room—she had closed in the balcony to make a narrow bedroom. "Wait here," she said, "you'll have company soon," and she shut the door.

He slept at last.

And was awakened by the woman who brought a cup of coffee and a glass of water. "There are some men to see you," she said.

A rabbi, or a man who looked like one, shook his hand and said, "We're ready, come with me."

This time the room wasn't dark but a curtain hung down the middle. Three men sat in a semicircle with Jimmy. He didn't know any of them, they all looked like rabbis with long beards, yarmulkes, and bushy eyebrows. It looked like a prayer group or a Talmudic study center. Jimmy nodded to each of them and took a seat. There were dry pastries on a table and glasses of water and orange soda. He looked around. It was a friendly room with family photos on the wall and the cupboard. A mongrel slept on the floor, twitching. They all appeared to be waiting for someone.

One of the men spoke through a mouth full of cake. "Did you read the report to President Truman about the survivors in the camps?"

"Yes," another man said.

"Listen," the first man said anyway, smoothing crumbs from his jacket, and began to read from the newspaper. His accent was more German when he read than when he spoke.

"This is an official American report, remember:

> *'As things stand now, we appear to be treating the Jews as the Nazis treated them, except that we do not exterminate them. They are in concentration camps, in large numbers under our military guard instead of SS troops. One is led to wonder whether the German people, seeing this, are not supposing that we are following or at least condoning Nazi policy.'"*

He pursed his lips and his beard twitched. *"Nu?"* So?

The other man said, "Yes, I know. But guess what they didn't print. And it's also in the report. I read all of it."

"What?"

Jimmy looked from one to the other, wondering why he was part of this meeting. Had they come to see him? Or did he just happen to be in the apartment? Who were these people? The leaders? Either way, he was proud to be there. He wondered what happened to the man he shot. Nothing good, that's for sure. That was so close!

"They did surveys asking the survivors where they want to go—home, America, where? Guess where most want to go?"

"Here," said the first man, pouring himself an orange juice.

"Exactly. They get two choices, and the first choice they write is Palestine and under second choice they write Palestine, too. In one

camp they were told not to write Palestine as second choice but a re-
alistic alternative. Guess what they wrote?"

"What?"

"Crematoria. We're failing them, you know. We have to do more,
we must bring them here."

"I know. Fifteen hundred a month, we're allowed. Eighteen thousand a year. It's nothing; there are hundreds of thousands of them.
I myself have two cousins of my own in a camp in Germany. In the
same camp there are German prisoners of war—concentration camp
guards. Can you imagine that? Jewish survivors sharing a shower
with their former guards, the murderers. Mad. We must do more
to get them out. We need them here. We need people, more people,
or when we chase out the British, we won't have enough to fight the
Arabs."

That broke Jimmy's reverie about the man he'd shot. He hadn't
thought about the British blockade like that. It was a double squeeze.
First, we can't help the poor survivors now. Then, they can't help us
later.

A voice cut in from behind the curtain. He'd been there all the
time. "Jimmy, you killed a policeman—Special Branch." Those same
sharp vowels, the singsong rhythm.

Killed?

"I didn't mean to. I had to get away."

"I know. You did the right thing. You did what you had to do.
They would have hung you anyway."

Jimmy thought, he does have a way with words. Our boys don't
want mercy. They don't accept the legitimacy of the British court in
Palestine, don't take a lawyer or defend themselves, they just sing the
Hatikvah and swing.

The voice continued and the bearded men and Jimmy looked at

the coarse grey blanket with a blue stripe along the edges. "I have news for you all. The Jewish underground movements are at last uniting against the British, thank God, we are forming a united resistance movement. This has long been our desire. The new government in London has changed everything. In opposition the British labor movement paid lip service to the mass repatriation to Zion and we hoped they meant it. They undertook to restore the land of Israel to the people of Israel in our own homeland. But now they won the election and have formed the new government, they have gone the traditional British route of denial and betrayal. They will not let our people go. The anti-Semite Bevin will prevent us from coming in sufficient numbers. Afraid of upsetting the natural balance with the Arabs, that's what they say. He believes that the natural place for our Hitler survivors is in their countries of birth. This man is a simpleton, a brute. He does not understand what has been done to us in Europe, and by our own neighbors, who will do it again if they have half a chance, which they won't, God willing. This foreign minister of Britain is not a worthy man, he is our enemy. This man compares us to the Nazis because we fight back. So we will unite against the betrayer. We will meet his fist with our fist and we will wage war till the end, war till victory. History offers us no choice."

The leader stopped. Jimmy looked at the blanket. It was a rousing message. If all the Jewish underground forces, the Haganah and the Irgun and Lehi, joined together, no more betrayals and recriminations, the British would soon run with their tails between their legs. All the soldiers want to do is go home anyway. We don't have that luxury, we don't have any other home, we'll fight till the end. But in the pause, in the silence, his mind leapt to Bella. Everything had moved so quickly he hadn't had time to think. He'd left her screaming, naked, in the bed. They wouldn't harm her. Would they? Now that the policeman's dead? She doesn't know anything anyway, doesn't even know who he really is, just knows him as Jimmy. They would soon know she's innocent.

He was lost in his thoughts, not paying attention as the other men talked with the leader. He had stopped wondering why he was there, whether they had another mission for him. He'd slept, been awoken and brought into the room with the leaders, he hadn't had time to think. But now . . . Bella. He prayed she would not be hurt. If they hurt a hair on her head . . .

The woman barged into the room and the men turned to her, startled. She never joined them, wasn't permitted. "They're closing the streets," she said breathlessly, as if she'd just run up the stairs. "Bren Carriers, jeeps, trucks, men, they're rolling out barbed wire, the whole area." The men stood, alarmed. Jimmy heard the chair scrape behind the curtain.

"Jimmy, go," the voice ordered, "run, now, immediately. Don't think. Go. They mustn't find you here."

Jimmy stood, unsure, turned, ran to the door, and was gone.

They heard loudspeakers, a threatening voice, in English and perfect Hebrew: *"Nobody leave the house, go inside."* Engines, running feet in the street, more vehicles stopping, officers yelling orders, dogs barking. They knew what would follow: The streets would be cut, they'd be inside a barbed wire box, every apartment would be searched, every resident interrogated. Who were they after? Did they know the killer of the Special Branch policeman was in the area? One of the men who killed the army officer? Did they follow Jimmy? Or was that just luck? If it was luck, why were they here? A spot-check, a routine operation? The men in the apartment tore down the curtain and folded it, pulled out the holy books and opened them, ready for the knock on the door. Their ID cards were in order. They all lived in the building. A regular study meeting. Hiding in plain view. The storm would pass. Where was Jimmy?

He was downstairs, crouching by a pillar. He knew he must put as much distance between himself and the leaders as possible, to put the British off the scent. Someone must have followed him after he realised his home was under surveillance, followed him to Bella, somehow followed him here. Did they know in which apartment he'd been? Or was this not about him at all? Just bad luck? He had no chance, they were everywhere. Only one way out. Walk out. Plead innocence. Nobody had seen him shoot the policeman, it was dark. They didn't know what he looked like. But the gun, the gun. Throw it or keep it? He didn't know . . . no time to think. He stood up and walked through the garden, straight into four poppies and another man.

"Hello. Where are you going, sir?" the plainclothes man asked.

"Home, I heard the noise and I didn't know where to go. I'm just on my way home, I don't live around here."

"On your way home? Through the garden?"

"It's just a shortcut, sir."

"What are you doing here, then?" the man asked, pleasantly enough.

"I was just, just walking by, I wanted to visit a friend but he's out, no answer, so now I'm on the way home."

"Not at home, was he? Do you mind showing us your ID?"

"Certainly." He tried to remember which one he had. He hoped it was the Jimmy one. And his pistol. It was in his shorts, stuck in the back, covered by his loose T-shirt. The short barrel dug between his buttocks. If they searched him, he could only run, run and shoot. His lungs felt like they'd explode but he must stay calm, his life depended on it.

The plainclothes man examined his card. "Jimmy? That's a strange name for you, isn't it?"

He shrugged and tried to smile. "My parents liked the name," he said. "it reminded them of Scotland. They like Scotland, or rather, the idea of it, they've never been there."

"People with taste, I see," the man said, smiling. "That's why your English is so good? Bit breathless, aren't you?"

"You're making me nervous, what can I say?"

"Yes, well, we can have that effect on people."

The poppies were looking away now, toward a commotion up the street. "Got someone, it looks like," one said, and the plainclothes man looked up, still holding Jimmy's ID. Jimmy's breath was almost under control now, he tried hard to breathe easy, slow, deep, slow down his heart. He looked up the street, too. A man was struggling with two soldiers who forced him to the ground while a third ran up and handcuffed his hands behind his back.

"Where does your friend live, then, when he's at home?"

Jimmy pointed beyond the buildings. "About half a mile away, sir, near the Eden Theater. I waited a bit and now I'm off home."

"I see. And work? It says here you're a hospital porter. Not working today?"

"I'm off shift. I work nights. I'm on at nine o'clock tonight, till seven in the morning."

The man nodded thoughtfully, staring past the ID card at Jimmy's feet. Two of the poppies entered the garden and poked among the bushes and the garbage cans. *Thank God I didn't throw the gun,* Jimmy thought.

One of the others wiped his forehead, took off his beret, ran his fingers through his hair and put it back on. "Bloody 'ot!"

Jimmy nodded in agreement. "It is."

People were looking from their balconies now, children pointing and mothers holding babies. A woman called to a neighbor on the balcony opposite. "Did you see Gila, she went shopping?"

"Don't worry, it won't take long," her neighbor called back. From the third floor of the apartment building, directly above, a woman looked down at Jimmy talking to the Special Branch officer. She couldn't make out what they were saying but if they talked loudly she would hear every word. She turned and said something to someone in the room, then turned back to listen.

"Can I go now, sir?" Jimmy asked.

"In a hurry, are you?"

"No, not at all, whatever you like."

"Well, you can't leave yet, the area's closed, you'll just get stopped up the road. Better wait over there, till the op's over. I'll hang on to your ID, for the moment, if you don't mind."

"Yes, sir." Jimmy took a couple of steps backward, away from the policeman, looking for somewhere to sit. The man watched him.

Jimmy's heart raced. His lips cracked. He forced himself not to lick them. He couldn't turn around. The man may see the bulge of the gun in his trouser band under the T-shirt. He should have worn a loose shirt. He backed up a couple of paces, smiled, sat down on the grass.

"That's a funny place to sit, sir, may I suggest that bench?"

"I like the grass. It's cooler."

"Do you? Not allowed to sit on the grass in England, you know. Bad for it. So they say. Don't know why, myself."

As he spoke he considered Jimmy and licked his lips, then took a step forward, beckoning to a soldier.

"Would you mind standing for a moment, sir?"

The soldier approached as Jimmy raised himself from the ground, poised to sprint. The soldier, a sergeant, raised his rifle till it pointed at Jimmy. The bayonet was fixed and the long blade glinted. Jimmy saw his finger flick the safety.

The policeman said, "Would you mind, sir, slowly, put your hands in the air and turn round, be a good fellow." Jimmy raised his hands, began to turn, and knew he was going to die but definitely not alone. As he turned he grabbed at the back of his pants and saw a flash of green grass and bright sun and thought, *Bye, bye Bella, I could have loved you,* his hand desperately scrabbling under his shirt for the handle. He whirled round, finger on the trigger . . .

"Gun!" the policeman yelled and threw himself to the ground and the soldier, already aiming at Jimmy's chest, shot him on automatic, three bullets, then three more. Stiched him up, good and proper. The women on the balconies screamed as the guns exploded, and ducked inside. Six slugs close to the speed of sound. Jimmy flew backward and was dead as he fell. His gun spun to the ground. Birds fluttered from the trees.

The woman on the third-floor balcony was the first to reemerge. She peered over the edge.

"Blow me down," the Special Branch officer said, supporting himself on one knee, staring at Jimmy's blood ooze from small round holes in his stomach and chest. Jimmy's mouth was wide open, as if shouting.

The officer stood, took another look at the ID card and examined the photo, shaking his head. "Jimmy Levy, it says, I wonder who the heck he was, then?"

"One of them terrorist bastards, that's for sure," the sergeant said, poking Jimmy's face with the bayonet. By now a dozen soldiers and police had run up and a jeep screamed to a halt.

Colonel Peters, with a dark blond mop of hair spilling under his maroon beret, stepped out and was quickly filled in. He picked up Jimmy's pistol and turned it over in his hand. "Czech job," he said, "bit basic, gets the job done. Well done, Bill, smart work, well done, Sergeant. What's your name, Sergeant?"

"Sir! Sergeant Barnes, sir!" the young soldier called, almost snapping his arm off in salute. "Eric Barnes."

"Well done, Sergeant Barnes, you all right?"

"Yessir!"

"Jolly good then, carry on. We'll let Special Branch take over, find out who he really is. Let's get on with it. Work to do. The big boss bastard's around here somewhere and we're not leaving without him."

Two more trucks drew up and more soldiers leapt out, pulling more rolls of barbed wire, which now stretched double thickness around two city blocks. The colonel looked up at the buildings and at the women who were reappearing on the balconies, staring down on them like owls. "He's here, all right. We'll find the bugger."

The woman on the third-floor balcony directly above watched the colonel and the soldiers disperse, turned into the room and said to the bearded men inside, "Sergeant Eric Barnes. That's the name of the soldier. Who killed Jimmy. Eric Barnes."

NINE

London

October 24, 1945

Edith was pacing. Three steps, turn, three steps, turn, that's all the space there was, like a prison cell. From the window to the table, where Georg sat, to Anna on the sofa. Back again. Turn. Three steps. Turn. "Stop it!" Georg said again, raising his voice. "Stop pacing!"

"I've got to do something!" she shouted. "There must be something we can do, I can't be happy here knowing Papi is out there somewhere."

"Happy? Who's happy? Stop making yourself a martyr," Georg shouted back. "You think I don't worry, too? We have to be thankful for what we have, not always crying about the past." He paused, watching Edith turn at the window, her mouth grim. "Sorry. I didn't mean that. Of course I want Papi to come back," he said, lowering his voice. "But we must think of ourselves, too, here and now, and that means the baby. Anything that is bad for the baby we must not do. So stop walking up and down all the time!" Georg grabbed Edith's arm as she walked by and pulled her to the sofa. She fell into the seat, squirming.

"Leave me alone! Don't touch me!"

Anna pushed herself up with a sigh and left the room.

"Stop it, Edith, you're becoming hysterical."

"You stop it! You're useless. Why don't you do something?" she said, pushing his arm away. Even as she said it she knew how unfair she was. What could he do? What could anybody do? "You can't even get a job!"

"Useless? I'm useless?" Georg sputtered in rage. He raised his hand, and quickly dropped it. His body shook with frustration. He let out the beginning of a roar, then stopped dead. He didn't want the neighbors to hear. He didn't want Edith to get even more upset. He didn't want any of this. Why were they fighting? About nothing. And everything. He felt a sob rise, and swallowed hard. And of course, she's right. I am useless. I'm offering her nothing, just to wait. But what else is there?

He went to the window, pushed it up, gripped the sill, breathing heavily. Cold wind came in, bringing drops of rain. It's always bloody raining. *Verdammtnochmal.* He closed the window again, turned to Edith on the sofa. She was watching him.

"Dit, I'm sorry," Georg said, taking her hand. "You're right. I'm useless. No real job, no money, no . . ." As he spoke, part of him knew what she would say next.

"Oh, no, you're not, I'm sorry, I should never have said that, it isn't true. What can we do? What can anyone do? Nothing."

"I know. And that's what's so hard."

She took his hand, kissed it, held it in her lap. "Poor Anna, she ran away." Edith chuckled. "Call her back, tell her we made up."

"In a moment. Look, I'm not saying there isn't more we could do to find Papi, I just don't know what it is. But I do know we have to find a way to accept what we have, here, now."

Edith smiled. "I feel a lecture coming on."

Georg smiled back. "I'm serious. Even if it's hard. Look, our life just goes on, day after day, waiting for something to happen, we've lost our freedom, we don't control our lives. All we have is the chance to work by day, if we're lucky, love at night, and to try to keep some magic." Georg stood up, and now it was his turn to pace, but for his tall frame it was hardly two steps between the sofa and the bed, the table and the window. He was in lawyer mode, his natural response to every argument. "Of course we're unhappy here. It's natural. That's why we mustn't fight. We've lost our home, everything. You know the origin of our German word *ausland*? Abroad?" *Yes I do,* Edith thought. *Still, tell me again.* He gestured around their single room, the peeling wallpaper, the little gas stove, the unmade bed. "It comes from the word *elend*. Misery. *Ausland* and *elend*, abroad and misery, have the same root. And that's how it is. He who lives abroad is not at home, and is therefore miserable. How true that is. For us it's even worse. We're miserable abroad but we don't have a home to return to, nothing else to look forward to, just this misery. So we must make the best of it. Not fight. We don't have anything else. Just each other."

He sat next to Edith on the sofa and kissed her cheek.

"Nice speech." She smiled. "I've heard it before."

"Thank you. Haven't finished yet. Another thing. We don't know when or how this will end. This chain of pain and hardship and uncertainty that we call life. It seems endless, for one sees only the beginning and not the end. The greatest grace of God is that he does not give us the knowledge of when the chain will end. So every day we get up and start again. And then, every adventure, every romance, ends with the return to reality, grey, sticky, the hard daily grind. So, Dit. We mustn't let it all overwhelm us. Let's not fight." He put his hand on Edith's belly and kissed her on the nose. "All I know is that I want this baby so very much. It's our way forward. Our new life."

They sat together for minutes, calmer now, stroking each other's hands. That's when Georg mentioned the lawyer in Vienna.

Edith licked the envelope, grimaced at the oily taste, and sealed it. It contained a request to Doctor Stinglwagner in Vienna to visit her home in Ghelengasse every week to inquire of the thieves whether any previous occupant had arrived. The Viennese could be relied upon to lie to a returning Jew but they would never tell an untruth to a man of standing, a lawyer, a gentleman of the bar. She didn't have a penny to pay him but neither, apparently, did he charge for the task. The lawyer was said to be a Christian man, a good man who did the same for other Jews, and her letter was full of thanks, while almost begging for any scrap of news.

So far she had discovered, from newspapers and the refugee organizations, that when the Russians liberated Auschwitz on January 27, they had found five thousand survivors, most of whom were sick. Many of these had died, even after liberation. Some had been taken to the hospital, others put in tents near the Russian army base, and the rest had stayed put, eating and drinking and recovering. One by one they had left, on foot, on carts, on army trucks, trains, any way they could, but because the war was still on in the west they had gone east, even farther away from home. They had drifted to Moscow and some even as far as India and China, anywhere they could reach that was safe and there was food.

But that was nine months ago. Assuming he'd survived, Papi could be anywhere in Europe, in Asia, who knows, maybe he even went to Palestine? If he was alive, surely he would have sent a message by now? But who would he send it to? She felt like traveling to Poland and searching for him, but she knew how impossible, and pointless, that was. Her best hope, as everyone said, was to wait for his name to appear on a list; and Bloomsbury House had all the lists. Or maybe he would make his way to London; he must have guessed she was married by now; he must wonder whether he was a grandfather. He will be soon! Every knock on the door, every ring on the bell or call on the telephone made her heart leap. She knew he was alive, she just knew it. But it was unbearable just to wait like everyone said, it made her feel so weak and helpless. And she took it out on Georg. *I must stop that,* she thought, even as another thought slipped in—*Why doesn't he go to Vienna? He could do it easily. What's he afraid of?*

Edith pushed the letter aside and drank some water. While Anna daydreamed on the lounge sofa, Edith emptied the bag of stockings onto the table and picked through them, deciding where to start until, unable to face another batch, she sat back with a sigh. She covered her swollen stomach with her hands, only to jerk forward.

"Ooh," she said with a laugh, "what a kick!" She looked down and even though the room was chilly, pulled up her sweater, two shirts, and vest. "Oh, Anna, look!" she called. Her belly rippled as if someone was tapping from inside. "Baby's kicking! Again. And again!" Anna jumped up and cupped Edith's navel. Edith took her hand and pulled it down the side of her pale belly and covered it with her own. They both smiled and waited with faraway looks. Seconds went by. "I don't feel anything," Anna said, disappointed. And then Edith squealed, "There, there, did you feel it?" and now they both laughed. "Yes, yes!"

"Can I feel?" Ismael came over.

"No, you can't," Edith said.

"Then cover yourself, you are offending me."

"How are you feeling, Dit?" Anna asked. "Really. You feel good?"

Edith smiled and tucked her clothes back in. Her top shirt was Georg's flannel Pioneer Corps work shirt, it was the warmest they had. "Everything's upside down, I don't know what to think. I feel good, yes, very good about the baby. Georg worries too much. We've been fighting a bit lately. I have headaches, backaches, but that's normal. Not always comfortable, though."

"And the rest?" Anna asked.

Edith's smile faded. She thought: What rest? Is Papi alive? Sometimes I doubt it. Maybe that's why I'm so nervous with Georg, because I know Papi is dead but can't face it. Did even one member of my family survive? Maybe not. How to live with that? And Georg, will he ever find work? That's upsetting him, too. And the stockings. If I darn another one I'll throw up. And the petition: Will we be thrown out of England with nowhere to go? And now another Jewish baby? In this world? Such a silly question. Do I feel good?

"Oh, I feel wonderful," Edith said. "But I should teach you to mend stockings, then all my problems would be over."

"Yes," Anna said. "It's time for me to earn my keep."

"You haven't even left the house in three weeks," Ismael said. "Come on. Today's the day."

"Yes," Edith said, "why don't you go out for once, just for a little walk." *I need a rest from you.*

"I'll take you," Ismael volunteered.

"In that case, better stay home," Edith said.

"Come on," Ismael said, stretching his hand to Anna. "Just once around the block. Pretend you're taking the dog for a walk."

"You said it," Edith said. He opened his palms as if to say, *I gave you that one.* Anna stood, too. "All right! I'm coming!"

"Hooray," Edith and Ismael said together and looked out of the window. It was pouring, the raindrops were bouncing. "Never mind, come on," Ismael said, "I have a big umbrella, but you'll have to stay close." Five minutes later the front door closed behind them and as

Edith hooked the first ladder and guided the thread through the sewing machine, a small smile formed: *Well, well, who'd have thought, Ismael and Anna.*

They strolled in silence, sheets of rain beating on the black umbrella. It was large and only their legs and waterproof galoshes were exposed. Rain coursed off the umbrella around them, a cosy cave inside a waterfall. "Take my arm, you'll be dryer," Ismael said, raising his elbow. But Anna didn't, so he swapped hands with the umbrella and took hers, pulling her closer. A car splashed through a puddle and they jumped to the side.

"That's why the man should always walk on the outside," Anna said, "to stop his lady from being splashed."

"His lady?"

"The lady," Anna smiled.

"I thought it was so that the man could draw his sword with his right hand to defend his lady. Excuse me, the lady."

"Well, apparently you don't need a sword," she said.

"So tell me, what do you think of England? What is it, three weeks now?"

Anna made a so-so gesture with her hand.

"I suppose you haven't seen it yet. You like the house?"

They walked on and he gave her time. Finally Anna said, "I like the house. I like Edith and Georg very much. I must say, I'd like my own room and I'm sure they'd like that, too. But I am very lucky when you think . . ." Her voice trailed away. Still Ismael didn't talk.

Anna continued in a rush. "What I find hardest to understand is why there is so much hostility toward the Jews. Everybody must know what we went through. What did we do to them?"

Ismael squeezed her arm. "You're right, but you know, not everyone thinks like that."

Another silence, broken by Anna: "Then why don't they say something? I saw what happens when people don't speak up."

Ismael didn't have an answer. He glanced at Anna. Her head covered in a tightly wound red scarf borrowed from Edith and her black coat collar pulled up. Loose black hair curling down her neck; it seemed to be growing back. Her gaunt face had already filled out, leaving finely etched lines of jaw and cheekbones, in shadow under the umbrella. Noble. Quite beautiful; but so distant, so detached. So defensive, careful.

She returned his gaze and almost smiled before turning away. "Anyway," she said, "where do you keep going at night? Sometimes you don't come home, and you come and go at strange hours. Edith says you're mysterious."

"Oh, she does, does she?" Ismael laughed. "The mystery man from the Nile! But tell me; England. Do you want to stay here? What will you do?"

"I know exactly what I want to do," she answered. "And I will do it."

"What?"

"I want to go to Palestine. Be safe among the Jews. I would have gone from Paris but it was too hard, the blockade is too tight. There were agents from Palestine organizing us, but everyone is being turned back, or interned. I could get into America more easily!"

"I doubt it."

"You know what I mean."

"There are ways to get into Palestine."

"I didn't find one. Not yet."

The rain eased until it stopped, but now the fog was settling—whispy and acrid, grey and damp. The Kilburn River that ran beneath the ground sent up its chill. The paving stones were uneven and cracked and they picked their way around the puddles. Ismael shook rain off the umbrella and while he furled it, it almost hit a man walking by. "Oh, sorry," they both said. Ismael pointed toward the house and guided Anna up the steps. "It's getting smoggy. I can smell it. Let's go home while we can still find it."

Their place on the sofa was taken by Georg, sunk back, staring at his feet, an airmail letter in his lap, and Edith holding his hand. The gas fire had gone out. Ismael took some change from his pocket, selected a couple of shillings, leaned down and put them in the slot. He put a match to the gas and the flame jumped up. Out of the corner of his eye he looked at Edith and Georg and knew this wasn't the time for a joke. His jacket cuff was damp and it began to steam in front of the fire. He stood up and held it out to dry.

Anna sat down next to Edith, who was leaning forward, her belly resting on her open legs. Anna took two cushions and stuffed them behind Edith and pushed her into them. Edith's lips tightened in acknowledgment and she patted Anna's hand. After a minute she took the letter from Georg and gave it to Anna to read. "It came right after you left." Anna held the letter forward to catch the dying light. It wasn't even midday and the light was fading.

Vienna, October 8, 1945

Dear Dr. Georg,

Yesterday Mr. Mayer visited me and I read your letter. Although it is very hard for me to write about it I am ready to tell you what I know about your dear parents. I met your mother in January 1942 on a transport from Vienna to Riga and we became so friendly that we ended up sharing a room for two years. Although I am twenty-five years younger than your mother, sisters could not have gotten on better. Even if I don't know you personally, dear Georg, and your sister, still I know everything about you from your earliest childhood. For there was nothing your mother liked better than to talk about her children and no day went by without us talking about our lovely past years. But unfortunately fate wanted it differently. In August 1944 we were dragged from Riga to a Polish concentration camp which was much worse than death. I don't want to make it any harder for your heart. The whole world knows what these brown beasts did with us. Nobody, dear Dr. Georg, can have as much understanding as I for at the same time I lost my own mother in a concentration camp. Your dear mother died of typhoid, as did my own mother. Maybe it is a comfort for you to know that she did not have to go through all the things that I did. One can hardly describe in words all the horrors we had to put up with. It is a miracle that I am still alive and it was only thanks to a deadly bomb attack that I and four other women were able to escape. As sad as fate can be, we can only console ourselves with the thought that there was nothing we could have changed. I also, dear Dr. Georg, will never forget your dear mother and will always remember her fondly. As for your father, who I did not know, the news is no more welcome. Your mother said she was separated from him and he was taken straight to Majdanek in Poland, from where we know of nobody who has returned.

Dear Dr. Georg, there is no relief for such great pain. I wish you for the future all the best and the dearest and send my most intimate greetings to you and your sister,

Yours affectionately,
Rosa Fried

Anna sat transfixed. Transported to her own place where she didn't want to go. Her hand shook as she gave the letter back to Edith. Georg was numb. Anna stood up, walked to the door. She felt sorry but she couldn't take it, the heaviness was unbearable; she did not want to, would not think about this. But as she turned the door handle, she hesitated; something had struck her, but she didn't know what. She turned and sat down, her senses alert. "You said Georg's mother died in Majdanek, they all did."

"That's what we thought," Edith sighed. "Early on. It was a relief to know that, in a way." After a moment, she added, "So Georg's mother lived much longer than we thought."

Ismael sat at the table and looked at his hands, locked his fingers, rested his chin on them, supported by his elbows. The clock on the mantelpiece chimed eleven times, singsong tones, ding donnng. Anna took back the letter and read it again, tutting. And then it dawned on her, what she had sensed, what made her return. She shivered. She slowly raised her head, understanding that Georg's numbness was from much more than his mother's death, which was reason enough. Anna looked again at the last lines, and she read, in a low, wondering voice, "Greetings to you and your sister."

A sob reached Georg's throat but he suppressed it with a choking sound.

"That's right," Edith said. "She thinks Ellie's alive."

The door swung open. Albert entered, took in the scene.

"What's wrong? Looks like a morgue in here."

Sally pushed past him, saying, "Look at this!"

She slapped the local newspaper on the table and spread it out. "Just look! Who'd have thought?"

It was the headline of the *Ham and High*: 2,000 RESI-
DENTS WILL SEND PETITION TO PARLIAMENT and beneath:
ALIENS SHOULD QUIT TO MAKE ROOM FOR SERVICEMEN

"Two thousand signatures," Sally said, "two thousand! That's an
awful lot, you know. There's only as about seventy thousand people
living in Hampstead, and half of them are Jews anyway. And with all
the kiddies too young to sign . . . They've done awfully well, haven't
they? And it says here . . . look, listen . . . they're hoping to get the
mayor of Hampstead to sign it, too, and take it to Parliament. That's
serious, if they do that. Not just some silly fascists, but it's real people. Two thousand—that's an awful lot."

"Very impressive," Albert added.

"But that's not all," Sally went on, and stopped, looking around.
"Here, come on you lot, don't act so glum, it may never happen!"

"This is not a good moment, Mrs. Barnes," Ismael said.

"Oh, come on, they've got a right to say what they want! Free
speech, and all that. Doesn't mean it'll happen. If you ask me, they
won't throw you out, they can't, that's not the way we do things round
here. That's not what we fought Hitler for. I was just going to say,
there's more, listen." She found the spot with her finger: "Other local
residents have refused to sign it and, it is understood, feel so strongly
about it that they are organizing countermeasures and hope to enlist
the support of other MPs and councillors in condemning it.' There,
you see, it'll come right in the end."

Albert said, "They've got a point, though."

Edith couldn't resist. "Did you sign it?"

"Good question, dearie," Sally said. "We don't know what to do,
talking about it all the time. Wondering, what'll happen when Eric

comes back, and his mates? You mustn't take it personally, you know. It's all about housing, really, that's all. We don't want to, Lord knows, but will we have to throw you out when he comes back? All weekend we've been at loggerheads, me and Albert."

There was a pause, interrupted by Anna, who asked, to be polite, "Where is Loggerheads?"

Sally screeched with laughter and Albert gave a good old chuckle. "That's a good one!" Sally said, elbowing Albert. "Isn't it?"

He said, "No dearie, loggerheads isn't a place, it's sort of, you know, when you can't agree about something, uh . . . you know, it's just the sort of thing you say. . . ."

Georg's voice came, as if from a distant place. "Loggerheads—to engage in dispute or confrontation; it's an English idiom. In a slightly different usage it has synonyms like blockhead, dunderhead."

He looked down at the letter. Can Ellie really be alive? This woman, Rosa Fried, Mutti must have told her that Ellie didn't go to Majdanek, and she doesn't mention her in Riga. Ellie must have gone somewhere else. She sends greetings to both of us. She assumes she's alive, too. But where? Where is Ellie?

"Come on, cheer up," Sally said again. "The war's over, you know! You know what, I've got some marmalade, Jean over the road made it. I got extra sugar rations, now don't ask me how, so I made marmalade cake and I'm going to bring some up and make a good cuppa for everyone. A good cuppa. That'll solve all your problems!"

TEN

Hampstead

November 1, 1945

"What a silly film!" Edith laughed as they left the Everyman Cinema on Heath Street a week later. "And that Tommy Trinder, *zum Schiessen!* He slays me!"

Georg smiled; he loved Edith in a good mood and that had been rare lately. "What do you mean, silly?" he said. "Stonehenge is a time machine. Two sailors and a Wren are transported to ancient Rome, where they can see into the future. What's silly about that? What shall we do now?"

"Go to Stonehenge," Edith said.

"Let's go then, I know a wonderful hotel where we can all stay," said Ismael. "I'm not paying, though."

"And then we can go back in time to before the war and start again."

"Failing that, shall we go for a tea, a walk, or both?" Georg said, practical as ever.

They linked arms and walked up the hill toward the Whitestone

Pond. "Where military horses drink," Georg said. They had decided on a quick walk on the Heath before dark, a drink at Jack Straw's Castle across from the pond, and the bus home.

The four of them took up most of the pavement so they split into twos, Edith and Georg and Ismael and Anna. "Did you enjoy the film?" Ismael asked.

"Yes, thank you."

"Was it funny?"

Anna tried to laugh. It was the first film she'd seen since Vienna, in that other life, and the normality of it all was shocking.

They walked on, past a sweet shop, the Cruel Sea Pub, an iron-mongers, a butcher. Georg, walking ahead with Edith, pointed out the sign: NO CHICKEN, NO SAUSAGES, NO KIDDING, and Ismael chuckled. Anna acknowledged with a nod. They crossed a cobbled road toward the Heath. The streetlights came on but wouldn't do much good. They only worked on half strength since August to save coal, orders from the Ministry of Fuel. Two steps ahead, Edith and Georg kissed as they walked.

"I understand what you're going through," Ismael, feeling helpless, said to Anna.

Before *Fiddlers Three* began, the Pathé Newsreel had shown the usual Welcome Home parade for demobbed soldiers in their country village, and the Royal Family waving somewhere and shaking hands with children, and something rolling off a factory production line. They had passed around the digestive biscuits while listening to the newsreel announcer's jaunty reassurance . . . *London folk are waiting patiently for delivery of* . . . and Edith had kicked off her shoes. And then there had been some American senators getting out of two large cars at . . . *the gates of the death camp of Auschwitz.* . . .

Anna had stiffened as she heard the name. The senators shook hands with some officials, who guided them through the gates beneath the now familiar wrought-iron sign: ARBEIT MACHT FREI. The pictures changed to newsreel of the first images from the camp, the ones that had so shocked the world nine months earlier. There were only a few groups of people scattered around the afternoon showing, and they all heard Anna's gasp.

Piles of skeletal naked corpses, expiring pale carcasses pulling themselves like white slugs across the earth, beseeching eyes and clawlike hands gripping barbed wire, striped pants and shirts, stacked bunks, human remains tumbling from trucks like so much waste—Anna had closed her eyes, stood, pushed Ismael's legs with her knees. She sucked in air, wanted out, out, but those pictures ended and moved on to the comic kicker: something about bushy-tailed squirrels in London parks. She fell back into her seat. They had those in the back garden, too.

Then Tommy Trinder's long chin and wacky smile and terrible songs and laughter, and someone clapping, which sounded like gunfire, miles away.

Anna had never seen such pictures before. That was her, or it could have been if she hadn't been force-marched away. Seeing the inmates, like torn rag dolls, herself, through the eyes of others, far away, unreal, just a flickering image in the dark, just grey faces on a screen—just a couple of oohs and aahs and sympathetic clucking and the main film starts and they're immediately laughing at that funny man—through most of the film her eyes were shut, trying not to think, and she felt nauseous. Sick. She wanted to vomit. Throw up. Puke. Reject it all. The blackness was her shelter. She mustn't see. But in her closed eyelids dark shapes swam and merged and floated, shouts and blows and screams. She heard her own breathing. It was only when Nero threw the sailors to the lions that Ismael's bellow jolted her back, and the rest of the film she smiled, trying not to think of her dead friends, as her new ones laughed.

Good news! In the nick of time the sailors were saved from the lion's jaws by the time machine.

They all knew what Anna must be thinking but there was nothing they could do to help, except hope she would enjoy Tommy Trinder.

As the road flattened toward the summit of Heath Street they saw two flags fluttering in the wind. The Red Cross of England, the Cross of St. George, which always flew from the white pole, marking London's highest point. The second, they now saw, the Union Jack, was raised above a platform on the grass and a crowd of people. Two large banners hung from a van parked nearby: THE BRITISH LEAGUE OF EX-SERVICEMEN and WOMEN'S GUILD OF EMPIRE. From the listeners a man was shouting at the speaker, his voice thin and high at this distance.

They couldn't make out what anyone was saying until they settled at the edge of the crowd, when it became all too clear.

It was the fascists again. Their British leaders had been locked up during the war as Nazi sympathizers but were now back on the streets. And while the target of the Hampstead petition was the local refugees, the fascist's target, a handy vote-getter in their march to power, was Britain's entire Jewish population. They were collecting crowds in outdoor meetings all over the country but especially in London and especially here, with local elections a few weeks away and everyone talking about the lack of housing and the anti-aliens petition.

The speaker had a dark quiff with a kindly face and a fixed smile, as though enjoying a private joke. Edith thought he looked pleasant, but not for long. He rushed his words and swallowed syllables but she could make out the standard phrases: "aliens among us" and "black-market profiteers" and "They were shirking while we were fighting."

"Let's go for the walk," Georg said, his heart sinking. He didn't want any more trouble. He couldn't see anyone else in the crowd who looked like a refugee, even though people like the speaker said you could spot one a mile away. Even Albert the landlord joked about the "enemy alien proboscis."

But Ismael pulled Georg back by the arm. The young man next to him had waved a fist and shouted, "You didn't fight, you were in jail, where you belong! I was in North Africa, Normandy!" The man was with three friends and they were all getting edgy.

"Watch," Ismael said. "This is going to get lively."

Georg looked closer at the men. It was unmistakable. Joking aside, it was obvious they were Jews. And hard, too. The one who had shouted hissed to his friend, "I'm going to shut that bastard up!"

"Who's he think he is, then?" the second one said, and shouted, "And I was in the paras, for five years, and I'm Jewish, so fuck off!"

Some people turned round and said, "Hear, hear, good for you," while one voice carried, "You're still a Jewish scumbag!" and another man, standing by the flagpole, yelled, "Hitler should have finished you off, then."

"Watch out, mate, or I'll shove that flagpole up your arse!" This from another of the Jewish ex-servicemen.

Anna looked disbelievingly at Edith, who shrugged. "This is what it's like. They hate us." Anna's mouth hung open. From Auschwitz, to this? Would it never end?

Four large young men selling copies of the fascist bulletin *Britain Awake* moved to the front of the platform, while the speaker ranted on. His smile had gone. Only occasional phrases could be distinguished: "Judaic-Communist conspiracy . . . perish Judah . . . Jewish terrorists in Palestine . . . Yids . . . only themselves to blame . . ."

"Let's go," Edith said, "this is disgusting." But such bare hatred had its own fascination and they found themselves rooted, wondering how many people agreed with the crazy speaker.

The four Jewish ex-soldiers seemed to be preparing themselves. Two were edging to the right, a step at a time, careful not to draw attention, and two proceeded forward, touching the shoulders of listeners who parted to let them through. Ismael elbowed Georg, pointing with his chin to their progress. One woman objected until the stocky one with an almost shaved head, the paratrooper, said he just wanted to buy a copy of *Britain Awake*. Two copies actually, one for the missus, she collects them. She smiled, said, Oh sorry ducks, I thought you was one of them, and let him through.

The four men reached the front, opposite the four fascist guards, who noticed too late. Ismael sniggered to Georg. "Watch. Four soldiers, four thugs. Most unfair."

He had hardly said it when one of the demobbed Jews, a tall man, grabbed the heads of two of the guards and smashed them together with a crack like a bat hitting a ball, and followed up with two quick punches to their noses. Blood poured from both of them. In the same instant another of the guards yelled and doubled up, grabbing his balls, while the man who had kneed him, head-butted him, bony forehead cracking his nose. The fourth guard ran, while the other two enraged Jews rushed, like linebacks, at the two front legs of the platform, and pushed the whole edifice down, tossing the speaker off the back. It all happened so fast the crowd was first shocked into silence, then erupted, half with derisive cheering and half with outrage. The speaker had tried to hang on to the flag as he fell and dragged it to the ground. Now he scrambled to his feet, nursing a shoulder, and hobbled with the flag to his van.

A man in the crowd called to the four ex-soldiers, "You better run for it, lads—the police'll be here quicker than Jack Robinson."

They ran away, laughing.

As usual they gathered in the lounge in the evening, all but Ismael who had gone off somewhere. The refugees didn't have anywhere to go and it was cheaper to heat one room than all the bedrooms. Not that the lounge was warm. Everyone wore a coat. Edith had wrapped a scarf around the cold tip of her nose. Sometimes friends dropped by, and this evening Max and Margit Wasser joined them, distant acquaintances from Vienna who had become good friends with Georg and Edith in London. Max and Margit made leather belts and handbags in their single room in Canfield Gardens and, like all the refugees, went to the Austrian Center or Bloomsbury House to meet friends and look for relatives on the lists. If Edith had had a good stockings day or the Wassers had sold some belts, they'd continue to Lyons Corner House or the Cosmo.

The guests had the place of honor on the sofa while Georg, Edith, Otto, and Frieda sat around the table, sipping tea and wiping up the last of the jam from the *Kaiserschmarrn,* Georg's favorite Austrian pancake dessert. "Apart from the fact there's no nuts, cherries, or plums, no sugar and not enough salt, the milk's gone off and the eggs are dried mix from a tin, this is pretty tasty," said Edith, licking the plate.

Anna drifted in and out, sometimes avoiding company, other times craving it, and this every few minutes. Each time she came in,

Margit wanted to ask a question, but she didn't know what to ask, and didn't dare anyway. Anna was the only concentration camp survivor she had met, but it was as if she had brought the barbed wire fence with her. Beyond banalities, there was no way to penetrate her prickly silence.

Conversation was about the punch-up at the Whitestone Pond two days earlier. They didn't know whether to be upset or encouraged. Was it good news or bad news to know that people hate you and someone is fighting back?

"They aren't the only ones," Max said, about the four Jewish ex-servicemen. "There's a group of them that meet at Maccabi in Compayne Gardens. I went to a meeting. They're organising to fight back. They say this is a street war and they're not going to give up the streets to the fascists."

"I told you already, there's a big difference, though," his wife said, shaking her head. "They don't care about us, either. They're English Jews, been here for generations, they fought in the wars and that's what they're defending, their own place in this country. They're not fighting for us, the refugees, nobody is."

"Nobody has to," Georg said. "We don't want this violence. There are plenty of good people here, lots of them, that petition will never work."

Margit continued, "Those Jews who were fighting, they're English. The government won't let the refugees become English, that's the difference."

Max said, "We don't want to be English."

"Oh, yes, we do!" Margit said, and everyone laughed in agreement.

Georg got up. "Talking about not wanting us, that reminds me. I'm going to get something," he said and left the room.

"Close the door, it's freezing," Edith called out. They heard his footsteps up the stairs.

Edith shook her head. "I don't know. I feel they don't want us here. Not really. And you know what, maybe they're right. When I see the soldiers come back, and there's no work, and nowhere to live . . ."

"Oh, come on, don't you start," Otto interrupted, smacking the table. "I get so tired of hearing that. They've got lots of work. Look at you two: stockings, belts, working from home. You're not taking anyone's job. You're making your own work. We're the ones who can't find work. I'm an accountant and I haven't worked in a year. Thank God my brother sends me money from America. Look at Georg, the fancy lawyer, makes buttons, for God's sake, if he's lucky. And as for houses, look around, half of them are empty. All they have to do is fix up the bomb sites and the problem's over. They just don't like us, never have and never will. All this is just an excuse."

Georg came back holding a sheaf of printed foolscap papers held together by a staple. "Listen to this, everyone."

Edith recognized the *Onchan Pioneer,* the newssheet from Georg's internment camp on the Isle of Man. He'd kept this copy because he'd written one of the letters. But she knew that wasn't what he was going to read aloud.

Anna slipped in and sat on the stool by the fire, rubbing her hands, wrapped in Edith's woolen cardigan.

"Listen to this, Anna, it's about us. This is so true, it's a poem." As he spoke, Georg resumed his seat at the table, carefully separating the dry pages. He'd already torn one and he wanted to keep this copy. He stopped at page five.

"It's by W. H. Auden. He's English, lives in America. But you'd think he's one of us. Listen. It's called 'Refugee Blues'—I'll just read bits of it." He cleared his throat, seemed to sigh and suck in air at the same time. His eyes scanned down as he tutted. And then Georg read aloud, those painful lines—of the city with its ten million souls . . . yet no room for us . . . our lost fair country where we can't go back . . . and Hitler saying we must die...

> Dreamed I saw a building with a thousand floors,
> A thousand windows and a thousand doors;
> Not one of them was ours, my dear, not one of them
> > was ours.
> Stood on a great plain in the falling snow;
> Ten thousand soldiers marched to and fro:
> Looking for you and me, my dear, looking for you and me.

Georg looked up. The last words always gave him goose bumps and he could see the poem had the same effect on the others. The first time he had read it, four years earlier in the camp, on the wrong side of the barbed wire, lying on the straw sack they called a mattress, he had felt an overwhelming sense, not of anger, or fear, or resentment, but of loss. To him the poem wasn't about how little he had here, how unwanted he was in England, though that was bad enough— they'd locked him up after all, the Enemy Alien (how those words hurt)—but how unwanted he had been at home, how all the certainties of life had been systematically stripped away, like chopping off his fingers one by one—can't study, can't work, can't buy in this shop, can't sit in that café—and then, finally crushing the body, they had razed everything: killed his family, stolen his home, wanted to destroy him.

Georg looked around at his friends' silent faces. Was that embarrassment he saw as they avoided his eyes? Max, Margit, Otto? Shame? They had all been laid bare. There was not a soul in the room, or among all their friends in London, who had not been robbed of everything essential: family, home, wealth, future, their very reasons to exist. That was then, but they were discovering that now was even worse. The reports from the camps, the trickle of news, like blood dripping through a rag: Dachau, Buchenwald, and Bergen-Belsen in Germany and the Nazi tentacles that spread east to Mauthausen, Theresienstadt, and Gross-Rosen and even farther east to Lodz, Auschwitz, Treblinka, Majdanek, and even more death camps farther away in Ukraine and Belarus; each name another thousand tons of earth and dirt burying family, friends, neighbors. All the refugees shared the terror of not knowing. Where is Mutti, Papi, my family, what is happening to them, are they dead or alive? It was unbearable. The German bombs on their London homes hardly affected them. Anyway, nobody understood why they of all their loved ones had been chosen to live, so what did it matter if they died in the blitz?

And now? We're still waiting, we still don't know what happened. Only Anna knows, Georg thought, looking at her hunched over by the fire, in Edith's cardigan, rubbing her hands, always trying to get warm, like a stray cat; Anna knows but she's not saying, no doubt for good reason. But there are things we must know. Ellie? Can she really be alive? And Papi? Until we know, we're stuck. We can't build new lives on such uncertainties, we can't move forward, but if we don't, we'll sink in a swamp of doubt and fear. Our only future is the baby.

Georg felt the emptiness pushed aside, a rush of warmth, of

gratitude, welled up inside, filling him, burning his eyes. He looked at Edith, who was looking at him, and who understood and shared it all. He put the poem down and smiled. He reached over and caressed her tummy, and felt like crying. Seven weeks to go, God willing.

ELEVEN

Palestine

October 20, 1945

"Open the door!"

The narrow corridors of the Bauhaus building shook under the boots of the troops who ran up the stone stairs and fanned out, automatic rifles cocked. A corporal or sergeant controlled his men from the stairwell on each floor. Plainclothes Special Branch officers followed with lists of names and apartment numbers. Outside, snipers aimed from roofs and on the ground soldiers stood at ten-yard intervals, boxing in each apartment building. Jeeps and tanks blocked access roads and double barbed wire encircled the whole area. On street corners, away from the buildings, where nobody could overhear them, or roll heavy objects off rooftops onto them, Special Branch and CID officers sat at tables interviewing suspects. The local curfew had been in place for two days; nobody could come or go and if they did, they could be shot. The orders: man or woman, arrest or kill.

Detective Bill Campbell banged on each door in turn. Campbell or "eagle-eyes, a Scot nicknamed as much for his intense stare from hooded dark eye sockets as for his legendary instincts, checked each name on his list against each occupant of each apartment. It was a mess and after two days he was tired. Either the man wasn't home or the male who was there shouldn't be. How many cousins or brothers can there be, anyway? Each male who wasn't registered for the apartment or seemed shifty was taken downstairs for interrogation in the screening cage and anyone who didn't pass muster went on to the station. *I'll get the evil bastard,* Campbell thought, wishing they knew more about Lehi's leader. But it was a hard slog. So far they'd found sweet fuck-all. Apart from that bit of luck with the murderer, Jimmy Levy, who'd killed two Brits. Scored a few brownie points there. Pity, though. "If I'd known who he was," Campbell told the colonel, "I'd have made sure to catch him alive."

There were eight apartments on each floor of the three-storey building. Outside number 16, the last apartment on the second floor, Campbell wiped his brow and walked back to the stairwell and called for some water. A soldier below tossed him a water bottle, which he caught like a cricket ball. He took a long swig, brushed his lips, sighing heavily, and passed the bottle to the two soldiers accompanying him, who drained it. Someone was frying liver and onions and he felt his saliva drool. He was starving.

He banged on the door of apartment 16: "Open the door!"

The usual alarmed muttering and bangs and knocks and shuffling of feet and the door opened, tentatively at first, and wide as he followed the soldiers in.

"Sarah Lichter?"

A young woman holding a baby to her breast nodded, holding out her ID card, which he examined and returned. Next to her a little boy hung on to her skirt. "You're wee Aaron?" Campbell said, and the boy took a step backward, peering from behind his mother's leg and she answered for him, "Yes." Campbell glanced around and walked from the small living room into a smaller bedroom where he found an older woman sitting on the bed, one hand in her lap and the other nervously fiddling with the frayed ends of a shawl that covered her head. He always looked for the hands first. Paid to be careful. You never know. She looked away. "You are?" he asked, glancing down at his list. "Rachel Sonderheim," she murmured, "Sarah's mother."

"Who else is here?" Campbell asked, as the soldiers poked behind a curtain concealing an alcove full of clothes and bags, and under the bed, and inside cupboards. Campbell moved along the walls, eyes hard and focused, tapping with his knuckle, and knocking on the floor with the steel toe of his shoe. Sounding like a woodpecker, he progressed slowly through the rooms. The buildings were made to last, with concrete floors and mortar walls. They all felt and sounded the same, dull and hard; he'd hear the emptiness of a false wall or a hollow space immediately, but there were none here. Above the hall entrance, where it met the first bedroom, the ceiling was lower and had a small door. One soldier stood on a chair and emptied the little attic: two empty suitcases, old shoes, blankets, books, a broken tennis racket in its wooden frame. With a broom handle he knocked against the farthest end of the crawl space, listening for a hollow sound, a false wall. It was solid. Nobody hiding.

Sarah Lichter followed the poppies with her eyes; there wasn't far to go, there were only three rooms. The soldiers went through the cupboard drawers, rifling through blouses, underpants, bras, and in the smaller chest of drawers, baby clothes, cloth nappies, pink knitted booties. They flipped through each book and poked the binding and put it back. In the kitchen one looked inside the kettle and emptied every cabinet, looked inside each cup, used a fork to poke inside each jar of spice, sugar, and tea. They looked in trouser pockets and sent any handwritten note to the translator they shared with other search parties. When he had finished his wall, ceiling, and floor inspection, and while the two soldiers searched every corner, Detective Campbell didn't take his eyes from the two women, who now sat together with the two children on a tatty brown sofa in the living room. They looked weary, rather than nervous; resigned, rather than scared; defensive, rather than defiant. Nothing to find here, he thought. "Where's Mr. Lichter, then?" he'd asked, and been told he was visiting his parents in Jerusalem. That's what they all said, but this time he believed them. These women weren't hiding anything. After twenty minutes he said to the two soldiers, "Okay, that's it," and to the women, "Thank you, Mrs. Lichter, sorry to disturb you. It'll all be over soon," and he closed the door gently as they left. They walked back along the corridor and climbed the stairs, past Hebrew graffiti and grimy grey hand smudges, to begin the search on the third and top floor.

It had all been so much easier the last nine months. The Jews had been fighting amongst one another and the main group, the Haganah, collaborated with Special Branch. Campbell grinned. That made it so easy. Lehi's assassination of Lord Moyne in Cairo had really put the wind up Haganah; they couldn't turn in the Lehi boys, and the Irgun, quick enough. Acting on information from the main Jewish group, he'd arrested dozens of them himself and they'd put away hundreds; sent half the leaders to camps in Africa. All that stuff about Zionist solidarity, that didn't last long when push came to shove. Bit of pressure, and they folded. Trouble is, the Season, as they called it, was over. Bevin's fault, really. Should have kept his big trap shut: just kept the immigrants out like before, not made a big deal in Parliament announcing the government's new policy, which was just like the old one anyway. Now the Jews were back together again, fighting the white paper. It's all about letting in more Jews. We can't have that.

It'll upset the Ay-rabs and make things worse. All we want is security. That's my job. Peace and quiet.

As he reached the top stairs and looked down at his list of names for the corridor's first apartment, number 17, Detective Campbell felt a jolt of adrenaline speed his heart: getting close. Otherwise what was that murderer doing here? Couldn't have been just a coincidence. Not after the tip-off about the leader living in the neighborhood. There's only a few hundred members all over town. The bastard's got to be here, he thought, the net's closing.

It occurred to him that maybe they should have more backup, but he looked around at the soldiers stationed along the corridor, and Sergeant Barnes, the quick-triggered one, covering him from the stairwell, and the troops and armored vehicles downstairs: We could take Arnhem with this lot, he thought, no problem.

He was just sucking in his breath to shout, and raising his fist to bang on the door, when a call rang out from the courtyard behind the house: "Sir, come and take a look."

In mid-knock, Campbell turned and walked downstairs. Colonel Peters was just arriving with his swagger stick tucked under his arm: "Hello, what have we here, then?"

"A stash," a soldier said. He was kneeling on the ground, pulling weapons from a hole in the concrete beneath the space for the rubbish bins. Grit dug into his bare knees like little nails and he kept stopping to wipe them. Two other soldiers were resting, hammers and a drill at their feet. Ragged blocks of concrete and white plaster were piled up in the garden where a mist of dust settled over the grass and bushes. "One of the fellows was going through the rubbish when he noticed the ground wasn't uniform," a captain informed the colonel. "They must have laid new concrete to make it look like the rest of the yard, but left a hole and covered it with plaster. It looks almost identical to the concrete. And with all the smelly rubbish bins on top, rats 'n' all, pretty good hidey-hole."

The kneeling soldier passed up another canvas sack. The captain unfurled the mouth and pulled out a Bren gun and its detached steel butt. The soldier continued to poke around, his body half disappearing into the ground, and emerged with another sack, of hand grenades. "That's the lot, sir," he said, standing up, rubbing his knees, "nothing else down there."

"You sure?" said the captain.

"Yessir."

"Well done," said Colonel Peters. "What's the haul?"

It was all laid out on the grass, in a row, Exhibit A. The captain reeled off: "Three Sten guns, sir, three Brens, fourteen hand grenades, all British-army issue, stolen or bought, six pistols, two Browning HPs, and four Berettas, good mix of distance and closeup stuff, sir."

"Yes, I do know that, thank you."

"And about a thousand rounds for the automatics, three hundred for the handguns."

Detective Campbell, standing next to the colonel, added, "It was stashed away quite recently, sir. Grease is fresh. No mould on the sacks. And look, that tea sacking is from Ceylon, Assamese tea from Uva province, only been making that open-leaf tea grade since August, ergo, recent terrorist activity."

Colonel Peters stared at Campbell. "You're joking, Sherlock, right?"

"Yes, sir," Campbell grinned, "about the sacking, anyway. But it's all recent stuff. Look, that's a silencer for the Sten. We've only had that ourselves for a year. I think our info's good. He's around here somewhere."

"Yes," Peters replied, "I think so, too. And we'll get him this time."

"How many have we taken in so far?" Campbell asked.

"Twenty-two men, two women. Their stories don't add up. Nothing serious, though. But we only need one, the right one, and anybody with him."

"Yes. Two more buildings to go, and the last floor of that one."

Campbell walked back up the stairs, thinking hard. Score so far, one ammo dump and the killer. Not bad but just scratching the surface. Been so close to capturing the leader before but we always missed him. Putting two and two together, there's no way he slipped away at night or through a tunnel or something like that. No. He's disguised, that's all, and a bloody good disguise, too, I bet. Wait a minute! Could the killer, that Jimmy Levy, be him? That's why he was trying to run away? No, way too young. Could he be a she? A woman as the leader? Possible. But no, don't look for the drama. Therein lies madness. Look for the ordinary, look for what's staring you in the face. There's nowhere to hide so he's just dressed up as an ordinary bloke, maybe even using his real name. The best cover is just to be yourself, that's what I learned.

Just that morning he'd briefed the extra SB men brought in for the search. Lehi's leader—the British didn't even have an alias for him, let alone his real name—had come to their attention two years ago. It was the Jews themselves who had tipped them; they were afraid he'd do more harm to the Zionist cause than the British themselves. A small band of frustrated and impatient underground fighters had split off from the Haganah and even from the much more radical Irgun and formed Lehi, a Hebrew acronym for Fighters for the Freedom of Israel. Just when the Jewish leadership was trying to ally with the British against their common enemy, the Nazis, Lehi embarked on a spree of mayhem—Campbell liked that word, *mayhem*—and killing, aimed at proving that only blood and fear would force the British out of Palestine and at the same time scare

the Arabs into accepting a Jewish state. Two of their agents assassi-
nated Lord Moyne, a hero of the Boer War, the highest-ranking British official in the Middle East, as he stepped out of his car in Cairo in
1944. Shot him three times and killed his driver, too.

It was part revenge for the murder two years earlier of Lehi's
founder and leader, Avraham Stern. With posters of his face all over
the country and a price of two hundred pounds on his head, Stern
had been reduced to wandering around Tel Aviv carrying a collaps-
ible cot in a suitcase and sleeping in apartment building stairwells
or on rooftops. But it was in a friend's rented apartment in dingy
Florentin that his luck ran out. Police, acting on a tip-off, searched
Tova Svorai's apartment on Mizrahi Street, going from room to room,
knocking on walls, emptying closets. Campbell had been there. They'd
found the unshaven Stern hiding among the trousers and coats and
took his pistol from his pocket. He hadn't tried to use it. They sat him
on the sofa with his hands handcuffed behind his back, with two
police officers pointing guns at him. They asked Tova Svorai to leave.
Later she said that as she walked downstairs she heard three gun-
shots. It was the execution of Lehi's leader, and this one could expect
the same.

"Open up!" Detective Campbell banged three times on the door
of apartment 17, and moved aside. Two soldiers stepped forward,
pointed their weapons at the door, one at chest height, one lower
down. A paratroop corporal covered them from the stairwell six feet
away. The next soldier covered the other doors along the corridor, in
case anyone ran out. The door opened, the soldiers pushed past the
woman and Campbell followed them into the small living room.
Bookshelves lined the two longer walls, crammed with dark red and
brown bound volumes. "Got our work cut out here," said one of the

soldiers, going straight to the bottom right-hand side of the lowest shelf and opening a heavy brown leather book with gold lettering.

"Good afternoon, IDs please," Detective Campbell said to the woman and the four bearded men sitting around a table covered with religious-looking books. They each wore crumpled white shirts and black trousers. "Sorry to disturb you," Campbell said, "won't take long." The Jews nodded and one of the men continued in Yiddish, tapping a page.

"Don't speak Jewish, if you don't mind," Campbell interrupted. "We'll be out of here soon."

The woman said something and the man who was speaking fell silent. One of the others sipped tea, with a subdued slurp, from a small glass with a brass handle encircling it.

"Manja Singer?" Campbell said to the woman, raising his head from her ID card. She nodded.

"I've seen you before, haven't I?" Campbell said, tapping her card. She stretched out her hand to receive it but he didn't offer it back.

"No, I don't believe so," the woman answered. "I'm sure we haven't met before."

"You're right about that, we haven't met. But I've seen you."

"Well, that's certainly possible," she smiled, stroking her grey hair, "but unfortunately I don't believe I'm as memorable as I may have been in my youth."

"Your English is very good, madam, where did you learn to speak so well?"

"My mother was English, God rest her soul."

The four men busied themselves looking out of the window. One, the oldest, got up, saying, "Zhe toilette."

"Please stay where you are," Campbell said sharply. "We won't

154

Martin Fletcher

detain you long." He looked around thoughtfully and went on his usual journey, tapping, knocking, in this case playing for time, while one soldier searched a bedroom and the other flipped through the holy books.

"Quite a collection you have here," Campbell said, looking over the shoulders of two of the men at the books on the table. "You rabbis, then?"

The man who wanted the bathroom answered, "*Nein,* students." Pronounced the German way—Stoo-dehn-ten.

"At your age? Students? You, too?" Campbell said, looking at the man opposite him. The man looked askance at the woman.

"He doesn't speak English. None of them do."

"*Vy, Manja, Ja,* I do!" the man who wanted the toilet said. "*Mein* English ist *gut!*" he laughed, pulling his beard. Manja smiled, wrinkles creasing her cheeks.

Campbell said to the woman, "You seemed very interested when I was talking to that young man who got shot. You know, the terrorist murderer. You were the first to come back after the shooting. Listening very hard from the balcony, you were. Did you know the murdering pig?" As he spoke, all Campbell's attention was focused on his peripheral vision, alert to any reaction to his provocation from the men at the table, who claimed to speak no English. Did they tense? He couldn't tell. Didn't seem to.

"No, I didn't," she said. "But if a Jewish boy is killed, of course I pay attention."

"You were paying more than attention, a lot more."

"Well, I can't judge."

"And you four, who lives here?"

The men looked at Manja again. She answered, "None of them, they all live in the building. This is their study room."

"And you, you live here alone?"

"No, with my husband."

"Where is he?"

"His mother is sick. He went to Haifa a few days ago."

"No children?"

"Not here. In Europe. One day they will come, God willing."

Campbell nodded. He pulled up a chair, turned it and sat down, his arms hanging over the back, gripping the frame. The fastest position to get up. The seat becomes a weapon.

"Would you like some tea?" the woman offered.

"That's very kind, but not on duty." He cleared his throat. "Serious business here." Hearing the code words, the soldier who had been looking through the books put one down and took up position in the nearest doorway where he could see everyone. His legs were apart, his arms loose, ready to raise his rifle in an instant. Gently, he cocked it.

Campbell leaned forward and looked closely into the face of each man, taking their measure without shame, putting them on the defensive. In turn, each shifted in his seat but met his gaze. What's the first thing a man does to conceal himself? Grow a beard. They all had a beard. It was a sign of wisdom and respect but to Campbell it could have been a Halloween mask. Behind their beards, each looked middle-aged. Two with wrinkles, two almost baby-faced. Red cheeks. Never seen the sun. One thing he had noticed about religious men— they all had smooth cheeks. Why should they have wrinkles? What did they have to worry about, reading books all day? He concentrated on the two with the wrinkles; not that a rabbi couldn't be a terrorist, but he liked to narrow the odds. At least to start with. One had worker's hands, the other didn't. Didn't mean much, a professor could also be a terrorist, but still, narrowing the odds. Of course, the leader didn't have to be a working man, probably wasn't, given the intellectual claptrap these bastards used to justify their mayhem. But let's start with him.

"Yosef Chernikowsky?" Campbell said, holding on to his ID card.

The man nodded.

"Thirty-five years old. Where do you live?"

He looked helplessly at the woman and raised the palms of his hands.

"Shall I translate?" she asked.

"No."

Campbell took the ID of the next man. "Chaim Segal?"

Same questioning look toward the woman, who shrugged back. The man who needed to piss kept crossing and uncrossing his legs.

Now Campbell looked at the third of the four men. Eyebrows slightly shaved and trimmed. Too even, and a cropped, fuzzy bit where he'd shaved them, hair growing back. Campbell stared at him; at his baby cheeks, his full, greying hair, a stray lock half covering one eye, an annoying irritation to most men but which this one made no attempt to push away. The man looked back with a satisfied, controlled gaze.

"And where do you live?" He glanced down at the ID card on top of the stack of five. "Mr. Steinmetz?"

Just as Steinmetz indicated he didn't understand, the first man interrupted with a plaintive whine, leaning forward, one hand on his stomach. "Pliss, toilette?"

Campbell called to the second soldier, who was still working his way through the first bedroom. "Maceda, take this one to the pisser, search it first, search him, leave the door open, don't take your eyes off him." He nodded and pointed toward the corridor and the man quickly raised himself from the chair and hurried to the bathroom, almost doubled over. "Sank you!"

"So, where do you live? Translate please," Campbell said to the woman. After a short response from the man called Steinmetz she began to translate but blushed and faltered to a stop, distracted and embarrassed by the loud and voluminous tinkling of urine into the water of the toilet bowl. It was like heavy rain on a tin roof. Campbell couldn't help smiling, especially at the long relieved sigh followed by the tearing sound of a zipper. "Sank you," the man said again, sighing as he took his seat at the table, the trace of a relieved smile on his face, "Zat's besser."

Campbell acknowledged his thanks with a glance and a nod, taking in the elderly man's labored walk and clear eyes and gentle hands. This is a man without cares, he thought, apart from a dodgy bladder.

"Steinmetz, eh?" Campbell said, turning back. "Thirty-three. What do you do for a living then?" As the woman translated and Steinmetz, with his cocky look, answered in German, and she translated his answer, Campbell made up his mind. He didn't need to hear what she said. It was all in their look, their body language, their shifting eyes, their swallowing, licking of lips, sweat, heartbeat, prickly hair on their hands. Their stories didn't matter. Everyone had a story and no doubt it stood up. Cunning lot, these. No, doesn't matter what they say, it's how they look and behave. Beards didn't count for much either, everybody in hiding grew a beard. Rabbis. Four of them in a room, studying the holy books. Just when we're searching the building? Pull the other one, it's got bells on. And this Steinmetz? One distinguishing factor is the eyebrows. You can add a lot to the face to change it: grow a beard, long scraggly ones, neat ones, moustache, all sorts, grow your hair, wear lipstick, rouge, earrings, wear glasses, a hat. But you can't take anything off, except hair. Trouble there is, you never know if it's different, if they tried to change themselves by wearing it long or short. You don't know how it was before. Only one thing on the face is a dead giveaway: shaving big bushy eyebrows. They always stand out. This chap trimmed his, shaped them. Didn't want to stand out.

Campbell pushed his chair forward and stood up. The second soldier was in the doorway now and the first halfway inside the room, directly behind the woman. Both pointed their weapons at the men at the table. Two other soldiers stood at the entrance to the apartment, alerted by one of the men accompanying Campbell. The corporal in the stairwell had warned the men below. The building was an armed camp.

"All right then, you three, stand up slowly and come with me. Tell them, please, ma'am." As he spoke he pointed at the three men, one by one, and gestured toward the door. They got the message before Manja translated. The three men looked at one another and at the soldiers and at Campbell, who didn't take his eyes from their hands. He pulled out a pistol. Used it to point toward the door and then pointed it at the man in the middle, flicking it to show he must move. The faces of the three men were blank, tense, lips tight. Beads of sweat gathered on the brow of one of them, not Steinmetz, cool bastard, but Campbell saw the rapid rise and fall of his chest. He twitched his gun again. "No funny ideas, all right?" They got up slowly and pushed past the elderly man, who was still seated, walked past the woman and out the door. One by one, with the corridor full of soldiers, a Special Branch officer took their hands, pulled them behind their backs and slipped on handcuffs.

At the door Detective Campbell handed back two of the identity cards, said, "Thank you, sorry for the disturbance, ma'am," and closed it quietly behind him. She could hear the tramping down the steps of the troupe of men and moments later, through the thin walls of the next apartment, the sound of banging and of the policeman again: "Open the door!"

She went toward the balcony to see what they were doing with the three men but the calm rasping voice of the remaining man stopped her. "Don't look out the window again, Manja. They're very sharp."

She sniffed and sat down heavily on the sofa. "You think so?" she said. He didn't move from the table.

"Not sharp enough, no."

TWELVE

Hampstead

November 8, 1945

Edith heard the tinny slam of the letterbox as the mail fell to the floor; it was a good excuse to take a break from the stockings—she'd been going for hours. Her neck felt like a board. She stretched, moved her head in a slow circle, hearing her tendons creak, went downstairs to gather the envelopes, and started: on top was a letter addressed to her, with an Austrian post horn stamp and Stinglwagner, the lawyer's name, on the back. That was fast! It must be good news! It must! She felt herself panting and tried to calm herself. Or bad? He must have received the letter, gone straight to the house, found something worth reporting and written right back. Her heart raced, beat against her ribs. Standing at the door, she held the envelope in one hand and with the other counted the days on her trembling fingers: Posted letter to the Vienna lawyer on the twenty-fourth of October. Twenty days hath September, April, June, and November. All the rest have thirty-one . . . her fingers popped up and down . . . fifteen days. She took the letter into the empty lounge, sat on the sofa, then at the table with her sewing machine, then decided to open it in her room upstairs, in case someone came in. She took the stairs slowly, resting every few steps, turning the envelope round, looking at the stamp and the post-mark, the lawyer's address on the back. It was a thin letter, probably one page. She was glad Georg and Anna were out, Georg for yet another job interview, the poor boy, and Anna for a walk by herself. They hadn't seen much of Ismael lately. Otto and Frieda seemed to be spending a lot of time in each other's rooms and missing breakfast. *Good. I want to be alone.* As she climbed the stairs she looked at the envelope in her hand.

It must be good news. It must! He can't be dead. It was unimagi-nable. He was too close.

Papi's face always accompanied her, she felt his presence over her shoulder, would look around, search for him in crowds, see his blurred reflection in windows, twirling his moustache, she'd close her eyes and there he was, in the shadowy fleshy shifting of her eyelids, like Papi clouds floating. The only one left.

She heard him calling, "Edith," and looked up. "*Komm hier ein moment. Komm, mein liebling.*" And she ran to his feet and sat on them while he stretched out his legs and lifted her straight up, his strong manly legs, and she crawled along them into his lap where he leaned forward and cupped her little head with his big hands and kissed her nose and eyes and she snuggled up against him, enveloped by his warmth and his musty smell of snug clothes and the tangy, apple-smelling tobacco smoke curling up from his pipe, the long wooden one with an ivory bowl carved in the shape of a Tyrolean head. It had a golden amber lid with a little silver handle. It was his favorite pipe for many years, and she even tried it herself when she was, what, eleven, twelve? The smoke caught in her throat and burned it. How she coughed and coughed! How he had laughed and Mutti brought her a glass of water which she spilled, she coughed so much.

That's how she saw him now, laughing and happy. Not the somber medical doctor in his clinic on Kaertner Strasse or his consultation room in the trauma ward of the Wiener Allgemeines Krankenhaus, or the gallant officer in the starched grey uniform of the Imperial Austrian Army with a row of medals and their colorful ribbons or even the relaxed gentleman in the suit and necktie discussing politics with his friends in the parlor. . . . Hitler's just a phase, this can't last long, we'll get through. No, Edith saw laughing, silly Papi with his nicotine-stained moustache, twirling it with delight, his eyes twinkling, carving the meat, pouring the wine, sitting back with a gentle burp followed by a satisfied "Excuse *me!*"

When they all went together to the Wienerwald and drank wine in Grinsing it seemed that everywhere was one of Papi's patients, greeting him, doffing his hat, wishing him and his family well, and once when Mutti drank too much and wanted to sleep he decided to take two rooms in a *Gasthaus* and they ate and drank and slept and only came home the next day. What a time we all had, Mutti, Papi, Lisa. A warmth filled Edith's veins, her very skin seemed to sigh.

He can't be dead. She can't be alone.

Edith sat on the sofa by the window in her small room and tore a hole in the corner of the envelope and after staring at the garden took a knife and slit the edge neatly all the way. She took out the single sheet of paper. Automatically her eyes went straight to the bottom of the page. No condolences! She read the first line: No sad preface, no "I am sorry to have to . . ."

Edith looked up, blinking away a tear, and had to force herself to look down and read.

Dear Mrs. Dr. Fleischer,

First, please allow me to thank you for giving me this opportunity to represent you in the matter of your home and search for your surviving family members. I consider this a task of the highest personal and national importance and will endeavor my utmost to be of service.

Upon receipt of your letter of the 24th inst. I followed your instructions to pay a visit to your family home at Ghelengasse, 4 Hietzing. I can inform you that the house is in good repair and is currently occupied by four families, one on each floor.

I encountered the occupant of the ground floor who was sweeping the leaves along the driveway and she was good enough to open the gate and allow me to inspect the exterior of the building, which is being properly maintained, as are the gardens, the garden outbuildings, and the surrounding exterior wall.

She further informed me that indeed, to the best of her memory, about two months ago an elderly man approached one of the other tenants inquiring about earlier occupants, but, in the words of my informant, was told "in no uncertain manner to be off about his business."

My informant said she did not know any more about the matter, as she assured me it was not her who sent the gentleman away, she would never have done such a thing, but she was cordial and polite and promised to inform me immediately if any further approaches are made on the subject by anybody, and in

particular by a gentleman fitting the age and appearance of your
father. Of course, I will be in further contact with you as circum-
stances warrant.

   Please, gracious madam, accept the expression of my high-
est goodwill.

Friedrich Stinglwagner,
advocat

Edith read the letter three times. The words *elderly man* tore at her heart. Papi, so tall and strong and noble, was never an elderly man. But who knew how he looked now? She hadn't recognized Anna at first, the war had aged her beyond belief although her recovery was so fast she already had that sparkle in her eyes and her beauty shone through her sadness. What would I give to have the chance to nurse Papi back to health! But it couldn't have been Papi. Her address was known to all the refugee organizations and international tracing services in Vienna; he would have found her with one call or visit. Maybe he was sick? Couldn't remember? Lost his memory? Where would he be? There must be hospitals, hostels, hospices where the sick or homeless can stay. Did the lawyer go there, too? I should send him there. Could Papi be there, waiting, lost? Could I ask the lawyer, for no money, to extend his search? Could I somehow pay? Are there any friends to look for me? They should talk to the person who sent the elderly man away from the house, get a description, some more information. How was he dressed? Did he look sick? Did he talk well or feebly or did he ramble as if he'd lost his memory or some of it? Did he ask for specific people, mention names, who he was looking for, not just "earlier occupants." Edith knew: There's only one thing to do. I must go to Vienna. I must. Or Georg.

• • •

Edith slipped the letter back into the envelope, the better to keep it. She couldn't wait to share the news with Georg. What other elderly man would have visited the house to ask about the people who used to live there? At last, a sign of life.

As the hours went by and Georg didn't come home, Edith decided to prepare a special meal. Why was he late? Maybe he'd gotten the job and started right away? At last maybe this would be the day to remember? As the afternoon wore on and she had tidied the room and wondered where Anna was, and cleaned away the clothes, she prepared for dinner.

She opened a tin of asparagus tips and a tin of tomato, and a tin of corned beef hash, reminding herself to add it only at the very last moment so that it wouldn't cook too long. It should be heated and nothing more. She put the dried scrambled egg powder to the side. She boiled the water for the package of chicken noodle soup and surveyed it all, lined up on the counter next to the little sink where they prepared food, washed, and brushed their teeth. On particularly cold nights Georg used it for something else, too, but not since Anna shared their bed. Edith boiled the water on the gas ring so that when Georg arrived she could begin straightaway to heat the soup, and while they ate that, she could heat the rest in the pot. Pudding was plum tart that she had made earlier, but she wasn't too proud of it: she had neither sugar, her ration had run out, nor plums, just pastry mix and plum jam.

She heard the door close two floors below and Georg's heavy, slow steps. Smiling, she took the soup package and emptied the powder into the simmering water. It would be ready in two minutes. When Georg came in she was waiting with her arms open, but he just took off his coat, threw it on the bed and sank into the sofa.

"Is Anna here?" he asked.

"No," Edith answered, "I think she went somewhere with Ismael."

"He's back, is he?"

"Yes. So what happened?" *This wouldn't be that day after all.*

"Nothing. Same as always."

"Oh, I'm so sorry," and Edith sat next to him and took his hand. "You're late, so I thought maybe they gave you the job."

Georg snorted. "Sure! He was all right, he kept talking, telling me about the job and the place, but it was obvious he wouldn't take me. Said I was overqualified. There were two other men there in their demob suits. I knew I didn't have a chance."

"So where have you been all day?"

"Walking around. I went to see the lists at Bloomsbury House and the Austrian Center. Nothing. Waste of a day. Again."

"Not completely," Edith said. She poured the soup into his bowl and sprinkled salt and pepper over it. He sat at the table, his head low, blowing on the hot soup. He sipped. "Just like Omi made it. *Omisuppe!*"

They laughed together, remembering the rich, full aromas of grandma's kitchen. Whenever she gave him the miserable package soup he said the same thing and they always laughed at their poor food.

When they finished their soup and Edith had heated the corned beef hash with reconstituted scrambled eggs on top and boiled asparagus tips and tomato on the side, and they had finished that, too, Edith said, "This came today."

Georg looked at the envelope, noticed the Austrian stamp and the lawyer's name, glanced with surprise at Edith, and pulled out the sheet of paper. She began to wash up, watching for Georg's reaction.

When he finished reading he swallowed and looked thoughtfully at the letter, and reread it. Edith emptied the last of the corned beef from the tin onto a plate, covered it with a piece of paper, opened the window and put it on the sill outside, next to the milk and a small slab of butter.

Finally Georg shook his head and said, "No. Definitely not. And nor can I."

"No what?" She banged down the dish she was about to dry with the towel.

"You know very well."

"I knew you'd say that, I knew it! We have to go."

"Look, obviously you can't go, in your condition. And I can't go. We don't have two pennies. There's nowhere to stay. Really, we just have to—"

"I knew it! We have to go, at least one of us. It could be Papi, he's looking for me." Tears welled in Edith's eyes.

"No! Of course you can't go. Look, Vienna is full of organizations helping the survivors, if he's there they'll find him. What if he comes here and we're there!"

"Then I'll go. Or you go. One of us. We can't just sit here. How long can we do nothing?" *How long will you do nothing?*

"Don't you understand? There's nothing to do! Just wait. I know it's hard, it's hard for everyone, we all—"

"You go, then! You must!" Edith shouted. Her voice broke, but became stronger, louder. "Just because you've given up hope . . . I haven't!"

"How can you say that?" Georg spluttered, furious. "What do you mean? Because I know my father is dead? And my mother . . ."

Edith slapped Georg with the towel. "That's not what I—"

"Let's not fight about this!"

"That's not what I meant, you know it. You always—"

"I don't know where Ellie is, either! But what can I do about it? You can't go. You know that. The baby comes first. We don't want to do anything stupid again. . . ."

"What do you mean, again? You never let me forget! It wasn't my fault, I fell over, I fell down the stairs, I didn't mean to . . ." Now Edith started to sob. It had been her fault, she knew it. She had jumped, without thinking, and hit her chest and the railing punched into her stomach. She had felt the blood immediately and knew. Otto had tried to lift her but she pushed him away and called for a doctor, her body doubled up on the carpet. Oh, Georg's face when he came to the hospital. How they both had cried. And now? She would do anything to keep this baby, stay in bed until she came. But Papi? How to find Papi? She knew there was nothing to do, that Georg was right, and that made it all so much worse. All she could do was wait. Wait for baby. Wait for Papi. Doing nothing was driving her crazy. She let out a wail of anguish, of frustration.

"Oh, stop it! I didn't say it was your fault! I'm saying we can't go to Vienna, you can't go to Vienna, because you have to think of the baby. That's all. It's obvious. Stop crying!"

Edith tried to stop and sniffled and blew her nose. "You go! You're afraid, that's why you don't want to go. Afraid to go alone, you—"

"Don't be ridiculous!" Georg shouted, trying so hard to hold in his anger that he twirled round and stamped on the floor. "Think about it for a moment instead of being hysterical as usual. You never think! Of course he hasn't lost his memory. Otherwise how would he have found the house? So he must know his own name! And if he knows his name he'll go to one of the agencies, and they all have your name." Georg waved the letter at Edith. "Anyway, that man, he couldn't have been your father. It was two weeks ago. Where's he been since then? Maybe he was a friend, a neighbor, looking for someone, anyone from the old neighborhood, just another old Jew looking for his family or friend or someone he knew or knew him. There are hundreds of thousands of people like this, looking. In Vienna alone, thousands.

If Papi was alive and in Vienna we'd know by now. Maybe he's alive somewhere else, but he isn't in Vienna!"

"If it wasn't for the baby I'd go anyway! Just in case." Edith sat on the sofa, torn as usual, tormented. She had opened her shirts and her hands were on her bare stomach, her thumbs tapping her navel. She imagined the little head, resting in its sack just an inch away. Tears rolled down her face. Filled with love for her baby, a surge of warmth made her skin prickle; or was it a chill of fear for Papi? Everything seemed to have a price. Why couldn't everything be perfect? She knew those days were gone, long gone.

She wiped her eyes and stroked her belly. Georg sat next to her and covered her hands with his own and their hands moved together. "It kicked," Georg said, and Edith nodded. "You mustn't excite the baby," Georg said, "it's bad, all the nerves and fighting. He hears it."

"She hears it."

"He."

"She!"

"All right, she."

"All right," she said. "He."

Together, they stroked her belly and waited for their baby to move, and as the light faded they sat in the gloom, lost in their thoughts, and the room became colder and colder.

Doors slammed and floors creaked and voices carried as the house filled at the end of the day. Edith and Georg decided to go to the lounge, for warmth and company. Maybe Anna was down there, and Otto and Frieda, even Ismael. But when they opened the door they found Albert and Sally, sitting glum and silent at the table. It was too late to change their mind so they entered and sat on the sofa. Georg rose to put the kettle on, while Edith looked at the ornaments on the mantelpiece: a ceramic duck with a chipped yellow beak, the clock with its annoying, tinny chime, a framed photo of their son in army uniform, and their prized possession, a King Edward coronation cup. It was part of the guided tour for new house residents and their commentary: "1902, just look at the blue and green and gold, would you, and the red background, priceless, you know," was always followed by a warning, "Don't touch it, though, it's the finest porcelain, you break it, you buy it!"

Above the mantelpiece, of veined Victorian marble, hung a faded painting of the sheer white cliffs of Dover, with a stormy sea and brooding clouds. A ray of light broke through to brighten patches of chalk. Edith liked it. It summed up the British: solitary, defiant, dour and yet a ray of hope in a dangerous, threatening world. And in her case, it was true. Nobody else let her in; only the British. They saved her life. "I like the painting," Edith said.

"Me too," Sally answered. Georg stood by the kettle, waiting for its whistle. Albert looked up, curled his lip in agreement and nodded.

As Georg served the tea and offered some to the landlords, Edith asked, "Is anything wrong, Mrs. Barnes? You're quieter than usual."

"Am I?" she said, sipping her tea, her pinky curled out.

"Nice day, isn't it?" Edith tried again.

"Yes, very nice," Sally answered.

"Three sugars in the tea as usual?" Georg asked.

"Yes, please, that would be nice," Albert replied. Edith said, "Three sugars? I don't have any. Do you have extra rations?"

After a lengthy pause, Albert volunteered. "We had some nice news from Palestine. Well, quite nice."

"That's nice," Edith said, and thought, *I'm learning to talk like them.*

"Our Eric. He's a hero," Albert said, but trailed off.

"Really?" Georg said, sitting next to Edith, holding his cup and saucer in one hand and resting his other hand on her knee. "What did he do?"

"He saved a man's life," Albert said. "Letter came today. He may get a medal. Apparently a terrorist was about to shoot a Special Branch officer and our Eric got in first, killed the terrorist on the spot, saved the officer's life."

"Trouble is, well, you know what they say . . . ," Sally said, but hesitated. "What do they say, dear?" she asked Albert. "You know, every cloud's got a silver lining. What's the opposite?"

After a moment's thought: "Don't count your chickens before they hatch?"

"No, no. Something about, um, for every hill there's a valley? Something like that. You know what I mean."

Georg thought best with his eyes closed. He loved playing with words. "The antonym," he said. "I know. How about: No good deed goes unpunished?"

"Exactly! That's it. Goodness, you do speak good English, Georg. Better than mine! That's exactly what I meant to say."

Albert just kept tapping on the table.

Punish was an unfortunate choice of word.

"Trouble is . . . ," Sally began, and stopped. "You say, Albert."

He spoke to the table. "Trouble is, apparently those terrorists put out some kind of leaflet. Had Eric's name on it. Something about re-venge. Eye for an eye, all that rubbish. I don't know what we're doing there, to be honest. The war's over, the boys should come home. Send the Jews to Palestine. Let the Yids and the Ay-rabs fight it out. Who cares? Why's it our business?"

"Eric may come home now," Sally said. "Anyway he's due a leave, been away for three years soon, they should let him go now, get away for a bit, let all the fuss die down."

"He's a soldier, remember?" Albert said. "They aren't going to run away from some terrorist threat. He'll stay there."

"Oh, I do hope he'll be all right, I really do," Sally said.

"I'm sure he will be, Mrs. Barnes," Edith said.

"Why, what happened?" Ismael asked. He had just entered the room with Anna and they were taking their coats off.

"Oh, never mind," Albert said.

"So, where have you two been all day?" Edith asked.

"I've been showing Anna the town. We had a good time, right?"

Anna folded her coat and laid it over the back of a chair. "Yes. Yes, it was quite nice."

"Quite nice. Quite nice!" Ismael laughed. "*Y'allah!* You've become so English. It was amazing, incredible, wonderful!"

"Did you let your hair down?" Georg asked. It was another favorite idiom.

Ismael peered into Anna's face and smiled and raised his eyebrows. "Did you? Well, maybe not exactly, but we're getting there, right, Anna. Are you letting your hair down yet?"

Anna smiled. "When it grows back maybe I'll let it down. It's growing though, yes?" she said, plumping down next to Edith.

Edith stroked her hair. "Yes, it really is. And so shiny, too. I'm getting my cousin back!" She laughed and patted Anna's knee. But she also thought, *Will I lose her to this Arab?*

Otto came in with Frieda, interrupting everyone as usual. "Guess what," he said. He was holding a page of printed light blue paper. Frieda beamed.

"Your visa to America?" Georg asked.

"You got married? It's your marriage certificate?" Edith said.

"You got a job?" From Ismael.

"You're moving out?" Albert said hopefully. "I've got ex-servicemen lining up all the way round the corner for a room here."

"None of the above," Otto said, and laughed. "Look, it's a petition against the petition."

"What do you mean, let me see," Georg said and tried to snatch the paper, but Otto pulled it away. "I'll read it," Otto said. "Listen, there's a meeting this evening, I just found out. Let's go. They call it a protest against prejudice. Here's what they want everyone to sign . . . pardon my French accent." He put on his glasses and began to read:

> We the undersigned, British residents in Hampstead, believing that the recently organized petition for the deportation of aliens from this Borough is contrary to the principles for which this country fought and for which so many have died, and is contrary to the tradition of safe refuge for which Britain has always stood; and furthermore, convinced that the admitted difficulties of the housing situation in Hampstead, as elsewhere, do not justify the action proposed in the above-mentioned petition, do earnestly pray the House of Commons to disregard such agitation as being against the best interests and the good name of the British people.

"What does all that mean?" Edith asked.

"It means, leave the Jews alone," Georg said.

"So we must go to support it, what time is it? And where?"

"Oh, no," Georg said, "let's stay at home."

"Of course we'll go," Otto said. "Holy Trinity Church at eight o'clock. Someone speaks up for us, and we don't support them? Whoever heard of such a thing?"

"You remember what happened last time?" Georg said.

"Don't worry so much," Otto said. "Ismael can come, and anyway, these are different people. They're on our side."

"No, we won't go," Georg said.

"Of course we will," Edith said. "Anyway, it's just up the road. Holy Trinity is the church at the top of Goldhurst Terrace. I bought our cups at a jumble sale there. It's just the other side of Finchleystrasse. Eight o'clock? That's in an hour. Let's get ready."

THIRTEEN

They were only allowed in because Edith was so heavily pregnant. At the door the stewards were turning away dozens of refugees who came in support; to allow in more Hampstead residents qualified to sign the petition, the stewards said. But Edith pointed to her tummy and fluttered her eyes and they were ushered through. They slid past some seated residents at the back of the hall and took their places.

"Where are all the flags? The signs?" Otto said, leaning over Ismael. "That Face the Facts meeting was like a zoo, this is like a coffee evening."

"Tea," said Georg.

"I've never been inside a church before," said Edith, looking around. "It's very bare."

"It's just the meeting hall," Georg said. "This isn't the real church, this isn't where they pray."

"We should pray this all does some good."

By ten past eight every chair was taken and people lined the walls and sat on the floor in the front. The stewards had to turn people away; fire risk, they said. The air was jolly, smug even, good people come together to do good. Which didn't mean they were a pushover. Reverend Cleverley Ford, Holy Trinity's vicar, called for a moment of prayer, which was immediately rejected by a lady in the front row who called out, "This is a political meeting, not a church affair," while a man several rows behind her shouted, "How dare you interrupt the vicar in the House of Our Lord?" and a man right behind him shouted, "Pipe down!"

Ismael laughed and nudged Otto. "They haven't even started yet!" But when the speeches began, without prayers, a wave of encouragement washed over the refugees. The Reverend Chalmers Lyon read warm messages of support from the biologist Julian Huxley and the actress Peggy Ashcroft and the philosopher C.E.M. Joad. Joad had written, "Fascism, with all its beastliness, is not the prerogative of one country. Its first beginnings are often hard to detect but this petition is, I think, one of them. Let us have no truck with it." The reverend, whose powerful build and almost aggressive stance surprised Edith, said "hear, hear" to the words he had just read, and sat down smiling.

A Mr. Brailsford spoke next. He could have been talking about Georg and Edith, and indeed surveyed the audience while he spoke, as if looking for examples. "Every avenue has been closed to refugees in this country and many of them have to earn money by working in their own homes. Some of them give music lessons, others do small household repairs, others try to start small businesses. Many of them I know live in one small room . . ."

Edith relaxed into her chair, her shoulders sagged with relief; she had been so uncertain. Despite Georg's dismissal of it, the prospect of being hounded from Britain just when her baby was born had terrified her, as if there was no place for her on earth to rest—in a world with a thousand doors, none opened for her—yet here, in church, she at last heard the words she longed to hear.

But it was a man wearing a colorful cravat and a checkered jacket with leather elbows who brought tears to her eyes.

"The people who have sponsored this petition have certainly chosen the most appropriate time if they wished to inflict the greatest possible distress on the unfortunate refugees. There is not a single one of them who is not just now receiving the ghastly details of the fate of his or her closest relatives, fathers, mothers, husbands, wives, sons or daughters . . ."

Edith wiped her tears. Before her she saw the painting of the white cliffs of Dover and the shaft of light, the ray of hope, their British haven given shape on canvas, and here, in this hall, their support given solid presence, like the stocky reverend and this kind man. In Vienna they had felt alone, and in truth they were. Here they felt alone, but in truth they weren't. These are the people, she thought, who saved us, and will again. For the first time since the anti-alien petition started, Edith understood what Georg kept telling her: It had no chance of succeeding.

A handful of petition supporters had heckled the speakers, jeering and shouting "That's because you're Jewish!" and laughing amongst themselves but applause drowned out their catcalls. Until one audience member toward the end provoked the hecklers by saying, "I hope and pray that those who have the honor of our country at heart will recognize this movement calling for the expulsion of refugees for what it is—a replica of that Nazi bigotry whose logical conclusion was exposed in Bergen-Belsen."

The fascists who had remained subdued apart from the occasional whistle or jeering now jumped to their feet, furious, screaming: "Honor of the country! How dare you! Who are you calling a

Nazi! You should go to Bergen-Belsen yourself you fat—!" The audience was by and large a genteel, fair-minded lot, but they, too, had just survived a war, and been hardened by it. Hampstead ladies leapt to their feet, yelling, cursing, jeering, giving as good as they got.

Reverend Ford ran up and down the stage in his black cloak, flapping his arms like a stork trying to take flight. "Please, Please . . ."

Out of respect for the vicar the pandemonium soon subsided, allowing one man's deep, authoritative voice to cut through the hall. "I would like to take the floor, Reverend Father, if I may . . ." He remained on his feet as everyone sat down, shuffling in their seats, some red and excited, others laughing.

"Thank you, thank you, everybody," the vicar said as he walked back, somewhat breathless, to take his place at the table. He pointed to the standing man. "Please identify yourself and proceed."

"Mr. White, 43B, Greville Road. Thank you. I would like to point out that the petition to repatriate the aliens amongst us has been prompted by many issues relating to our past and present situations but there is also a growing element of future risk in allowing our foreign friends to remain. I refer of course to Palestine. We are all aware of the growing tensions in that unfortunate arena and we read more and more of the Jewish terrorists threatening to take the battle to our very own island, whose freedom from Nazi menace we defended for so many hard years. After we saw off the Nazis are we now to tolerate threats from bands of foreign terrorists against our own homes? These aliens amongst us could very well one day—no very soon, today even—be plotting to support their brothers and sisters in Palestine by attacking us here in our homes. Not all of them, of course, but some of them, there are always a few rotten apples. We must beware of a foreign fifth column fighting us from within. We must listen to Ernie Bevin. He knows what he's talking about. That is why we interned the enemy aliens during the war and now we face a similar danger. Our boys are trying to keep the peace in Palestine, but . . . For that reason alone we should support the petition for the repatriation . . ."

He went on and the audience listened intently to Mr. White's reasoned, mellifluous voice. They supported the rights of the Jewish refugees in Britain but they supported their army in Palestine more. Letter bombs had already been mailed to the London addresses of army officers who had served there. Only a week earlier a man in London was killed when he opened a package, because he had the same initial as his brother, a former soldier to whom it had been addressed.

When he finished there were murmurs of support; he'd struck a nerve, but with Edith, too. She was feeling a surge of sympathy for these good people, they were so fair and honest and good, and now he was ruining it. While she was listening Edith had pulled her hand from Georg's and now she found herself rising to her feet with one hand in the air. As the vicar pointed to her she wasn't too sure what she wanted to say, and at first the words came out timidly. She was speaking without thinking. "My name is Edith Fleischer. I just want to say thank you. I am a Jewish refugee and . . ."

"Speak up, we can't hear," a man in the front called out.

"I just wanted to say that as a Jewish refugee I am very grateful to you for your support. I just want to say that the idea that because of Palestine we Jewish refugees would do something bad here to you people who have sheltered us and given us food and saved our lives, that is not possible, not possible at all. There is no reason to be afraid of us. On the contrary, we owe you our lives and we know that and we thank you. We really do. Thank you." And she sat down, heavily, her eyes brimming.

FOURTEEN

London

November 11, 1945

All the more shocking the next day when Edith heard that Hampstead's mayor, Alderman S.A. Boyd, had signed the petition to send the refugees home, as had several of the borough councillors, as well as the influential and popular headmistress of South Hampstead Girls School. Hampstead's member of Parliament, flight lieutenant Charles Challen, promised to present the petition to the House of Commons, saying, "I hope we shall view this matter with a balanced judgment. The best way to find a sane solution to any problem surely lies in recognizing its existence, and in free and temperate discussion." His more private views were hinted at in the local newspaper, the *Hampstead and Highgate Express:* "The fashion of charging with anti-Semitism anyone who realizes the difficulties of a problem such as this seems likely to exacerbate controversy and to be lamentable. This problem must be handled in the most sympathetic manner possible, with the greatest kindness toward all those who have been welcomed with hospitality to this country. But to ignore it is to be in the last degree unstatesmanlike."

"Unsta . . . sta . . . unstates . . . man . . . like!" Otto roared, stumbling over the unfamiliar word. "Kindness!"

Heads turned in the Lyons Corner House café.

"Otto, quiet," Georg said.

"Quiet! *Kannstmichamarschlecken!*" Kiss my ass!

"Now look!" Georg said, stretching down to pick up the piece of cake Otto had knocked to the floor. "But you're right. You know what they say here? 'Although I loathe anti-Semitism, I do dislike Jews.'"

"How quickly it all changes," Edith said. "Yesterday at church the petition seemed to have no chance, and now it's being sent to Parliament."

"Yes, but they won't pass it," Georg said, blowing on the cake and taking a bite. "As someone at the church said, anyway there's nowhere to send us, and there isn't enough food in Europe already."

"You never heard of the DP camps?" Otto said. "They have plenty of room. And since when does anyone care if we're hungry? And give me that cake back."

Georg quickly swallowed the rest.

"Amazing," Edith said. "They don't want us here, they don't want us in Europe, and the one place that does want us, they won't let us go to. Allowing the Jews into Palestine would solve all their problems."

"And start a whole lot more, that's the trouble," Georg said.

The addition of the mayor's signature and the MP's promise to present it to Parliament were the main topics of discussion that morning at Bloomsbury House. What had seemed a futile gesture by a few blowhards had been adopted by the local establishment leaders. After commiserating with two friends who had discovered relatives, one a cousin and one an aunt, on the lists of death camp victims, a morose group gathered in the basement lounge. Fortunately, cheery Stanislav Chomsky was among them. He was about thirty years old but looked prematurely aged, with an imperial moustache and thick grey hair. He had a solution. "Naturalisation. We must get British citizenship. Then they can't throw us out."

"That's why they won't give it to us," another refugee said, "so they can throw us out when they want."

"But they'll have to, they're talking about it now," Stanislav said. "Look, a lot of refugees joined the forces. They're British soldiers. Most of us were in the Pioneer Corps. That was valuable service. What, you can be a British soldier but you can't be British? No, sir!"

Everyone burst into laughter. They knew what he meant. With Hitler's ashes still warm, the move to throw the Jewish refugees out of England had already begun. On May 15, a week after VE day, the Honorable Austin Hopkinson, MP for the northern constituency of Mossley, had stood up in the House of Commons and asked the Prime Minister whether, now that the war was over and they had no further need for refuge, he would "make arrangements for the immediate repatriation of the Jewish refugees." Winston Churchill's instant response: "No, sir!"

"And by the way," Stanislav shouted when the laughter died down. "When I'm naturalised I'm going to get a new name: Stanley!"

Again, the room erupted.

"Stanley Churchill!"

Edith's eyes streamed with tears of laughter.

Standing next to Stanley, George Mikes shouted that in England the only way to be taken seriously is to laugh at yourself. He proposed a book: *How to Be an Alien*. He was laughed down—who'll buy that?

"Georg," Mikes said, "what name do you want? Rupert?"

"Let's get nationalized first," Georg said, and added smugly, remembering Albert, "Let's not count our chickens before they hatch."

"There's just one problem," someone said. "Churchill isn't prime minister anymore."

"Yes, it's all very well," someone else began in Hungarian.

"Speak in English," another voice called. A dozen languages were represented by the two dozen people in the room, and English was their common tongue, in all its mangled forms.

"Oh, sorry. It's all very well relying on hope, but *tachles*—"

"English!"

"*Tachles,* do you think we can really be thrown out?"

"Anything can happen," Georg said, "but of course not. . . ."

"Anything happened already!" Otto interrupted. "Look at the death camps, did anybody expect that? And it happened. So what's being thrown out compared to that? *Bupkes!*"

Everyone laughed and said together: "English!"

Georg opened the door for Edith so she was the first to see Ismael lying on their bed, propped up against the pillows, and Anna standing by the window, staring out. "If you must lie on my bed, take your shoes off," she said, entering the room. Georg took Edith's coat, shook off the raindrops and hung it over his on the door hook. Ismael didn't answer and Anna didn't turn. "Oh you my good," said Georg, translating directly from the German. "Oh dear. What's wrong?"

Still no response. "Ismael?" asked Edith. There was no point asking Anna. He looked at her and shrugged. "Well, as Sally would say," Edith said, "let's have a nice cuppa. Georg, can you go downstairs and see if there's any sugar in the lounge? We've run out." He left the room.

Edith sat next to Ismael on the bed and he plumped up a pillow for her to sit against. "Haven't seen you much lately," Edith said.

"I've had a lot on," Ismael said.

Edith indicated with her chin toward Anna.

Ismael shrugged again, this time with a pained grin that quickly vanished. Edith turned her palms up, miming—so what happened? Without turning, Anna said, "Stop talking about me. I can see you in the glass."

Edith and Ismael laughed. Georg came in with a sheet of paper containing a small pile of sugar, which he distributed evenly in four cups. "Glad to hear that everything's all right," he said.

But it wasn't, and they drank their tea in silence.

Finally Ismael said, "Anna, come and sit down, the sofa's empty." Anna's right shoulder barely twitched and she remained at the window, looking out on another grey, drizzly autumn afternoon. She breathed on the glass and drew on it and moved her head as if talking. Silhouetted in the window frame, she looked like a shadow of herself.

"Please," Ismael said.

Edith got up, went to the window, took Anna's hand and brought her to the sofa where they sat together, holding hands. Anna's face was a blank.

"All right. This is what happened. I kissed her," Ismael said. "I tried to, anyway."

"Oh," Edith said. She felt Anna's hand tense up.

Georg put the water on. He glanced at Anna and suppressed the start of a smile. When had she last been kissed?

"And she got upset."

Anna pulled her hand from Edith's and leaned forward, elbows resting on her knees, hands cupping her chin, looking at the floor.

"She said she liked me and I kissed her. That's what boys and girls do. Sorry about that." But Ismael didn't look as flippant as he sounded. Georg poured water into each cup and added milk. Edith's pregnancy permitted them an extra half-pint ration.

Anna's whole upper body moved with her sigh. She licked her lips and said, "Stop looking at me." She wore a white blouse underneath a soft sky blue pullover that belonged to Edith and little imitation pearl earrings that Ismael had given her as a present. She had a pleated checkered skirt and blue slippers. Her hair, which now reached her ears, was glossy black. The curls, beginning to find their natural waves, brushed pearly, almost translucent skin. Her lips, which had seemed tight and drawn, looked fuller and relaxed. Edith thought, she looks beautiful, and vulnerable. Edith saw her hand tremble.

Georg refilled the tea but the cup and saucer rattled in Anna's hand so much she couldn't hold it, so she put the cup on the floor and within an instant had knocked it with her foot and spilled the tea over the wooden floorboards. A tear coursed down one cheek and another and she silently wept. "I'm sorry," she said. "I'm so sorry."

"That's all right," Edith said, holding her while Georg wiped up the tea with a cloth. "It's nothing, just hot water, we'll make another cup."

"No need to cry over spilled milk," Georg said.

But it wasn't the tea, or the kiss. Ismael's strong grasp and his suddenly looming face had shocked her, taken Anna to that place in her nightmares, a cell of stinking serpents, the place that today, among these new friends, seemed as if it could not possibly have existed. Was there really such a place? Did those things really happen to her? Really? Yes, they did. She just had to look at the number branded on her arm, blue marks like a secret code that unlocked all the evil, that she could never wipe away. What she had done was tattooed on her soul.

"I want to tell you what happened there. But I can't. I just can't. I don't have the words." Anna hid her face and tried to cry.

The next morning Edith and Georg left Hampstead tube station into the pouring rain and hurried right on Heath Street and right again into the New End Hospital. The tiles at the entrance were sunken from years of wear and the rain Georg shook from his umbrella added to the puddle. Edith stepped clumsily over the water. They walked along the narrow corridor and climbed two flights of stairs to the obstetrics department, gave Edith's name to the nurse in a glass booth and sat at the end of a long row of chairs, each occupied. It was her first visit since she had booked a delivery bed five months earlier. Her GP, Doctor Goldscheider, had recommended as much rest and care as possible, given her earlier miscarriage, but now, with about six weeks to go, it was time for a hospital examination.

They waited an hour, amid the sour, tangy odour of drugs and disinfectant. Ismael should leave Anna alone, Edith had said, she isn't ready, he should have more sense. No, Georg had said, he's helping her, she needs help, something terrible happened to her. She needs to talk about it. The Arab doesn't care about that, Edith said, we all know what he wants. Georg bristled but dropped it. They were arguing too much lately, and about nothing.

"Mrs. Flasher?" The nurse called, looking around the room.

Edith rose. "Fleischer?"

"Close enough. Follow me, please. I'm Nurse Parkinson." The cheerful nurse turned and they followed her bustling squat frame into a small room. "Not you," Nurse Parkinson said at the door, blocking Georg's path. "This is ladies' business. Take a seat, there's a dear, the little lady won't be long. Have a cigarette in the waiting room, if you like."

Twenty minutes later Edith was back, frowning. Georg took her hand and they walked slowly to the exit. *"Nu?"* he said. So? Worried, he waited for her to say something.

She took his hand. "It's nothing. He said I've got hypertension. Higher than normal blood pressure, but not too high, that's what the doctor said. Doesn't have to be a problem, but can be."

"Is there anything you should do?"

"Come back next week to monitor me. I did a urine test. But that's all. He asked if I have headaches, blurry vision, stomach pains, swollen hands or feet. I don't have any of that." She didn't want to get into her lower back pain, Georg would nag her to death.

"What does he mean by hypertension? You worry too much? Nothing actually wrong?"

"No, nothing."

"So it's all right, then?"

"Yes. I told him I had a lot on my mind. He said, welcome to the real world."

"That's helpful." He held the door open. It had stopped raining, although the sky was still a swollen grey and a few drops fell and a sharp wind blew as they walked toward the High Street, the sign of an approaching storm.

"I don't think what he worries about and what I worry about are the same."

Georg laughed. "No. No, you're right there."

FIFTEEN

Palestine

October 22, 1945

"We must move fast," the man with the bushy moustache, known as Miki, said. "That Detective Campbell has seen my face, even if he didn't know who I am. One day he will, and then he'll remember. He'll remember me, the one with the weak bladder!" He chortled, his smooth red cheeks pinching into dimples hidden for two years. "And then he'll curse himself."

"As he is already cursed by the Name," a bearded man said, "may our tormenters be blotted from the earth."

"Tfut, tfut," said another Orthodox-looking Jew, known as Shimon, spitting over his shoulder for good luck, to antagonize the truly observant man to his left. "Knock on wood," he added, to deepen the insult. Last time he had said knock on wood, the Orthodox man had been scandalized: "Jews don't say knock on wood! That wood is the cross of Jesus."

Night had fallen by the time the British had loaded the barbed wire onto their trucks and the soldiers driven away. After two of his men made sure no plainclothes detectives were lurking among the residents stretching their legs in the streets, after their two and a half days of confinement, Miki had slipped away from the house carrying a small holdall. He walked two blocks and caught a taxi to the bus station, where a commotion caused by a noisy crowd of people trying to stop British police from arresting a young man helped him pass unnoticed. By the southern felafel stand a boy and a girl appeared and he followed them to this house in south Tel Aviv where he had spent the night. Now they were assembled in the basement, four men and a woman, to make their most momentous decision since the assassination of Lord Moyne a year earlier. That assassination had provoked the fury of not only the British and Winston Churchill, who was a close friend of the murdered minister, but also of the Jewish Agency, which had turned against them with all its power, arrested leaders and tortured members, and had sworn to destroy them before they did more harm to the Zionist cause. Miki himself had been detained but had escaped from the agency prison before they had time to discover how important their captive was.

None of the five had ever been in this damp, grease-smelling basement room before, and would probably never see it again. It was the storage room of a hardware store; they were surrounded by piles of lumber, rolls of tubing and coils of wire, and boxes of nails and screws. There were no bodyguards; not to draw attention and anyway, if the British came, resistance was futile. They trusted in luck, and their ability to bluff; they had no choice. They were too few.

The British were persistent and sometimes lucky and the net was closing. Even though the agency had now formed a joint resistance with Irgun and Lehi against the British blockade, Miki's men were vulnerable and running out of safe houses. This was their third generation of leaders in four years. Only Miki had survived the British hunt; the rest were either dead or in detention camps in Africa. This was the first gathering of the new leadership in one room. Old comrades, there was no need to hide behind a blanket.

Around a flimsy table with a plate of flaky bourekas in the middle and glasses of orange juice and water, they had exchanged personal news for a few minutes: three bearded men, one newly clean-shaven but for a moustache, and the lone woman. Four lived with their families and had normal jobs: hiding in plain sight. Only Miki changed shelters every few days or weeks.

He got straight to the point. "We must decide quickly, and move fast."

His introduction was terse and brief: "We're losing. They're closing in on us and we can't operate. We need to change the rules of the game. We need to take the battle to the British. In London. And this is why." Though his own resources were limited, his information was excellent. It came from within the heart of the intelligence arm of the Jewish Agency itself, where a young woman, a Pole from his hometown of Andrespol, copied or stole documents for him. He received many of the same briefing papers as the agency leader, David Ben-Gurion, and he read the same field reports from Europe, but his conclusions differed wildly. He explained slowly, precisely, preparing his friends for his dramatic proposal.

"President Truman's request to the British to permit a hundred thousand European Jewish survivors into Palestine immediately has been rejected. Outright. This is encouraging the Arabs. Arab scout formations are organising and are being trained by Arab instructors demobilised from the British military in preparation for the future battle with us. We are not the only ones who see it coming. Every day becomes more urgent for us, every day is a day closer to the fight, the true fight for our existence in Palestine. We need our brothers in Europe, and they need us. And what does our friend Mr. Bevin do?

In response to the Yishuv's call for help? A committee! Another committee! He has invited the United States government to join an Anglo-American committee, under a rotating chairmanship no less, that's how much time they have, to rotate! To examine the question of European Jewry and to make a further review of the Palestine problem in light of that examination. You see? First an examination, and then a review of their examination. Trust me, I am quoting from Parliament's very own minutes. It's like a joke. Bevin said Truman accepted. Of course this is just a continuation of the white paper. By the time they finish their review, how many more of our people will be dead, those survivors of the charnel houses of Europe, or will be killed here at the hands of the Arabs? Bevin is backtracking. The right of return to a Jewish homeland guaranteed to the Jews by the Balfour Declaration in 1917 is now being pulled from under our feet. Bevin is still limiting us to eighteen thousand Jews a year. Any immigrants we can bring in unofficially, illegally as the British put it, will be taken off that total. Even the agency, even Ben-Gurion, the dunderhead, has lost faith in diplomacy. As for us, we will remain faithful to our promise to redeem the people of Zion, to end the exile, and we will remain faithful to the millions of our helpless families who have been murdered. But how? We will not permit another Anglo-American delaying tactic. But what can we do?"

The others looked intently at Miki. They knew him. He wouldn't ask a question if he didn't have the answer. He went on.

"Europe is teeming with Jews who want to come here, but the British won't let them. The agency is trying but failing. A hundred and fifty Jews slipped in on the SS *Ville d'Oran* last month. A handful managed to walk in from Syria. The Greek boat *Dimitrios* nearly landed a couple of hundred but the British caught them. And the Arabs are still not satisfied. They're angry so many are getting in!

Although Truman's heart is in the right place he's cooperating with the British government despite pressure within the American Senate, especially from Senators Wagner and Taft. They want to open the doors of Palestine to Jews. But the British will always delay and prevaricate. They'll review their examination under rotating chairmen! They'll try to satisfy their old friends the Arabs. Why? Simple. Because there are more of them. And listen to this. I will read to you one paragraph from Mr. Bevin's recent speech to Parliament that will show you how little they care about us, how the Jews have become a mere *loch im kopf,* a bureaucratic headache." He took a piece of paper from his pocket and smoothed it. "Again, this is from Parliament's own minutes, this is what Mr. Bevin wants to do. His rotating committee!"

He read, his voice dripping with scorn, speeding up as he became angrier:

> *To hear the views of competent witnesses and to consult representative Arabs and Jews on this problem of Palestine as such problems are affected by conditions subject to examination under paragraph 1 and paragraph 2 above, and by other relevant facts and circumstances and to make recommendations to His Majesty's Government and to the Government of the United States for ad interim handling of those problems, as well as for their permanent solution.*

Miki wanted to shout, but didn't permit himself in case shoppers upstairs heard. Instead his fury seeped out in drool over his chin. He could only splutter: "Paragraph one! Paragraph two! How much time does Bevin think we have!" His face swelled, his eyes bulged. "Relevant facts and circumstances!" He looked set to explode, and his hand trembled as he tapped the table, unable, because of their need for quiet, to smash it with his fist as he longed to. "We need our people today!" His colleagues were hardly less angry. What did the British care? It wasn't their problem. So they had to make it their problem. One of the men interrupted.

"We need to shock them. Terrify them. An officer here, a whipping there, it doesn't work."

"Exactly," Miki said. "We must change the rules, we must tear up the rules. You think we're the real issue? We're just another pawn. Listen to this."

Again Miki looked down at his piece of paper. "If you really want to know what Mr. Bevin's true imperial concerns are, listen to this. He says if Britain doesn't stick to its commitments to the Arabs to limit the Jews coming to Palestine, and I'm quoting from his speech to Parliament again, 'It would arouse widespread anxiety in India.' India! Widespread anxiety in India! That's what he cares about, the reaction of ninety million Moslems in India against British rule there! What does he care about the fate of a few Jews rotting in DP camps in Europe? He cares about Britain keeping India! A pink map!"

Miki looked around the table, his shoulders heaving, out of breath. He sipped water and took a bite of bourekas. The others all spoke at the same time, whispering, hissing, What to do? What was big enough?

"So we are left with only one option," he continued, quieting them with a wave of his hand. "To be more effective in our attempts to force the British out of Palestine. But again, so far they are defeating us, we are stinging them here and there but we are no more than a nuisance. We need to change the rules of the game. More attacks on their police posts and catching a few soldiers won't change things.

Ben-Gurion has finally ordered the Hagana to start a campaign of sabotage. Good. But that's too little. Begin has the right idea; he said we must take the battle to the dogs in their home. But what has he done? *Gurnicht.* Nothing. So we will do it. We must. I have a proposal. That is why I asked for this meeting." He poured himself another glass of water and licked the last flakes of bourekas from his fingers.

"*Nu?*" the woman said in Yiddish. So?

All looked at Miki, who hesitated. The Orthodox man gestured with his open hands—*Nu?* Miki took a deep breath and leaned forward. "We have to cut off the head of the beast. We must strike a blow that will rock the British. Against the true terrorist who hides behind a pile of papers and fine words. In short, we must be bold and brave and in one act exhaust and terrify the British, shock the Arabs, and stiffen the Jews. I have a target." Miki paused. Not for effect or fear, but at the enormity of what he was about to propose. When he spoke it was with the finality of a judge.

"The British foreign minister, Bevin," Miki said. "The head of the snake." Everyone at the table stared at Miki who paused again. He wouldn't. Would he? "My proposal is we assassinate Ernest Bevin. Quickly." They gasped, spoke at once, interrupted each other, where, when, how . . . Miki went on, "And we have just the man to do it. He's already in London."

SIXTEEN

London

November 15, 1945

Edith was curled on the sofa with a blanket over her knees and whenever someone asked her what she was drinking, shouted "Orange juice and cod liver oil!" If someone asked why, she shouted louder, "I'm going to have a baby!" She was drunk, on happiness. Five and a half weeks to go, thirty-eight days to be precise. "Edith!" Doctor Goldscheider said, then laughed, swigging from a bottle of stout. "I can't believe you're taking my advice! You're really taking it easy?"

"Dit isn't taking your advice," Georg put in too loudly from over the doctor's shoulder, "she's following my orders! Yes. I forbid Dit to go out until baby is born!"

"You're slurring your words," Dr. Goldscheider said, "and the remarkable thing would be if Edith ever listened to you for once."

"True, too true," Georg said, "but in this instance, the proof is in the pudding . . ." Edith laughed, said, "I've got a bun in the oven," and toasted Georg with her cup of juice: "My lord and master!" Georg had taught her the phrase that very day. "You see, I am king of my castle!" he said.

The lounge was crammed with refugees and more were arriving, crowding the corridor and the staircase. Whenever someone spoke in German or Polish or Hungarian or Czech everyone shouted, "Speak in English!" Otto drank gin and ginger and Gina was half-way through her second bottle of champagne cider. She was wrapped around a dark young man with long black hair whom nobody knew. Two Slavs with their arms entwined fell onto the sofa next to Edith, their weight bouncing her into the air, prompting Georg to call out, "Careful!" The radio played loud in the background, English songs that nobody knew but they sang along with anyway.

Sally and Albert had smiled from the doorway, sipping their favor-ite orange gins until, seeing a gaunt man in a beret and a buttoned three-piece suit spill his drink on their carpet, had retreated to their rooms. "Fair enough," Albert said on the way downstairs, "they got a lot to celebrate, and about time, too." A historic success for the refugees that morning in Parliament had followed another a few days earlier.

Hampstead town hall had agreed to a compromise that removed the threat to throw them out of England. Within minutes the news had raced from the civic center to Bloomsbury House, the Austrian Center, the Czech Club, the Cosmo, and Dorice; telephones rang across the borough and everybody knew—they would stay in their homes, and the mayor and councillors who had supported the peti-tion to repatriate "enemy aliens" were crawling to the cross, or as the English said, eating humble pie, explaining, apologising.

The rout began with the eminent Hampstead residents who signed the "Protest Against Prejudice" petition, and gained momen-tum with the support of the local branch of the Left Book Club. The final blow was dealt by the vicar of St. Cuthbert's in his Sunday ser-mon, whose theme was the Good Samaritan in relation to the Jewish refugees. "The Good Samaritan remembered the First Command-ment," the vicar told his flock, "Thou shalt love thy neighbor as thy-self. He gave the Jew his ass and took him to the wayside inn and fed him from his own purse. All this the stranger did for the Jew. Jesus had remarked, 'Go out and do thou likewise.' And in face of this," the vicar intoned, and his words were printed in the *Ham and High* for all to read, "in face of this the present-day response is 'Let us petition the Home Secretary to secure the deportation of aliens.'

"If the true Christians who sought to obey Christ's Command-ment, Love thy neighbor, took no action," he went on, "the community might lose men who potentially possessed the genius of a Disraeli, an Einstein, or a Kreisler." He even credited the Jews for helping save Brit-ain. "Sir Philip Sassoon, who was a Jew, was almost alone in prewar days in advocating a great expansion of the Royal Air Force."

"Forgive me," the vicar concluded to his congregation, "if I have spoken words that may hurt you this morning, but I worship a Jew, Jesus Christ, who is my lord and my master, and I reverence a book by which my life is ordered, the Bible, of which all the writers save one were Jews, and I belong to a Church where all the first members were from God's chosen race."

Shaking the congregant's hands at the church exit, the vicar urged them to sign the counterpetition, and many did. The petition to eject the Jewish refugees from Britain and the petition to throw out the petition were neck and neck, with around two and a half thousand signatures each.

It was then that other councillors took the lead at town hall. Councillor Stephen Murray, who put forward a motion to condemn the anti-alien petition, said, and his words also reached the whole borough through the pages of the *Ham and High,* that the petition was "a piece of blatant anti-Semitism and if carried through would lead to another Bergen-Belsen." He told his fellow councillors, "If they supported the petition they would be in grave danger of adopting the fascist precept of divide and rule. It was up to the members to reestablish Hampstead's good name by giving a decisive vote against the petition."

After bitter exchanges in the council, Hampstead's leaders reached a compromise, which acknowledged the housing problem yet removed the threat to the Jews:

> *The Council:*
>
> *Notes with regret the organisation of a petition in the Borough to Parliament purporting to seek a resolution of the housing problem;*
>
> *Expresses the view that the question of repatriation of aliens in Hampstead cannot be pursued without discrimination or regard to the many considerations involved; and*
>
> *Urges the government to expedite the demobilisation of building trade operatives as the only method by which the bomb-damaged houses in Hampstead and elsewhere can be adequately repaired and the housing schemes go forward and the present shortage of accommodation made good.*

The refugees were safe. And getting drunker by the moment. Nobody knew all the words but everyone joined in with Bing Crosby on the radio, making it up, humming, swaying together, Edith belting bits of it out from the sofa, waving her empty bottle of cod liver oil:

I'm dreaming of a white Christmas ...

The lounge became thick with cigarette smoke and alcohol and noise and laughter. A blast of cold air cut in from the window, and died when the sash cord tore and the window fell with a bang, scaring everyone. Relieved laughter followed, and more drinks. It was a room of reprieved people. The death of the petition didn't make them feel more accepted, just less rejected, and that was good enough, for most of the loved ones of everybody in the room had been murdered.

Edith, her mood suddenly changing, lay back, observing the party, a little smile playing on her lips, satisfaction spreading across her face. The room was warm, she felt safe with her friends. So Mr. Scarfe at the newsagents and her English customers were right: They had kept telling her not to take the petition seriously. But it was all right for them, they weren't about to be expelled. What a relief, she thought. Her hands rested comfortably on her stomach, which stood straight up, firm and pointy, a little mountain prodding from within. Sometimes she could feel an elbow or a foot pushing out and would try to grasp it through the skin. We have a home, she told her baby, don't worry anymore. For a moment she saw her real home, the house in Ghelengasse, she saw her family quietly at dinner and she saw her friends in the little alpine hut in the garden as it rained outside, all the boys and girls, crowding in and laughing and shouting, lying across one another, a quick kiss in the dark, hands near breasts, thigh against thigh, someone's hand too close and pushed away, never quite daring. Pity, she thought.

Now, half of them dead, the rest, God knows where.

Gina brought her young man to Edith who swung her legs to the floor to make room on the sofa. Edith raised an eyebrow in appreciation and Gina said, "My nephew, Tomac. He's such a dear. Doesn't speak a word of English. Just arrived." Now Edith understood: so that's who he is. Gina had told her his story. A farming family on the

Danube outside Budapest hid him in a hole in the ground under their boat shed. "For nine months," she had said over coffee at the Cosmo, after receiving a short note that he was alive and coming to London. "With three other people. In a hole in the ground. Can you imagine? I can't."

Tomac smiled and kissed Edith's hand. Edith fluttered her hand across her heart and they all laughed.

"Gina Hayworth, what do you think?" Gina said.

"Perfect," Edith said, grinning, stroking Gina's long, lush hair. "You look just like Rita Hayworth."

They'd called it a naming party and said everyone should bring a bottle and think of an English name. For that afternoon had marked their second breakthrough. The Home Secretary, Chuter Ede, had announced the government's new naturalization policy: Foreign residents who had been in the country for five years could become British. As the refugees had all come before the end of 1939 and most had never been able to leave, it meant that Jewish refugees could become citizens. No more enemy aliens: as Otto joked—"Mee Eeenglith at lest!"

"Kurt Giebel has the best name," Edith said. "Clark Gable!"

"Edith Fleischer," Gina said, "let me think—"

Otto interrupted, putting his arm around Gina. "Edith Flyshit."

Edith ignored him. Everyone knew that Flyshit was Fleischer's nickname in the button factory. "Georg wants to change his name to George," she said. "George Fletcher. He thinks he may seem more English and get a proper job at last."

"Oh, sure," Otto said, and laughed, "mein name iss Chorch Fletscher, pliss gif me zhe jhop!"

They all burst into laughter and Otto kissed Gina on the ear.

"Stop licking my ear," she said.

"Oh, I didn't think of that," he said, and licked her ear.

"Uuummhh," Gina purred. "Don't put your tongue in my ear," so he did. "Where's Frieda?" she asked.

Edith took Tomac's hand and said the only word she knew in Hungarian: "*Szeretlek.*"

The young man threw his head back and roared.

"What does that mean, anyway?" Edith asked.

"As if you didn't know," Gina said. "I love you."

"Oh, dear. Please tell him I didn't mean it."

"Tell him yourself," Gina said, nuzzling Otto.

"I don't know how."

"What a party," Gina said to Edith the next morning, drying the glasses in the lounge sink. She was wearing Otto's slippers. "I don't think Frieda likes me anymore."

"I wonder why."

"Where was Anna, though, I didn't see her, was she here at all?"

"No, she was upstairs in the room. That sort of thing is too loud for her. Too many people." Edith slumped back into her chair as the Vitos whirred down and came to a clacking halt. She crumpled her shopping bag full of torn stockings and threw it to the floor. "I hate stockings!" she yelled. "Georg, get a job!"

"It isn't his fault," Gina said. "Anyway, about Anna, Ismael wasn't here, either."

"Another reason for her not to join in."

"Exactly. They're pretty close, aren't they?"

"Too close."

Gina turned as she put the last glass away. "Only four broken glasses, not bad. What do you mean, too close?"

"You know what I mean."

Gina smiled. "Is there such a thing as too close?"

Edith moved to the sofa and Gina joined her. Edith was losing patience with Anna but didn't want to tell Gina. She'd tell Otto and then everyone would know. But sharing the small room with Anna was beginning to wear. She could see Georg trying not to look as Anna dressed and undressed, especially undressed. She may have less hair but her figure was the same. And sleeping in the same bed every night . . .

"One thing I keep wanting to ask her," Edith said, "is how she survived. I mean, all those years in the camps, so beautiful, what did she do? She never says. She once told us the general story, but not a word about what she did. But I don't dare ask."

"I know," Gina said. "I mean, with so many people dead, what did you have to do to live? That's what I don't understand. No one does. It's her silence that is so bad, that's what got people talking."

"Who? What are they saying?"

They heard footsteps in the corridor and fell silent. Gina quickly changed the subject. "By the way, did you hear from that lawyer in Vienna again?"

"No, I didn't," Edith said. The footsteps continued past the door. "Mrs. Wilson at Bloomsbury House said the same as Georg. The old man who came to the house was probably a neighbor. Otherwise Papi's name would be on a list somewhere in Vienna, and it isn't."

"Is there anything else you can do?"

Anything else? Edith lay back on the sofa and pulled the blanket up to her chest, and didn't answer. I'm so tired, she thought: a few hours' sleep on and off at night, listening to Anna groaning and mumbling, and a few minutes dozing during the day. Everything seems to hurt, especially down below, and nipples like sandpaper. If only Mutti could be here to help, and Lisa. And Papi. He had wanted so much to be a grandfather. In his professional way he'd have it all arranged by now, clothes bought and arranged, nappies washed and neatly piled, a wooden cot, blankets and bedding, what else is there? I don't even know. He wouldn't think much of her own preparations, which so far consisted of unfinished knitting by friends and a plan to empty out the top drawer, line it with a blanket, and make it baby's bed. Sometimes she felt Papi looking at her, arms folded, pipe dangling, frowning.

Papi had always said he felt linked to his twin brother who had died at birth; not in a spiritual but in a very bodily way. He still took up space in his life. He felt him in the room. Now Edith felt Papi's presence, too, close and intimate, like a second skin. Warm and protective. She called out to him at night in her dreams, in which he always appeared moving away, on a train, walking, flying, a sad face, looking at her as he faded into the distance and sometimes this would merge with a baby face, little and round with huge staring eyes. She would wake breathless and feel pressure inside; she never knew if this was caused by the dream, or by the weight of baby pressing down. But just as she knew baby was coming, so she knew Papi was alive. I know, I just know, you're here somewhere, I can feel it. Come to me, come quickly, don't miss the birth of your grandchild.

Other times, she felt, he must be dead.

"Hello? Hello? Anyone there?" Gina said, putting her face into Edith's. "I said, is there anything else to do?"

The door opened and Georg and Anna came in. "About what?" Georg asked, heading straight for the kettle.

"Some party that must have been," Anna said, "I couldn't sleep. People were creeping in and out of rooms all night. Those squeaky stairs." Edith closed her eyes and flexed her neck muscles. "Georg, would you?"

Georg stood behind Edith and covered the top of her head with one hand and kneaded her neck with the other, working upward, digging with his fingers, massaging her skull. "Gina, you're here early," he said. "Or are you here late?"

"All I can do is wait," Edith said to Gina, answering her question at last. "It's terrible."

"I know those slippers," Georg said with a smirk.

"Look at Tomac," Gina said, "a note, and then he appeared. Out of nowhere."

"Like Anna," Georg said. "Wait, that's all we can do."

"I can't bear any more of those news films at the pictures," Anna said. "I keep looking for someone I know."

"Especially the camps in the East," Georg went on, his hands busy on Edith's neck and head. "The survivors scattered. Could be anywhere. There's nowhere to look for them. Can only wait." He felt Edith's sigh. "Dit, how do you feel, better? Anywhere else?" Anna looked at Edith and smiled. It made a nice picture. Georg massaging pregnant Edith on the sofa. A homey picture. Edith didn't smile back, just bent her head so Georg could get at all of her neck.

They heard the front door open and close and a man's heavy tread up the stairs. "That's Ismael," Anna said, then smiled and opened the lounge door. Edith looked up at Gina and raised an eyebrow.

They heard Anna shriek from the corridor, "What happened to you?" followed by muted words from Ismael. "No, come in," Anna called. She pulled a resisting Ismael into the lounge. A white bandage was wrapped around the top of his head, one of his eyes was bruised

and dark and the right side of his lower lip was swollen and cut. A
trouser leg was torn at the knee.

They all stared. Ismael shrugged and pulled up a chair to the table.
He slurred through a swollen lip, "You should see the other guys." He
tried to smile, but winced. His lip felt as if it filled his mouth. Anna sat
next to him, her hand on his shoulder in concern. "But what happened, Ismael? Where have you been all night? The hospital?"

"Yes, for hours. Just a few stitches. I got hit by a bottle, I think."

"Who by?" Georg said. "Why?"

He'd been coming home last night to join the party when he'd
seen a group of young men on West End Lane following two Jews,
swearing at them and making fun of them. He couldn't resist so he
crossed the road and doubled back, following them to see what
would happen. It was early evening, the shops around the tube station were closing and the streets emptying. The Jews were scared and
hurried forward, and turned right onto Broadhurst Gardens. They
should have stayed on the main road where there were more people
and streetlights; this street was empty and dark. One of the men
threw a stone at the Jews who started running. One stumbled and
fell over. The men attacked him, kicking and punching, so Ismael
piled in. The two Jews ran away and Ismael tried to get away, too, but
they were a tough bunch of lads and got stuck in. Luckily two bob-
bies from the West End Lane police station had just begun their foot
patrol and ran up blowing their whistles and the thugs ran away. Not
without Ismael, who was on the ground, stretching out his arm and
grabbing one by his ankle, who tripped straight into a wall and
knocked himself out. The police arrested him and drove them both
to the hospital.

"So I missed the party. I was there all night."

Anna was stroking his hand. The knuckles were grazed and red.

"You know, Ismael," Georg said, "for an Egyptian anti-Semite you sure get in a lot of trouble helping the Jews."

Ismael tried to smile. "In Egypt we say, know your enemy." He rose stiffly. "I'm going to my room."

Anna stood with him and they left together.

SEVENTEEN

London

November 17, 1945

Edith had worried most of the night, easing herself past Georg half a dozen times to go to the freezing toilet. The constant throbbing in her right leg had spread to her upper thigh and abdomen, and baby seemed to have the hiccups for hours on end. It gave her the hiccups, too, her whole torso lurching, and she worried: Is baby all right? It moved so much and took up so much room. She sometimes had a choking feeling as if her organs were squeezed, competing for space. Doctor Goldscheider had said not to worry, couldn't be better, quite normal at this stage to be so tired. But that wasn't why she couldn't sleep. Her mind was racing with anticipation.

As she dozed on the bed, chin on chest, a magazine lying on her lap, a bag of stockings half sorted on the floor, a pot of tea untouched on the night table, her heart thumped.

A visitor was coming with news of Papi.

Next to the tea was the bombshell: a postcard from a Herr Andreas Kellerman requesting, with the politest Viennese formality, for permission to visit at gracious madame's earliest convenience, to bring some news about her father, Max Epstein. Included was the request to confirm by telephone at the local number indicated: HAM 2992.

When Georg brought her the card the day before, with a warning not to get too excited, Edith was sure her heart had stopped for an instant; then it pounded so hard she could hardly catch her breath. What could this mean? What did this man Kellerman know? Who is he?

They reviewed what they already knew, and it wasn't much. Anna had said Papi was alive days before the Russians freed the prisoners in Auschwitz, but also that he was very sick. The old man looking for occupants of the house in Vienna couldn't have been Papi because his name didn't appear on any lists. So all they really knew was that he may have survived the war, but if so had been missing for ten months. Plenty of people survived the camps and then died right after liberation, from disease, neglect, plain bad luck. Yet survivors were turning up all the time, in Palestine, in British internment camps, displaced people camps, on Red Cross lists, discovered in hospitals across Europe, living in their old homes with no way of contacting anybody, scattered as far away as India, China, Russia after fleeing the fighting.

The Continent, one big graveyard for Jews, also teemed with ragged souls seeking their loved ones. Some were lucky. The fifteen-year-old nephew of Trudi, a waitress at the Dorice, survived Dachau, became the mascot of an American army unit as they fought through Germany, made his way to London three months after the war ended, and met his father by chance waiting for the number 13 bus in St. John's Wood. Anything was possible. And now this man Kellerman.

"If he knew him in Auschwitz or earlier it doesn't tell us anything about where he is today," she had said to Georg. "But maybe he knew him later, maybe even where he is now? What do you think?"

"I don't know. You were sleeping so I called him and left a message that he should come as soon as possible. He rang back last night and told Albert he'll be here today at seven o'clock." That was in eight hours.

At midday Ismael tapped on Georg's door. "Could you come to my room for a moment?" he asked. Georg looked over his shoulder. "Sure, what's up?" As they walked downstairs, he asked, "Is it about Anna? Where is she?"

"She's gone out."

"What does she see in you?" Georg asked.

"Ah, there you have me, my friend." Ismael opened the door to number 6. "It isn't about Anna, though." They went in and there was an awkward silence. Georg looked around. The room was neat and spacious and the bed was made. Some packages were stacked in one corner, half covered by a cloth. Georg could see American stamps. A thick envelope was lying on the table.

"I'm feeling a bit rough right now," Ismael said, gliding his finger over his split lip. "Would you do me a favor? I have to drop this off in town and you said you're going in for an interview. I thought maybe you could drop it off for me."

"Where?"

"Wigmore Street. You're going to Oxford Street, right? They're very close."

"Certainly. What's in it?"

"Oh, just a few things. I'll give you the address. Don't ring the bell, just knock on the door lightly and give it to the person who answers. The name is Len Smith."

"Do you want a receipt or anything?"

"No, no need, just ask for the name and only give it if the person says Len Smith."

"What if it isn't Len Smith?"

"It will be."

"But if not?"

"Bring it back. But Smith will be there. They're expecting it."

"All right." Georg couldn't resist. "You and Anna seem to be hitting it off. . . ."

"She's beautiful. Becoming more beautiful every day."

"Telling me," Georg said, and paused. "Vulnerable, too."

"What do you mean? Easy prey for a handsome Arab?"

"That's not what I meant, Ismael. I mean, after all she's been through, she's very sensitive. Sad. Damaged, actually. You know, Edith's cousin, we've been sharing a room for weeks, I feel kind of responsible. I hope she's all right, that's all."

Ismael put his hand on Georg's shoulder. "I know what you mean, Georg, I feel the same. We may have more in common than you think. A lot more. I like Anna very much. Very, very much. I don't want to hurt her."

"She wouldn't deserve that."

"I know. Trust me, I know."

"I don't trust him one inch," Edith said while Georg was dressing. "Anyway, what's in it?"

"I don't know, he didn't say. He just said 'some things.'"

"Oh, very helpful. Where is it?"

"He's still got it. Said he had to put something else in. He'll give it to me on the way out."

"Huh. There's something about that man, something fishy, I've always thought that." Edith was still lying on the bed, and leaned over to pour herself some tea.

"Anna likes him," Georg said.

"That worries me even more. No good can come of it."

"Maybe. But you must admit she's loosening up, coming back to herself, according to what you said about her, anyway."

"That's true. Not because of him, though. Well—what do I know?"

Several evenings that week Anna had tiptoed into their room after they had gone to bed, and undressed quietly, trying not to waken them. And each time Edith had whispered variations on "Did you have a nice time?" and Anna would whisper "Yes." And Georg, pretending to sleep, straining to see Anna undress in the dim room, couldn't help but think, *Lucky Arab!*

Georg was late for his interview so he rushed to the lawyer's office first and only afterward, glum at another polite brush-off, walked to Wigmore Street to deliver Ismael's package. It was a thick brown envelope which seemed to contain some papers and a thin box, possibly made of wood. It was heavier than it looked. Ismael had written the name on the package, Len Smith, but not the address, which he said Georg should remember.

Turning left from Marylebone Lane onto Wigmore Street, Georg was wondering whether he would ever get a lawyer's position. He couldn't compete for jobs with returning soldiers. Maybe there was work in a refugee aid organization? It isn't what he wanted but he was running out of time. With another mouth to feed in a few weeks they would soon need a larger place, a place of their own. Right now they could barely feed themselves. The first hadn't been born yet and already he wanted another baby. Maybe work as a full-time translator? A clerk? Not what his glowing parents had imagined when he graduated cum laude from the Law Department of Vienna University. But anything's better than making buttons. He stopped dead. What number was it? Oh no! He had clean forgotten. Twenty-three? Thirty-two? One hundred thirty-two? *Verdammtnochmal!* Just when he needed to get home quickly to meet this Herr Kellerman.

After ten irritating minutes Georg went into a pub, which was just opening, found the public phone, dropped in a coin and dialed the house phone. Albert answered, disappeared, and returned, wheezing. "He isn't in his room. I called. He isn't in the house." Georg thanked him. Damn! He only had the package because Ismael said he couldn't leave the house, and now he'd gone out. What is it with that guy? Dit's right, a shady character. Now what? What on earth was the number? He walked down the street looking at the elegant Georgian homes, few of which remained intact after the bombing. Yet even with their damaged roofs and shrapnel-pocked facades and boarded windows they were pleasant, with their lace curtains and tiny flower gardens behind spiked metal railings. But what was that number! He didn't have time. He had to be home by seven, Dit would want him there when Kellerman came. He'd been right, though. He'd been right to say all they could do was wait. Wait for some sign of life, a call, a letter, a message. And then Mr. Kellerman's postcard came. Maybe this will be the breakthrough. Maybe this would stop Edith being so angry with him. He was beginning to feel that maybe he was as useless as Edith said. She was becoming impossible. But it's the hormones. The baby. It's normal. But damn! What's the number? Maybe I am useless, can't even remember a street number.

Forty-eight. It came from nowhere, just popped back into his mind. Thank goodness. He walked halfway down the street and came to the tall house with half a dozen bells, most of them doctors. He knocked on the door, as Ismael had instructed. It opened immediately and a young woman with a floppy hat that covered half her face came out. "Oh," Georg said, "I'm looking for a man, by the name—" She interrupted: "I'm Len Smith. You have a package for me."

"Somehow I expected a man," Georg said, handing it over.

"Which way are you going now?"

"Oh, uh, there, to the tube," Georg said, pointing vaguely.

"Good-bye then," she said, and walked the other way.

It was dark when Georg left the tube station. He made it home just after seven and found the lounge empty. *They don't want to be interrupted. They're upstairs in the room.* He took the steps two at a time. Edith and Mr. Kellerman, a bony, forty-something man in a faded suit, with thinning brown hair slicked backward, were sitting on the sofa with Anna leaning forward from the hard kitchen chair. Edith looked up, her eyes intense, her face drawn.

"Mr. Kellerman just arrived," Edith said immediately. "He spent two months with Papi after Auschwitz, after Anna saw him." Georg felt his heart go hollow. *So Papi did survive the war. But Edith doesn't look good. What else is there?*

Mr. Kellerman stood up to shake hands, smiling thinly. *This is not the face of a man with good news.*

"Please, don't let me interrupt," Georg said, taking off his coat and sitting on the bed. "Continue, please." The ceiling light kept dimming. He thought, *time to change the bulb.*

"May I have a glass of water?" Mr. Kellerman asked.

Anna jumped up and fetched it.

"Thank you. Forgive me, this is very hard for me. Your father was . . . is . . . a fine, noble man. He spoke so much about Edith. Georg, I was just telling Edith and Anna, we traveled together for two months and nursed each other, we were both unwell, and swore to stay together till we reached Vienna, but then we lost each other, somewhere in Poland. Max spoke all the time about Edith, about her growing up, as a baby, hoping she was safe in London. And then at the Cosmo somebody mentioned Edith from Hietzing, and I said, can this be? Could this be Max Epstein's Edith? And the woman said yes, the same, but nobody knows where he is. And the Austrian Center gave me your address. I know so much about you," he said, taking Edith's hand, "and here you are, about to have a baby." Tears welled in his eyes, he couldn't continue, he put his hand to his chest and gripped it as if to massage his heart. He breathed heavily and drank some water, and waited for his emotions to subside. "Forgive me," he kept saying, "forgive me." They stared at him, impatient.

He took a deep breath and blew it out loudly. "You see, when the Russians came and freed us, and after we recovered a bit, we set off to go home. We had survived an unimaginable hell and now that we were free, we thought that everybody outside must be waiting to help us. How naïve. It wasn't like that. Not at all. Everyone had their own problems. What were we to them? Our troubles just changed.

"I met your father for the first time on the rail track outside Kato-wice. We had both got rides on different carriages of a local freight train and when it stopped we found ourselves in the same empty waiting room. We slept there together. It was freezing but at least it stopped the wind. Of course, Max was a good deal older than me. He had a coat and good shoes but otherwise was in rags, and so was I. He wasn't well, I'm sorry to say. He was recovering from scarlet fever. He'd had rheumatic fever and symptoms of meningitis. He had terrible headaches and felt nauseous. We didn't have any food or money. When I found some stale bread he chewed a chunk and vomited almost immediately. But he never complained. Not once. All he wanted was to go home. *Nu,* what else did anybody want?

"The track we were on was off the main line by a good thirty miles. It ended inside a big coal mine. We couldn't stay where we were, we didn't have anything to eat or drink and when we asked for help the locals slammed their doors on us. So we had to walk. It was bitter cold, there was sleet and rain and the track was heavy with mud. We helped each other along but we were wet and freezing and it was dark again. To survive the fires of Auschwitz and freeze to death in freedom? We thought that was to be our fate. Then we saw a tiny glow in the darkness. It was like the star of Bethlehem, our guiding light. We reached it, and knocked. When the man opened the door, a young man with a bald head, I couldn't talk. Nor could Max. We could hardly stand. We just stood there with our teeth chattering, our bodies shaking. But he wasn't a young Pole. He was an angel. Two days we spent in his home, him and his mother, they had a wood stove, and fresh eggs. Max slept most of the time.

"Your father told me how he and Anna were saved by the man whose life Max saved on the train in the Great War. How extraordinary. But you know, everybody who survived has an extraordinary story. Otherwise he'd be dead. When we were stronger the man drove us to Kielce, to an assembly camp where refugees waited together for transport to the west. And there another incredible thing happened.

"Of course, wherever Max went he offered to help and even though he wasn't well himself he worked in the clinic. We were there for about two weeks. Everybody came for help, refugees, Russian soldiers, German prisoners, the locals, every nationality you can name, everybody was desperate, trying to stay alive, trying to go home, it was so crowded. Everybody was weak from hunger and if ever they found some scraps of food, what do you think, they got food poisoning. Now, in a Grimm's fairy tale you wouldn't believe this coincidence, but it's true, I swear. One morning Russian soldiers brought some German prisoners for treatment, and then came a man, all by himself, he said he was Swiss, a Swiss-German, that he had been a diplomat. He wanted to see the doctor, he needed urgent treatment for a wound he had suffered on his thigh, he said a stray bullet had hit him and the wound was turning gangrenous. Now, because he said he was a Swiss diplomat and spoke a few words of Russian the Russian soldiers let him go before their German prisoners. And when the diplomat reached your father, they both froze. Because the man, the Swiss diplomat, had a deep hollow scar on his throat. It was the man who had saved Max's life. He was an SS Hauptsturmführer, hiding, pretending to be Swiss."

Anna's hand flew to her mouth, which hung open. She had hoped he was dead. Could nothing kill him?

"He must have been a very evil man," Kellerman was saying. "But Max owed him his life. On the other hand, he had saved his life once already, so they were even. What to do? The Russian soldiers stood behind the Nazi. One word and he would be finished. Regular soldiers were treated quite well as prisoners of war. But SS? I saw survivors from Auschwitz recognize an SS guard and tear him to pieces, like a pack of dogs with a fox. Max? He treated this man, dressed his wound and gave him some medicines, I don't know what, and the man left. Europe is full of them, Nazis running and hiding. They should rot in hell, and they will.

"In Kielce we were told that there was another camp eighty miles north, closer to Warsaw, just for Austrian and German survivors, and that if we went there we could be sure that when the time came we would all be taken home together. But we had bad luck—that's a surprise? Our train was stopped in the middle of the night and taken over by Russian soldiers returning from the front. Their own train had broken down and they took ours. Rather than be abandoned again on the rail tracks and die of cold we stayed on the train with them. We thought we would meet another train in a city along the way. They had hardly any food, but at every stop locals gave them bread and vodka. There was no sleep to be had on this train. It was freezing cold, some of the carriages had no roof, and of course we were in one of these, we were hungry and thirsty, the soldiers were drunk and singing, and all day and night we hugged each other on our corner of the bench, trying to get warm and sleep. Your father was looking older by the day and he was shivering and weak. Close to the Belarus border we finally left the train. Anything was better than going into the Soviet Union; with our luck we'd end up in a gulag.

"So now we found ourselves not only freezing, hungry, sick, and penniless but much farther from home than in the beginning. Again we started to walk, looking for the nearest village. In this part of Poland we were lucky, people gave us food and shelter, sometimes a lift in a horse and cart, and finally we got a train back to Kielce. A month of terrible hardship and we were back in the assembly camp where we started. Of course, in this time Max and I became more than friends, more than brothers, we were hanging on to life only thanks to each other. We were past talking. I am sorry to say that I did not think Max would live long. His cheeks were sunken, his skin damp and grey like chalk, his eyes so hollow you couldn't see his pupils in the shadow, his neck was like a chicken and an old one at that—I am sorry to describe your father like this but that's how it was. By now his shoes were like mine, torn and flapping, and we stuffed them with whatever there was, paper, twigs, leaves, anything to give them some shape, and we tied it all onto our feet with any string and rags we could find. I am so sorry to tell you, but for two days I even carried him on my back and as you can see I am no Max Baer myself. He weighed less than a sack of earth and believe me I know, I carried them for months in Auschwitz myself, don't be fooled if I look weak, fifty pounds and a hundred pounds, and he was less than a hundred pounder.

"Then the Russians came, they were nervous. The Germans were fighting back on another front and they needed defences so one day soldiers came to the camp and took hundreds of us in trucks, another awful journey, packed together like worms in a can, for a week they made us dig trenches for them, fill sacks, even your father, I saw him fading. It was a shame, a scandal, but the Russians, these peasants, they had no mercy.

"But Max, it was strange. People dropped all the time, they survived the camps and then they died of weakness, cold, hunger, disease. But your father? He was the oldest survivor I ever saw. Yet however sick he looked, however weak, whatever he had to do, he did it. Slowly, painfully, but he did it. I know why, too. Because of you, Edith. Because of you. You gave him strength, the idea of you, alive somewhere, waiting for him, he would say, Edith is waiting for me and he said, maybe I have a grandchild, I want to see him before I die. That's what he said. And look, soon he will have a grandchild. Can you believe?"

Edith's mouth was open, she was staring at Mr. Kellerman, tears streaming down her face. Anna and Georg were hardly breathing.

"It was there that I lost Max, although I found him again later, and then we were separated for good. The first time I lost him was at the Russian work camp, he became so frail that even the Russians realised he would die in their arms, so they sent him to a hospital, at least that's what they said, how would I know? One day they just came and took him, I saw him go, we kissed each other farewell, there was nothing I could do, we were all just like feathers in the wind. For all I knew they would shoot him in the forest. But by then I thought anything was better than digging the trenches in that cold, the earth was hard like rock and then when it rained it was mud till your knees and then that froze like a glacier and we still had to dig, they were so afraid of the Germans, what a godforsaken place. I thought I would die there and at least Max would go quickly.

"I didn't see Max again until the day the war ended. The eighth of May. What a day. I was back in Kielce, somehow, how the people laughed and hugged, there was such a celebration that you didn't know who was a Pole, who was a Jew or a Russian or even a German prisoner, everybody was in the streets laughing and singing and drinking, oh, how they drink, but this was a time to drink, if ever there was one. Polish partisans came in from the woods, they shot their guns in the air, not a few people were killed by mistake, I swear they killed more people on that day than they ever did in the war.

And then, another miracle, I look around and there in the crowd is Max! How we fell on each other! And he looked well! He had been in the hospital for three weeks, recovered, and he was back working in the clinic. He danced and sang along with everyone, because until then we couldn't even try to go home, there was too much fighting and the Germans could have found us, but now the road was open, we just had to find a way. Of course, it still wasn't so easy, everywhere you need permissions, passes, stamped in triplicate, but now we knew it was just a matter of time.

And then I made a big mistake, another big mistake. A train was leaving for Warsaw and Budapest, that's what everyone said, so I joined a crowd of people, I ran, really ran, to the station, and your father stayed, it was too much for him. Twenty of us made the train and guess what? After a day it picked up hundreds of Russian soldiers, turned round, and went east. Can you imagine? Just like that. Oh, these Russians. With the Germans that would never have happened. They say a train goes to Budapest, it goes to Budapest. The Russians? It means nothing. By the time we realised what was going on, how could we know, east, west, it all looks the same, we were back near the Belarus border. How we cursed. How we cried. And I never saw Max again."

Mr. Kellerman described his journey back to Warsaw, Budapest, finally to Vienna, where he found not a familiar soul, and decided to continue to London, unable to spend another instant of his life among the killers and their stooges. But by now Edith, Georg, and Anna were barely listening, each was lost in thought, sifting through what they had heard. Mr. Kellerman felt he had lost them and stopped. The room was cold but nobody noticed.

Anna sat with her legs crossed, still leaning forward, frowning, deep in her own memories. The man with the scar. He had helped her to live, but his kind of help and that kind of life, he should burn in hell. She had hoped he was dead. And Papi saved him. Where is he now, the evil bastard? And that second man, another SS pig, it was even worse with him and his friends. Sick, evil. How many times did she wish she could die? Her eyes hardened, she went blank, as she did then, blotting it out, imagined her blood flowing cold, her body hard like a marble sculpture. It wasn't really her. It was happening to someone else, far away, far away. And Papi saved his life! He should have let him rot in hell. One day he will. Now she looked at Edith. How she longed to tell her everything. But she knew she would never tell anyone anything.

Edith seemed bewildered, restless. Her mouth hung open. Georg busied himself: put a coin in the meter, switched on the second light, boiled more water, made some sandwiches. All the while thinking, *So where is Max now?* Mr. Kellerman sat in silence, looking at all three in wonder. Max had described them perfectly, even Georg, whom he knew only from Edith's letters. Max, who fought death for Edith.

Edith smiled to herself. So as she celebrated the end of the war at Buckingham Palace at the same instant Papi was celebrating the same thing in Kielce. Apart, they had been joined for a moment, like lovers across the globe looking at the moon together. Another cause for hope. She was the first to break the silence.

"If Papi was in Kielce on May eighth, and so were you, and you made it here even after that long detour, then Papi could be here, too. More easily than you. And if he isn't, why not? What would have stopped him? And somehow he knew I'm having a baby. Nothing would stop him, especially if, as you say, nothing was too much for him. So where is he? Why isn't his name on a list somewhere? What could have happened to him? There was no more fighting. In Poland they sometimes killed Jews who went home, but not in Austria. So where is he? Where is Papi?"

She took Mr. Kellerman's hand, looked at it in a kind of wonder. She was thinking, He's gone through so much and here he is, he seems all right, but who knows—like Anna. Who knows what is really happening inside. And how will Papi be? If he's alive at all. Old and sick? She didn't care. She'd nurse him, nurse the baby, share her milk, do anything, anything at all. "But what can we do to find Papi?" she asked of nobody, wondering aloud.

Georg brought the tea. What could he say? He didn't want to say that Papi could arrive any day, like Mr. Kellerman or Anna or Tomac, because there could have been another outcome. The Poles could have killed him before he left Poland, they killed lots of Jews after the war. They were hearing stories every day. He could have fallen sick again and died. Plenty did, especially the older, weaker ones. Or had a terrible accident. Who knows? If he was alive he would have been in touch by now. The war ended six months ago, in May. Auschwitz was liberated well before that, in January. He gave Edith a cup of tea and took her other hand.

Fortunately, Mr. Kellerman answered Edith.

He removed his hand, took Edith's, and looked into her eyes. "We can only wait."

That night was the first that Anna didn't come to their room. After hearing Mr. Kellerman she needed to tell her own story, or at least some of it, to relieve herself of its burden, to lighten the terrible load. At last. But not to Edith and Georg. They were too close, they would try to comfort her, give her sympathy, try to understand, but that was not what she needed. Nobody could understand who had not been to such a place, and there had never been such a place before on earth. That was why she really wanted to go to Palestine: to be somewhere safe, in silence, among people who didn't need to ask, because they knew.

I feel safe with Ismael, too, she thought. *He didn't know me before, he knows next to nothing about me now. He isn't looking and judging, waiting for me to change, to become someone they once knew. He just loves me as I am and tonight I will tell him what happened to me. As much as he can take. Some of it. Maybe.*

But Ismael didn't come home till the middle of the night. When he turned the light on and saw Anna fast asleep in his bed he snapped it off again. He knew how hard it was for Anna to sleep; he didn't want to waken her. He tiptoed to the table in the dark, found the small lamp, put it under the table and lit it. The shaded light cast a warm glow. He locked the packages inside the cupboard, read the list of names a last time, placed it on a saucer, struck a match, and burned it. He flushed the ashes down the sink, brushed his teeth and gargled, undressed down to his shorts and slid into bed, moving the covers delicately, careful not to suck in the air and expose Anna to the cold.

He snuggled into Anna's warmth, rested his head against her hair and stroked it. Every day it seemed longer and softer. Gently, he put his arm around her shoulder and as she lay on her side, breathing deeply and evenly, he reached and cupped her breast through her shirt and wriggled closer. They had kissed and cuddled on the bed but she had never been in his bed before. Now Ismael felt her heat as he pressed against her. He was panting and waited for his breath to calm. He slid his hand down and up again beneath the shirt and cupped her breast again; it was bare, and warm and full, and her nipple soft and sleepy. It hardened to his touch. For minutes he lay, eyes heavy, happy. He brought his hand down again and it hovered like a butterfly over her thigh and came down softly on her warm skin, feeling an edge of fabric. She wore soft loose panties. Gently he kissed her neck and her shoulder and she sighed and straightened her top leg. Ismael moved his hand to her inside thigh, feeling its nighttime moistness. His breathing labored as he inched his hand inside her panties and rested it on her stomach, below her navel, his fingers grazing her pubic hair, and he pressed slightly, stroking her, his fingers searching. His body tensed, ready, needy. He felt her legs tighten and her groin muscles go taut and her body rise as she turned, with a grunt, turned him too in her sleep, away from her, and now he lay on his side, legs bent, with her spooned tightly behind him, hold-ing him to her, her hand on his arm, still breathing evenly and deeply, and that is how they spent the rest of the night, Anna in a deep and peaceful sleep, Ismael wide awake.

Soon he would leave the house. He loved Anna. He didn't want to hurt her. Georg was right, she was so vulnerable, like a wounded bird. But he'd have to leave her anyway.

EIGHTEEN

London

November 19, 1945

"Would you *look* at *this!*"

It was never clear to Edith whether Albert just wanted an audience or whether he held his resident refugees complicit in every Jewish act of terror in Palestine. She let the sewing machine whir to a halt and looked up with polite attention as he came to her in the lounge, shaking out his *Daily Graphic*.

"Here it is, in black and white! I told you! 'Terrorists Target Soldiers in London Bomb Outrage.' It's the Jews, of course it is, excuse me, the bastards, listen. . . ."

> *A letter bomb exploded in the Chelsea home of Colonel John Steele yesterday morning, destroying the door, shattering windows and scattering shrapnel across the street. The colonel was not at home. His wife, Margaret, 47, miraculously escaped death when the bomb exploded prematurely. Colonel Steele serves in the Sixth Airborne Division currently*

active in Palestine, from where he returned last month. Also lightly wounded in two more separate letter bomb attacks were two enlisted men from the same division, both of whom escaped serious injuries or death when letter bombs sent to their homes failed to explode. Sergeants M. Lefcoe and L. Smith . . .

Georg looked up sharply.

. . . returned recently from Palestine on furlough. Their return to duty will be delayed pending investigations, an army spokesman said. He added that police expect a break in the case soon. It is the second letter bomb campaign in a month.

That's a coincidence, Georg thought.

Albert shook his head. "I don't know what we're doing there, I really don't. You know what? That petition to throw you lot out is dead, good riddance, too, but that Oswald Mosley and his lot, this is grist for their mill, that's what this is, grist for their mill!"

The British Union of Fascists had met nearby on Prince Arthur Road and was gaining members. The Hampstead petition had failed but had laid the groundwork for a more disturbing issue than Jews taking jobs and homes: Jews in England supporting terrorists in Palestine. It was a story line tailor-made for resurgent fascists.

"These bombs shows they're right," Albert said, "that's the trouble. It isn't just a fairy tale, it's true. Look," he said, his voice rising, tapping the paper, "the proof is in the pudding."

Edith said, "Lucky they were only slightly hurt."

Otto added, "More like a warning than trying to do real damage, no?"

"There's a head of steam building up here," Albert continued. "People don't like Mosley and his fascists but they don't like terrorists more, especially not here at home, on the doorstep, so to speak. Eric and his mates got their hands full enough as it is over there, trying to keep the peace, and this is the thanks we get. . . ." He went on but Georg was deep in thought.

Of course it's a coincidence. But strange. That woman. So rude. Why? He'd been late and rushed back to meet Mr. Kellerman, and then had been so intrigued by his story, and talked it all over later with Edith, that he hadn't given the rude woman a thought. Come to think about it, another strange thing. The bells. Why knock on the door with all those bells? Wouldn't she be waiting in her flat? Ismael had said to knock lightly. That's also strange. What, she was waiting by the door? Maybe she was, actually; she opened the door immediately. But they didn't know exactly what time he'd come. What, she was just waiting there, inside the door? Why? It didn't make any sense. But not much about Ismael did.

Later that morning Georg and Edith joined Gina and two other friends at the Cosmo. Willi Landsman and Yogi Mayer, close friends from Berlin, had been checking the lists at Bloombury House, and had both found names: Willi, his sister, and Yogi, an uncle.

"At least I know, now," Willi said, staring at his coffee. "Beckie was the last one. I had a feeling, I knew."

They didn't have to ask. All his family was now confirmed dead. Edith wiped an eye and stirred her tea.

"Sobibor," Willi said.

Georg sat with his arms folded, looking around without seeing, absently nodding. Sobibor was one of the worst camps. Not that there were any good ones.

"Onkel Rudi, he was my mother's brother," Yogi said, "I didn't know him very well. He lived in Hamburg."

They nodded.

"Now what?" Willi said.

Again they knew what he meant. They were all living the same blocked life. They couldn't go anywhere till they knew. For most people, death was an ending. For the refugees, it was a beginning. Knowing was a relief, it slammed the door on the past, it opened the door to the future, knowing allowed them to move on.

"Where will you go?" Georg asked.

"America, I hope," Willi said. "There's nothing for me here. Or in Berlin. Or anywhere, really."

"So why not stay here then, with your friends, with us?" Edith said.

"Maybe Palestine. But it's very hard there and I don't have the strength. America's easier. If I can get in."

"Did you apply for a visa?" Georg asked.

"Of course, who didn't? Two years ago. But my number won't come up for years."

"England?" Georg asked. "At least we can stay now."

"No, I don't want to stay here. It's too close. I want to go far away. Australia? A long way away. Somewhere new."

"Me too," Yogi said. "I don't have much hope anyone's alive."

"Don't say that!" Edith said. "You must have hope. What if someone's looking for you, you have to believe, you're betraying them if you don't."

"But I feel paralysed," Yogi said. "I can't do anything with myself, I'm stuck, I have to get on with my life, I'm dying here." He slumped back and lit a cigarette, offered his pack of Kensitas around. "Of course I hope my parents are alive. But inside, I just know they're not. I'm not betraying them. To be honest, I just feel empty inside, like a scooped-out apple. I keep asking why all this happened."

Gina put her coffee cup down with a bang and slid a cigarette out of the pack. "Let me know when you find out."

Ismael fell into step with Edith and Georg as they turned onto Goldhurst Terrace. "Hello, where have you been?" Edith asked.

"Nowhere special," Ismael said.

She told him about Willi and Yogi.

"Lucky you have something to look forward to," Ismael said. "How are you feeling?"

"Taking it easy," Edith said. "Avoiding stress." They all laughed.

Inside the door, Ismael asked Georg into his room again. A few minutes later, after making sure Edith, who said she had a headache, really would lie down and not work at the sewing machine, Georg knocked and entered.

"What is it?" he asked.

"Would you do me another favor?" Ismael said. "I'm sorry to ask you again but could you take another package for me? This afternoon? I know it's a lot to ask but I'm so busy lately."

Somehow Georg had known that's what Ismael wanted. And he'd been thinking. If it was all so innocent, why didn't Ismael take it himself, or just post it? And if it wasn't innocent, why bring me into it? What does he want from me? What's he up to? I can't come straight out and ask, Is this a bomb? That's crazy.

"What's in it?"

"Important papers. And a small gift. Would you take it?"

"What about Otto? Can't you ask him?"

"He'd lose it."

Georg chuckled. "Yes, he probably would." He didn't have anything else to do and anyway, he was intrigued. Who is this man,
really? He knew nothing about him; Ismael always avoided giving
real answers to anything. Edith didn't trust him, and neither did he.
Yet Ismael was so sweet with Anna, it was clear they were falling in
love and Georg didn't want to ruin things for Anna. *My imagination's running away with me.* Letter bombs indeed! Ismael was looking at him, waiting, a small smile on his lips.

"All right, I'll take it. You owe me dinner."

"Deal. Thank you. I'll cook."

This time the address was on the envelope: 12 Gower Street.

"Take the tube to Euston Square, it's a short walk from there."

"I know, it isn't far from Bloomsbury House, I'll go there afterward, I wanted to go there anyway. Who shall I give it to?"

"Same person as last time. Just knock on the door. She'll come
right out."

"No bell?"

"Don't ring the bell, just knock. And don't give it to anybody else.
All right?"

"She was quite rude, by the way, hardly said thank you. Just took
the package and walked off."

Ismael laughed. "Yes, she's not very talkative. She's pretty, though.
Did you see her face?"

"No, not really, had a big hat on."

Ismael nodded, as if in approval.

"Thank you, Georg, I appreciate it."

Edith wasn't happy about it but didn't feel well enough to argue. Her
headache had passed but now her stomach hurt and she was lying on
the bed. Georg offered to stay but she felt like sleeping anyway.

Don't be long, she had said.

Georg found the house, a medical practice with a row of brass bells and consultants' names. As instructed, he knocked softly. On cue, the door opened, and the same young woman, wearing the same floppy hat, took the envelope, muttered something, and walked away. He looked after her. Someone should teach her some manners, he thought, and set off for Bloomsbury House, a ten-minute walk away.

It was getting chilly, London's damp cold that got into the bones. He pulled up his coat collar and bunched his scarf around his neck. His trilby hat was snug and helped keep him warm. It was another grey day in London, with gathering dark clouds. He missed Vienna's clarity. It rained a lot there, too, but the colors were clearer, brighter, the sun illuminated the clouds, warmed them. Here it was just dim and dreary, raining, about to rain, or had just rained. Yet he loved London. Like Vienna, it was dense, drenched with history and pomp, which fascinated Georg, a student of trivia. But whereas in Vienna he knew where he was going, had always felt part of the place, until he was booted out, in London he felt he was a visitor, as if he was admiring someone else's property, with no clear direction of his own. He snorted. Yes, Auden's thousand doors had opened. But they led to a thousand corridors.

He strolled along Gower Street, past the classical columns of University College, England's first university to welcome all religions and races, toward Bloomsbury Square, where Virginia Woolf and friends had dominated Britain's literary and social life. Nearby was Dickens House, the writer's last home which he had rented for eighty pounds a year, and could afford thanks to the success of *The Pickwick Papers.* And the British Museum and the grand redbrick Russell Hotel on Russell Square and the barrister's courts at Lincoln's Inn.

And Covent Garden and Bow Street police station. The Bow Street Runners were London's first policemen, the precursors of Britain's police force. They were founded by Henry Fielding, the barrister and author who wrote *Tom Jones.*

But London's special place in Georg's heart was as a refuge. Nobody welcomed Jewish refugees as Britain did. Reluctant? Yes. Suspicious? Yes. Even with some hostility toward Jews? Yes. The anti-alien petition showed what some people thought of the Jews, but ultimately it had failed, was outvoted by traditional British fair play. And now the refugees can all become citizens, even if not the most popular ones. If you judge a person not by what he says but by what he does, Georg doffed his hat to London.

As the first drops of rain spotted the street he pulled his hat down and quickened his pace. And he thought again, What's in the packages? They can't be bombs. I would never harm London. But Ismael was secretive, strange, charming in a menacing way, and so tough and violent; who knew what he was up to? He was a true anti-Semite in his language, but in his deeds? Not at all. If anything, he keeps defending us. Weird. And if they are bombs, just for the sake of argument, that would make me an accessory before the fact. Ismael would know that. Why would he want to implicate me? He seems to be drawing me closer on purpose. But closer to what?

Georg chuckled as he walked through the drizzle. My imagination's going wild. I do Ismael a couple of favors and next I'm in jail. Get a grip! But that woman? She's weird, too. So rude. Hardly a thank you. And that hat. I still didn't see her face. That seemed to please Ismael. Maybe I'm not imagining things. And if I'm not, what to do?

In Bloomsbury House Georg met Willi and Yogi again. They had come to sign some papers. After two hours there, meeting other friends, all worrying about the usual—family search, job search, house search—they went for a coffee, shared a scrambled egg and tomato sandwich, two bites each, and commiserated with each other. Everybody's life was on hold, and had been for six years.

It was eight o'clock by the time Georg returned home.

"Where have you been?" Edith was in panic, her hair dishevelled. "You said you wouldn't be long. My tummy hurts, it's like a rock. I can't feel baby, she isn't moving." She was lying on the bed, flat out on her back, arms by her sides, a small pillow under her head. Her face was red, eyes swollen. Georg's heart fluttered and a nervous pang shot through his gut. He sprung forward. "What do you mean, you can't feel the baby?"

"I can't feel the baby, is what I mean, she isn't moving." Her voice quavered and he could see she'd been crying. Her shirt was open, her vest pulled up, her belly exposed. He felt it gently, pressed it. It felt like a table.

"Why is it like that?"

"I don't know!"

He rested his hands on her belly, moved them down the sides, waited, tried to feel the baby but her stomach was hard as a rock. "What's going on?"

"I don't know! I was making a salad and then when I sat down suddenly it hurt, I think I screamed, it was like cement, it's gone all hard."

"Why?"

"Stop asking silly questions! I don't know!"

"Can you sit up?"

"No, it hurts too much. I tried. Everything's hard inside."

Georg stood up, sat down, stood up.

"Since when?"

"An hour. Where have you been? I'm so scared. Oh, baby." She started to cry again.

Georg fetched a glass of water but Edith knocked it out of his hand onto the sheet as she tried to raise herself. She fell back in pain.

"I called Doctor Goldscheider. He said just to wait. Wait! Ouch!" Edith panted in pain.

"Stay still, does it hurt if you don't move?"

"Not so much. It all feels tight."

"Shouldn't you go to the hospital?"

"Doctor Goldscheider said no. He says it's just a false contraction. It'll pass by itself."

"Oh, good." Georg felt faint with relief. "Why didn't you say that straightaway? I had visions of losing the baby again."

Edith tried to roll onto her side but a spasm of pain shot through her back.

"Can I do something, get something? Would you like a cup of tea?"

"You've been in England too long."

"How about *Kamillegewurzemitzitronenwasser*?"

Edith's laugh came out as a gasp of pain.

"Let's not talk," Georg said. "If Doctor Goldscheider said it will pass, all we can do is wait." He thought, *The one thing I know how to do.*

It seemed that Edith urinated every ten minutes that night, and each time she felt her stomach for any sign of movement. There was none. Georg woke with her, worried. He padded to the toilet to empty her potty and it was full again by the morning. Still no movement.

"How long is it now without feeling anything?" Georg asked, dressing.

Edith was sitting by the gas stove, waiting for the kettle to boil. She counted on her fingers. "Thirteen hours." Even as she said it, her heart raced, she felt the blood suck from her face. It hit her: each breakfast baby tried to beat his way out early; it was a kickfest in there. And now: nothing. She gripped the counter and felt her legs sag.

Tears streamed down her cheeks. "Georg, call Doctor Gold-scheider, *sofort*. This can't be right." He stared, went white, buttoned his trousers, darted to the door and down the stairs, then reappeared, grabbed some coins from the bedside table and ran.

Edith didn't move. She closed her eyes, in terror.

"I called a taxi, get ready," Georg shouted before he reached the door. Anna appeared in Ismael's shirt.

"What's wrong? Why are you shouting?" She saw Edith, her face twisted, trying to stay calm. "What is it?"

Georg said, "Goldscheider said not to panic, it can be quite normal, but to go immediately to the hospital."

"Immediately? Why?" Anna asked. "Edith, what is it? The baby? What's wrong?"

Edith was too panicky to say anything. She looked around, wondering what to take. Georg quickly explained. Anna ran downstairs, threw her clothes on and all three left in the cab. Sprawled in the backseat, Edith's heart beat so hard she thought it would explode. But in her stomach she felt nothing. A phrase rattled round her head, beating against her skull, in time with a ferocious headache: the silence of the tomb.

Doctor Goldscheider had called ahead and Edith, frightened, catching her breath, was taken through the waiting room straight to the ward. A young doctor was there, with the same cheerful nurse. Again, she pushed Georg back.

"Hello, Mrs. Flasher," Nurse Parkinson said.

"*Flei*scher."

"Little problem? Don't worry, we have this all the time. Soon have you sorted out." But Edith could see the doctor looked worried.

"How many weeks?" he asked.

"Thirty-three."

As they closed the curtain around her bed, he asked, "Any discharge? Water broken? Backaches?" They pulled her clothes away and the doctor felt her stomach.

"No. No. Yes."

He pressed and prodded, his eyes distant, his lips pursed. Each push was agony. Edith yelped and gasped.

"Have the baby's movements slowed down?"

"They've stopped." It came with a shout. She felt sick and tears came again. She hated the cloying hospital smells of disinfectant and gauze and the two-tone walls and the up-close faces.

"There, there, dear," Nurse Parkinson said. "It's all right, it really is. Lots of people have this."

Edith groaned as the doctor pushed. He clamped a fetal stethoscope to his ears and placed the steel chest piece on her belly. She flinched at the cold touch. He listened, moved the chest piece, traveling up and around, nodding his head. Edith couldn't bear it.

"Can you hear anything?"

The doctor was concentrating too hard to hear her.

The nurse squeezed her hand and smiled in encouragement.

"Can you?"

The doctor's eyes were creased in concentration and his lips pressed tight together. Edith felt she could scream, and did.

"Can you hear it?"

The doctor looked startled, nodded, and took the stethoscope from his ears.

"A very strong heartbeat. But also very irregular. That's what I was listening for. But yes, you have nothing to worry about, there is a very strong heartbeat and your baby is well. No movement happens, for many reasons. So don't worry, you'll be feeling him again very soon."

Edith felt every muscle relax, and that very passing of tension softened her stomach.

"The baby appears to be halfway between transverse and cephalic, so we need to monitor that, but that doesn't have to be a problem at all."

"What does that mean?"

"It means that your baby's position is about midway between lying horizontally across your stomach and the head down position, which is what we need for birth. It seems it's in no hurry to come out but is getting ready in its own good time. A baby with a mind of its own, it seems," he said with a smile.

"Just like his mother," Georg said when Edith told him.

"I was so scared," Anna said, resting her head on Edith's shoulder in the taxi home.

"Apparently it was just a prolonged contraction. Like the abdomen practicing for the real thing. It's rare to last so long but it happens," Edith explained.

"I thought I'd die," Georg said. "If we lost the baby now, I'd die."

"They want to see me again one more time before delivery," Edith said, "to make sure baby's in the birth position. And my blood pressure's still a bit high, too. Otherwise everything's fine."

"You must rest, too," Georg said. "No excitement, no stress, we have to keep you as quiet as possible." He stroked her hand and felt the heat of tears rising. He had imagined the worst, always did. He wiped away a tear, hoping no one noticed.

"You baby," Edith said, squeezing his hand. "I'm fine now."

November 23

A rare bright sun in a clear blue sky. It stood in the south, a beacon of something good, warming the lounge. Four days had passed since Edith's scare. She wanted the window open, Ismael wanted it closed, so it was half open, the lace curtains fluttering in the unusually warm breeze, hard light beams playing on the floor and walls. The air made the gas fire sputter on the stove. Georg was silent, glancing occasionally at Ismael. He didn't know what to do. There had been more bombs.

"Why don't you start your own business?" Otto was saying. "You'll never get a job with that accent, even with your noble name, George Fletcher."

He looked up when he heard the name. "What? Yes, I will."

"Not a real one. Not as a lawyer."

"Don't be so sure. Fletcher is an old Scottish name. I checked. From the MacGregor clan. It means arrow maker. From the French for arrow, *fleche*. If I change my name to Fletcher I can get a tie or a kilt in the MacGregor tartan. Then I'll get a job anywhere."

"Yes, on the Isle of Skye."

"Where's that?" Ismael asked. "Anyway, what does Fleischer mean?"

"Butcher."

"So why not call yourself Butcher? Then instead of Flyshit they can call you Butch."

"Do I look butch?"

"You don't scare me, that's for sure," Ismael said. "You wouldn't scare a fly."

"Why would I want to? They're sentient creatures." He couldn't help it. He laughed to himself. He'd been looking for an opportunity to use that phrase.

"Stop it, you two," Edith said, sorting through her stockings, making two piles, ladders and holes. "You heard Eric Barnes is coming home?"

"Who, the landlord's son?" said Ismael sharply. "The one in Palestine? The soldier?"

"Yes."

"When?"

"In a day or two."

"Really. Staying here?" Ismael said. His intense dark eyes met Georg's and held them.

"Wonder why. And how long for."

As if on cue Albert came in with his newspaper and sat heavily on the sofa. He'd brought his own cup of tea which he had brewed downstairs. It was the sign that something was on his mind and he meant to stay awhile.

"Good morning, Mr. Barnes."

Mr. Barnes took a deep breath and let it out slowly, shaking his head. Clearly Mr. Barnes was about to pronounce. In black and white. There was only one question: Would he shout while standing or sitting?

But he did neither. He seemed under the weather. "It's all here in black and white, you know. As clear as water. It's going to get worse in London. More bloody letter bombs. We got lucky this time. But who knows next time?"

Ismael stared at Albert. Opposite him, at the table, Georg looked up, too. The news had spread the night before from the wireless. Strangest was one early news report that was dropped from later

BBC bulletins and wasn't in the morning papers, either. Georg had already looked. The former foreign secretary, Mr. Anthony Eden, had walked around with a letter bomb in his briefcase all day and never opened it. How lucky was that? Another, addressed to a brigadier in army intelligence, exploded prematurely in a post office, injuring two postal workers. A third, addressed to Foreign Secretary Ernest Bevin, was intercepted by Scotland Yard.

Ismael frowned thoughtfully at Albert, rubbing his chin. Albert suddenly smiled. "Did Sally tell you? My lad Eric's coming in a day or two," he said, changing his mood. "Bit of R 'n' R, and going to get a medal, too. Bravery. Quick-thinking lad, always was."

"That's wonderful," Edith said, stretching a stocking over the wooden mushroom, sewing a hole by hand. "I hope he stays here nice and safe for a long time. How long will he be here?"

"Dunno yet. If the missus had her way he wouldn't go back. Get a nice cushy job in Whitehall."

"It's just as dangerous here, with all these bombs," Otto said.

Georg was putting two and two together and getting thirty-seven. Two letters. He'd delivered two letters. Followed by letter bombs. Does that mean they were the same letters? Of course not. Did that make Ismael a terrorist? Just because he's a strange one? Of course not. Anyway, why would an Egyptian Arab blow up the British? They're on the same side. It didn't seem possible that he shared a roof with a terrorist. But a terrorist had to live somewhere. And that look when our eyes met. When Ismael heard Sergeant Barnes was coming home. The one who had killed a Jewish terrorist. It was the look of a hunter. Or was it? What do I know about a hunter's look? Could something happen here in the house? What about Edith? A shiver ran through him. What to do? Why not just ask Ismael, confront him? What good would that do? He'd just deny it. And then he'd know I'm suspicious. Maybe I'll be in danger. Go to the police? Tell them. Tell them what? I delivered a couple of suspicious packages? That could make me an accomplice, even if they believed me, which they wouldn't. Edith. She'd know what to do. She'd accuse Ismael on the spot, regardless of consequences. But that's the last thing I want. Baby comes first. No stress. No hypertension. We've already had one scare. No. Best thing. Stay out of it. First, I may be imagining the whole thing. Second, all I care about is Edith and the baby. If anything went wrong. It doesn't bear thinking about. Baby is my first responsibility. Do not, do not mention anything to Edith.

NINETEEN

London

November 26, 1945

The Barnes put on quite a spread and all the neighbors came. There were cheese straws and biscuits and cheeses, with Worcestershire sauce and ketchup. All kinds of sandwiches: watercress, liver sausage, delicatessen savory, scrambled egg and tomato, cheese and onion. There was a jar of prawns that was gobbled up and another with pickled sardines as well as cream crackers, and small scones in buttered halves and peanut butter sweets. Somehow they'd got hold of bananas and little Gerry Cotton from next door, who'd never seen a banana before, ate one with the skin on and spat it out. Everyone roared with laughter: Little Gerry ate the skin! There was port and sherry to drink and beer and homemade wine from the Abbotts on the other side who'd known Eric since he was born. And now look at him! A hero.

Even the sun was celebrating Eric's homecoming, beaming down through scattered clouds, heating the grey street, so that friends and neighbors spilled down the steps into the little front garden and sat on the low wall dividing them from number 179. "You've never seen such a proud mum," said Mrs. Cowen from over the road, and she called out, "Sally, you look lovely today." Sally acknowledged with a tipsy laugh and raised her glass. "Come on over, plenty more where this came from," and Mrs. Cowen came over to get a glass of sherry, and plenty more.

There hadn't been much to celebrate since VE day in May. VJ day, August 15 it was, wasn't the same, in London it had been pouring rain and if it hadn't coincided with the state opening of Parliament there was a good chance nobody would have turned out. By the time they'd defeated the Japs the truth had sunk in: There was no magic wand, no great victory handout, no reward for six years of hardship and danger at home, for the loss of four hundred thousand British lives at war, just the chance to roll up your sleeves and get on with it, if you can find a job at all.

The young men who'd come to welcome Eric were his old mates from the street, they'd played together since they were kids, now they turned up in demob suits and caps. They counted off dead friends and thanked their lucky stars they could work, even if it was only in the building trade. They had all moved back in with their mums and dads, only for the time being of course, till they got back on their feet. Most people didn't agree, but good luck to Eric's folks, let them have those Jews upstairs, at least they can pay the rent, God knows we can't.

Edith and Georg leaned out of the lounge window, looking down on the crowded steps, smiling. Ismael and Otto, crammed together, watched from the side window, wineglasses in their hands, Otto flicking ash on the windowsill.

Eric came out from the salon, he'd been getting an earful from the vicar thanking him for doing God's work in the Holy Land. He handed round a pack of Woodbines and struck a match and managed to light five cigarettes with it. Each time he held out the match another friend pushed his head forward, like a tortoise from its shell, with a fag hanging from its mouth. He lit them all from the same match, till it burnt his finger, and he threw it to the ground.

"You're lucky," Eric said. Two of his mates were with the Desert Rats, Roger and Gordon, sergeants, they'd fought in North Africa and ended up in Berlin, not many made the whole journey in one piece. Tony had been an Air Force tech, got shrapnel in the jaw when German fighters strafed the runway, had to drink beer out of the side of his mouth which got a good laugh, he looked like a gerbil or a platypus, not that anyone knew what they looked like but it sounded right. Bob had been a driver for a succession of majors in the Black Watch, Scottish lads, always made fun of him, didn't know what a Londoner was doing driving them around, but he was the best driver, the others were all used to riding sheep, he said.

They had a merry time, standing around, drinking, swapping wars, till Willy Kentridge's mother came over and they all patted her on the back and said sorry. Her youngest, Jeremy, he was only four, had drowned last month in one of the bomb sites. They were all playing, him and his mates, hide and seek, and they couldn't find him, they thought he'd won, but it turned out he'd slipped and fallen into one of the basements full of water and couldn't swim. None of them could. Probably he'd knocked himself out or something. Drowned at number 153, three bombed houses in a row, all with flooded basements from the rain, should put up a sign, bloody dangerous. Really sorry, Mrs. Kentridge. She was wearing her dressing gown and her hair was a mess.

"Well, I just wanted to say hello to you all, that's all, wanted to thank you for what you've done for England, you heard about my little Jeremy, have you?" Even though they'd already given their condolences. She turned and walked back home, it took a long time for her to reach her house. They looked after her and swigged their drinks.

"You're lucky," Eric said. "I don't know when I'll be demobbed. I think we're up for another tour in Palestine."

"You and half the army," Bob said.

Eric was still in uniform. "I haven't had time to get changed," he said. "Mum and Dad are so over the moon they arranged this whole thing. Quite a reception. I thought I'd slip back quiet like."

"Good grub!" Roger said. "Dunno where you find the food, our windowsill can hardly feed the pigeons."

"Lucky, that's all, mate," Eric said. "Got the lodgers. Pays the bills, and then some." They looked up to see the lounge windows full of people looking out. Ismael raised a glass and they toasted him back.

"And then quite a lot, apparently," Tony said, angling a glass to pour beer into the side of his mouth, dribbling some. "They said I can get this seen to, couple of ops, right as rain."

"Sure," Eric said, "that's nothing. You'll have a new jaw in a jiffy."

"And if not you can drink through a straw instead of slobbering all over yourself," said Bob. "Just joking. They'll sort that out, not a problem. You should see some of the blokes in our squad. Anyway Eric, so what happened, word is you saved an officer? What for? Shoulda let the bugger get topped."

"Now you're even sounding like the Black Watch."

"Yeh dinna wat?" They all laughed and clashed glasses and toasted Sally as she smiled at them from across the street.

Mister Rogers had been drilling Sally again about throwing the refugees out and giving the soldiers a place to live, but she'd told him where to get off. Who's he to tell me what to do? Anyway, she felt sorry for them, what right-thinking person wouldn't?

Later that evening, Sally grinned as she led her son into the lounge to meet the lodgers, who waited with cups of tea and biscuits. She hadn't noticed before but they all looked much of a muchness, a bit taller or squatter but they all, sort of, looked the sameish. Dark hair, darkish skin, certainly not white or even pale, and sort of, strong, how do you say, dominant, features. Ismael's a bit different, built like a brick shithouse actually, but then he isn't really one of them, different, he's an Arab. They're not like Eric, that's what makes me notice. Sally smiled with pride. Eric's so tall, carries himself well, light brown hair gone blond in the sun, tanned, fit, buffed up. A soldier.

"Well, everybody," she beamed, chest out, taking up the room, "this is our Eric, our one and only, who I may have mentioned once or twice, that's him on the mantelpiece. Back on leave from Palestine, aren't you, sweetheart."

Eric stepped forward with a smile and everyone stood and shook his hand. Albert came in with a tray of cakes, laid it on the table, left and reappeared immediately with a bag of bottles. "To Eric," Albert toasted, and the lodgers said, "To Eric. Welcome home."

"Not for long enough, unfortunately," he said.

"How long have you got, dear?" Sally said.

"I'll find out soon. It's possible I'll get reassigned, but unlikely. Probably back there in a couple of weeks."

They chatted, about life in Palestine for the soldiers and the beach and the desert and the Jews and the Arabs, and the difficulty of playing piggy in the middle, until it was Anna, Anna who wanted nothing more than to go to Palestine, who couldn't resist: "Why not let the Jews into Palestine? Why stop us?"

"Oh, that's above my rank, miss," Eric said.

"You just do what you're told?" Anna said.

Edith interrupted: "Come on Anna, Eric is a soldier, he has his duty."

"He can think, can't he?"

"Don't be rude," Edith said in German.

"Forgive me, I don't mean to be rude, I may sound more blunt than I mean to be because my English is not so good. What I mean is, why not just let Jews go there if they want to go?"

"As I said, ma'am, I'm a soldier, I do what I'm told. But if you ask me, and I hope I'm not being rude, either, if you ask me, there's enough Jews there already. The locals don't want more. It's just making more trouble. I think the word is that those who are there can stay, a few more will be allowed in, and the rest will have to go somewhere else. It isn't me as makes the rules. But that's how I understand it."

"But there's nowhere else to go."

"Yes there is. For a start you can stay in England now. And you can go to other places. And you can go home—the war's over, why not go home?"

It was familiar territory: Palestine, America, stay in Britain, go somewhere else, go home, what home? Georg tried to change the subject and asked how Eric found his home, after so many years at war. Sally interrupted. "Tell them, Eric, what happened, go on, tell them, he's a hero, you know. Going to get a medal."

"Oh, Mum," Eric said, like any bashful kid. But she insisted he tell the story.

During a search a terrorist had been caught. Stood there, looked suspicious from the start. When he was told to go and sit down he wouldn't turn round, he backed away.

"I knew right away he had a gun in the back of his trousers. I just knew it. I was already aiming right at his heart when he turned and grabbed it. I stitched him up. Didn't have a choice. It was him or me, or rather, the SB officer who'd stopped him. Do or die it was, one of those. He shouldn't have gone for the gun. If he'd put his arms up, he'd be in the slammer now, doing time. Or maybe not. Turned out he'd just murdered another SB officer the night before. So he probably knew he was done for either way. Anyway, ma'am, as you said before, I'm just doing my duty, and my duty at that moment was to kill or be killed. Didn't feel good about it, not at all. You never do. But that's what I was there for, to protect the SB chaps, and that's what I did. I was just doing my duty. Trust me, I'd rather be here with you lot in this house, taking it easy, making lots of money, nothing to worry about and getting on with my life. Instead I'm stuck over there, keeping the peace, trying to be fair to everyone."

Everyone was speaking at the same time but Ismael's voice cut through. "Well, I think you Jews should say thank you to Hitler," he said. Georg groaned. Here we go, another provocative rant from the Arab. It just didn't add up. Ismael can't be behind the bombs. Why would an Arab, an anti-Semitic one at that, attack the English?

"No, I really do, and here's why. Why does Bevin hate the Jews so much? Because right now just about every Jew in Europe wants to go to Palestine, and he has to stop them. All Jews are needed in Palestine. But why do they want to go? Because they love the idea of living in the desert heat among Arabs who don't want them? Of course not. It's because they finally realised they don't have anywhere better or safer. What, you think the British love the Jews more than the Germans? They just hate them less. Hitler is the modern Moses."

"What rubbish . . . ," Georg began.

"Wait, I'll tell you why. Why did Moses wander the desert for forty years?"

Edith said, "Because he lost his wallet?"

Sally shrieked with laughter. "That's a good one," she said, "ain't it, Albert. Have to remember that one."

"Ha, ha," Ismael went on, "the real reason he wandered so long was in order to take Egypt out of the Jews, to give them time to lose their slave mentality, so that a generation of Jews, the slaves, would die out, and a new generation, of free men, would take their place and have greater dreams and be stronger and be able to fulfill them. And now look at Hitler. What did he do? He killed the Jews, millions of them. And what did that achieve? It took away their modern slavery, their foolish notion that they could be absorbed, assimilated, live equally among gentiles. He showed it's a myth. Hitler took that away from the Jewish mind. Tore it out. Finally they realize they have no future in someone else's world. They need their own country. Same as Moses. Thank Hitler for that!"

Sally looked at Eric as if to say, what's he talking about? Albert began, "That's all well and good . . . but you have to consider . . ."

Georg was inwardly nodding to himself. Too clever by half. He's smug. He's playing us. He's reeling us in. Me, at least. Their eyes met for a moment and Ismael held his gaze. He didn't wink but he may as well have. And then, very suddenly, Georg understood. A hint of a smile began to play on his lips. I get it. Why didn't I realize earlier? The cunning bastard.

That evening Georg left Anna massaging Edith's feet on the bed, after another hospital checkup: blood pressure still high, not better, but not worse. As long as there was no sudden change there was no cause for alarm, the doctor had reassured her. Baby hadn't moved position but that didn't have to mean much, there was still plenty of time, they often don't assume the full birth position until the very last moment. When Edith asked, What happens if she doesn't, his response hadn't helped: "We'll panic when the time comes."

Georg went downstairs and knocked on Ismael's door. The room was clean, tidy, barren. Ismael said, "I was expecting you."

"No packages?"

"No packages."

"No letters?"

"No."

"Why not?"

"Since you ask, bigger fish to fry."

"I see. Or rather, I don't. What do you mean by that?" Georg sat on the sofa by the window, the room's only furniture beside the bed, table, and two chairs. There was no ornament, no picture, no spare clothing. Ismael could have moved in yesterday, and could move out tomorrow.

"What fish?"

Silence.

"Who are you, Ismael?"

"Who are you, Georg?"

"Don't be silly. I'm Georg Fleischer and I am who I say I am, but who are you? Who is Ismael—I don't even know your family name."

Ismael looked at Georg, looked past him, turned to face the window. "We are all here for a reason, right?" he said, as if he'd been preparing for this conversation. "What is your reason to be here, Georg?"

"That's easy. I am waiting to have a baby. And I want to get on with the rest of my life. That's why I am here. Why are you here?"

"One moment. But why are you waiting here? Why not somewhere else?"

"You know why, I can't go anywhere else. But don't change the subject. I asked you first—who are you, Ismael?"

"You should be in Palestine, where your people need you."

Georg stared at Ismael, nodding thoughtfully. A calmness enveloped him, as if he'd reached a destination. "I knew it. You aren't an Arab, are you?"

"Oh, yes, I am. I am an Arab, from Cairo."

"An Arab Jew."

"Congratulations. Yes, I am an Arab Jew."

"What is your real name, Ismael?"

"Change one letter."

"What do you mean?"

"*M*. Make it an *R*."

Georg thought, and had to smile. "Ismael. Israel?"

"Clever, no?" Israel laughed. "One letter. A little word game."

He lit a cigarette, took a deep breath, blew it toward Georg. "So, now you know."

Georg waved away the smoke, he hated cigarettes.

"This isn't funny, far from it. Why did you involve me with the letters?"

"Because, my friend, I need you. And by the way, you need me, some may consider you now an accomplice. You took not one of those letters but two, so it's good that we're on the same side. Not that it matters, but it's good that we understand each other."

"Don't be ridiculous. I had no idea what was in those letters. I was just doing you a favor."

"I'm sure the police will believe you."

"You set me up. You asked me to help."

"And you did, Georg, you did. Just like I helped you when those fascist thugs attacked you. We are on the same side. And I'm not asking you to do anything. Well, not much. Just one more small thing. But not yet."

Georg felt himself go pale, clammy. His voice sounded hollow. "What are you up to? Why are you sucking me into this?" Georg's calm was giving way to panic. *I helped deliver bombs. I'm an accomplice.* It was dawning: This maniac was threatening his entire life in England, which admittedly wasn't much. But Edith, the baby, the safe place he had found . . . Georg felt his heart racing. *What have I got myself into? Me, a lawyer. I'll go to the police. Say I didn't know anything. Just naïve. This man is a terrorist. What to do? Mustn't tell Edith, keep her relaxed.* "Who are you, though? What do you want?"

"Ah, not so fast."

Georg was calculating, as fast as he could. The damage that Israel could cause. What was he capable of? "What about Eric?"

"What about him?"

"He's a British soldier. He killed a terrorist in Palestine."

"Freedom fighter. Yes, he did."

"You wouldn't?"

"Here? You think I want an Agatha Christie whodunit in my own house? No, trust me, I don't need that."

"And Anna. I think she loves you."

Israel turned to the window, lit another cigarette, went to the bed, lay on it, his feet hanging over the side.

Georg said, "You could really hurt her. She's so vulnerable. And she's getting better. Every day she looks more beautiful and she seems to be opening up a bit. Edith says it's because of you."

Israel tapped the ash onto a saucer. "Not everything works out the way you plan it."

"You're telling me."

"Sometimes it turns out better. Sometimes it doesn't. I didn't plan on Anna."

"I'm sure Anna didn't plan any of the things that happened to her. So the question is what happens next. To you and Anna?"

Israel's cigarette, glowing and diminishing.

"I suppose that's between me and Anna."

Georg looked at him: Ismael's lips pursed, sucking smoke deep, exhaling toward him through the nose. Callous bastard. After a long silence Georg got up to leave and for want of anything else to say, said, "Don't count on me." But even as he shut the door, he knew he couldn't go to the police. He felt his body tremble as he climbed the stairs. At best they'd throw him and Edith out of the country, just as the baby was born. More likely, he'd spend years in jail. He was trapped.

"Good night," Anna whispered, as Edith and Georg held each other and their breathing slowed and became more even. She looked at them, their heads touching, and felt at peace. Her shadow followed her as she slipped out of bed and tiptoed downstairs to Ismael. She unlocked the door and slipped between his icy sheets. She sighed deeply, curled up, her hands tight beneath her chin, and felt her heat warm the bed, her mind drifting, as always, she couldn't stop it.

It always went to the same place, where she didn't want to go. Such bedtime warmth saved her not once but many times, yet each time her mind went there she tried to stop it. It was a place she would not go. She refused all evil. Sometimes she lay for hours, forcing only happy memories, as she did in the camps, digging deep into her childhood, taking her to another time and place, to ward off what was being done to her. The nursery at home. Nanny cooing. Mummy singing. Daddy playing with her fingers and toes, one little piggy went to market, one little piggy stayed at home, one little piggy had roast beef, one little piggy had none, one little piggy was a good little piggy and he ran all the way home. . . . Everyone talking and laughing around the table and light flashing off the silver cutlery and crystal bowls with fresh flowers in the middle and raising glasses and saying "Prosit!" Holidays in the Tyrolean Mountains and the Salzkammergut lakes, swimming, rowing, climbing the trails. Sunshine. Going to bed late. Even just sitting in the parlor, knitting, everyone together, content. Humming. Edith, in the garden. All the friends. Once life seemed like a bunch of beautiful flowers, all the good things, so abundant, so bountiful, so much to enjoy, and then the sun went in, this flower faded and that one died and this friend plucked and that one missing and slowly her life narrowed and narrowed to a few dry stems until one day, impossible to say exactly when, all was dust.

And stayed bad for so long. And whenever there was a change, it was for the worse. And worst of all was what saved her. And there she wouldn't go.

When Ismael came to bed and wrapped himself around her, she was dozing. Her voice was very quiet, from another place.

"Where have you been? What time is it?"

"I had to see someone. It's about three o'clock."

She snuggled against him and he moved against her, slipped his hand under her shirt and held her breast, warm, friendly.

"Have you been sleeping?"

"Not really. Trying."

"The usual?" He covered her neck with little kisses and sucked the nape into his mouth. It made her shiver.

"Yes. My mind is crazy, I can't stop it."

"Would you like to lie on top of me?"

"Yes."

Anna rolled on top of Ismael, kissed him gently, and rested her head on his breast and he trailed his fingers down the small of her back. She wiggled her hips to get comfortable. Stomach on stomach, everything fitted as it should, with only her shirt between them. She pulled up one leg and he held her even tighter, stroking her. She felt safe in his powerful grip. He kissed her on the lips, very long. They moved, now lying side by side, kissing. Slowly Anna's lips slackened, her breathing eased, and if there was light, and if he could see so close, Israel would have seen Anna drifting off to sleep, with a smile on her lips: back in a safe place. He didn't mind that she wouldn't make love. That, too, would come. *Inshallah*.

December 2, 1945

The number 13 bus slowed on Wellington Street as it passed Lord's cricket ground. The placards were still up from England's victory test against Australia.

"Miller scored a hundred and ten," Georg read.

"Who's Miller?" Israel asked.

"A hundred and ten what?" Georg said.

"How is Edith?"

"Big. Happy. Sad. Frustrated. Confused, like all of us."

"Come to Palestine, your problems will be solved."

"Why aren't they planning a cricket game there, too, for the soldiers? They're playing victory tests here, in India, Australia, why not Palestine?"

"Nothing to celebrate."

Georg thought, *You're telling me.*

He had decided: tell Edith nothing, go along with Israel, don't touch any more letters, do as little as possible.

They got off at the end of the line, the Strand, and immediately split up. Israel had gone over it twice at home. They should leave the bus separately and not acknowledge each other again. Georg should go to the base of Nelson's column and wander around it, like a tourist, but should watch Israel, who would walk around Trafalgar Square. When Israel turned onto Cockspur Street toward Pall Mall, all Georg had to do was watch from a hundred yards back.

"I need to know if anyone's looking out for me, following me, " Israel had said. Apart from a brown trilby worn fashionably forward and tilted, he hadn't tried to disguise himself. When Georg asked why he was doing all this Israel had said, "If I tell you, I'll have to kill you."

"Joke, right?"

"Oh, of course."

Georg stepped from the bus onto the pavement, waited for a break in the traffic, and walked over to the southeast African lion. He'd never been up close to it before, it was bronze and magnificent, huge, one of four. He examined the bronze relief at the column's base, its carving picked out neatly by the faint morning sun. It showed the death of Nelson at the Battle of Trafalgar. A life-size Nelson was being carried from the quarterdeck to the cockpit by a marine and two seamen while the battle raged. Beneath Georg read the inscription: "England expects that every man will do his duty." Looking straight up, he could only see the column and Nelson's hat. Pigeons fluttered by his head. He waved one away, looked up, squinted at the crowd. Damn, where's Israel, have I lost him already? But there he was, taking his time, hands in his coat pockets, making way for a lady carry-

list, it do
turned u
westward
list. But i
maybe Pa
transferre

"Yes, i
"So wl
Georg
"This
What else
he didn't
called hir
crossed o

Now Otto
"Move," h
ding an ap
never gue
"What
crowded,
calling "o
with a tra
"Anotl
"I thou
said.
"The p
it." Otto p
footprint.
Georg

ing some bags. Georg looked to see if anyone was following him. How would he know, anyway? There were lots of men walking the same way. Women, too. *And why am I doing this?* He walked slowly around the statue, as if examining the lion at each corner, instead checking behind Israel. Dozens of people could be following him. Israel had said: Look for one person who follows me around the square, and then takes a left onto Cockspur Street after me. Nobody would do that. If they wanted to go down that street they would have gone straight there. So pay attention when I take the left, see if anyone does the same, and follow from a hundred yards. If the same person follows me right into St. James Square, halfway down Pall Mall, stop following, turn round, and go home. You can tell me later.

Israel wouldn't say why. And Georg couldn't say no. Not yet, anyway. He'd have to go along with Israel until he could find a way out. Still, all this stuff about Palestine being the last refuge for Jews was nonsense. Many wanted to go there, fine, but all these scare stories about throwing the Jews out of England, that was just a crazy minority. Noisy, nasty, but fascists, and they'd just lost the war, in Germany, Italy, and earlier in Spain. Nothing to fear from them anymore. Britain won. *Ve von!* He smiled at Edith's accent, and trailed his hand across the smooth cold flank of another bronze lion as he watched Israel progress around the square, waiting now at a zebra crossing.

What about Anna? Obviously she was in love, but did she know who with? She still thought Israel was Ismael, an Egyptian Arab. Israel had persuaded Georg to stay out of it. He hadn't even told Edith, didn't want to worry her. And now he was getting sucked in deeper. But deeper into what? Israel wouldn't say. No more packages. Just that phrase: Bigger fish to fry. *What is he up to? And what does he really want from me? This is the last favor I'm doing him. I won't be blackmailed. I'll just say no. What can he do?*

Is
the tı
at Bu
conti
into (
yards
typic:
the r
Surel
Stree
mark
The o
side c
must

Jo
on th

Gina
sweat
"I
Ge
"A
foldec
He fir
his th
"G
"I
"P
"Y
with l

hole in the middle and a rip, as if it had been torn from someone's hand. It had a symbol in the upper left hand corner: "43" inside a Star of David. He made out one paragraph:

> *Public sympathy, aggravated by the happenings in Palestine, turns against the Jew. Anti-Jewish signs appear in the streets, on our shop windows, our houses and Synagogues. Windows of Jewish properties have been broken; our sacred places of worship have been desecrated. The Fascists openly, unchecked, state "Clear out the Jews"—this is happening in England TO-DAY.*

Gina interrupted, "So what? Someone scrawled PJ by the bus stop, Perish Judea. Who cares what they say?"

"Remember that big bald soldier at Hampstead Heath?" Otto continued. "Who attacked the speaker's platform? About a month ago? He was there, today. I recognized him. It was the same thing again. There were a whole bunch of them. English Jews."

"I know, I heard of them," Georg said, looking at the ragged leaflet. Jewish ex-servicemen were organising. They called themselves the 43 Group because forty-three had turned up for a meeting at the Maccabi building in Compayne Gardens, just a few streets from their boardinghouse. They'd had enough of the insults, the threats. For them it wasn't about Jewish refugees from Europe. It was about their own lives in England. Their families came over from Russia and Poland at the turn of the century, they fought in the wars, and now the fascists said throw them out. Hitler started with just a handful, too. Not again! They decided to fight back. They found themselves on the same side as the communists, against the fascists, with the police in the middle, and ordinary folk aghast at the thugs taking over their streets.

"It isn't only Kilburn, it's everywhere. I spoke to two of them, they're looking for members," Otto said. "The fascists are getting back on their feet, led by Mosley of course, and the Jews say they'll stop them talking, break up all their events. It got ugly. There was blood, the fascists were ready, they threw potatoes with razor blades sticking out. Lucky the police were there, they broke it up quickly. But it was horrible. People were running everywhere."

"What were you doing there?" Edith asked.

"I was shopping. My shopping bag split and the bastards trod on my tomatoes." They all laughed.

"It's not funny, though. It's a serious matter. That was my dinner."

Georg slapped Otto's leg. Otto leaned across and pecked Gina on the lips.

"Oh, ho," Edith said, "what have we here? Getting serious?"

"Not as serious as you, my dear," Gina said, putting her hand on Edith's belly. "How are you feeling now?"

"Very good. Apart from the backache. Headache. Leg ache, which I have all the time. Exhaustion. Heartburn. Stretch marks. Wonderful. I can't wait for it to be over."

"How long now?"

"About two weeks."

"About?"

Edith moved her lips and fingers. "Sixteen days. December eighteenth."

"Nearly a Christmas baby."

"You mean, a Chanukah baby."

"When is Chanukah?"

Edith looked round. Georg shrugged. Nobody knew.

"Fine lot of Jews we are," Georg said.

Eleven o'clock. It had been a long day, and a strange one. Georg plumped up two pillows and Edith sunk into them, lying on her back, her only vaguely comfortable position. He stretched his arm and switched off the light, kissed her cheek and said good night. She smiled and patted his arm. "How is baby?" Georg whispered. "Can you feel him?"

"Her."

He smiled. It didn't matter how many times they said the same thing.

His smile faded. He didn't want to think about him, didn't want him to intrude. But there he was. Israel: the packages, the bombs, lucky he hadn't killed anyone, or I would have gone to the police. And this strange request to follow him. What was he up to now? I wish I could tell Edith. But again he forced himself to stay quiet. This was such a special time, waiting for the baby, he didn't want to ruin it, it was hard enough already. Edith was on edge all the time; impossible to think of the baby, starting a new family, without thinking of her old one, and as if she sensed his thoughts, she murmured, "I thought about Papi. I know he's alive." Georg squeezed her arm. She said, "I dream about him, you know, I see his face. His itchy moustache. Nice dreams."

Georg felt himself nodding and turned onto his back, too. When Edith talked of her father, he didn't know what to say. She didn't talk of her mother or her sister, and he didn't talk about his family, each kept it inside. It was too much to bear, yet they did, in silence. Like everyone else. Carrying on. He felt his eyes burn. In the dark, he permitted himself a tear, it felt warm, brimming out of his eye socket and trickling down his cheek, tickling.

Edith shifted her weight and reached, feeling for his eyes, and wiped them, and kissed them.

They lay on their backs, in silence.

"Are you asleep?" Edith whispered.

"No. Thinking."

"It's going to be very strange."

"What?"

"Having a baby. I wonder sometimes. How it will be. Sometimes I'm almost in panic. I feel my heart beat, and then I realise, it isn't mine, it's someone else's. This little person inside me."

Georg laid his hand on her belly. It was firm, quiet, sleeping, rising and falling with her breath.

"I mean, this little thing is totally dependent on me. Everywhere I go, she comes, everything I eat, she eats, everything I hear, she hears. What will she be like? Crying? Calm?" She swallowed, and now her voice was anxious. "And sometimes, I think, what kind of life can we give her? Who will give her birthday presents? Who else will care if she's sick? I had so many people around me, when I grew up. Mutti, Papi, Lisa, nanny, aunties, uncles, cousins . . ."

"Don't," Georg said.

"I think, she won't have anyone, just us. It will be so lonely. And other children will make fun of her, because she's Jewish. And we haven't got any money, we can't always live in this room. Sometimes I'm frightened, Georg. What will happen? And what if there's something wrong with her, when she's born, you never know—"

"Stop it, Dit, stop it, now."

"I'm sorry, I'm sorry." And then, "Can you get me some water?"

Georg felt his way to the sink, filled a glass, and held it to Edith's lips. She put her hands over his, drained the glass, and sighed back into the pillows. "Thank you."

Georg got back into bed. As Edith tried to turn toward him she gasped in pain, that ache in the right leg again, it shot up to the groin. Why was it all so hard?

And then she caught herself—hard? Hard? *I'm alive, I'm having a beautiful baby with the man I love, I have friends, I am safe, I am warm, I am able to mend stockings. Why, I even have extra cod liver oil.*

She lay quietly on her back, Georg's warm hand resting on her hip.

TWENTY

London

December 10, 1945

"I made love with Ismael tonight."

Anna twisted the sheet in her hands, glanced at her feet sticking up under the blanket, smiled down at Edith. Who struggled to a sitting position. "What!"

"I'm trying to sleep," Georg whined.

"The first time."

"The first time, what?" Georg said, yawning. "What time is it?"

"One o'clock. Made love. With Ismael tonight, for the first time."

Now she had Georg's attention, all right. He sat up with a start. "Why? I mean—what did you say?"

Anna played with her hair, curled the locks below her ear. "I wanted to for a long time, but I couldn't. Suddenly, I could. So I did."

Edith knew she should be pleased. "Do you love him?"

"I think so."

But Edith wasn't pleased. She was thinking, I don't trust that anti-Semite. He doesn't deserve her. Yet he was helping Anna, that was sure. Slowly she was coming out from that silent, frozen, stuck place she had been in when she first arrived. When was it? More than two months ago. True, she still hadn't said a word about what she really went through in Auschwitz, but . . .

"I'm telling you this because, in Auschwitz, some things happened to me . . ."

Georg shivered. *I don't want to know.*

"And not only there . . . that I thought, I would never get over. And I won't. But I thought, I could never love a man, I hated them all. And, especially, I hated myself. And now I have something good . . ." Tears came to her eyes. "And I like Ismael very much. At first I couldn't bear to have him touch me. Now I want him to." She began to cry. "I'm sorry, to tell you this."

She had cried with Ismael, too, cried her heart out, while he held her, and kissed her, and made love to her. She had held him as if she would never let go, she hung on as if to a life raft, at the end he had to pry her arms from his body. He didn't ask.

"You must, you must," Edith said gently, taking Anna's hand into her lap.

"I've been so alone. I've tried to be strong. I, I've lost everyone . . ." Now her body shook, as she sobbed freely. Georg sat up and reached over Edith and put a hand on Anna's shoulder. She was wearing his shirt. "I thought I couldn't carry on. I didn't know what to do. Oh, it's so horrible. I wanted to kill myself. I've been so lonely. You've both been so good to me, so kind, I love you both. And you're having a baby, and you're so afraid for Papi, and then I come along, with all my troubles, I'm so sorry." She wiped her face, it was wet, she dried her hands on the sheet. A sigh shook her body.

"Anna," Georg said, "please, don't think we mind."

"We love you, too," Edith said. "Don't forget, we don't have anyone else, either, only you." Now Edith's tears came. And Anna cried again. Georg held them both, thinking: What to do? He's an evil man.

"Can I sleep here tonight?" Anna asked, blowing her nose.

"Of course," Edith said. "But don't you want to sleep with Ismael?"

"He had to go out."

"What, at this time?"

"Yes. He often does. He comes and goes at all hours. Georg, he said he'd like to see you in the morning, will you be here?"

Now what?

"I may be busy."

Israel paced the room, his hands flat together at his mouth, like a Christian at prayer. He was thinking, and he wasn't in the mood for Georg's questions. Things were coming to a head.

The Foreign Ministers were meeting, the venue scheduled, the time fixed. He was under pressure from Palestine to get it done. Two more agents had come out of the woodwork. He hadn't realised how many Miki had in London, and that was good; keep it tight, everyone in their box. They met on street corners once during the day, once at night, in different places. They talked, split up, met on another street corner a few minutes later, and so on, arranging it as they went, never more than ten minutes in one place, kept moving. Everything face-to-face, no more letter drops, coded messages, brief calls to public phones. They didn't know one another's real names, where they lived, anything.

Only that one of the others was a plant in one of the fascist groups. He didn't say which and Israel didn't need to know. He'd make sure two fascist thugs were in the area when it went down; they'd get picked up, divert attention.

The shooter was in town. Done it before, cool as ice. Was already checking out the area and the building. One of the other agents would bring two weapons for him to choose from; both regular army issue with serial numbers filed off. Untraceable. Wear gloves. He'd do it and drop the gun on the spot.

The taxi driver, a hundred percent to be trusted. He'll drive by with an orange balloon—nice touch, Christmas after all, can't miss it, pick him up, when he's in the cab, pop it, gone, lost in the traffic.

This would have nothing to do with the letter bombs. Different people entirely. May need them again. But everyone involved with the hit would have to leave immediately. Back home. Disappear.

He had it all figured out. Total speed and surprise. Nothing could go wrong. Like hell. That's what they thought in Cairo last year when they did Lord Moyne. Tried to escape on bicycles and got caught. Dopes. Both shooters caught and killed.

He needed just one more person. Someone totally uninvolved. Just in case. To watch and report. Just to be on the other side of the street, a hundred yards away, walking slowly. If it all went to shit, to tell him what happened. Because he wouldn't be there himself. Miki's orders. Too valuable.

"It's a simple thing I'm asking you," Israel said, pointing. "You can't say no."

"Oh, yes, I can."

"Trust me, you can't. Listen, you do me a favor, I do you one. We have people all over Europe, everywhere. And guess what? That lawyer you found in Vienna isn't going to do anything. All he can do is wait, and that's what you're doing here. I've already asked my people to look for Edith's father, I did it for Anna and Edith. I haven't even told them about it, I'd rather get results first. Now I'm asking you for this one last thing. I promise, I'll never ask you for anything else. But I need you to do this. It isn't much."

"Look, I don't know who you really are or what you're mixed up in, but I'm a lawyer, I'm about to be a father, I don't want anything to do with any of this. Anyway, this is all wrong. This is England. They saved us. What are you planning now, anyway?"

"You *were* a lawyer. And it doesn't matter. All that matters is that you do this."

"I can't. No. I won't. I don't want to be involved."

"Georg. You *are* involved. You carried the letters. You know what they were. You're part of the team."

"Are you mad? I had no idea what they were."

"Tell that to Special Branch. When they hear your name, if worse comes to worst."

"You *are* mad." *This maniac can ruin my whole life in England.*

"There are bigger things going on here than you and me and whether I'm mad. How can I put this politely? You're fucked."

Georg went to the door, and stopped. His heart was thumping, he was almost gulping for air. He felt himself going white. How had he gotten into this?

"And as for Max Epstein, I can call off the search."

Georg froze.

"You wouldn't."

He moved slowly back into the room, felt himself being reeled in.

"How do I even know it's true, that you have people looking for Papi. What people? You . . . evil man."

"On my mother's life, it's true. We have people in the DP camps, train stations, all the major towns, checking hospitals, synagogues, all over Europe, they all have his name. We're trying to get people to Palestine. I'm not talking about my people, I'm talking about the Jewish Agency, they're everywhere. We have friends with them, too. They have his name. They're looking for Max Epstein or someone who knows what happened to him. They're asking. Right now. I can call them off, you know. I can just tell them to stop looking, he's dead. It's up to you."

There was a knock on the door. "Georg, are you there?"

Israel looked sharply at Georg, raised his eyebrows. "Decision time."

Georg opened the door. "Morning, Edith, come in."

"That's all right. Georg, are you coming? Gina's waiting."

Georg forced a smile. "I'll be right down."

"All right. Come on, though, I'll be in the lounge with Anna." She waved at Israel, took a deep breath and set off down the stairs, gripping the banister.

"What are you going to do, anyway?"

"Georg, it's better if I don't tell you. You don't have to do anything yourself. All you have to do is walk slowly when and where I say, watch, and report. Whatever happens, happens. I'll give you a phone number to call me on."

"Another letter bomb?"

"No."

"Bigger fish, you said."

"Don't go on, Georg, you don't want to know."

"You said Pall Mall, walk up Pall Mall."

"Georg, stop. So you're still a lawyer. Stop putting two and two together. You may make four. And then you're in trouble."

Georg looked hard at Israel.

Bigger fish.

Bigger fish to fry.

A shout from downstairs: "Georg. Come on. We're going."

He opened the door. "Dit, do you mind going on without me? I'll see you there. I'm just talking to Ismael about something."

"No, come on, let's go. Chop chop!"

"I'll see you there, I'll come soon."

"Oh, all right then, we'll walk slowly, catch us up." The front door closed. He turned.

Bigger fish.

Bigger than a letter bomb.

Jewish terrorists had been in the news a lot lately. Palestine. Georg tried to remember, *What had been in the papers? Something big had happened.* He sat down, frowning at Israel.

"Don't think so much, Georg. Will you do it? You don't have any choice, you know."

What did I read?

"Yes or no, I need to know."

Yes! Of course.

Last month, November sixth, the day after all the fireworks on Guy Fawkes Day. The papers had been full of stories, newspapers love anniversary stories, especially one year after. November sixth last year. When the Jewish terrorists from Lehi murdered Lord Moyne in Cairo. The top British official in the Middle East. Gunned down getting into his car. His driver was killed, too. They caught the killers. They'd tried to get away on bicycles. That was a strange twist.

"What?" Israel said.

"You haven't got a bicycle, have you?"

"What are you talking about?"

"Are you from Lehi?"

Israel lifted his chin, his lips went tight. "You're too clever for your own good, Georg."

"What are you planning? If you want to blackmail me into helping, at least let me know."

"No."

"A bomb? Bigger? An assassination?"

"Shut up, Georg." Israel's shoulders bunched, he looked ready to throw a punch. But Georg went on.

"Who?"

"I said shut up. This is getting dangerous."

"Who would you want to assassinate? Who's going to be in Pall Mall? Soon?"

Israel stepped forward, pulled Georg from the chair, pushed him backward, took his head, hit it against the wall, hard, with a thud.

"Shut up now, Georg."

"You're crazy," Georg said, shaken, holding on to Israel's wrists, trying to pull them down. "What, you're going to kill me, too?"

Israel released him but his face stayed close. His brow was sweaty, Georg smelled his breath. Georg pushed past him toward the door.

"You're mad. Do you know what would happen if you kill someone? And who? A military leader? A politician, an English politician? In London? My God! After all they did to help us? It's wrong! Keep your war far away from here. In Palestine, maybe you have a point. But here? Oh, my God, you must be mad." Georg reached the door, turned. He was almost spluttering. But he saw clearly. "And you want to blackmail me into being part of this? No! Anything but that. Anything! There are thousands of us living here. You know what would happen? Everyone would say, those crackpot fascists in Hampstead were right, after all. A Jewish fifth column in England. Can you imagine? They really would throw us out. Naturalisation? Who would want us? And they'd be right."

Israel stalked forward, jabbing with his finger. "Good. Good! Let them throw you out. Why are you here anyway, what do you have here? We need you in Palestine. The Bible says about the Amalekites— destroy them completely. We're not shedding innocent blood. They kill us, why is Jewish blood cheaper than theirs? They are bloodsuckers, and not only the soldiers, policemen, clerks in Palestine who exploit and obey orders, but also the people who give those orders, safe here in London. Well, it isn't safe here, and it will never be safe for them here as long as it isn't safe for us there. They want to stop the Jews from coming to Palestine. They guard imperialist rule and prevent the rescue of the Jews. We should surrender to the white paper? It will lead us to a new Auschwitz, Bevin will take us there by the hand and we should go quietly. No, we can't let him. No! This time we will protect ourselves."

"Bevin?"

Israel, red in the face, and furious, stopped. Moved to Georg. Pointed to the chair. Georg sat. He moved closer. Georg flinched.

"I told you to stop. Now you've gone too far. Lives are on the line, Jewish lives. If I can't trust you, believe me, I'll have to do what has to be done. This is not only about you or me."

He's mad. He can do anything. The baby.

"I won't say anything."

"I know you won't."

"I will say one thing, though."

"What?"

"I have no clue what Anna sees in you."

Israel slapped him in the face. He fell off the chair, cheek stinging, tried to get up, Israel held him down, leaned over him.

He shouted, "I love . . ." And dropped his voice to a whisper. "I love Anna."

He turned away. Came back. Pulled Georg to his feet. Georg flinched and put a hand up to ward off a blow. "I'm sorry, Georg. I shouldn't have hit you."

Georg's head spun, he felt nauseous, he stood with his hand to his cheek, could feel it burning. He moved toward the door and began to open it, when Israel said, quietly, "They killed my brother, you know. And another boy, who was like my brother."

Georg stopped, his hand on the doorknob.

"I'd like to tell you about it."

Israel looked stricken. Georg thought, everyone has his story, his reasons, maybe I can listen, talk him out of whatever he's planning. He closed the door, turned and sat on the chair by the table, leaning forward, a hand cradling his tingling cheek.

Israel propped himself against the window, looking into the street. The window was hazy with drizzle.

"He was my youngest brother, wasn't even twenty years old. We were very close once, I took care of him. He was a fighter. Began by posting leaflets at night, like they all did, running, hiding. I didn't see him for the last six years." He paused, turned toward Georg, as if wondering how much to say. How much to give away. Or judging the effect. His look made Georg think, *Is he really opening up at last, or is he still trying to play me?*

"When the war broke out I went to Europe, I was a British soldier, believe it or not. Special unit. Jews fighting with the British, sometimes behind German lines. I speak Arabic, I did special missions in North Africa. Explosives, sabotage, that kind of thing. But my heart was with the resistance in Palestine, they had sent me to join the British, to learn, we knew one day we'd end up fighting the British, for our own country. I was wounded, got demobbed early and came straight here, been active here ever since. But my brother, he was helping the illegal immigration, getting Jews into Palestine. They caught him and I don't know why, but in Atlit they beat him, and he died. They beat him to death. Just a couple of months ago. His name was Sami. It nearly broke me. You didn't notice, right?"

"No. No, I didn't. You didn't say anything."

"Of course not, how could I?" He sat at the table. "I never thought about revenge. That isn't what this is about. It isn't personal. That's my point."

"I'm sorry about your brother."

"Yes."

"But Israel, you can't assassinate Ernest Bevin. The Foreign Minister. It's just insane. Just because you want Jews to come to Palestine. That isn't the way. How many are you, in Lehi? A few hundred? Not more, according to the papers. How can you dare do this? Nobody agrees with you. I don't. No one does. This is madness. What, because your brother was killed, we all have to pay?"

"I told you, Georg, this isn't personal. It has nothing to do with my brother. If I wanted revenge, trust me, I know how to take revenge. This is about the future of—"

"Of course it's about revenge, you said yourself you were so close to your brother—"

"No! It isn't. I told you. His best friend was killed, too, not long after, six weeks ago maybe, he was like my brother, that boy, they played together in the market, it was a tough neighborhood, I looked after them both. They killed him, too. Shot him down in cold blood. And believe me when I say, I could take revenge, if I want."

"How? Killing another minister?"

"No. Killing the killer."

"What do you mean?"

"I know the name of the soldier who killed him."

"And?"

"He's downstairs."

Georg stared. "Eric?"

"Sergeant Eric Barnes, C company, Eighth Parachute Batallion, Sixth Airborne Division, big fucking hero."

· · ·

"Well, look at you, Mrs. Barnes."

They crossed at the door, Edith and Georg coming back, Mr. and Mrs. Barnes leaving. "Call me Sally, after all this time, how many times have I said it? This is a big day," Sally trilled, her voice rising on the last words. "Our Eric's getting his medal, we're off to celebrate. You like?" she said, spreading her arms. Sky blue coat, sky blue hat with green and red feathers on top of piled-up hair, enough rouge for all the girls at the Windmill. She twirled round, beaming, knocked over the milk bottles. "Oops!"

"Careful, dear, we'll be late," Arthur said, stooping to pick them up, while Georg stuck out his leg to stop one as it clattered down the steps.

"Oh, dear. May have partaken just a little too much, get some courage, you know. Big day, this."

"Well, congratulations," Edith said, "you have a wonderful time, and Eric, too. Where is he?"

"Don't know, we'll see him there. And how about you then, you look lovely, too." She touched Edith's belly. "How much longer, then?"

"Any day, a week or so, not a moment too soon."

"Can't wait to see what you got in there! Oops." The milk bottles again.

"I'll get them," Georg said, bending. "Or you'll never go."

"By-yyyeee," from Sally, as she jolted down the steps toward the bus stop.

Edith began the climb upstairs, a step at a time, breathing heavily. She rested on the landing, almost doubled over, holding the banister. "Ooof, I'm so clumsy."

"How long now?" Georg said, coming from below.

"Two more flights."

"I mean the baby, of course."

"Eight days. But it feels like I can't take another eight minutes."
Edith, gripping the banister, pulling herself up the stairs, Georg
putting his hands against Edith's bottom and pushing.

What to do? He always reached the same conclusion. Nothing.
Israel's got me over a barrel. I can't tell Edith anything, certainly not
till the baby's safely delivered; I can't tell the police, I'm an accomplice;
I can't tell Anna who he is, it'll kill her. What an evil bastard. He's
got us all tied up in knots. But he loves her. That can only end badly.
What to do?

As they reached the top landing, the phone rang. It kept ringing
as he unlocked the door and Edith fell onto the bed and tried and
failed to raise her leg while he pulled her shoes off.

"Nobody's in," he said.

"Let it ring."

Georg took his shoes off, too, hung up their coats, emptied his
pockets as usual: change, handkerchief, keys. He put everything in
the night-table drawer. He put the kettle on while Edith sighed and
sighed again. "Ooof." She looked around. "Do we have everything
ready?"

"No."

Big sigh. "Gina said she'd help. And Frieda."

"Sally?"

"Oh, no," Edith laughed. "Can you imagine? She's very nice,
though, but keep her away. They have a different way of doing things,
here. My first job in Leeds I had to wash the baby in olive oil. They
said it was healthier. What a smelly baby, poor little thing!"

The phone rang again. "Leave it," Edith said. But it kept ringing so Georg put on his slippers and went downstairs.

Edith was asleep when he returned. He sat down heavily on the bed.

"Where have you been?" She groaned.

"In the lounge."

"In the lounge? Why? I was waiting for you. I thought, we could, maybe . . . you know . . ."

He stood up, went to the window, looked out. Squirrels playing. Slight drizzle. Each hazy droplet standing out on the windowpane. Sighing, he went to his drawer and pulled out his family list, held it in his hands, stared at it, put it back.

"What is it?" Edith asked. She was lying on her back, looking at him across her belly.

"That was Mrs. Wilson."

"Yes?"

He began to cry. Edith struggled up. She went cold. "What?"

Georg came to the bed, lay facedown. He struggled to breathe, crying, trying not to cry, stopping sobs, some escaping.

"Darling, what is it? What did she say? Papi?"

"Ellie. She isn't here after all."

Edith shivered. She stroked his head.

"It isn't fair. She died of typhoid two weeks before the end of the war. Two weeks." His shoulders rose and fell, shuddering from his gut, as if every breath was torn from him. "That's everyone on my side."

It grew cold. They got under the covers with their clothes on. He had never felt so alone. He found her hand and held it to his mouth.

Yitgaddal veyitqaddash shmeh rabba
Be'alma di vra khir'uteh

veyatzmakh purqaneh viqarev ketz meshiheh
behayekhon uvyomekhon
uvkhaye dekhol bet yisrael
be'agala uvizman qariv ve'imru amen

"Amen."

In the lounge, nodding and responding, as Georg said Kaddish, were Edith, Otto, Anna, Frieda, Gina, Israel, Sally, Albert, and Eric.

It was complicated. Nobody knew the procedure. Otto and Gina had burst in bearing presents and candles, saying, Guess what! It's the first day of Chanukah! That surprised everyone. But Georg had just invited them all to join him in the prayer for the dead. He wanted to light a memorial candle for Ellie, but now they also wanted to light a candle for Chanukah. Was this allowed?

To mourn, and to celebrate?

Was it blasphemous to say Kaddish for the dead and immediately rejoice with a Chanukah candle, one after the other? They didn't know. In the life that had been forced upon them, it seemed natural; but was it right?

Georg decided: We will never celebrate again without mourning those who cannot celebrate with us, those who were taken from us. They will always be in the room. So we may as well get used to it.

Yehe shlama rabba min shmayya
Ve hayyim tovim
vesava vishu'a venekhama veshezava
urfu'a ug'ulla usliha v'khappara

verevah vehatzala
l anu ulkhol 'ammo yisrael ve'imru amen

He could read Aramaic but couldn't understand it, nor could anyone else, so he read the translation of the Kaddish, too.

May there be abundant peace from heaven and good life
Satisfaction, help, comfort, refuge,
Healing, redemption, forgiveness, atonement,
Relief and salvation
For us and for all His people Israel; and say, Amen

Amen, they all said, and the refugees thought, *It could be written for us.* Georg closed the prayer book.

Nobody wanted to break the silence. They all looked at the single memorial candle on the mantelpiece in its round tin, with its little orange flame. The only warmth in the cold room. Edith sat on the sofa, rubbing hands with Anna. Everybody else was standing. Otto gestured to the seats and the Barneses sat with grim smiles. As he watched the fragile flame sputter in a slight draft, Georg thought: Me and Edith, Gina and Otto, Anna, if you add up all our relatives who were murdered in the last three or four years, it must be a hundred people. At least. Our mothers, fathers. Brothers, sisters, cousins, aunts, uncles. Others lost husbands, wives, children. Only Anna has come back. He looked at her, and their eyes met. But only half of her. Will that bastard bring the other half back to life? Or will he destroy the half that remains? He glanced at Eric, sitting next to his mother, his head bowed, sun-bleached hair falling over his eyes. What about him?

"Excuse me a moment," Georg said, "I'll be right back." Edith watched him leave and the door close. She knew where he was going.

He was going upstairs to his list. He was going to put a line through Ellie's name.

She was right.

As Georg walked slowly upstairs, Heinrich Heine spoke to him from his schoolboy years. How often had he and Ellie read his poems aloud to each other, tried to learn them by heart for class? Heine was a prophet as well as a poet.

Ich hatte einst ein schönes Vaterland.
Der Eichenbaum
Wuchs dort so hoch, die Veilchen nickten sanft. Es war ein
    Traum.

Once I had a beautiful fatherland.
The oak tree
Grew so high there, violets nodded softly.
It was a dream.

Sitting on the edge of the bed, Georg opened the drawer and took the sheet of paper with the list and rested it on his book of Heine's poems. He took his pencil and stared at Ellie's name as if saying a final farewell. He tried to see her face but failed. She was gone. He heard the silence of the house. He made a kissing sound, brought his hand down and put a line through her name. After a blank moment he looked at the second list on the paper, Edith's family, a column next to his. He sighed and crossed out Mutti and Lisa, too, at last.

He sat on the bed with his head in his hands.

"A fine lot you are," Georg heard Sally say, as the lounge door opened and closed.

He came slowly down the stairs, trying to change his mood, and followed her in. Edith smiled and pulled him to her on the sofa, held his hand, rubbed it.

"Here, Otto, presents under the tree. Just joking!" Sally said, laying down all the presents she'd prepared for the baby. She piled packages on the table while Otto studiously lined up eight egg cups and placed a ninth in front, a makeshift menorah. He lit a match, held it to the bottom of a thin red candle until the wax began to drop, and set it in the first egg cup. "At home we had a glorious silver menorah," he said, balancing the candle, which kept drooping to the side. "It was huge with carvings of animals and buildings, it was in a glass case all year."

"So did we," Edith said. "I wonder where it all is now. Melted down somewhere."

"There, there," Albert said. "Have a drink, do that littl'un inside of you a world of good. Cider? Gin and orange? Fancy a cigarette?"

"I don't smoke, thank you."

"More's the pity. Cheer you up. Here, Eric, show them your medal."

"I don't think so, Dad, it's downstairs."

"Go on, Eric, get it," said Sally.

"Don't bother," Israel said.

"Another time," Eric said, looking at Israel. *What's his problem?*

"My turn," Otto said, calling for quiet. He struck a match, lit a candle, and read from Georg's prayer book:

Blessed are you, Lord, our God, king of the universe who has sanctified us with His commandments and commanded us to light the candles of Chanukah. Amen.

Everyone repeated Amen and smiled. Edith began to sing a Chanukah song but nobody knew the words so they ended up humming, Otto waving his arms like a conductor.

"You know what Chanukah is, don't you," Israel said to the Barneses.

"Of course," Albert said, "it's their Christmas."

"Not quite. It celebrates a Jewish revolt against their occupiers in Palestine. The Greeks. Sort of a Greek Mandate," he said, to Eric.

"Don't look at me," Eric said, raising a beer. "I'm happy to get out of there soon as possible. Anyway, you're an Arab, what do you care?"

"Now, now girls," Albert said, "it's pressie time."

Apart from Sally, only Otto and Gina had brought presents. "We'll give ours when we light tomorrow's candle," Edith said, "we didn't know."

Israel eyed Eric. "I'll give you your present another time."

"Save it for Christmas."

"Why wait?"

Sally jiggled with excitement as Edith unwrapped one present, and then another, as everyone laughed and applauded. Each present was for the baby. "I didn't know if it's a boy or a girl," Sally said, clapping her hands. "So I got green."

"Oh, Mrs. Barnes, sorry, Sally, you shouldn't have." Tiny green pyjamas, the sweetest things, woolly socks, booties, nappies, a tiny sweater with a matching cap, pacifiers, even a weighing scale. Each present produced squeals and coos and laughter. Gina had already given Edith the blue sweater she had knitted, but brought more presents. More pacifiers, in all colors, a little rattle, bibs with deers running around the edges. Otto said, Wait a moment. He ran downstairs, two steps at a time, and came back, accompanied by clattering, rattling, knocking sounds. He pushed open the door. "Da danh!" and there was Otto grinning, wheeling in a pram, patting the hood. "We all clubbed together, we had a collection at the Cosmo."

Edith wiped a tear. "Oh, thank you. Thank you. We really didn't have anything."

"Isn't there something about not buying things for a baby, until it's born, bad luck?" Georg asked.

"Nonsense," Gina said. "Buy before, during, and after. That's the recommended way, it's in all the books."

Edith lifted her mouth to kiss Gina and Otto. She blew kisses to Sally, Albert, and Eric, but that wasn't enough for Sally, who came over and planted a big wet one on Edith's lips and hugged her. "Now don't you worry about a thing, my dear," she said, "when the little'un's born I'll know exactly what to do, you'll be in good hands, Lord knows I haven't got much to do, and with all your family gone 'n' all, don't worry, I'll be here to help, Edith, all day, don't you worry about that."

"Now you're in trouble," Eric said, and laughed.

Edith smiled. "Thank you." She turned to Gina. "What a lovely pram," she said. "What, you organised a collection?"

"Didn't have to," Otto said. "Everyone wanted to give you something."

"Oh, but that's so sweet."

"It's like everyone's first baby. It's the first Jewish refugee baby born here."

"Really?"

"Of course. Certainly in our crowd. It's the new generation."

"This is going to be one spoilt boy," Georg smiled.

"Girl."

TWENTY-ONE

London

December 12, 1945

Anna came to Israel like a bride. She gave herself to him. And when she came, her back arched like a bow, this time she didn't cry, she laughed. When she came again she laughed so hard, she cried, tears of laughter. "I see, this is what you like," Israel said, and gently made her laugh again. "Ssssh, you'll wake everyone up."

She lay back, panting, her legs open and her pink and pinker skin damp, and Israel put his head there and tasted the damp, up and down and around, oh, so close, until she forced his head with her hands to where she needed him.

And then she did the same to him.

"Ssssh," she said, "you'll wake everyone up."

They fell asleep in each other's arms, but not for long. Anna woke and pushed Israel off. He moaned and rolled back, moving a leg and an arm across her, pinning her down. She lay on her back, eyes open, feeling his deadweight, and she couldn't help herself, her mind returned to that place. She closed her eyes, tight, tighter. Trying to block it out. Her body seemed to turn cold and stiff. A little bit of her died each time she went there. She felt scarred, dirty. Filthy. Violently, she pushed Israel away.

He woke with a start. "What?" He sat up. "Anna?"

And just as suddenly, it went. Gone, the weight lifted. A flood of relief as her mind cleared. She was back.

All she felt now was what was growing in her hand. She placed her head against Israel's chest, her hair caressing his, and gently pushed until he lay on his back and she raised her mouth to his and kissed him and raised her hips to take him and held him a very long time, and even longer, until he groaned and shook and that is how they fell asleep again.

Georg strode along Finchley Road, swinging his arms in excitement. He had an idea and couldn't wait to tell Edith. It came to him at Bloomsbury House, after he gave advice to a German-speaking Pole who had just arrived and wanted to change his name, but didn't have his original birth certificate, or any documents, and didn't speak enough English to go from office to office to get everything done. Georg had drawn up a list of offices, phone numbers, and addresses, explained which forms to take to which office, and offered to fill out the forms and to go with him, for a small fee, to translate if necessary.

When he turned into the top end of Goldhurst Terrace the hairs on his neck stood as he realised how smart, how simple, how doable his idea was. Why hadn't he thought of it before? Why keep on being rejected by English law firms? He'd never get work that way, with his accent. Otto was right: Can I haf zhe jop pliss? No, he'd start his own law practice, just for refugees. It was time to take his own life into his own hands. To do something instead of always waiting. Edith would be thrilled: at last, a way forward. He shivered with excitement. It all fell into place on the journey home. What with naturalisation, name changes, and now that the war was over, growing communications with home and the need for coordination between lawyers' offices in Europe and Britain, and all his languages, French, Italian, as well as German and English, he'd have more business than he could handle. The English lawyers would come to him for help. He chuckled at the fees he would charge them. There was already talk of German reparations. There would be lots of work—gathering documents, translating them, filling out applications. Refugees tracing families, trying to reclaim their homes and businesses, retrieve their assets. They can't all keep phoning and writing to Europe, relying on unknown lawyers, half of them former Nazis who'd do no more than steal their money. And the English have no idea of the German legal system. Much better for refugees, thousands of them, to deal with one of their own, a specialist, here in London. He'd handle everything for them. He could charge by the item, or an inclusive fee for a whole package of services, or even charge a percentage of the money he retrieved. He could start a translation business on the side, legal translations.

By now he was almost running down the hill. The more he thought it through, the better it felt. Refugees couldn't pay much, but by helping them now, and charging low, fair prices, he'd build up a loyal client base. And soon their needs would change: from helping them reclaim their lives and assets to helping them in their developing business lives. Commercial law. That was the future. As his clients got money, invested, worked, grew wealthier, so would he. Yes, that's the way forward. Rent a small office near Bloomsbury House, maybe hire an assistant, a refugee who needs work, too, someone fluent in several languages . . . He hurried home to tell Edith, goose bumps on his neck he was so excited. This could change everything. At last, something to do, not just to wait for things to happen and hope and beg, but to take control, lead the way, begin to build their future. Until now, everything was happening to him, waiting for news, waiting for baby; time to change! Make things happen.

When he unlocked the door, he came upon Israel in the lobby, finishing a phone call. He stretched out an arm to stop Georg, said good-bye, and hung up. "Georg, I need to talk to you." Georg tried to brush past, he was in a hurry to continue to his room, to Edith, but Israel pushed him into the empty lounge.

"Now what? I said I'd do it. You said you wouldn't ask anything else."

"Well, good news. I don't need you after all."

"What do you mean?"

"Slight change of plan. You're off the hook. We have someone else to watch. So we don't need you."

"So, you don't want me to do anything?"

"Right. Happy?"

Georg shook his head, in disbelief.

"What? I thought you'd be glad."

"I am. But all that stuff you put me through. For nothing."

"The plan changed. That's what plans do. One thing hasn't changed, though."

"What?"

"Keep your mouth shut. Do not say a word. Otherwise, nothing's changed. I'm serious. This is not only me, other people are involved."

"Did you hear anything about Max Epstein?"

"No, not yet, but I promise you, if he's alive, the Agency will find him."

"You promise?"

"It isn't only you, Georg," he said, laying his hand on Georg's shoulder. "I know what he means to Anna, too, don't forget, they spent years together. I also want to find him, Georg. For Anna."

December 14

"Georg. Georg. Wake up. Psss. *Nu!* Psssss. Oooofff! Georg." Georg pushed her hand away and rolled over, moaning. Edith sat on the edge of the bed in the dark, in her slippers and dressing gown. She rubbed her hands, blew into them: It's freezing. She put her hand on her heart, felt the beat, put it on her tummy, felt it hard. "Georg! Wake up."

"What!" He'd been dreaming of how to decorate his new office. Edith was his assistant. Otto was translating and getting it all wrong.

"I'm having contractions."

"How often?"

"About every ten minutes."

"Go to sleeeep. You know what Goldscheider said. Every five minutes. Then we go. Sleep."

"But some stringy, jelly stuff came out. With blood."

She had to pee several times an hour, and the last time a thick discharge plopped out. "Should we go to the hospital?"

"Sleep."

"Babies get born at night, you know. Sorry, but it's a fact."

Georg sighed, propped himself up on an elbow, yawned, Edith came into focus, a shadow by his head. He stretched out his arm, put his hand on her tummy. "You feel it?"

"No, hard as a board. Then it goes soft again."

"What do you want to do?"

"I don't know, what do you think?"

"How should I know? You should know."

Edith slumped. "I can't wait to get this over with. I know it's going to hurt a lot, and take a long time, I just know it."

"Your blood pressure's down."

"No, it's the same, much too high. But the baby's in the right position, head down, bum up."

"That's good. What else did they say?"

"Not much. Any moment now, she said, the nurse. She didn't feel her moving, but I feel the kicking. Very strong."

"If we don't need to go to the hospital, let's go back to sleep."

"What about the jelly stuff?" Edith said, getting back into bed.

"No idea. Did the waters break?"

"No."

"There, you see." Georg rolled over and was already asleep.

Edith jerked with another contraction, tighter than the last, like someone had a knee in her back, pulling her belt, sharply. Her groin ached. Just as suddenly it relaxed. She waited for it to come again, looking at her watch, timing the gap. She began to perspire. Baby's coming. This is it. She spoke to her: Hello, baby.

TWENTY-TWO

Pall Mall

December 16, 1945

Okay, here they come. He glanced at his watch. 5:17. Bang on time. Just like the Arab said.

Four goons, bunched up, down the steps. Dark suits, hats. Lanky one holds the car door open. Quick look-around. Fifteen seconds . . . twenty . . . thirty, like clockwork, here they are now, the Foreign Ministers, that's Bevin in the middle, big fat bastard. Bit dark but enough light from inside the building. Don't pop the Yank, or the Frog. Bevin's much bigger than the others, broad shoulders, heavy. No problem.

Five yards from the last step to the car door when it's open. Four guards, a funnel to the car. But they're letting people walk through. Stupid. Simple, like Ismael said. Pass him, turn, shoot, three times, in the head, turn again. Walk. Calm-like. Jump in the cab, the one pulling up, with the orange balloon. Tomorrow night.

Fifty yards down Pall Mall, from St. James Square, two men approached, side by side, hunched against the cold, towards the British Foreign Minister's sleek black Humber. Their mouths were tight and their eyes creased in the wind, spotting the ministers in their dark suits and open coats, talking between the stone columns. Their steps faltered as they approached the politicians but the bodyguards parted and the two men walked through. The smaller one looked at his watch. 5:17. On the dot. That's what they'd been told: Pass the Humber at 5:17. Don't say anything, don't do anything, just act natural and walk by at 5:17. Same thing the next night, only then they'll be following another man. Stay fifteen yards behind him, they'd been told, don't do or say anything, just walk by the black Humber. Nobody told them why and they didn't ask. Used to following orders.

Back on the other side of the road a young woman, who could be a domestic servant in her faded grey coat and flannel hat which half covered her face, wheeled a black hooded pram past the man watching from the doorway of the bombed building. She didn't acknowledge him but looked across as the bodyguards made way for the two men walking past the official black car. That's a smart move, she thought. Let two of the fascist scum get caught. They'll run, say it wasn't them, didn't know what was going on. But nobody trusts the fascists: What were they doing there then? That'll keep the heat off us. Smart.

The pram squeaked as she pushed it over a cracked paving stone. That left wheel needs some grease, the young woman thought, looking at the blue glass eyes of the tucked-up doll.

Israel met the shooter by the tube on the corner of Oxford and Regent streets. They talked briefly, set a new rendezvous, and twenty minutes later shared a bench in Hanover Square; half an hour later they met at the number 13 bus stop at Oxford Circus. Anyone looking would see two talkative friends who met by chance. They rode together to Trafalgar Square, and split up.

The shooter had checked out the area, approved the plan. The driver and the watcher were all good to go. Susie, her code name, would wheel the pram, with a bomb inside the baby doll, and would only set it off, push it from the other side of the road, if everything went wrong. It was only three pounds of gelignite, just enough to divert attention, and give everyone time to escape. It had a five-second timer, with a detonator switch on the pram handle; tight, but enough for Susie to get out of the way. Israel had put it together himself.

The shooter would choose his gun tonight.

They would never meet again. Maybe one day in Palestine. Or in court.

Now Israel had to tell Anna. That he had to leave. Tomorrow. And she couldn't come with him. He would catch the eight p.m. ferry to Calais, make his way to Marseilles, where Alain, whoever he really was, would take care of him. He'd have to disappear for a while. A letter bomb here or there was one thing; killing the Foreign Minister would crash the whole house down.

There was a parallel plan, he didn't know much about it, didn't need to, to finger the fascists. It might work, it might not. It would buy time, certainly. But Miki didn't want him to take any chances. He was needed back home, the real fight was just beginning in Palestine. His London venture was over.

But he hadn't planned on Anna. Beautiful, fragile Anna, who loved him, and whom he loved. His stomach lurched, he almost felt sick. She still thought he was Ismael the Arab. What was he doing to her? Her whole world would collapse. Again, before she'd even recovered. What would she do, what would she think? He couldn't tell her the truth; she'd have to believe him: that he was going away, suddenly, he had no choice, but he loved her and would send for her. He clenched his jaw, ready to do what he had to do.

He folded his few pairs of trousers and shirts, placed them in his carryall on the table. He scooped his underpants and T-shirts from one drawer and dropped them in, and two pairs of shoes which he placed around the sides. Two jackets on top. He'd wear the coat. It wasn't much. Wasn't much left. He'd started weeks ago, bit by bit, to avoid attention, taking every piece of paper, most of his clothes, all his books, every tiny thing that could possibly help identify him, and dumped them around the area. Only Georg knew anything at all about him. Shouldn't have told him about his brother but too late now. He surveyed the room. It had been a good room. It was empty now.

Here today, gone tomorrow.

Except for Anna.

I love her.

Just as the thought warmed him, there was a light tap on the door, and it made him smile, and also made his stomach lurch. It was Anna and he had to tell her now. He walked to the door, could hear his heart beat, louder than his footsteps.

Her lips were ready. She pressed them to his, and pushed him backward till he buckled on the bed, and she fell on top of him. "Got you," Anna said. She covered his face in kisses, put her hand between his legs. "Edith's having a baby any moment," she said, "and I want one, too."

And then she saw his bag. And the empty room.

"I love you, Anna, you know I do. Anna, please. Anna."

"Anna?"

Life hadn't prepared her for any of the things she had survived, yet she had survived.

Why should he be any different?

"Anna?"

I'll survive, she thought. *And then, one day, I'll die. The sooner the better.*

Israel was scared. She hadn't said a word. She had seen the bag, looked back at him, sat on the edge of the bed, and hadn't moved a muscle since.

"Anna? Are you all right?"

It is nice here. Mummy singing, everyone talking and laughing, fresh flowers on the table. Wiener schnitzel, cold white wine, Salzkammergut, the lakes, swimming. It was nice, those holidays in the Tyrol. And in the garden, with Edith, all the friends. Sunlight dappled yellow dandelions.

"Anna?"

I'm not tied up anymore, no ropes, I can get up. So she got up. She stood and seemed to savor standing. She felt light, light-headed, as if she were rising, above it all. She glanced at Israel, unseeing, and walked to the door, but he was faster, blocked it with his body.

"Anna, have you heard anything I've been saying?"

She looked at him, and now she heard him, too. Slowly, she shook her head, the garden faded, she came back. "No," she said. "Where are you going? Why didn't you tell me?"

"Where were you? Anna, you scared me."

"Where are you going?"

What to say? She has been hurt so much, she is so vulnerable, so weak. Only the truth. But the one thing he can't say is the truth.

"Anna." He took her hand, led her back to the bed. He kissed her brow and her eyes. "Anna, there's something I can't tell you. Not yet. But please believe me: I love you so much, I've never loved anyone anything like this. You know that, don't you?"

"You've been playing with me. How can you leave without telling me?"

"Of course I was going to tell you. I'm leaving tomorrow, I don't want to, but I don't have a choice."

Tears welled in Anna's eyes. "I love you," she said. "I'll go with you."

He sat next to her, took her hands.

"Anna, I have a strange story. I can't tell you all of it. I know you haven't told me everything, and I didn't ask. I never will. One day maybe you'll tell me what happened, when you're ready. And one day I'll tell you everything, too. But not now. So we're even. All right?"

She nodded, she wanted to believe him, she needed to. He smiled and kissed her nose and wiped away her tears.

"You want to go to Palestine, don't you?"

Nod.

"You'll go there. Soon. I promise. But first, I have to go away. And then I'll send for you. And we'll go together. All right?"

"Are you going home to Cairo?"

"No. I'm never going to Cairo. I can't tell you why, either. I can only ask you to believe me. Let my love speak for me."

"You haven't told me anything. Only that you're going away."

"And that I will send for you. As soon as I can."

The room was even colder bare and Anna went to bed with her clothes on, although he took them off piece by piece under the covers. They didn't talk much; there wasn't much to say. Their bodies spoke for them, declared their love, made their promises. There were tears, and fear, and soaring moments and Ismael's glowing cigarettes. The tips of Anna's fingers traced the scar ridge on his shoulder, and he told her of being shot in Benghazi. He told her of his childhood, and when she said, But where was it? he put a gentle finger to her lips. No more lies.

When she spoke of her own childhood, without mentioning her family once, he didn't ask.

Their bodies were more open, and honest; they said it all, left nothing to the imagination. And then they slept. And in the morning, when she woke, he was gone.

"Gone? Gone where?" Edith said. She was dressing after a hot shower. Trying to relieve the back pain.

Georg, drying the dishes, could feel his hands tremble. He put the cups down and dried his hands on the cloth, to steady them as he listened.

As Anna helped Edith with her socks, she tried to explain, but it came out all wrong. She didn't know where he had gone, or why, or if he would return, or how to contact him, or, in fact, anything.

"But you say you love each other?"

"Yes."

"What kind of love is that?"

Anna gazed into the distance. She began to say, I don't know, when Edith fell back on the sofa, her legs wide open, clutching her belly. "Ouch, ouch! Ow! It hurts!"

Anna stretched out her hand in concern.

"It's all right." Edith, like a puffer fish, blowing hard.

"It's the baby. Contractions. It's close."

"How close?"

"A few minutes."

"Is it time? Shall we go to the hospital? Georg?"

"Not yet," Georg said. *Israel. Where has he gone? He's going to do it.*

"It hurts more," Edith said. "But it's still about every ten minutes, maybe a bit less, when it's five minutes, I'll go. She's due tomorrow."

"Tomorrow?" Anna said in alarm. "Then let's go now. Georg?"

"Not yet. Shouldn't bother them until it's really time," Edith said, puffing on the sofa, holding her stomach.

"Georg?" Anna said.

"Edith knows best."

But he was thinking of Israel. Gone. Just like that. That can only mean one thing. They're going to kill the British Foreign Minister. Soon. Maybe today. I must do something. But what? He's got me over a barrel. All those threats: to call off the hunt for Papi; to denounce me to the police, after he entrapped me in the first place; and Anna, she loves him, this would destroy her, after all she's been through. Oh, what to do? We could get in trouble, just when the baby's born. Just when I finally get a business going. It'll be the end of everything. And what will this do to all of us, all the refugees, all the Jews, for that matter? A Jewish terrorist assassinates the British Foreign Minister in London. Oh, my God! They must be mad. He looked at Edith, sprawled back on the sofa, calling out in pain, her legs open, Anna terrified. "Taxi?" he said.

"Oh, I don't know." Edith, her mouth open, fearing pain.

I can't let this happen. I can't. It would destroy us all. And it's so wrong. An insane tiny group would ruin everything.

Suddenly it hit him. Of course. A phone call. An anonymous phone call to the police, tipping them off, an assassination plot today to kill Ernest Bevin. Yes! That's it. That'll stop it, and I'll stay out of it. So obvious. Why didn't I think of it before?

Anna was yelling now. "Georg! We should go!"

Edith stood up, holding her stomach. "It's so hard. It's the muscle. It's the baby."

"Just a moment," Georg said, putting down the dishcloth. Decided. "I have to make a phone call."

"What! A phone call? Now?" Anna was almost spluttering, holding Edith by the elbow, while Edith tried to bend double in pain, prevented by her rock of a belly. Anna yelled, "Where are you going!"

"I'll be right back," and Georg left them. What is the damn emergency number? In his panic he couldn't remember. One-zero-zero. Is that London? Or Vienna? Or none? Damn. Just before he reached the lobby, it came to him: nine-nine-nine.

He picked up the phone to call the police and heard a scream and a bang. He turned and looked, and another scream. Oh, God. He ran upstairs, two, three at a time, his long legs buckling. Edith stood in the middle of the room, her legs apart, clutching her groin, dripping, Anna looking aghast. She had knocked the chair over.

"The waters broke," Edith said, in shock.

"It's all right," Georg said, "that's good. Good. What should we do?"

"Call a taxi. Immediately," Anna said.

"Ow, ow, another contraction. Baby!"

"Now," Anna shouted.

Georg turned and ran down the stairs again. Picked up the phone. Scanned the phone list pinned to the wall. Where is it? Where? "Where's the taxi number?" he yelled at the wall. He scanned the list again, tapping each number as he read and there it was. SWI 1122.

"Five minutes," he called, just as Mr. and Mrs. Barnes came in. "What is it, Georg, why the shouting, is it Edith?" Sally said.

"Yes," he shouted back, running upstairs, "the waters broke."

"Dear, dear, what a to-do. It happens to everyone, you know, calm down."

But Georg was already in the room, supporting Edith with one hand, holding her valise in the other. Anna was on her hands and knees with a rag. "Never mind that," Georg shouted, pushing her head with his knee, "give me a hand."

Edith, face contorted, trying to shrug him off. "Georg, you're making things worse, please," but his panicked eyes grew even wider.

Sally had reached the top by now, and understood with a glance. "Georg, stop panting. Edith's having the baby, not you. Now calm down."

Georg was white. "Useless, men, always are," Sally said. "Now, follow me slowly down the stairs, Edith, there's a good girl, put your hand on my back and lean on me if you like, and hold the banister, too."

Georg carried the valise in one hand, slung Edith's coat over a shoulder, and had a pair of her shoes in his other hand.

"Men," Sally continued as they proceeded downstairs. "When I had our Eric, Albert didn't even come with me to the hospital. Put me in a cab, had a whisky, and went back to bed. And Mrs. Cowen over the road, when her waters broke, what did Mr. Cowen do? Called his mum. And Georg, Edith won't need those shoes where she's going."

TWENTY-THREE

London

December 22, 1945

Morning

"We'll have you there in a jiffy, missus, not to worry," the cabby said, looking over his shoulder, in alarm. He honked his horn and flashed his lights. Bloody Sunday driver! "Put yer foot down," he yelled. The car in front finally turned left and the cabby swung hard right into Fairhazel Gardens, sped up around the traffic circle with the weeping willow and kept his foot down along Belsize Road. Dear God, not another one who can't hold it in. Cost a fortune to clean the seats. Should get leather next time, easier to wash.

Sprawled across Georg and Anna, Edith muttered, "But I'm not ready." It was all happening so suddenly. A baby! Another life. It seemed incredible. She was wet between the legs; hadn't thought to put a cloth there. She felt herself, found blood on her fingers. "Oh no. Look. What does this mean?" Georg shook his head. Anna didn't know, either. Can't be good. Another contraction. "Ow, owww." Papi. If only you were here, you'd know what to do.

Georg leaned forward. Shouted, "Quickly, driver." And then, his voice rising a pitch, "There's blood, do you know what that means?"

The cabby looked over his shoulder. Blood? Oh, for Gawd's sake, not again. His foot was flat down as the cab labored up Fitzjohn's Avenue toward Hampstead, but the steep climb was winning and the old car slowing as it barely reached the top. "Quickly!" Georg shouted again and the cabby felt like saying, "Shut up, yer bloody foreign . . ." but didn't.

The cabby ran into New End Hospital, shouting "Emergency!" as Georg and Anna manoeuvred Edith out of the narrow door. She hobbled with her legs apart, holding her stomach, panting. *Just get me inside. I need to lie down. My back, like a knife. Blood, more blood. Oh, my baby!* "What's wrong?" she gasped at Georg, "What's wrong?"

"Nurse," Georg shouted, pushing aside a trolley blocking the way. It clanged into the wall. "Nurse! We have an emergency!"

Nurse Parkinson came running, with two orderlies rolling a stretcher. Edith, Anna, Georg, yelling and tottering toward her, patients and visitors in their seats following them with interest. "What is it, Mrs. Flasher?"

What bloody fool question is that?

Georg explained, between gasps: Can't you see? Contractions, blood, back pain, hurry, hurry.

"Stop fussing, it all sounds quite normal. You had us in a tizzy for a moment. Mrs. Flasher, there's nothing to worry about. Mr. Flasher, would you mind sitting down over there. I said sit down over there. Now. We'll handle it from here." She supported Edith's elbow and the orderlies went off for a cup of tea. As they moved down the corridor, Georg heard, "How long between contractions?" and then, "Oh, good that you came, but no hurry."

The clock above the telephone showed 11:10.

. . .

Two hours later Otto and Gina arrived, bearing flowers, beaming. "*Nu?* Boy? Girl?"

Georg was sitting miserably, with Anna looking tired. "They won't let me see her."

Gina sat down but there wasn't a seat for Otto. He hated hospitals. They heard a girl crying, her parents hugging her, and the girl saying, between sobs, "Why me?"

Otto lit two cigarettes, handed one to Gina. "Where's Edith?"

"Just down there. In one of the rooms."

It was a long, narrow two-tone corridor with doors on both sides. Busy nurses in white dresses and bonnets came and went, and sometimes a doctor in a white coat, looking important. "Sally's very excited. She may come here," Otto said.

"No." Georg groaned.

"Albert said they'd only get in the way."

"Oh, pray she listens to him, for a change."

They watched a nurse walk up to a man, talking, explaining, his face lighting up, the excitement, he kissed her. He walked quickly to the telephone, jingling change in his pocket, grinning as he passed them: "It's a boy. Took all night and half the day. It's a boy."

After twenty minutes Otto said, "This can take hours. Georg, it's a nice day for a change, you aren't doing any good here. Let's go for a walk on the Heath, we won't miss anything."

A nurse confirmed: contractions two to three minutes apart, you have time. Georg let himself be persuaded.

Edith, alone in the labor room, stared at the ceiling. She was naked beneath the hospital gown, her hands at her sides, tense, anticipating the next contraction. Blood pressure 140 over 90, high but not dangerous; baby's heart rate in the 150s. But Nurse Parkinson had frowned when she said it, and had brought the delivery doctor to listen, too.

"Hello. I'm Doctor Cummings. So, are you ready to be a mum?" he said kindly, as he placed the stethoscope on her belly.

"No."

"Jolly good. Let's see what we have here." He listened intently, moving the chest piece. Moved it again, staying longer in each position. Placed his hands around her stomach, dug in with his fingers, probed. "Good, your baby is in the vertex position. Everything fine there." He moved the stethoscope again, listening.

"Irregular heartbeat. Not a problem, though," he said, glancing at his chart, "Mrs. Fleischer."

"How do you feel?" he said, examining her.

Her face twisted. "It hurts a lot."

"Not long now. Let's see. Dilated two inches. Call when you think it's time, my dear, when you need to push. Nurse is here."

Alone again, Edith followed a crack in the ceiling, its jagged splinters, like tributaries, reaching down the wall. Bomb damage? Will plaster flakes fall down? Will the wall collapse? What else can go wrong? Her eyes closed. Irregular heartbeat? What does that mean? "Ow!" Edith lurched in pain. She took a deep breath from a mouthpiece, gas and air, half oxygen, half nitrous oxide, and then another, deep and long. It entered her bloodstream and dulled the pain, but not for long. She measured time in wrenches, sharp, piercing pain, as if someone was trying to twist off the upper part of her body, like grinding pepper, while someone else kicked her in the back with heavy boots. Each time the contraction stabbed through her, she sucked on the mouthpiece like a starving baby.

"It's really diluted laughing gas," a nurse said when she came in to monitor Edith's groans and yelps. "Breathe in each time there's a contraction. They'll get longer and it will help."

She came in every twenty minutes, for hours, dabbed Edith's tongue with a damp cloth, as Edith squirmed in pain, calling out, groaning. Down from three minutes apart and sixty seconds long to one minute apart and eighty. A midwife checked her. "Good, dilation four inches." The gas relieved some pain but also made her lightheaded, the room turned, until it steadied and the pain came back. More hours. Thirty seconds apart and ninety seconds long. This is unbearable! Where is Georg! She vomited and called for help, and heard, "Mrs. Flasher. Mrs. Flasher!" Another contraction, like someone pulling her pelvis apart from inside.

She screamed, "Nurse! I can't do this. It hurts too much. Give me something." She held her breath against the pain and went red and looked as if her eyes would pop, and Nurse Parkinson shouted, "Breathe, breathe," and finally she had to, and sucked in air, more gas and air, and kept sucking until she sucked in pressure and there was no air left in the cylinder and her chest felt like it would collapse and she would drown. She tore away the mouthpiece, gulping, screaming, "Gas and air, more gas and air." Another contraction, like the heat of a volcano bursting inside her, hot lava filling her, pushing out everywhere, she screamed in pain.

"That's enough!" Nurse Parkinson said, and slapped her sharply on the cheek.

Edith gasped, her eyes opened wide in shock.

"Stop it now. Don't make an exhibition of yourself. You're at the perfect age to give birth." And with that, Nurse Parkinson marched out of the room.

A moment later, another twist on the grinder and Edith squirmed and arched her back, sweating. But no scream. Another. And another silent contraction. She was panting, in pain, until a nurse brought more gas and air and she grabbed it and sucked in like she planned to hold her breath underwater for two weeks.

It felt like she was floating away and the hint of a smile appeared on her lips. *Georg,* she called out inside her head. *Baby's coming.* And then she screamed, and shouted, and pushed. The nurse started, and ran for help.

They wheeled Edith to the delivery room, with her screaming all the way.

"Oh, my God, that's Edith!" Georg jumped out of his seat in alarm, her screams seemed to bounce off the corridor walls and around the waiting room and terrified the life out of him. Where are they taking her? What's going on? Why doesn't someone tell me? He looked around for a nurse, where are they when you want one?

"Nu?" Otto said, walking in and taking a seat. "Any news?" He'd gone home to rest, complaining that this giving birth thing was tiring. "How much longer?"

At that moment, Georg remembered. "Oh, my God," he said again, falling back into the chair.

"What?" Otto said, turning in alarm, "what is it?"

The drama at home, rushing to the hospital, Edith's pain, wanting so much to be with her, frustration at the hospital rules that kept them apart, lapsing into long memories of his family who would never share this, would never know he was becoming a father, the smells and bustle of the hospital, Georg clean forgot.

Israel. The assassination. Suddenly it seemed impossible. Did he imagine all that? Israel and his plan intruded from another planet. He had been going to call the police. He was going to stop it. *I must,* he thought.

He looked at the public phone, in the corner. One person talking, he could hear every word, two waiting right behind. Israel would kill the Foreign Minister while Edith was having a baby. He had to warn someone. Anonymously. What to do? He looked around, panicking.

"Relax, Georg," Otto said, taking him by the elbow. "You're looking nervous. It can't be good for you. Let's go for a drink and come back."

Georg pulled away. "It's something else," he said.

"What now?"

Anna came over. "What is it?"

"I have to make a phone call."

"Now? Why now? Anyway, the phone's over there."

"No, I have to speak privately. I need another phone."

"What are you talking about? Edith—"

"Mr. Flasher? I just wanted to let you know what's going on. Everything is fine. Your wife was transferred to the delivery room, a little discomfort, but nothing out of the ordinary. Very soon you'll have your baby. It's your first, isn't it?" Nurse Parkinson asked, smiling with encouragement.

"Yes, yes, it is."

"Good. Well, won't be long now, you stay right here and I'll be back with the good news just as soon as we have some. Your wife is an angel. Very brave." She smiled and walked briskly back along the corridor, taking with her the waft of blood and drugs and disinfectant.

Georg looked at the phone. There was no privacy. Now there were three people waiting and even from this distance, in this bare white room, he could hear clearly ". . . waiting, can you bring some sandwiches, chutney . . ."

Now Georg knew he had to act. He had to stop Israel from killing Bevin. An image flashed before him: Napoleon, the lion, the engraving . . . "England expects every man will do his duty" . . . Time was running out. He heard Otto say again, "Let's go for a drink."

"No, you and Gina go, Otto, take Anna, she needs a break, I'll stay here."

"You sure?"

"Yes, definitely, I don't feel like a drink, but you all go, this can take hours." Otto, leaving with the girls, looked over his shoulder to see Georg waiting in line to make a phone call.

Impatiently. Hurry up! "It wasn't even full to the top," the man on the phone was saying. "Even with the head it wasn't full, I had a good mind to give him a piece of my mind. What? No, I didn't . . . Pubs today, not the same. I remember when . . ." Hurry up! Now Georg had decided to make the call, he was nervous, fit to burst. He wanted to call before anybody else got in line behind him, before the others returned, before anything happened with Edith, before Israel did anything. *Verdammtnochmal*, get on with it! "What?" the man was saying. "How many runs did he hit? Bloody sissies, can't play cricket to save—" He felt a tap on the shoulder. He looked round, as if he'd seen a rat in the corridor. Georg made a desperate face, shrugged an apology, put his hand on his heart, said, "Sorry, emergency." The man held the phone away from his ear. "What? I'm talking."

"I'm sorry. An emergency. I need to make an urgent phone call. I won't be a moment. Please."

The man tutted, and said into the speaker, "I'll call you back in a moment, someone here in a tizzy," and hung up. "Here you are, then."

"Thank you, thank you," Georg said, taking the phone and putting the pennies in the slot. One fell and rolled away, stopping against the man's foot. Georg leaned down and retrieved it. "I'm afraid it's private," Georg said with a grimace. The man looked at him, shook his head and walked away. Georg could imagine what he was think-ing. Bloody foreigners . . .

Now Georg had the phone to his ear and his finger in the dial, he hesitated. What to say? But he didn't have time. The man was look-ing at him and at any moment somebody else could come and stand right behind him. He dialed, three times, nine-nine-nine. A wom-an's voice said, "Fire, police, or ambulance?"

"Ambulance. Uh, no. Police."

A click, a tone, some more clicks. "Police, may I help you?"

Georg looked around, turned into the wall, hunched his shoul-ders and whispered, "Listen carefully. All right? Can you hear me? Someone is trying to assassinate the Foreign Minister, Ernest Bevin." Even as he said it, it sounded crazy.

"What? Louder. I can't hear you."

"Listen. Someone is trying to assassinate the Foreign Minister. Can you hear me? I can't speak louder. Ernest Bevin. Someone is try-ing to kill him. Today. Or soon. I don't know exactly when. In Pall Mall. Can you hear me?"

"Yes, I heard. What is your name. Your address? Who is trying to kill him?"

"Did you hear?" Georg said, a tiny bit louder, his heart beating like a piston engine, "Bevin. Kill. Maybe today. Tomorrow, I don't know when. Pall Mall. It's to do with Palestine."

"Who are you? Is this a hoax?"

"Check. Check . . . if Bevin will be in Pall Mall . . . within a day or two. He mustn't go there. There is a plot to kill him. Jews from Pales-tine."

He hung up. Stared at the phone. Looked around. The man was looking at him strangely, but Georg was sure he couldn't have heard a word, he was five yards away and Georg had whispered with his back to him. Georg tried to smile, said thank you, and offered him the phone.

The man just looked at him. That bloody foreigner's sweating like a pig . . .

Georg's heart was pounding, he was sweating. Would they believe him? She had asked if it was a hoax. They must get dozens of calls a day like that. Should he call again, give more information? But what? All he could give was Israel's name and address. But that would only get himself in trouble. Just when the baby's born. That wouldn't do, not at all. But would the police believe the call, would they do anything? Well . . . he'd done all he could. It's out of his hands now. But if Israel kills Bevin . . . oh, my God.

Two more hours, and Edith was still pushing. And yelling. "Push. Push down," the doctor called. The nurse's head was next to hers. "Push, six, five, four, three, two, one . . ."

Edith's torso came up as she strained, her legs wide open, strained, pushed, and fell back, hoarse from shouting. Come! Come already, damn you! No, no, I didn't mean that! Pain, tearing her apart, can be no worse! Sweat rolling off her, cursing, screaming, *Verdammtnochmal! Komm schon!* Another push and an even greater push, she felt her lungs, and her stomach, and everything inside, being expelled. Her liver would come out, too! She looked down, between her knees, the doctor, a midwife, nurses, someone else. Nothing. She yelled and pushed and the nurse at her head saying six, five, four, three, two, one, *push.* She fell back, desperate. How long can this go on for? How long can I bear it? I didn't know it could be like this. She creased her eyes against the blinding ceiling light. A moment of calm, and then another push, and another, harder, longer: "*Push,* six, five, four . . ." and then she felt a tearing, a rending, and heard a nurse calling, "The crown," and this is it and now it peaked, this torture, and she pushed and pushed. She heard the quiet voice of the doctor say, "I'll need to enter, turn the shoulder," and she felt more pushing, inward this time. What's he doing? He's going the wrong way. There's no room! Get out! More pressure there, more pushing, and suddenly, her whole body relaxed, went slack, like a paper bag bursting, she fell back, it was over. She cried, tears pouring, rolling down her cheeks. "Oh, my God, Oh, my God. Oh, my God." She sobbed with happiness, catching her breath, sobbing again. "Oh, thank you, thank you, thank you. Show me my baby. Please. Is it a girl? A boy? Oh, let me see, let me see, oh, thank you, oh, my God. Show me my baby!"

When Georg saw Nurse Parkinson approaching with a doctor he leapt up and sprung toward her. How long had it been? Ten hours? Anna, who had only left his side once for twenty minutes, was exhausted, and only raised her head. Otto and Gina, well rested, sat up, with huge smiles and sparkling eyes. This is it. How happy they were to share this moment. Georg's smile was even broader. He opened his arms, welcoming Nurse Parkinson as well as the news.

But their steps seemed deliberate, tentative. Their eyes, calculating. Their mouths, tight. He stopped. These were not the bearers of good tidings.

His smile faded as he saw their grim faces, the blood on the doctor's white coat; Georg's arms dropped to his sides. The blood drained from his face.

"Mr. Fleischer?" Dr. Cummings said, taking him by the shoulder and steering him to a corner. "Rest assured, your wife is fine, just fine." He looked around and lowered his voice. "Unfortunately, we have some bad news, however. Apparently there were complications in the womb or the birth canal, we have not yet established what precisely, we will examine the fetus, but I'm terribly sorry to have to inform you, that the fetus was stillborn."

Georg stared. His lips moved, he tried to talk, but no sound came. His head spun and he leaned on the wall for support. Stillborn? *Tot geboren?* "Not . . . alive?" he managed to say.

"I'm terribly sorry. We did everything possible. We don't know what happened yet. We heard a heartbeat, loud and clear. A bit irregular, but strong. It's very strange. I am so sorry."

Georg's face collapsed. He sobbed: Edith, poor Edith, can nothing go right? Oh, beautiful baby. Our dreams. A miscarriage. And now a stillbirth. Nurse Parkinson tried to comfort him. Her eyes were wet, too. She stroked his hands and said: "There, there, Mr. Flasher. There, there. Heaven has another angel now."

Anna stared into the distance. She was unable to cry. There really is no end, she was thinking. There is no end to all the bad things that can happen. Why? She remembered the little girl she had heard when they arrived, who must have been told she was very sick. "Why me?" she had said to her parents. They could only hug her silently. She hugged Georg, and also had no words, and no tears.

He, too, fell quickly silent, an occasional sob breaking past his throat. He could see Edith as soon as they had cleaned her up. He longed to hold her. What must she be feeling? What would he say? All their plans. All their love and joy. Everything was to change. All those presents, the baby clothes. It was to be the beginning of a new life, looking forward instead of backward, at last, a new beginning. They wanted a baby for themselves, and also for their families. It was what their parents would have most wanted. To know it isn't all over, that their lives continue in the baby. One baby, the first of many, for all of them. It goes on, despite Mr. Hitler. And then: First a miscarriage, and now this? Why? Oh, why? And Edith, poor Edith.

He yearned to see her, but Nurse Parkinson had insisted, almost pushed him into a chair. "We must clean her, give her a moment to rest. She may need a tranquiliser. She's very upset. I'll come and get you."

He looked at the clock. That was twenty minutes ago. He became frantic, Edith must be waiting desperately for him. *She doesn't need a tranquiliser, she needs me.* He stood, determined to find her by himself, cleaning be damned, manners be damned, when he heard running feet in the corridor and a young nurse appeared, looking around. "Mr. Fleischer, Mr. Fleischer."

Edith? What's wrong? His heart seemed to stop. *No, No.*

"Yes, that's me."

"Oh, Mr. Fleischer, the doctor sent me, he told me to tell you, wait here. There's another one. There's another baby," and she turned and ran back.

Push, push! Edith was pushing and screaming and yelling and Nurse Parkinson now was also shouting *Push, push.* The nurse by her head called, as calmly as she could, which wasn't very calmly, "Six, five, four, three, two, one, *push!*" Dr. Cummings was trying to contain his excitement. Another crown had appeared. Edith was straining, pushing, shouting, and now the shoulders followed more easily, birth canal prepared, vagina already stretched, and then the whole body, curled, wrinkled, mushy, the doctor holding it upside down by its feet, tapping its bottom, a first howl of life. The doctor snipped the cord and said triumphantly, "It's a girl, a perfect little girl." A nurse took her, wiped her clean as she yowled, a tiny piping cry, and wrapped her in a white towel. And handed her to Edith.

Who was beyond tears, beyond shock, beyond comprehension.

"Oh, oh, oh . . ." A hundred times she said "Oh!" Edith hugged her baby girl, brought her to her lips and kissed her eyes, her brown eyes, kissed her forehead and her little hairy head, wispy and damp and black, and every finger and toe. To pass from such despair to such bliss in moments. All she could say was "Oh!" and she kept saying it. She looked around her, shaking her head in wonder, and everyone was laughing and Nurse Parkinson began to clap and they all joined in, even the doctor. And then Edith's tears flowed like a river, dripping on her baby, who balled her fists and went red.

"Please, please, get Georg. I want to see my husband."

"Oh, no," Nurse Parkinson said. "Not yet, we have to . . ."

"Oh, come on, nurse," Dr. Cummings said, "just this once, poor boy, what we've put him through."

The young nurse ran out again to fetch Georg, who could hardly believe her. "Me? You're sure?" He looked at Anna, and ran after the nurse, scrambling into the gown she had handed him.

Georg entered the delivery room just as Edith felt violent cramps in her uterus and yelled and pushed and expelled the placenta in a great gush of blood and stringy matter which cascaded onto the floor. Georg took in Edith, his baby, the gushing blood, the knotty stuff, and fainted on the spot.

TWENTY-FOUR

London

December 23, 1945

Evening

"What a baby!" Otto laughed, hooting at the story, clinking glasses with Sally, who said, "Men, useless!" Gina, kissing Georg on the nose, said, "Nonsense, I think it's sweet," and opened a beer, and poured it for Albert, who said when he was born his dad got lost on the way to the hospital, what was its name? Damn, what was the hospital's name, again, Sally?—and nobody cared because they weren't listening anyway, everyone was drinking and talking at the same time, congratulating Georg, who was still reeling.

Twins. Who would have thought of that? Nurse Parkinson had explained: The irregular heartbeat had been two hearts beating when they expected only one. Somehow they had missed all signs of multiple fetuses. It happens. They didn't know why one had died during birth. But Edith and Georg were so excited, so relieved, at having a healthy baby after all that they couldn't yet mourn its stillborn twin, which had been spirited away and they had never seen.

The new father was on his second gin and ginger, after a champagne cider, and was feeling pleasantly light-headed, when he saw

Eric come into the lounge and heard him ask Albert, "Did you hear the news?"

Georg froze. News? Bevin? Israel? He did it. His call came too late? His heart began to pound. He couldn't hear what Eric was saying, he'd lowered his voice. Albert was nodding, tight-lipped. He was a big man, the type who became big, paunchy, flabby, and so didn't dominate his space. Now he seemed to diminish, droop. Georg looked past Gina, who was babbling on. He didn't hear a word she was saying. He waited for Albert's outrage. It was the kind of news where you raised your arm and demanded silence. But they just kept on talking, until Eric left the room, leaving Albert looking worried and thoughtful, his beer arm raised. Georg nodded to Gina, smiled at whatever Otto said. What happened? He hadn't heard the radio all day. They'd been in their bubble in the hospital, and then come home last night, and today was a daze.

Albert sat on the sofa, next to Frieda, who was looking lost, as usual. Georg had to know. He crossed the room and sat on the sofa's arm, leaning down to Albert. "Are you all right," Georg said, "did you get some news? From Eric."

"Yes, I'm afraid so." But he didn't say what.

"Did something happen?"

"It's what I was afraid of. Eric is going back, to Palestine. He's happy enough. But what's the point, I say, what are we doing there?"

Georg nodded. His body sagged in relief. Maybe it wasn't too late.

"And what with that bother with that lad he shot, he got a medal and all, but there's this revenge threat. I don't know, I don't like it, not at all."

Georg felt the gin and cider swirl in his head, he was giddy with relief. "Yes, I see."

"I think he's safer here in London. The war's over, he should come home."

What a couple of days, Georg thought, as he got up. The call to the police. The tension in the hospital, it took so long, ten hours, although everyone said it could have been a lot worse. He'd almost collapsed when they told him the baby was dead, and then, when he saw the second baby alive, and the blood, he really had collapsed. He was supposed to look after Edith and she'd ended up looking after him. Mrs. Barnes was right: Useless men.

He looked over at Anna, sitting alone by the table. After the two-day roller-coaster, she had fallen silent and was nursing a drink. She looked drained. Must be thinking of Israel. Why, she still doesn't even know his real name, or that he's Jewish, yet she says she trusts him, that he'll send for her. He thought of Israel's threats. An evil man. If nothing's happened so far, should he call the police again? He put his drink on the table and turned toward the door, when it opened.

And in walked Israel. Hands out, offering a fluffy white rabbit with long ears. Georg's jaw dropped. So did Anna's.

"Present for you, Georg. Your baby can play with it, too. Congratulations." He hugged him, Georg felt his barrel chest. Georg stared, holding the rabbit.

Israel went to Anna, who was looking up at him, openmouthed. He shrugged. "Change of plan," he said, and pulled her up and kissed her on the mouth. Everyone applauded. He sat next to her, whispered into her ear. "I want you to come with me."

Anna felt her eyes begin to burn, her breath quickening.

"I thought I wouldn't see you again," she whispered back.

"Will you?"

"Already?"

"Yes."

"I thought . . . I thought . . . I didn't know what to think . . ."

"I wish I could tell you everything, I will, soon, but first, I just need to know, will you come with me? Immediately. I love you so much."

Her first thought was Edith, her cousin, her only surviving relative, and Georg and the baby. The new family, a beautiful family. Rising from the ashes. And Ismael—she wanted a baby, too, her own family. One day, she knew, she would tell Ismael what had happened to her. She also knew, she would never tell Edith and Georg, she couldn't, it would make their own pain even greater. Yes, leave. Start again, somewhere else. How lucky that someone loved her, someone who she loved back, she, who thought she would never love in her lifetime.

She whispered back. "Of course I will."

"I think you'll like where we're going."

"Not Cairo?"

"Not Cairo."

"Where?"

"You'll see."

"When?"

"Now."

"Now?"

"Yes, do you have many things?"

She laughed. "All I need is you." And how she kissed him. Sally shrieked: "We'll be back at New End in nine months, or you can call me a silly moo!"

"Can you pack?" Israel said in her ear.

"Really, so suddenly?"

"I'm sorry, but yes. And don't tell anyone, yet, please. I'll tell Georg myself, now."

Anna left the room.

Israel made a motion with his head and Georg followed him out, into Israel's room.

"What's happening?"

"The best-laid plans . . . read this." He handed Georg a telegram. Nine words: "DO NOT DO THE FAT MAN. STOP. RETURN FASTEST."

"It just came. In the nick of time, too."

"To where? You weren't here."

"That doesn't matter. To another place."

"Who's it from?"

"My chief in Palestine. You know what it means?"

"Of course not. How could I?"

Israel snorted, turned to the window, looked outside, back at Georg. "It's off, the whole thing's off. Do not do the fat man—that's Bevin. Do not kill Bevin. Return: Back to Palestine."

Oh . . . my . . . God . . . it worked, the phone call worked. Georg nodded, slowly, felt his heart pounding. A small smile began to form. A wave of relief, like a load lifting, swept through him, he seemed to rise from the ground. He breathed in, deeply, and let out a sigh. You don't assassinate a Foreign Minister and get away with it. Sooner or later, he knew, the police would have traced it all back to Goldhurst Terrace. His small role would have come out, been magnified; he'd have been ruined. Jailed. Edith . . . the baby . . . the fears that Georg had not permitted himself now streamed through his mind and out the other side. It's off. Thank God I made that phone call! Framed in the window, side on, the light played on Israel's face, softening it. *Go home,* Georg thought. *Do what has to be done, somewhere else. Leave us alone. We want to build a life here, not destroy it.*

"Georg, I want you to know, Anna is coming with me."

His first thought was of the baby. So she won't have even one relative here. And Edith; will she miss Anna? Will she be hurt? No. Surprised, maybe. "I guessed. Does she know you're going to Palestine?"

"Not yet. She doesn't even know I'm a Jew. I feel like the poor girl fell in love with a millionaire without knowing he's rich."

"Don't flatter yourself. You think it's such a good thing to be a Jew in this world?"

"Good point. It doesn't matter, though. I am what I am, and some of us want to fight back."

"It's over, Israel. The war's over. We survived, some of us. All we want now is to live in peace, make a new family, get on with our lives."

"That's exactly what I want."

"You won't find it there."

"Maybe I will, maybe I won't. But I'll be among my own."

"Huh. You'll be among the Arabs and the British."

"We'll see about that. That's why I'm going back. That's where the real fight will be. And you think you'll be so happy here? You think they like you, they like the Jews?"

"I don't care if they like the Jews. I care if my family will be safe. Anyway, with all their little insults and snide jokes, it isn't that they don't like the Jews. They don't like anyone different. It could be us, Negroes . . ."

"You think? The Nazis didn't kill six million Negroes. They killed six million Jews."

"All I care about is being safe, and I feel safe here."

"Your parents felt safe in Vienna."

"True."

"Good luck, Georg. I'll have a home in Palestine, with Anna, you'll always be welcome, when you need somewhere to hide."

Georg couldn't resist. "What happened with Bevin? Why was it called off?"

"I honestly don't know. I got the telegram, that's all I know. Cold feet? Afraid of the consequences? Maybe Ben-Gurion found out and killed it? Maybe the British found out? If so, that could be bad for the organisation. I don't know."

"Do you mind, that it was called off, though? After all your planning?"

"I told you before, this isn't personal. My chief is a brilliant man. He must have had a good reason, he always thinks ten steps ahead. Or the British found out somehow. I don't know. But I know I have to get out of here right away, just in case."

Georg thought of Eric Barnes, who had killed Israel's young brother, in the line of duty. He seemed a nice man, he'd been friendly. All he really wanted was to stay at home. "You say it isn't personal," Georg said. "What about Eric Barnes?"

"What about him?"

"You know what I mean."

Israel stared back at Georg, blankly, no trace of emotion. "Well, I've been thinking about that. I never did give him his Christmas present. We'll both be in Palestine at the same time. So maybe I'll get another opportunity."

"Leave him alone," Georg said.

Israel nodded, his face suddenly cold and flat, his eyes hard, like stones. "Of course, Georg, whatever you say."

As Georg stared back, unsure what to say, the door flew open and Anna returned with the same small bag she'd brought eleven weeks earlier. "He told you?" she said to Georg, hugging him. He nodded and took her hand. She looked at Israel. "Can we go to the hospital, to say good-bye to Edith? You haven't seen the baby."

He shook his head. "I'm sorry, Anna, no. Don't ask me why. Tomorrow I'll tell you."

"But we must. I can't leave without saying good-bye. She's been so good to me. . . ." She glanced at Georg. Anna was also thinking, *Edith will be upset. I'm leaving just when she needs me, to help with the baby. . . .*

Israel said, "Trust me, we must leave immediately. Right now. I'll explain . . ."

When we're out of England.

Georg kissed Anna, hugged her tight, she felt his heart beat. "It's all right, Anna. We love you, too, Anna, we'll see you again. I'll tell Edith how sorry you are not to say good-bye. I'll explain. She won't mind. She only wants the best for you. We'll send you photos of the baby."

"And we'll send you a picture of ours."

What?

Israel looked at her. "You're not . . ."

"No, of course not, silly." She laughed. "Not yet, anyway."

Georg kissed her again and held her. He knew she would soon be happy, where she wanted to be, in Palestine, and he wondered when they would see her again.

Over her shoulder he mouthed silently to Israel: Papi?

His shrug said it all. Nothing yet, not very hopeful.

TWENTY-FIVE

Tel Aviv, Palestine

December 23, 1945

Morning

It was over in an instant.

The old cleaning lady was taking a rest in the corridor, sitting on her upturned pail, picking at half a pita with hummus, taking small bites from a pickled cucumber, when the middle-aged woman opened the door to apartment 12 at 27 Balfour Street. The cleaning lady heaved herself up, rubbing her back and complaining, and waved her empty flask, asking in Polish for a top-up of water. The woman at the door hesitated, unsure whether to go back inside for a glass of water or to close the door and continue on her errand. She hadn't seen this cleaning lady before, in fact didn't even know someone had been hired to clean the common parts, although it was certainly about time, and at first didn't grasp how or why the stooped babushka in the red and black headscarf somehow transformed into a man with a gun at her temple and his hand pressing over her mouth. Two other women, guns drawn, stepped past her and into the apartment. The big hand smothered her scream. She could only kick and tremble in fear, not for herself.

She heard a door pushed back, a loud command, tense voices. She closed her eyes, her body rigid: Please, no gunshot! Miki, go quietly.

He did. Miki passed her, the two men in dresses gripping his arms, as other men with guns ran up the stairs. Within moments her apartment was crowded with Special Branch and soldiers, taking it apart.

At Special Branch HQ off the interior courtyard of the Dizengoff police station, Detective Bill Campbell watched the jeeps arrive with the terrorist leader and followed the prisoner into the holding pen. Above its steel door some joker had stuck a sprig of mistletoe. As soon as the hood was removed Campbell recognized Miki, even with a moustache instead of a beard. The chap who couldn't hold it in. "Need a piss, do you?" he said.

Miki's expression didn't change. He was thinking, He'd only been in the safe house two days. A precision raid like that, they knew he was there, even in which room he was. They came straight to his bedroom. It must have been a tip-off.

He was right.

Campbell glanced at the file, preparing for the interrogation. Following an anonymous phone call in London, Special Branch had contacted the Haganah with a warning: If the Jewish assassin in London so much as farts, the entire Jewish leadership in Palestine, including David Ben-Gurion, will be shipped off to the prison camps in Eritrea, no questions asked.

What Jewish assassin?

Haganah didn't know and the British didn't admit they didn't know, either. It was an inspired guess: Who else to do with Palestine would try to kill their Foreign Minister? And if it wasn't Haganah, they'd find whoever it was.

Rather than bring the wrath of Satan down upon them, just when they were gearing up to fight the Arabs, the Jewish leadership caved. Knowing only Lehi would both be so foolish and have the team to carry out such a hit, they shopped Miki to the British. It was about time. He was too much of a loose cannon anyway.

Campbell allowed Miki one phone call only: Call off the hit. In return he, and the woman who sheltered him, would live. Merry Christmas.

TWENTY-SIX

London

December 29, 1945

Seven days after giving birth, four days after Christmas, beaming Edith brought her baby home. The happy word had spread and friends crowded into the lounge at 181, bringing beer and wine and snacks, to pay homage to little Lisa. The surviving twin. The *Ham and High* wanted to do a story on the Chanukah miracle. Lisa's was the first birth to be recorded in the Association of Jewish Refugees' new bulletin. Friends came from the Cosmo, Dorice, the Austrian Center, Bloomsbury House, even Mrs. Wilson arrived with a box of chocolates. They were all fascinated by the new arrival. Otto kept saying, The best thing is, she'll have a British passport! Before any of us! He even blew cigarette smoke out of the corner of his mouth rather than into Lisa's face.

So tiny and beautiful, lying wide-eyed in Georg's arms. He paced the room, displaying his daughter, grinning from ear to ear. "Look, this is how you hold her, see, I support her head with my elbow." Someone said, "Georg, just one problem. She looks like you."

To be honest, Lisa's scrunched-up eyes and wrinkled red skin and dark patchy hair reminded Edith of a monkey, a wise old monkey head sticking out of a pink blanket. Her tiny hands bunched up into little pink fists by her angry mouth and she made everybody laugh as she swiveled her head to keep up with the action. Now she was sleeping, red eyelids pulled tight. Edith kissed each fist and smiled as Gina sat next to her, sighing heavily, bringing with her a heavy scent of rose and morning dew, a perfect scarlet outline of her luscious lips on her wineglass. "Want a drink?" she said, holding the glass to Edith's mouth. "Gin." Edith declined.

"Lucky Sally's here," Edith said. "She showed me how to give Lisa a bath in the sink. And to tie a nappy."

"Are you tired? You must be exhausted."

"Not really. Seven days' rest in the hospital. They wanted me to stay longer but I couldn't wait to come home. And so far Lisa is sleeping well."

As if on cue, Lisa awoke, became even redder, holding her breath, which exploded in a sudden, furious wail. Everyone turned, holding their drinks, as if about to hear a speech. "What's wrong?" Gina said. Edith, alarmed, began to shake Lisa, side to side, up and down, bounce her on her knees, she cooed cookie, bookie, cookie, bookie, but Lisa would have none of it, wailing, a surprisingly deep, hoarse voice from such a tiny body, a contralto foghorn. "My God," Otto said, "would you listen to that! Those lungs! An opera singer, I tell you."

Edith looked stricken: cookie, bookie, cookie, bookie, up and down, side to side, bouncing knees.

Sally bustled over. "No good shaking her brains out, dearie. It's your tittie she wants, she's hungry, that's all."

She brought a towel and covered Edith, who extracted her breast and manoeuvred her nipple into Lisa's mouth, which clamped down like a leech. The crying turned into slurping and sighing. Edith sighed, too, and settled back. In the hospital she hadn't had much milk at first and the nurse gave Lisa a bottle. But soon her breast became full and painful and Lisa, to Edith's relief, rejected the bottle for the breast.

Edith shifted and the towel slipped off, and there was the full, pale smoothness of her breast, with Lisa stuck to it. Slurp, sigh, slurp, sigh. Milk dribbled from the side of her mouth over Edith's aureola, and Edith dabbed at it with the corner of the towel, smiling dreamy and distant like the Mona Lisa, and as mysterious, her chest gently rising and falling, and Lisa's head with it.

Nobody covered her breast, the tableau was too pleasing and moving. The refugees fell silent, savoring the contented sighs of mother and child. With each draw, Lisa's head moved. Edith looked down, and the light glimmered in her auburn hair, which fell over her face and reached her breast. She gently brushed it away, grazing Lisa's cheek, and Lisa, sucking, stared back with big brown eyes. Satisfaction bathed the room, all warmed by their glow.

Georg moved forward and knelt by Edith, taking Lisa's pink-bootied foot in his hand, gently, not to disturb, and he brushed his lips against Edith's cheek. She gave the hint of a smile, couldn't take her eyes off Lisa's, and all the friends couldn't take their eyes off her.

It's good to have friends, she thought, looking up, but it's better to have family. And this is mine. All of it. Georg and Lisa. If only Mutti could be here, and Papi, and Lisa, and Lotte, Markus, Berta, Ada, all the aunts and uncles, cousins and everyone. But they can't. Names on a list, most crossed out. Maybe Papi will come, maybe he'll knock on the door even now, oh, if only. But with Lisa's birth a quiet came over her, Edith had calmed, wanted to give all of herself to her baby, become accepting. Papi would want that, would have wanted that.

She'd have to wait, and would never give up waiting. Until she had to. I hope and pray, Edith thought as she gazed into her baby's eyes as Lisa suckled at her breast, I hope and pray that Papi will come to us. Otherwise there is only Anna. Beautiful Anna. Good luck to her in Palestine. She'll need it with that strange man.

This is my family now, she thought. Georg's head, bent over Lisa. His thinning hair's familiar nutty odour, and the fresh sweetness of baby skin and mother's milk. She breathed in deeply, part sigh, part to take them deeper into her. This is all I have. She leaned down and kissed Georg's neck. She thought, *This is enough for what is left of me. The little I have is all I have room for. But the part of me that I have lost will always ache, I'll always feel it, like a missing limb. Georg will light his candles, say his prayers, and we will cry.*

Our greatest memorial will be Lisa, and more children, many more, God willing. They will be our revenge.

She thought of the shock of her delivery. It seemed God had sent a message with the twin who died: that joy is rationed. Rebuild slowly and carefully. That is how Georg explained it, as they lay together on the narrow hospital bed, as they tried to understand.

It was a boy, Lisa's elder brother. They agreed never to tell her. That she had shared the womb with a boy, who was born thirty minutes before her, yet chose not to stay.

A sudden blinding white light and a cheer erupted. When Edith could see again, there was a young man kneeling, pointing a large camera, and another flash. And another. Georg stood, one arm up, as if to defend himself. The young man stood, too, and stretched out a hand.

"Hello, Mr. Fleischer, I'm Peter Jordan from the *Ham and High*." Gina called out, "Let's have a group photo," and Peter said, yes, that's a good idea.

"He phoned and I said come right over, we're having a party," Sally said. "I hope that's all right."

"But my breast, you can see my breast," Edith said, horrified.

"No, you can't," Peter said, "I made sure of that, they'd never print it anyway. The baby's face and your husband's head cover it. It's a lovely picture, I promise you, your three heads together, Leonardo da Vinci couldn't have composed it better, even if I say so myself."

"Everybody, everybody, line up behind the sofa," Gina called out, "come on." She clapped her hands. "Come on, come on."

Edith held Lisa, who had drifted off again, satisfied, and Georg sat next to her, still holding Lisa's foot. Gina sat on the other side. Behind, Otto, a cigarette hanging from the side of his mouth, massaged Edith's shoulders. Frieda stood next to him, touching his knee with hers, and then Mrs. Wilson, beaming, holding up a pair of green baby pyjamas. On the other side of Otto was Mr. Kellerman and Tomac, with Kate, his delicious new English girlfriend. More friends pushed into the frame and Sally and Albert, huffing and puffing, helped each other to the floor at Edith's feet.

"Not so hard, Otto," Edith hissed, trying to make herself heard above the laughing, without waking Lisa.

"I thought you liked it hard."

"No, that's me," Gina said, waving the wine bottle.

"Move together, I'm not in the picture," someone shouted.

"Good, you won't break the camera, then."

"Ow, my knees," Sally said, "I'll never get up again."

"That's how I like it." Albert slapped her on the thigh.

"All right, everybody, I'm ready," the photographer said, waving with his left arm for the group to move closer together. "All right, cheese."

Everybody smiled, went silent, and the phone rang.

"Take the bloody picture, then," Albert said. "That's the phone."

"Oh, I thought it was the teakettle," Sally said.

"Go on, take it," Albert said.

"Cheese."

Another white light in everybody's eyes, they blinked. As Albert struggled to his feet, with the phone still ringing, Peter Jordan said, "One more."

"Got to get the phone first," Albert said, leaving the room. "It may be Eric, they're going through France, to Palestine. Hang on. Won't be a tick."

"Hurry up," Sally shouted after him. "If it's Eric, I'll come down, too."

As everyone broke up, chattering and laughing, Peter pleaded, "Move together again, please, one more photo. Get ready to smile."

They heard Albert laboring up the stairs. He reached the door, puffing. Between breaths, he managed to say, "Cor, blimey. I've got. To go. On a diet. It's for you. Georg."

He looked up from Lisa. "For me?"

"Yes. Ismael. From France. I told him to look out for Eric. Said not to worry, he'll find him all right. Wants to congratulate you."

"Won't be a minute," Georg said, glancing at Edith, hiding his surprise. *He's already congratulated me.* "I'll be right back."

"Hurry," Edith said, "we can't take photos without the daddy. Give my love to Anna."

Georg walked quickly down the stairs, holding on to the railing as he turned the bends. The receiver was lying on its side. "Israel?"

His brow furrowed as he listened in silence. It was a poor line and he had to strain to hear through the crackling, but Israel's voice was slow and precise. All Georg said when Israel finished was, "This is certain? No room for doubt?" And then, "Thank you, Israel. Give our love to Anna. Stay in touch." He hung up the phone, looked thought-fully at it, and walked up the stairs, pausing every few steps. He lis-tened at the lounge, frowning at the laughter and excited chatter that penetrated the door, and decided to continue upstairs to his room. He felt his heart beat fast and it wasn't the effort of climbing the stairs.

He sat on the bed. He lay back, stretched out, with his hands folded under his head, feet poking over the edge, staring at the ceil-ing, a sense of calm enveloping him, despite his palpitating heart. He took in the familiar cracks in the wallpaper, followed them like riv-ers. How long had they been there? Not the cracks, him and Edith? They had thought it would be for a few months—what, four years now? Already? He looked around: a sofa, a couple of chairs, the table, a few kitchen things piled on the cream-colored shelves, clothes stuffed in the narrow cupboard. His dented hats. He shook his head and sighed. They lived, ate, slept here for four years. In Vienna, just his own bedroom was bigger than this. He wondered, as he often had, what his parents' lives had been like before they married. He'd always intended to ask but never had. And now he never could. Such a pity, he thought. So much, lost. He studied the heavy folds of the blackout curtains, which had concealed their life in this little room, and decided to write everything down, write about all that had happened in the last few years. For Lisa, for her children, and her children's children. So that nothing would be forgotten. He'd make a family tree, too, so they'd know where they came from. Well: a family stump. But it would grow again. With children and more children, that would be the Jewish revenge, to raise a large and healthy family, God willing. A family tree. It didn't all start in this lousy little room on the third floor of 181 Goldhurst Terrace. A refuge, a sanctuary, a nest, yes, but now it was time to move on. Somehow. Somewhere. Maybe he'd find an office to start his law practice with a room or two above where they could live. To begin with; just to get away from here, to start anew. It's time. Eric and his friends can move in. After a moment he looked at the sullen, dreary clouds through the window, and went over to it. What endless grey days, he thought. It never changes. And yet there's something safe and strong about these bare trees and flinty streets. London is our home now, where we can face the past and build our future. Those of us still standing.

Georg sighed and went to the night table, opened the drawer, took out his pencil and his list of names. He could hear more laughter from downstairs. Somebody was calling his name. More photographs. He had never seen Edith so happy.

He sat on the bed and rested his Heine volume on his knees. He placed the list on it and steeled himself. And drew a grey lead line through Max Epstein.

He wouldn't tell Edith just yet. How often can we celebrate?

The past can wait.

He counted: sixteen names in Edith's column crossed out, five without lines through them. On the other side of the paper was his family's list. Four could still be alive, fourteen he knew were dead. He felt quite calm as he looked at the list, like a ship that had reached quiet waters, even if it was a ghost ship. He'd never held out much hope and he still didn't for the rest, it was just a matter of time. It is so much easier to know than not to know. There is a closure, yet such a sad one. He sighed again.

Mothers, fathers, sisters. Neither he nor Edith had one close relative left.

He thought of Heinrich Heine:

Aus meinen grossen Schmerzen
Mach ich die kleinen Lieder:

From my own great woe,
I make my little songs.

And then he smiled, and a warm rush filled his veins, he straightened just a little.

Georg drew a downward line from the bottom of his list toward the center of the page, and another from Edith's list, so that they joined in the middle, and then he drew one short line down. It was the beginning of a new list, and he wrote the first name: Lisa, b. December 22, 1945.

Author's Note

Events that took place over a year and a half have been compressed into three months. Otherwise the background to the story is accurate: Hampstead's anti-Semitic petition in October 1945, Lehi's plot to assassinate Ernest Bevin in 1946, the resurgence of British fascism and the Group of 43's street battles against them, all are factual.

My key source for the assassination plot was the man sent to London to plan the operation. He was a lawyer in Tel Aviv. The telegram calling it off with twenty-four hours to go read, "Do not do the fat man." He is nothing like Israel, though, and all details, beyond the principal ones of the hit in Pall Mall, are fictitious. He did not live with friends at Goldhurst Terrace. The truth is even more mundane. He lived with his mother on Abbey Road.

Because the material is so inflammatory, all anti-Semitic speeches and comments are taken from contemporary speeches, letters to the editor, and newspaper articles. Nothing is invented. The same goes for the pro-Jewish responses. All are taken from contemporary accounts as well as dozens of author interviews with elderly Group of 43 street fighters, Jewish refugees, former British soldiers in Palestine, and former fascists in London.

My parents, Edith and George, Jewish refugees from Austria, moved into 181 Goldhurst Terrace in 1944 and lived there until they died almost sixty years later. They lived through the events described, but this is not their story.

Discard